Asimov's Gho
Asimov's Mo

Asimov's Ghosts
Asimov's Monsters

Edited by Isaac Asimov,
Martin Greenberg and
Charles Waugh

ARMADA

This Armada *Isaac Asimov Two-in-One* was
first published in the U.K. in Armada in 1988
by William Collins Sons & Co. Ltd

Armada is an imprint of the Children's Division,
part of the Collins Publishing Group,
8 Grafton Street, London W1X 3LA

Printed and bound in Great Britain by
William Collins Sons & Co. Ltd, Glasgow

Asimov's Ghosts

Asimov's Ghosts was
first published in Great Britain
in a single volume
by Dragon Books in 1986

Acknowledgements

'Poor Little Saturday' by Madeleine L'Engle. Copyright © 1956 by King-Size Publications. Reprinted by permission of Lescher & Lescher, Ltd.

'The Lake' by Ray Bradbury. Copyright 1944 by Ray Bradbury, renewed 1972. Reprinted by permission of Don Congdon Associates, Inc.

'The Twilight Road' by Hesta Brimsmead. Copyright © 1968 by Hesta Fay Brimsmead. Reprinted by permission of the author.

'The Voices of El Dorado' by Howard Goldsmith. Copyright © 1974 by Howard Goldsmith. Reprinted by permission of the author.

'The Changing of the Guard' by Anne Serling-Sutton. Copyright © 1985 by Anne Serling-Sutton. Reprinted by permission of the International Creative Management

Contents

by Isaac Asimov

Ghosts

Do you believe in ghosts?

Actually, I don't and never have, but if you believe in ghosts you're in good company—or at least in lots of company. Almost everywhere, and at all times, people have taken it for granted that the dead continue to exist in some fashion and can make themselves seen, or somehow sensed, at crucial moments.

And even if a person *doesn't* think that this can be so or that ghosts exist, so widespread is the feeling and so much are ghosts talked about that the most hardened skeptic may get a little nervous in the dark, or in an abandoned house that creaks in the silent night.

Tell the truth: would you be willing to spend the night alone in an isolated house that had the reputation of being "haunted"? Even though I am absolutely convinced ghosts don't exist, I think I would rather spend my nights in other ways.

Oddly enough, if we are in a position to feel secure, it is always fun to read ghost stories. They have always been popular in the past, and they are still popular today. I certainly love to read them, because the feeling of fright, or at least nervousness, that they can arouse, even in a nonbeliever, has a kind of pleasantness about it if you know underneath that you are actually perfectly safe.

So here we have in this collection a dozen ghost stories, none of which, as it happens, are truly gruesome, but all of which will produce, perhaps, a little of the chill in the bones that we do enjoy in moderation.

But where do ghosts come from? How did the notion arise?

Actually, that's hard to say because the idea stretches far back into prehistoric times and may even be older than modern humanity. There's no record, therefore, of people beginning to think of ghosts, and we can only speculate as to how it came about. Here are my speculations on the subject.

In the first place, human beings are the only kind of living thing, as far as we know, who have made the discovery that no living thing, made up of more than one cell, can live forever. Every animal, every plant, must someday die. There are trees called bristlecone pines that may live as long as five thousand years, but in the end, they, too, must die.

And in particular, every human being must someday die. In some far-off ancient time when human beings came to this conclusion, think what a sadness it must have cast over life. Imagine knowing, *in advance*, that you *must* grow old and someday die, even if you protect yourself from accident, disease, starvation, and everything else that might kill you.

That is a terribly hard thing to accept, and even today most of us sometimes have secret feelings that perhaps we might be exceptions. Other people might die, but perhaps we will just keep going and maybe won't even grow old. Maybe that's why people feel so terrible when they notice their hair beginning to get gray, or that they can no longer see as well as they used to, or can't run as far or as fast, and so on. It means that, after all, they're *not* an exception.

We are bound to rebel. We might decide that we don't *really* die. Our body might die, but something in it, the something that we think of as "I," must continue to exist without the body. In other words, there must be an "afterlife." We have uncovered graves of Neanderthal people, who lived over fifty thousand years ago, in which some possessions of the dead person were buried with him, as though he might have a use for them in the afterlife.

But what was this something that kept on living after the body was dead?

e word "ghost" carries with it the notion of "some-
ɡ that terrifies." The words "ghastly" and "aghast"
are related to it. But "ghost" is also related to the
German word "geist" and that means "spirit." In fact,
even in English the word "spirit" is used as a synonym
of "ghost." "Spirit" is a less frightening notion. Things
of this world that can be seen and felt and are made
up of "matter" are "material." Things that are not of
this world are "spiritual," and that is a fine word. Of
course, if we want to think of spirits as frightening
and as capable of doing harm, we can speak of an "evil
spirit," but the point is that spirits don't have to be
evil.

And where does the word "spirit" come from? It
comes from the Latin word "spiritus," which can mean
"pride" or "courage," as when we say that someone
"has the spirit to stand up to a bully." The chief meaning of "spiritus," however, is "breath," or "air." Thus,
we speak of the process of breathing as "respiration,"
which, if you break it down into syllables, means "taking in air over and over."

This gives us a good hint as to how the notions of
ghosts and spirits may have arisen. Perhaps human
beings, very early in history, noticed that everyone
breathed and that if the breathing were stopped force-
fully, as by choking a person, that person would die.
What's more, as soon as a person died for any reason,
he or she stopped breathing.

It was as though breathing and living were the same

14

thing. With breath you were alive, and without breath you were dead. Perhaps breath *was* life. In that case, it might be that breath was the real you and your body was only what breath inhabited for a while. Thus, the Bible, in describing the creation of Adam, says that God "breathed into his nostrils the breath of life."

Well, then, what is breath? Breath is air, but pre-historic human beings didn't know what air was. They knew it was there because they could feel it whenever there was a wind, and winds could be strong enough to knock down houses and trees.

However, you couldn't see air, you couldn't feel air with your fingers. It could penetrate into every nook and cranny. It wasn't matter of the familiar sort, like water and rocks and wood. Air was "immaterial."

Ghosts and spirits were imagined to be made up of the breath that left the body when someone died, and, therefore, to be like air. At best, a ghost might have a cloudy appearance. You could see things through it. You couldn't feel it; your hand would pass right through it. If it took on a shape, it would be the shape of the body it had once had. (Otherwise how could you tell whose ghost it was?)

Strictly speaking, it should take on the shape of the body without clothes. After all, the clothes weren't alive and hadn't died. However, a naked ghost wouldn't seem very respectable, so they would naturally be imagined to consist of an immaterial body wearing immaterial clothes. Since dead bodies were often wrapped in long pieces of cloth, or "winding sheets," before being buried, that might be the kind of clothes they would wear. That gave rise to the common notion that ghosts appeared in long white nightgowns.

So it may be that the whole notion of ghosts comes about, first, from a reluctance to admit that people really die, and, second, from a feeling that breath is life, and can exist separately when the body dies. If you should happen to think that people really do die and that breath is not life and cannot live by itself, then you are not likely to believe ghosts exist—but I suspect very strongly that you would enjoy ghost stories just the same.

Therefore, turn to the stories and prepare to enjoy yourself.

M. R. James

Lost Hearts

Mr. Abney of this story, regardless of his crimes, is one of literature's most heartless villains.

It was, as far as I can ascertain, in September of the year 1811 that a post-chaise drew up before the door of Aswarby Hall, in the heart of Lincolnshire. The little boy who was the only passenger in the chaise, and who jumped out as soon as it had stopped, looked about him with the keenest curiosity during the short interval that elapsed between the ringing of the bell and the opening of the hall door. He saw a tall, square, red-brick house, built in the reign of Anne; a stone-pillared porch had been added in the purer classical style of 1790; the windows of the house were many, tall and narrow, with small panes and thick white woodwork. A pediment, pierced with a round window, crowned the front. There were wings to right and left, connected by curious glazed galleries, supported by colonnades, with the central block. These wings plainly contained the stables and offices of the house. Each was surmounted by an ornamental cupola with a gilded vane.

An evening light shone on the building, making the window-panes glow like so many fires. Away from the Hall in front stretched a flat park studded with oaks and fringed with firs, which stood out against the sky. The clock in the church-tower, buried in trees on the edge of the park, only its golden weather-cock catching the light, was striking six, and the sound came gently beating down the wind. It was altogether a pleasant impression, though tinged with the sort of melancholy appropriate to an evening in early autumn, that was conveyed to the mind of the boy who was standing in the porch waiting for the door to open to him.

The post-chaise had brought him from Warwick-shire, where, some six months before, he had been left an orphan. Now, owing to the generous offer of his elderly cousin, Mr. Abney, he had come to live at Aswarby. The offer was unexpected, because all who knew anything of Mr. Abney looked upon him as a somewhat austere recluse, into whose steady-going household the advent of a small boy would import a new and, it seemed, incongruous element. The truth is that very little was known of Mr. Abney's pursuits or temper. The Professor of Greek at Cambridge had been heard to say that no one knew more of the religious beliefs of the later pagans than did the owner of

Aswarby. Certainly his library contained all the then available books bearing on the Mysteries, the Orphic poems, the worship of Mithras, and the Neo-Platonists. In the marble-paved hall stood a fine group of Mithras slaying a bull, which had been imported from the Levant at great expense by the owner. He had contributed a description of it to the *Gentleman's Magazine*, and he had written a remarkable series of articles in the *Critical Museum* on the superstitions of the Romans of the Lower Empire. He was looked upon, in fine, as a man wrapped up in his books, and it was a matter of quiet surprise among his neighbors that he should ever have heard of his orphan cousin, Stephen Elliott, much more that he should have volunteered to make him an inmate of Aswarby Hall.

Whatever may have been expected by his neighbors, it is certain that Mr. Abney—the tall, the thin, the austere—seemed inclined to give his young cousin a kindly reception. The moment the front-door was opened he darted out of his study, rubbing his hands with delight.

"How are you, my boy?—how are you? How old are you?" said he—"that is, you are not too much tired, I hope, by your journey to eat your supper?"

"No, thank you, sir," said Master Elliott; "I am pretty well."

"That's a good lad," said Mr. Abney. "And how old are you, my boy?"

It seemed a little odd that he should have asked the

question twice in the first two minutes of their acquaintance.

"I'm twelve years old next birthday, sir," said Stephen.

"And when is your birthday, my dear boy? Eleventh of September, eh? That's well—that's very well. Nearly a year hence, isn't it? I like—ha, ha!—I like to get these things down in my book. Sure it's twelve? Certain?"

"Yes, quite sure, sir."

"Well, well! Take him to Mrs. Bunch's room, Parkes, and let him have his tea—supper—whatever it is."

"Yes, sir," answered the staid Mr. Parkes; and conducted Stephen to the lower regions.

Mrs. Bunch was the most comfortable and human person whom Stephen had as yet met in Aswarby. She made him completely at home; they were great friends in a quarter of an hour: and great friends they remained. Mrs. Bunch had been born in the neighborhood some fifty-five years before the date of Stephen's arrival, and her residence at the Hall was of twenty years' standing. Consequently, if anyone knew the ins and outs of the house and the district, Mrs. Bunch knew them; and she was by no means disinclined to communicate her information.

Certainly there were plenty of things about the Hall and the Hall gardens which Stephen, who was of an adventurous and inquiring turn, was anxious to have explained to him. "Who built the temple at the end of the laurel walk? Who was the old man whose picture hung on the staircase, sitting at a table, with a skull under his hand?" These and many similar points were cleared up by the resources of Mrs. Bunch's powerful intellect. There were others, however, of which the explanations furnished were less satisfactory.

One November evening Stephen was sitting by the fire in the housekeeper's room reflecting on his surroundings.

"Is Mr. Abney a good man, and will he go to heaven?" he suddenly asked, with the peculiar confidence which children possess in the ability of their elders to settle these questions, the decision of which is believed to be reserved for other tribunals.

"Good?—bless the child?" said Mrs. Bunch. "Master's as kind a soul as ever I see! Didn't I never tell you of the little boy as he took in out of the street, as you may say, this seven years back? and the little girl, two years after I first come here?"

"No. Do tell me all about them, Mrs. Bunch—now this minute!"

"Well," said Mrs. Bunch, "the little girl I don't seem to recollect so much about. I know master brought her back with him from his walk one day, and give orders to Mrs. Ellis, as was housekeeper then, as she should be took every care with. And the pore child hadn't no one belonging to her—she told me so her own self— and here she lived with us a matter of three weeks it might be; and then, whether she were somethink of a

21

gypsy in her blood or what not, but one morning she out of her bed afore any of us had opened a eye, and neither track nor yet trace of her have I set eyes on since. Master was wonderful put about, and had all the ponds dragged; but it's my belief she was had away by them gypsies, for there was singing round the house for as much as an hour the night she went; and Parkes, he declare as he heard them a-calling in the woods all that afternoon. Dear, dear! a hodd child she was, so silent in her ways and all, but I was wonderful taken up with her, so domesticated she was—surprising."

"And what about the little boy?" said Stephen.

"Ah, that pore boy!" sighed Mrs. Bunch. "He were a foreigner—Jevanny he called hisself—and he come a-tweaking his 'urdy-gurdy round and about the drive one winter day, and master 'ad him in that minute, and ast all about where he came from, and how old he was, and how he made his way, and where was his relatives, and all as kind as heart could wish. But it went the same way with him. They're a hunruly lot, them foreign nations, I do suppose, and he was off one fine morning just the same as the girl. Why he went and what he done was our question for as much as a year after; for he never took his 'urdy-gurdy, and there it lays on the shelf."

The remainder of the evening was spent by Stephen in miscellaneous cross-examination of Mrs. Bunch and in efforts to extract a tune from the hurdy-gurdy.

That night he had a curious dream. At the end of the passage at the top of the house, in which his bedroom was situated, there was an old disused bathroom. It was kept locked, but the upper half of the door was glazed, and, since the muslin curtains which used to hang there had long been gone, you could look in and see the lead-lined bath affixed to the wall on the right hand, with its head towards the window.

On the night of which I am speaking, Stephen Elliott found himself, as he thought, looking through the glazed door. The moon was shining through the window, and he was gazing at a figure which lay in the bath.

His description of what he saw reminds me of what I once beheld myself in the famous vaults of St. Michan's Church in Dublin, which possesses the horrid property of preserving corpses from decay for centuries. A figure inexpressibly thin and pathetic, of a dusty leaden color, enveloped in a shroud-like garment, the thin lips crooked into a faint and dreadful smile, the hands pressed tightly over the region of the heart.

As he looked upon it, a distant, almost inaudible moan seemed to issue from its lips, and the arms began to stir. The terror of the sight forced Stephen backwards, and he awoke to the fact that he was indeed standing on the cold boarded floor of the passage in the full light of the moon. With a courage which I do not think can be common among boys of his age, he went to the door of the bathroom to ascertain if the figure of his dream were really there. It was not, and he went back to bed.

Mrs. Bunch was much impressed next morning by his story, and went so far as to replace the muslin curtain over the glazed door of the bathroom. Mr. Abney, moreover, to whom he confided his experiences at breakfast, was greatly interested, and made notes of the matter in what he called "his book."

The spring equinox was approaching, as Mr. Abney frequently reminded his cousin, adding that this had been always considered by the ancients to be a critical time for the young: that Stephen would do well to take care of himself, and to shut his bedroom window at night; and that Censorinus had some valuable remarks on the subject. Two incidents that occurred about this time made an impression upon Stephen's mind.

The first was after an unusually uneasy and oppressed night that he had passed—though he could not recall any particular dream that he had had.

The following evening Mrs. Bunch was occupying herself in mending his nightgown.

"Gracious me, Master Stephen!" she broke forth rather irritably, "how do you manage to tear your nightdress all to flinders this way? Look here, sir, what trouble you do give to poor servants that have to darn and mend after you!"

There was indeed a most destructive and apparently wanton series of slits or scorings in the garment, which would undoubtedly require a skilful needle to make good. They were confined to the left side of the chest—long, parallel slits, about six inches in length, some of them not quite piercing the texture of the linen. Stephen could only express his entire ignorance of their origin: he was sure they were not there the night before.

"But," he said, "Mrs. Bunch, they are just the same as the scratches on the outside of my bedroom door: and I'm sure I never had anything to do with making *them*."

Mrs. Bunch gazed at him open-mouthed, then snatched up a candle, departed hastily from the room, and was heard making her way upstairs. In a few minutes she came down.

"Well," she said, "Master Stephen, it's a funny thing to me how them marks and scratches can 'a' come there—too high up for any cat or dog to 'ave made 'em, much less a rat: for all the world like a Chinaman's finger-nails, as my uncle in the tea-trade used to tell us of when we was girls together. I wouldn't say nothing to master, not if I was you, Master Stephen, my dear; and just turn the key of the door when you go to your bed."

"I always do, Mrs. Bunch, as soon as I've said my prayers."

"Ah, that's a good child: always say your prayers, and then no one can't hurt you."

Herewith Mrs. Bunch addressed herself to mending

the injured nightgown, with intervals of meditation, until bed-time. This was on a Friday night in March, 1812.

On the following evening the usual duet of Stephen and Mrs. Bunch was augmented by the sudden arrival of Mr. Parkes, the butler, who as a rule kept himself rather *to* himself in his own pantry. He did not see that Stephen was there: he was, moreover, flustered and less slow of speech than was his wont.

"Master may get up his own wine, if he likes, of an evening," was his first remark. "Either I do it in the daytime or not at all, Mrs. Bunch. I don't know what it may be: very like it's the rats, or the wind got into the cellars; but I'm not so young as I was, and I can't go through with it as I have done."

"Well, Mr. Parkes, you know it is a surprising place for the rats, is the Hall."

"I'm not denying that, Mrs. Bunch; and, to be sure, many a time I've heard the tale from the men in the shipyards about the rat that could speak. I never laid no confidence in that before; but tonight, if I'd de-meaned myself to lay my ear to the door of the further bin, I could pretty much have heard what they was saying."

"Oh, there, Mr. Parkes, I've no patience with your fancies! Rats talking in the wine-cellar indeed!"

"Well, Mrs. Bunch, I've no wish to argue with you: all I say is, if you choose to go to the far bin, and lay

26

your ear to the door, you may prove my words this minute."

"What nonsense you do talk, Mr. Parkes—not fit for children to listen to! Why, you'll be frightening Master Stephen there out of his wits."

"What! Master Stephen?" said Parkes, awaking to the consciousness of the boy's presence. "Master Stephen knows well enough when I'm a-playing a joke with you, Mrs. Bunch."

In fact, Master Stephen knew much too well to suppose that Mr. Parkes had in the first instance intended a joke. He was interested, not altogether pleasantly, in the situation; but all his questions were unsuccessful in inducing the butler to give any more detailed account of his experiences in the wine-cellar.

We have now arrived at March 24, 1812. It was a day of curious experiences for Stephen: a windy, noisy day, which filled the house and the gardens with a restless impression. As Stephen stood by the fence of the grounds, and looked out into the park, he felt as if an endless procession of unseen people were sweeping past him on the wind, borne on resistlessly and aimlessly, vainly striving to stop themselves, to catch at something that might arrest their flight and bring them once again into contact with the living world of which they had formed a part. After luncheon that day Mr. Abney said:

"Stephen, my boy, do you think you could manage to come to me tonight as late as eleven o'clock in my study? I shall be busy until that time, and I wish to show you something connected with your future life which it is most important that you should know. You are not to mention this matter to Mrs. Bunch nor to anyone else in the house; and you had better go to your room at the usual time."

Here was a new excitement added to life: Stephen eagerly grasped at the opportunity of sitting up till eleven o'clock. He looked in at the library door on his way upstairs that evening, and saw a brazier, which he had often noticed in the corner of the room, moved out before the fire: an old silver-gilt cup stood on the table, filled with red wine, and some written sheets of paper lay near it. Mr. Abney was sprinkling some incense on the brazier from a round silver box as Stephen passed, but did not seem to notice his step.

The wind had fallen, and there was a still night and a full moon. At about ten o'clock Stephen was standing at the open window of his bedroom, looking out over the country. Still as the night was, the mysterious population of the distant moon-lit woods was not yet lulled to rest. From time to time strange cries as of lost and despairing wanderers sounded from across the mere. They might be the notes of owls or water-birds, yet they did not quite resemble either sound. Were not they coming nearer? Now they sounded from the nearer side of the water, and in a few moments they seemed to be floating about among the shrubberies. Then they ceased; but just as Stephen was thinking of shutting the window and resuming his reading of *Robinson Crusoe*, he caught sight of two figures standing on the gravelled terrace that ran along the garden side of the Hall—the figures of a boy and girl, as it seemed; they stood side by side, looking up at the windows. Something in the form of the girl recalled irresistibly his dream of the figure in the bath. The boy inspired him with more acute fear.

Whilst the girl stood still, half smiling, with her hands clasped over her heart, the boy, a thin shape, with black hair and ragged clothing, raised his arms in the air with an appearance of menace and of un-appeasable hunger and longing. The moon shone upon his almost transparent hands, and Stephen saw that the nails were fearfully long and that the light shone through them. As he stood with his arms thus raised, he disclosed a terrifying spectacle. On the left side of his chest there opened a black and gaping rent; and there fell upon Stephen's brain, rather than upon his ear, the impression of one of those hungry and desolate cries that he had heard resounding over the woods of Aswarby all that evening. In another moment this dreadful pair had moved swiftly and noiselessly over the dry gravel, and he saw them no more.

Inexpressibly frightened as he was, he determined to take his candle and go down to Mr. Abney's study, for the hour appointed for their meeting was near at hand. The study or library opened out of the front-hall on one side, and Stephen, urged on by his terrors, did not take long in getting there. To effect an entrance was not so easy. It was not locked, he felt sure, for the key was on the outside of the door as usual. His repeated knocks produced no answer. Mr. Abney was engaged: he was speaking. What! why did he try to cry out? and why was the cry choked in his throat? Had he, too, seen the mysterious children? But now everything was quiet and the door yielded to Stephen's terrified and frantic pushing.

On the table in Mr. Abney's study certain papers were found which explained the situation to Stephen Elliott when he was of an age to understand them. The most important sentences were as follows:

"It was a belief very strongly and generally held by the ancients—of whose wisdom in these matters I have had such experience as induces me to place confidence in their assertions—that by enacting certain processes, which to us moderns have something of a barbaric complexion, a very remarkable enlightenment of the spiritual faculties in man may be attained: that, for example, by absorbing the personalities of a certain number of his fellow-creatures, an individual may gain a complete ascendancy over those orders of spiritual beings which control the elemental forces of our universe.

"It is recorded of Simon Magus that he was able to

fly in the air, to become invisible, or to assume any form he pleased, by the agency of the soul of a boy whom, to use the libellous phrase employed by the author of the *Clementine Recognitions*, he had "murdered." I find it set down, moreover, with considerable detail in the writings of Hermes Trismegistus, that similar happy results may be produced by the absorption of the hearts of not less than three human beings below the age of twenty-one years. To the testing of the truth of this receipt I have devoted the greater part of the last twenty years, selecting as the *corpora vilia* of my experiment such persons as could conveniently be removed without occasioning a sensible gap in society. The first step I effected by the removal of one Phoebe Stanley, a girl of gypsy extraction, on March 24, 1792. The second, by the removal of a wandering Italian lad, named Giovanni Paoli, on the night of March 23, 1805. The final "victim"—to employ a word repugnant in the highest degree to my feelings— must be my cousin, Stephen Elliott. His day must be this March 24, 1812.

"The best means of effecting the required absorption is to remove the heart from the *living* subject, to reduce it to ashes, and to mingle them with about a pint of some red wine, preferably port. The remains of the first two subjects, at least, it will be well to conceal: a disused bathroom or wine-cellar will be found convenient for such a purpose. Some annoyance may be experienced from the psychic portion of the subjects, which popular language dignifies with the name of ghosts. But the man of philosophic temperament—to whom alone the experiment is appropriate—will be little prone to attach importance to the feeble efforts of these beings to wreak their vengeance on him. I contemplate with the liveliest satisfaction the enlarged and emancipated existence which the experiment, if successful, will confer on me; not only placing me beyond the reach of human justice (so-called), but eliminating to a great extent the prospect of death itself."

Mr. Abney was found in his chair, his head thrown back, his face stamped with an expression of rage, fright, and mortal pain. In his left side was a terrible lacerated wound, exposing the heart. There was no blood on his hands, and a long knife that lay on the table was perfectly clean. A savage wild-cat might have inflicted the injuries. The window of the study was open, and it was the opinion of the coroner that Mr. Abney had met his death by the agency of some wild creature. But Stephen Elliott's study of the papers I have quoted led him to a very different conclusion.

Richard Middleton

On the Brighton Road

We like to think that death brings peace, but sometimes it may not.

Slowly the sun had climbed up the hard white downs, till it broke with little of the mysterious ritual of dawn upon a sparkling world of snow. There had been a hard frost during the night, and the birds, who hopped about here and there with scant tolerance of life, left no trace of their passage on the silver pavements. In places the sheltered caverns of the hedges broke the monotony of the whiteness that had fallen upon the colored earth, and overhead the sky melted from orange to deep blue, from deep blue to a blue so pale that it suggested a thin paper screen rather than illimitable space. Across the level fields there came a cold, silent wind which blew fine dust of snow from the trees, but hardly stirred the crested hedges. Once above the sky-line, the sun seemed to climb more quickly, and as it rose higher it

33

began to give out a heat that blended with the keenness of the wind.

It may have been this strange alternation of heat and cold that disturbed the tramp in his dreams, for he struggled for a moment with the snow that covered him, like a man who finds himself twisted uncomfortably in the bedclothes, and then sat up with staring, questioning eyes. "Lord! I thought I was in bed," he said to himself as he took in the vacant landscape, "and all the while I was out here." He stretched his limbs, and, rising carefully to his feet, shook the snow off his body. As he did so the wind set him shivering, and he knew that his bed had been warm.

"Come, I feel pretty fit," he thought. "I suppose I am lucky to wake at all in this. Or unlucky—it isn't much of a business to come back to." He looked up and saw the downs shining against the blue like the Alps on a picture-postcard. "That means another forty miles or so, I suppose," he continued grimly. "Lord knows what I did yesterday. Walked till I was done, and now I'm only about twelve miles from Brighton. Damn the snow, damn Brighton, damn everything!" The sun crept up higher and higher, and he started walking patiently along the road with his back turned to the hills.

"Am I glad or sorry that it was only sleep that took me, glad or sorry, glad or sorry?" His thoughts seemed to arrange themselves in a metrical accompaniment to the steady thud of his footsteps, and he hardly sought an answer to his question. It was good enough to walk to.

Presently, when three milestones had loitered past, he overtook a boy who was stooping to light a cigarette. He wore no overcoat, and looked unspeakably fragile against the snow. "Are you on the road, guv'nor?" asked the boy huskily as he passed.

"I think I am," the tramp said.

"Oh, then I'll come a bit of the way with you if you don't walk too fast. It's a bit lonesome walking this time of day." The tramp nodded his head, and the boy started limping along by his side.

"I'm eighteen," he said casually. "I bet you thought I was younger."

"Fifteen, I'd have said."

"You'd have backed a loser. Eighteen last August, and I've been on the road six years. I ran away from home five times when I was a little 'un, and the police took me back each time. Very good to me, the police was. Now I haven't got a home to run away from."

"Nor have I," the tramp said calmly.

"Oh, I can see what you are," the boy panted; "you're a gentleman come down. It's harder for you than for me." The tramp glanced at the limping, feeble figure and lessened his pace.

"I haven't been at it as long as you have," he admitted.

"No, I could tell that by the way you walk. You haven't got tired yet. Perhaps you expect something the other end?"

The tramp reflected for a moment. "I don't know," he said bitterly, "I'm always expecting things."

"You'll grow out of that," the boy commented. "It's warmer in London, but it's harder to come by grub. There isn't much in it really."

"Still, there's the chance of meeting somebody there who will understand—"

"Country people are better," the boy interrupted. "Last night I took a lease of a barn for nothing and slept with the cows, and this morning the farmer routed me out and gave me tea and toke because I was little. Of course, I score there; but in London, soup on the Embankment at night, and all the rest of the time coppers moving you on."

"I dropped by the roadside last night and slept where I fell. It's a wonder I didn't die," the tramp said. The boy looked at him sharply.

"How do you know you didn't?" he said.

"I don't see it," the tramp said, after a pause.

"I tell you," the boy said hoarsely, "people like us can't get away from this sort of thing if we want to. Always hungry and thirsty and dog-tired and walking all the time. And yet if anyone offers me a nice home and work my stomach feels sick. Do I look strong? I know I'm little for my age, but I've been knocking about like this for six years, and do you think I'm not dead? I was drowned bathing at Margate, and I was killed by a gipsy with a spike; he knocked my head right in, and twice I was froze like you last night, and a motor cut me down on this very road, and yet I'm walking along here now, walking to London to walk away from it again, because I can't help it. Dead! I tell you we can't get away if we want to."

The boy broke off in a fit of coughing, and the tramp paused while he recovered.

"You'd better borrow my coat for a bit, Tommy," he said, "your cough's pretty bad."

"You go to hell!" the boy said fiercely, puffing at his cigarette; "I'm all right. I was telling you about the road. You haven't got down to it yet, but you'll find out presently. We're all dead, all of us who're on it, and we're all tired, yet somehow we can't leave it. There's nice smells in the summer, dust and hay and the wind smack in your face on a hot day; and it's nice waking up in the wet grass on a fine morning. I don't know, I don't know—" He lurched forward suddenly, and the tramp caught him in his arms.

"I'm sick," the boy whispered—"sick."

The tramp looked up and down the road, but he could see no houses or any sign of help. Yet even as he supported the boy doubtfully in the middle of the road a motor-car suddenly flashed in the middle distance, and came smoothly through the snow.

"What's the trouble?" said the driver quietly as he pulled up. "I'm a doctor." He looked at the boy keenly and listened to his strained breathing.

"Pneumonia," he commented. "I'll give him a lift to the infirmary, and you, too, if you like."

The tramp thought of the workhouse and shook his head. "I'd rather walk," he said.

The boy winked faintly as they lifted him into the car.

"I'll meet you beyond Reigate," he murmured to the tramp. "You'll see." And the car vanished along the white road.

All the morning the tramp splashed through the thawing snow, but at midday he begged some bread at a cottage door and crept into a lonely barn to eat it. It was warm in there, and after his meal he fell asleep among the hay. It was dark when he woke, and started trudging once more through the slushy roads.

Two miles beyond Reigate a figure, a fragile figure, slipped out of the darkness to meet him.

"On the road, guv'nor?" said a husky voice. "Then I'll come a bit of the way with you if you don't walk too fast. It's a bit lonesome walking this time of day."

"But the pneumonia!" cried the tramp aghast.

"I died at Crawley this morning," said the boy.

Madeleine L'Engle

Poor Little Saturday

*Here is a story about a young boy and a witch and
a love that was generations old.*

The witch woman lived in a deserted, boarded-up plantation house, and nobody knew about her but me. Nobody in the nosey little town in south Georgia where I lived when I was a boy knew that if you walked down the dusty main street to where the post office ended it, and then turned left and followed that road a piece until you got to the rusty iron gates of the drive to the plantation house, you could find goings on would make your eyes pop out. It was just luck that I found out. Or maybe it wasn't luck at all. Maybe the witch woman wanted me to find out because of Alexandra. But now I wish I hadn't because the witch woman and Alexandra are gone forever and it's much worse than if I'd never known them.

Nobody'd lived in the plantation house since the Civil

War when Colonel Londermaine was killed and Alexandra Londermaine, his beautiful young wife, hung herself on the chandelier in the ballroom. A while before I was born some northerners bought it but after a few years they stopped coming and people said it was because the house was haunted. Every few years a gang of boys or men would set out to explore the house but nobody ever found anything, and it was so well boarded up it was hard to force an entrance, so by and by the town lost interest in it. No one climbed the wall and wandered around the grounds except me.

I used to go there often during the summer because I had bad spells of malaria when sometimes I couldn't bear to lie on the iron bedstead in my room with the flies buzzing around my face, or out on the hammock on the porch with the screams and laughter of the other kids as they played torturing my ears. My aching head made it impossible for me to read, and I would drag myself down the road, scuffling my bare sunburned toes in the dust, wearing the tattered straw hat that was supposed to protect me from the heat of the sun, shivering and sweating by turns. Sometimes it would seem hours before I got to the iron gates near which the brick wall was lowest. Often I would have to lie panting on the tall prickly grass for minutes until I gathered strength to scale the wall and drop down on the other side.

But once inside the grounds it seemed cooler. One funny thing about my chills was that I didn't seem to shiver nearly as much when I could keep cool as I did at home where even the walls and the floors, if you touched them, were hot. The grounds were filled with live oaks that had grown up unchecked everywhere and afforded an almost continuous green shade. The ground was covered with ferns which were soft and cool to lie on, and when I flung myself down on my back and looked up, the roof of leaves was so thick that sometimes I couldn't see the sky at all. The sun that managed to filter through lost its bright pitiless glare and came in soft yellow shafts that didn't burn you when they touched you.

One afternoon, a scorcher early in September, which is usually our hottest month (and by then you're fagged out by the heat anyhow), I set out for the plantation. The heat lay coiled and shimmering on the road. When you looked at anything through it, it was like looking through a defective pane of glass. The dirt road was so hot that it burned even through my calloused feet, and as I walked clouds of dust rose in front of me and mixed with the shimmying of the heat. I thought I'd never make the plantation. Sweat was running into my eyes, but it was cold sweat, and I was shivering so that my teeth chattered as I walked. When I managed finally to fling myself down on my soft green bed of ferns inside the grounds I was seized with one of the worst chills I'd ever had in spite of the fact that my mother had given me an extra dose of quinine that

morning and some 666 Malaria Medicine to boot. I shut
my eyes tight and clutched the ferns with my hands
and teeth to wait until the chill had passed, when I
heard a soft voice call:

"Boy."

I thought at first I was delirious, because sometimes
I got light-headed when my bad attacks came on; only
then I remembered that when I was delirious I didn't
know it: all the strange things I saw and heard seemed
perfectly natural. So when the voice said, "Boy," again,
as soft and clear as the mocking bird at sunrise, I
opened my eyes.

Kneeling near me on the ferns was a girl. She must
have been about a year younger than I. I was almost
sixteen so I guess she was fourteen or fifteen. She was
dressed in a blue and white gingham dress; her face
was very pale, but the kind of paleness that's supposed
to be, not the sickly pale kind that was like mine showing even under the tan. Her eyes were big and very
blue. Her hair was dark brown and she wore it parted
in the middle in two heavy braids that were swinging
in front of her shoulders as she peered into my face.

"You don't feel well, do you?" she asked. There was
no trace of concern or worry in her voice. Just scientific
interest.

I shook my head. "No," I whispered, almost afraid
that if I talked she would vanish, because I had never
seen anyone here before, and I thought that maybe I

was dying because I felt so awful, and I thought maybe that gave me the power to see the ghost. But the girl in blue and white checked gingham seemed as I watched her to be good flesh and blood.

"You'd better come with me," she said. "She'll make you all right."

"Who's she?"

"Oh—just Her," she said.

My chill had begun to recede by now, so when she got up off her knees, I scrambled up, too. When she stood up her dress showed a white ruffled petticoat underneath it, and bits of green moss had left patterns on her knees and I didn't think that would happen to the knees of a ghost, so I followed her as she led the way towards the house. She did not go up the sagging, half-rotted steps which led to the veranda about whose white pillars wisteria vines climbed in wild profusion, but went around to the side of the house where there were slanting doors to a cellar. The sun and rain had long since blistered and washed off the paint, but the doors looked clean and were free of the bits of bark from the eucalyptus tree which leaned nearby and which had dropped its bits of dusty peel on either side; so I knew that these cellar stairs must frequently be used.

The girl opened the cellar doors. "You go down first," she said. I went down the cellar steps which were stone, and cool against my bare feet. As she followed me she closed the cellar doors after her and as I reached the bottom of the stairs we were in pitch darkness. I began to be very frightened until her soft voice came out of the black.

"Boy, where are you?"

"Right here."

"You'd better take my hand. You might stumble."

We reached out and found each other's hands in the darkness. Her fingers were long and cool and they closed firmly around mine. She moved with authority as though she knew her way with the familiarity born of custom.

"Poor Sat's all in the dark," she said, "but he likes it that way. He likes to sleep for weeks at a time. Sometimes he snores awfully. Sat, darling!" she called gently. A soft, bubbly, blowing sound came in answer, and she laughed happily. "Oh, Sat, you are sweet!" she said, and the bubbly sound came again. Then the girl pulled at my hand and we came out into a huge and dusty kitchen. Iron skillets, pots and pans, were still hanging on either side of the huge stove, and there was a rolling pin and a bowl of flour on the marble topped table in the middle of the room. The girl took a lighted candle off the shelf.

"I'm going to make cookies," she said as she saw me looking at the flour and the rolling pin. She slipped her hand out of mine. "Come along." She began to walk more rapidly. We left the kitchen, crossed the hall, went through the dining room, its old mahogany table thick with dust although sheets covered the pictures on the walls. Then we went into the ballroom. The mirrors lining the walls were spotted and discolored; against one wall was a single delicate gold chair, its seat cushioned with pale rose and silver woven silk; it seemed extraordinarily well preserved. From the ceiling hung the huge chandelier from which Alexandra Londermaine had hung herself, its prisms catching and breaking up into a hundred colors the flickering of the candle and the few shafts of light that managed to slide in through the boarded-up windows. As we crossed the ballroom the girl began to dance by herself, gracefully, lightly, so that her full blue and white checked gingham skirts flew out around her. She looked at herself with pleasure in the old mirrors as she danced, the candle flaring and guttering in her right hand.

"You've stopped shaking. Now what will I tell Her?" she said as we started to climb the broad mahogany staircase. It was very dark so she took my hand again, and before we had reached the top of the stairs I obliged her by being seized by another chill. She felt my trembling fingers with satisfaction. "Oh, you've started again. That's good." She slid open one of the huge double doors at the head of the stairs.

As I looked into what once must have been Colonel Londermaine's study I thought that surely what I saw was a scene in a dream or a vision in delirium. Seated at the huge table in the center of the room was the most extraordinary woman I had ever seen. I felt that she must be very beautiful, although she would never have fulfilled any of the standards of beauty set by our town. Even though she was seated I felt that she must be immensely tall. Piled up on the table in front of her were several huge volumes, and her finger was marking the place in the open one in front of her, but she was not reading. She was leaning back in the carved chair, her head resting against a piece of blue and gold embroidered silk that was flung across the chair back, one hand gently stroking a fawn that lay sleeping in her lap. Her eyes were closed and somehow I couldn't imagine what color they would be. It wouldn't have surprised me if they had been shining amber or the deep purple of her velvet robe. She had a great quantity of hair, the color of mahogany in firelight, which was cut quite short and seemed to be blown wildly about her head like flame. Under her closed eyes were deep shadows, and lines of pain about her mouth. Otherwise there were no marks of age on her face but I would not have been surprised to learn that she was any age in the world—a hundred, or twenty-five. Her mouth was large and mobile and she was singing something in a deep, rich voice. Two cats, one black, one white, were coiled up, each on a book, and as we opened the doors a leopard stood up quietly beside her, but did not snarl or move. It simply stood there and waited, watching us.

The girl nudged me and held her finger to her lips to warn me to be quiet, but I would not have spoken—

could not, anyhow, my teeth were chattering so from my chill which I had completely forgotten, so fascinated was I by this woman sitting back with her head against the embroidered silk, soft deep sounds coming out of her throat. At last these sounds resolved themselves into words, and we listened to her as she sang. The cats slept indifferently, but the leopard listened, too:

I sit high in my ivory tower,
    The heavy curtains drawn.
I've many a strange and lustrous flower,
    A leopard and a fawn

Together sleeping by my chair
    And strange birds softly winging,
And ever pleasant to my ear
    Twelve maidens' voices singing.

Here is my magic maps' array,
    My mystic circle's flame.
With symbol's art He lets me play,
    The unknown my domain,

And as I sit here in my dream
    I see myself awake,
Hearing a torn and bloody scream,
    Feeling my castle shake . . .

Her song wasn't finished but she opened her eyes and looked at us. Now that his mistress knew we were here the leopard seemed ready to spring and devour me at one gulp, but she put her hand on his sapphire-studded collar to restrain him.

"Well, Alexandra," she said, "Who have we here?"

The girl, who still held my hand in her long, cool fingers, answered, "It's a boy."

"So I see. Where did you find him?"

The voice sent shivers up and down my spine.

"In the fern bed. He was shaking. See? He's shaking now. Is he having a fit?" Alexandra's voice was filled with pleased interest.

"Come here, boy," the woman said.

As I didn't move, Alexandra gave me a push, and I advanced slowly. As I came near, the woman pulled one of the leopard's ears gently, saying, "Lie down, Thammuz." The beast obeyed, flinging itself at her feet. She held her hand out to me as I approached the table. If Alexandra's fingers felt firm and cool, hers had the strength of the ocean and the coolness of jade. She looked at me for a long time and I saw that her eyes were deep blue, much bluer than Alexandra's, so dark as to be almost black. When she spoke again her voice was warm and tender: "You're burning up with fever. One of the malaria bugs?" I nodded. "Well, we'll fix that for you."

When she stood and put the sleeping fawn down by the leopard, she was not as tall as I had expected her to be; nevertheless she gave an impression of great height. Several of the bookshelves in one corner were emptied of books and filled with various shaped bottles and retorts. Nearby was a large skeleton. There was an acid-stained wash basin, too; that whole section of the room looked like part of a chemist's or physicist's laboratory. She selected from among the bottles a small amber colored one, and poured a drop of the liquid it contained into a glass of water. As the drop hit the water there was a loud hiss and clouds of dense smoke arose. When it had drifted away she handed the glass to me and said, "Drink. Drink, my boy!"

My hand was trembling so that I could scarcely hold the glass. Seeing this, she took it from me and held it to my lips.

"What is it?" I asked.

"Drink it," she said, pressing the rim of the glass against my teeth. On the first swallow I started to choke and would have pushed the stuff away, but she forced the rest of the burning liquid down my throat. My whole body felt on fire. I felt flame flickering in every vein and the room and everything in it swirled around. When I had regained my equilibrium to a certain extent I managed to gasp out again, "What is it?"

She smiled and answered,

"Nine peacocks' hearts, four bats tongues,
    A pinch of moondust and a hummingbird's lungs."

Then I asked a question I would never have dared ask if it hadn't been that I was still half drunk from the potion I had swallowed, "Are you a witch?"

She smiled again, and answered, "I make it my profession."

Since she hadn't struck me down with a flash of lightning, I went on. "Do you ride a broomstick?"

This time she laughed. "I can when I like."

"Is it—is it very hard?"

"Rather like a bucking bronco at first, but I've always been a good horsewoman, and now I can manage very nicely. I've finally progressed to sidesaddle, though I still feel safer astride. I always rode my horse astride. Still, the best witches ride sidesaddle, so . . . Now run along home. Alexandra has lessons to study and I must work. Can you hold your tongue or must I make you forget?"

"I can hold my tongue."

She looked at me and her eyes burnt into me like the potion she had given me to drink. "Yes, I think you can," she said. "Come back tomorrow if you like. Thammuz will show you out."

The leopard rose and led the way to the door. As I hesitated, unwilling to tear myself away, it came back and pulled gently but firmly on my trouser leg.

"Good-bye, boy," the witch woman said. "And you won't have any more chills and fever."

"Good-bye," I answered. I didn't say thank you. I didn't say good-bye to Alexandra. I followed the leopard out.

She let me come every day. I think she must have been lonely. After all I was the only thing there with

50

a life apart from hers. And in the long run the only reason I have had a life of my own is because of her. I am as much a creation of the witch woman's as Thammuz the leopard was, or the two cats, Ashtaroth and Orus (it wasn't until many years after the last day I saw the witch woman that I learned that those were the names of the fallen angels).

She did cure my malaria, too. My parents and the townspeople thought that I had outgrown it. I grew angry when they talked about it so lightly and wanted to tell them that it was the witch woman, but I knew that if ever I breathed a word about her I would be eternally damned. Mamma thought we should write a testimonial letter to the 666 Malaria Medicine people, and maybe they'd send us a couple of dollars.

Alexandra and I became very good friends. She was a strange, aloof creature. She liked me to watch her while she danced alone in the ballroom or played on an imaginary harp—though sometimes I fancied I could hear the music. One day she took me into the drawing room and uncovered a portrait that was hung between two of the long boarded-up windows. Then she stepped back and held her candle high so as to throw the best light on the picture. It might have been a picture of Alexandra herself, or Alexandra as she might be in five years.

"That's my mother," she said. "Alexandra Londermaine."

As far as I knew from the tales that went about

town, Alexandra Londermaine had given birth to only one child, and that still-born, before she had hung herself on the chandelier in the ballroom—and anyhow, any child of hers would have been Alexandra's mother or grandmother. But I didn't say anything because when Alexandra got angry she became ferocious like one of the cats, and was given to leaping on me, scratching and biting. I looked at the portrait long and silently.

"You see, she has on a ring like mine," Alexandra said, holding out her left hand, on the fourth finger of which was the most beautiful sapphire and diamond ring I had ever seen, or rather, that I could ever have imagined, for it was a ring apart from any owned by even the most wealthy of the townsfolk. Then I realized that Alexandra had brought me in here and unveiled the portrait simply that she might show me the ring to better advantage, for she had never worn a ring before.

"Where did you get it?"

"Oh, she got it for me las' night."

"Alexandra," I asked suddenly, "how long have you been here?"

"Oh, a while."

"But how long?"

"Oh, I don't remember."

"But you must remember."

"I don't. I just came—like Poor Sat."

"Who's Poor Sat?" I asked, thinking for the first

time of whoever it was that had made the gentle bubbly noises at Alexandra the day she found me in the fern bed.

"Why, we've never showed you Sat, have we!" she exclaimed, "I'm sure it's all right, but we'd better ask Her first."

So we went to the witch woman's room and knocked. Thammuz pulled the door open with his strong teeth and the witch woman looked up from some sort of experiment she was making with test tubes and retorts. The fawn, as usual, lay sleeping near her feet. "Well?" she said.

"Is it all right if I take him to see Poor Little Saturday?" Alexandra asked her.

"Yes, I suppose so," she answered. "But no teasing," and turned her back to us and bent again over her test tubes as Thammuz nosed us out of the room.

We went down to the cellar. Alexandra lit a lamp and took me back to the corner furthest from the doors, where there was a stall. In the stall was a two-humped camel. I couldn't help laughing as I looked at him because he grinned at Alexandra so foolishly, displaying all his huge buck teeth and blowing bubbles through them.

"She said we weren't to tease him," Alexandra said severely, rubbing her cheek against the preposterous splotchy hair that seemed to be coming out, leaving bald pink spots of skin on his long nose.

"But what—" I started.

"She rides him sometimes." Alexandra held out her hand while he nuzzled against it, scratching his rubbery lips against the diamond and sapphire of her ring. "Mostly She talks to him. She says he is very wise. He goes up to Her room sometimes and they talk and talk. I can't understand a word they say. She says it's Hindustani and Arabic. Sometimes I can remember little bits of it, like: *iderow*, *sorcabatcha*, and *anna bibed bech*. She says I can learn to speak with them when I finish learning French and Greek."

Poor Little Saturday was rolling his eyes in delight as Alexandra scratched behind his ears. "Why is he called Poor Little Saturday?" I asked.

Alexandra spoke wth a ring of pride in her voice. "I named him. She let me."

"But why did you name him that?"

"Because he came last winter on the Saturday that was the shortest day of the year, and it rained all day so it got light later and dark earlier than it would have if it had been nice, so it really didn't have as much of itself as it should, and I felt so sorry for it I thought maybe it would feel better if we named him after it . . . She thought it was a nice name!" she turned on me suddenly.

"Oh, it is! It's a fine name!" I said quickly, smiling to myself as I realized how much greater was this compassion of Alexandra's for a day than any she might have for a human being. "How did She get him?" I asked.

"Oh, he just came."

"What do you mean?"

"She wanted him so he came. From the desert."

"He *walked!*"

"Yes. And swam part of the way. She met him at the beach and flew him here on the broomstick. You should have seen him. She was still all wet and looked so funny. She gave him hot coffee with things in it."

"What things?"

"Oh, just things."

Then the witch woman's voice came from behind us. "Well, children?"

It was the first time I had seen her out of her room. Thammuz was at her right heel, the fawn at her left. The cats, Ashtaroth and Orus, had evidently stayed upstairs. "Would you like to ride Saturday?" she asked me.

Speechless, I nodded. She put her hand against the wall and a portion of it slid down into the earth so that Poor Little Saturday was free to go out. "She's sweet, isn't she?" the witch woman asked me, looking affectionately at the strange, bumpy-kneed, splay-footed creature. "Her grandmother was very good to me in Egypt once. Besides, I love camel's milk."

"But Alexandra said she was a he!" I exclaimed.

"Alexandra's the kind of woman to whom all animals are he except cats, and all cats are she. As a matter of fact, Ashtaroth and Orus are she, but it wouldn't make any difference to Alexandra if they weren't. Go on out, Saturday. Come on!"

55

Saturday backed out, bumping her bulging knees and ankles against her stall, and stood under a live oak tree. "Down," the witch woman said. Saturday leered at me and didn't move. "Down, sorcabatcha!" the witch woman commanded, and Saturday obediently got down on her knees. I clambered up onto her, and before I had managed to get at all settled she rose with such a jerky motion that I knocked my chin against her front hump and nearly bit my tongue off. Round and round Saturday danced while I clung wildly to her front hump and the witch woman and Alexandra rolled on the ground with laughter. I felt as though I were on a very unseaworthy vessel on the high seas, and it wasn't long before I felt violently seasick as Saturday pranced among the live oak trees, sneezing delicately.

At last the witch woman called out, "Enough!" and Saturday stopped in her traces, nearly throwing me, and kneeling laboriously. "It was mean to tease you," the witch woman said, pulling my nose gently. "You may come sit in my room with me for a while if you like."

There was nothing I liked better than to sit in the witch woman's room and to watch her while she studied from her books, worked out strange-looking mathematical problems, argued with the zodiac, or conducted complicated experiments with her test tubes and retorts, sometimes filling the room with sulphurous odors or flooding it with red or blue light. Only once was I afraid of her, and that was when she danced with the skeleton in the corner. She had the room flooded with a strange red glow and I almost thought I could see the flesh covering the bones of the skeleton as they danced together like lovers. I think she had forgotten that I was sitting there, half hidden in the wing chair, because when they had finished dancing and the skeleton stood in the corner again, his bones shining and polished, devoid of any living trappings, she stood with her forehead against one of the deep red velvet curtains that covered the boarded-up windows and tears streamed down her cheeks. Then she went back to her test tubes and worked feverishly. She never alluded to the incident and neither did I.

As winter drew on she let me spend more and more time in the room. Once I gathered up courage enough to ask her about herself, but I got precious little satisfaction.

"Well, then, are you maybe one of the northerners who bought the place?"

"Let's leave it at that, boy. We'll say that's who I am. Did you know that my skeleton was old Colonel Londermaine? Not so old, as a matter of fact; he was only thirty-seven when he was killed at the battle of Bunker Hill—or am I getting him confused with his great grandfather, Rudolph Londermaine? Anyhow he was only thirty-seven, and a fine figure of a man, and Alexandra only thirty when she hung herself for love of him on the chandelier in the ballroom. Did you know that the fat man with the red mustaches has been trying to cheat your father? His cow will give sour milk for seven days. Run along now and talk to Alexandra. She's lonely."

When the winter had turned to spring and the camellias and azaleas and Cape Jessamine had given way to the more lush blooms of early May, I kissed Alexandra for the first time, very clumsily. The next evening when I managed to get away from the chores at home and hurried out to the plantation, she gave me her sapphire and diamond ring which she had strung for me on a narrow bit of turquoise satin. "It will keep us both safe," she said, "if you wear it always. And then when we're older we can get married and you can give it back to me. Only you mustn't let anyone see it, ever, ever, or She'd be very angry."

I was afraid to take the ring but when I demurred Alexandra grew furious and started kicking and biting and I had to give in.

Summer was almost over before my father discovered the ring hanging about my neck. I fought like a witch boy to keep him from pulling out the narrow ribbon and seeing the ring, and indeed the ring seemed to give me added strength and I had grown, in any case, much stronger during the winter than I had ever been in my life. But my father was still stronger than I, and he pulled it out. He looked at it in dead silence for a moment and then the storm broke. That was the famous Londermaine ring that had disappeared the night Alexandra Londermaine hung herself. That ring was worth a fortune. Where had I got it?

No one believed me when I said I had found it on the grounds near the house—I chose the grounds because I didn't want anybody to think I had been in the house or indeed that I was able to get in. I don't know why they didn't believe me; it still seems quite logical to me that I might have found it buried among the ferns.

It had been a long, dull year, and the men of the town were all bored. They took me and forced me to swallow quantities of corn liquor until I didn't know what I was saying or doing. When they had finished with me I didn't even manage to reach home before I was violently sick and then I was in my mother's arms and she was weeping over me. It was morning before I was able to slip away to the plantation house. I ran pounding up the mahogany stairs to the witch woman's room and opened the heavy sliding doors without knocking. She stood in the center of the room in her purple robe, her arms around Alexandra, who was weeping bitterly. Overnight the room had completely changed. The skeleton of Colonel Londermaine was gone, and books filled the shelves in the corner of the room that had been her laboratory. Cobwebs were everywhere, and broken glass lay on the floor; dust was inches thick on her work table. There was no sign of Thammuz, Ashtaroth or Orus, or the fawn, but four birds were flying about her, beating their wings against her hair.

She did not look at me or in any way acknowledge my presence. Her arm about Alexandra, she led her out of the room and to the drawing room where the portrait hung. The birds followed, flying around and around them. Alexandra had stopped weeping now. Her face was very proud and pale and if she saw me miserably trailing behind them she gave no notice. When the witch woman stood in front of the portrait the sheet fell from it. She raised her arms; there was a great cloud of smoke; the smell of sulphur filled my nostrils, and when the smoke was gone, Alexandra was gone, too. Only the portrait was there, the fourth finger of the left hand now bearing no ring. The witch woman raised her hand again and the sheet lifted itself up and covered the portrait. Then she went, with the birds, slowly back to what had once been her room, and still I tailed after, frightened as I had never been before in my life, or have been since.

She stood without moving in the center of the room for a long time. At last she turned and spoke to me.

"Well, boy, where is the ring?"

"They have it."

"They made you drunk, didn't they?"

"Yes."

"I was afraid something like this would happen when I gave Alexandra the ring. But it doesn't matter . . . I'm tired . . ." She drew her hand wearily across her forehead.

"Did I—did I tell them everything?"

"You did."

"I—I didn't know."

"I know you didn't know, boy."

"Do you hate me now?"

"No, boy, I don't hate you."

"Do you have to go away?"

"Yes."

"I bowed my head. "I'm so sorry . . ."

She smiled slightly. "The sands of time . . . Cities crumble and rise and will crumble again and breath dies down and blows once more . . ."

The birds flew madly about her head, pulling at her hair, calling into her ears. Downstairs we could hear a loud pounding, and then the crack of boards being pulled away from a window.

"Go, boy," she said to me. I stood rooted, motionless, unable to move. "GO!" she commanded, giving me a mighty push so that I stumbled out of the room. They were waiting for me by the cellar doors and caught me as I climbed out. I had to stand there and watch when they came out with her. But it wasn't the witch woman, my witch woman. It was *their* idea of a witch woman, someone thousands of years old, a disheveled old creature in rusty black, with long wisps of gray hair, a hooked nose, and four wiry black hairs springing out of the mole on her chin. Behind her flew the four birds and suddenly they went up, up, into the sky, directly in the path of the sun until they were lost in its burning glare.

Two of the men stood holding her tightly, although she wasn't struggling, but standing there, very quiet, while the others searched the house, searched it in vain. Then as a group of them went down into the cellar I remembered, and by a flicker of the old light in the witch woman's eyes I could see that she remembered, too. Poor Little Saturday had been forgotten. Out she came, prancing absurdly up the cellar steps, her rubbery lips stretched back over her gigantic teeth, her eyes bulging with terror. When she saw the witch woman, her lord and master, held captive by two dirty, insensitive men, she let out a shriek and began to kick and lunge wildly, biting, screaming with the blood-curdling, heart-rending screams that only a camel can make. One of the men fell to the ground, holding a leg in which the bone had snapped from one of Saturday's kicks. The others scattered in terror, leaving the witch woman standing on the veranda supporting herself by clinging to one of the huge wisteria vines that curled around the columns. Saturday clambered up onto the veranda, and knelt while she flung herself between the two humps. Then off they ran, Saturday still screaming, her knees knocking together, the ground shaking as she pounded along. Down from the sun plummeted the four birds and flew after them.

Up and down I danced, waving my arms, shouting wildly until Saturday and the witch woman and the birds were lost in a cloud of dust, while the man with the broken leg lay moaning on the ground beside me.

Ray Bradbury

The Lake

Even if there were no ghosts, our childhood loves
would haunt us always.

They cut the sky down to my size and threw it over the Michigan lake, put some kids yelling on yellow sand with bouncing balls, a gull or two, a criticizing parent, and me breaking out of a wet wave and finding this world bleary and moist.

I ran up on the beach.

Mama swabbed me with a furry towel. "Stand there and dry," she said.

I stood there and watched the sun take away the water beads on my arms. I replaced them with goose-pimples.

"My, there's a wind," said Mama. "Put on your sweater."

"Wait'll I watch my goose-bumps," I said.

"Harold," said Mama.

I inserted me into my sweater and watched the waves come up and fall down on the beach. But not clumsily. On purpose, with a green sort of elegance. Even a drunken man could not collapse with such elegance as those waves.

It was September. In the last days when things are getting sad for no reason. The beach was so long and lonely with only about six people on it. The kids quit bouncing the ball because somehow the wind made them sad, too, whistling the way it did, and they sat down and felt autumn come along the long beach.

All the hot dog places were boarded up with strips of golden planking, sealing in all the mustard, onion, meat odors of the long, joyful summer. It was like nailing summer into a series of coffins. One by one the places slammed their covers down, padlocked their doors, and the wind came and touched the sand, blowing away all of the million footprints of July and August. It got so that now, in September, there was nothing but the mark of my rubber tennis shoes and Donald and Delaus Schabold's feet, and their father down by the water curve.

Sand blew up in curtains on the sidewalks, and the merry-go-round was hidden with canvas, all the horses frozen in mid-air on their brass poles, showing teeth, galloping on. With only the wind for music, slipping through canvas.

I stood there. Everyone else was in school. I was not. Tomorrow I would be on my way westward across the United States on a train. Mom and I had come to the beach for one last brief moment.

There was something about the loneliness that made me want to get away by myself. "Mama, I want to run up the beach aways," I said.

"All right, but hurry back, and don't go near the water."

I ran. Sand spun under me and the wind lifted me. You know how it is, running, arms out so you feel veils from your fingers, caused by wind. Like wings.

Mama withdrew into the distance, sitting. Soon she was only a brown speck and I was all alone. Being alone is a newness to a twelve-year-old child. He is so used to people around. The only way he can be alone is in his mind. That's why children imagine such fantastic things. There are so many real people around, telling children what and how to do, that a boy has to run off down a beach, even if it's only in his mind, to get by himself in his own world with his own miniature values.

So now I was really alone.

I went down to the water and let it cool up to my stomach. Always before, with the crowd, I hadn't dared to look. But now—Sawing a man in half. A magician. Water is like that. It feels as if you were sawed in half and part of you, sugar, is dissolving away. Cool water, and once in a while a very elegantly stumbling wave that fell with a flourish of lace.

I called her name. A dozen times I called it.

"Tally! Tally! Oh, Tally!"

Funny, but you really expect answers to your calling when you are young. You feel that whatever you may think can be real. And sometimes maybe that is not so wrong.

I thought of Tally, swimming out into the water last May, with her pigtails trailing, blonde. She went laughing, and the sun was on her small twelve-year-old shoulders. I thought of the water settling quiet, of the life-guard leaping into it, of Tally's mother screaming, and how Tally never came out . . .

The life-guard tried to persuade her to come out, but she did not. He came back with only bits of water weed in his big knuckled fingers, and Tally was gone. She would not sit across from me at school any longer, or chase indoor balls on the brick street on summer nights. She had gone too far out, and the lake would not let her come back in.

And now in the lonely autumn when the sky was huge and the water was huge and the beach was so very long, I had come down for the last time, alone.

I called her name over and over. Tally, oh, Tally!

The wind blew so very softly, over my ears, the way wind blows over the mouth of seashells and sets them whispering. The water rose and embraced my chest and then to my knees, and up and down, one way and another, sucking under my heels.

"Tally! Come back, oh, Tally!"

I was only twelve. But I know how much I loved

her. It was that love that comes before all significance of body and morals. It was that love that is no more bad than wind and sea and sand lying side by side forever. It was made of all the warm long days together at the beach, and the humming quiet days of droning education at the school. All the long autumn days of the years past when I had carried her books home from school.

Tally!

I called her name for the last time. I shivered. I felt water on my face and did not know how it got there. The waves had not splashed that high.

Turning, I retreated to the sand and stood there for half an hour, hoping for one glimpse, one sign, one little bit of Tally to remember. Then, in a sort of symbol, I knelt and built a castle of sand, shaping it fine and building it up as Tally and I had often built them, so many of them. But this time I only built half of it. Then I got up.

"Tally, if you hear me, come in and build the rest."

I began to walk off toward that faraway speck that was Mama. The water came in and blended the sea castle circle by circle, smashing it down little by little, into the original smoothness.

I could not help but think that there are no castles in life that one builds that some wave does not spread down into the old, old formlessness.

Silently, I walked up the beach.

Far away, a merry-go-round jangled faintly, but it was only the wind.

I went away on the train the next day.

Across the cornlands of Illinois. A train has a poor memory. It soon puts all behind it. It forgets the rivers of childhood, the bridges, the lakes, the valleys, the cottages, the pains and joys. It spreads them out behind and they drop back of a horizon.

I lengthened my bones, put flesh on them, changed my young mind for an older one, threw away clothes as they no longer fitted, shifted from grammar to high-school, to college books, to law-books. And then there was a young woman in Sacramento, there was a preacher, and there were words and kisses.

I continued with my law study. By the time I was twenty-two, I had almost forgotten what the East was like.

Margaret suggested that our delayed honeymoon trip be taken back in that direction.

A train works both ways, like a memory. It brings rushing back all those things you left behind so many years before.

Lake Bluff, population 10,000, came up over the sky. Margaret looked so handsome in her fine new clothes. She kept watching me as I watched my old world gather me back into its living. Her strong white hands held onto mine as the train slid into Bluff station and our baggage was escorted out.

So many years, and the things they do to people's faces and bodies. When we walked through the town, arm in arm, I saw no one I recognized. There were faces with echoes in them. Echoes of hikes on ravine trails. Faces with small laughter in them from closed grammar schools and swinging on metal-linked swings and going up and down on teeter-totters. But I didn't speak. I just walked and looked and filled up inside with all those memories, like leaves stacked for burning in autumn.

Our days were happy there. Two weeks in all, revisiting all the places together. I thought I loved Margaret very well. At least I thought I did.

It was on one of the last days that we walked down by the shore. It was not quite as late in the year as that day so many years before, but the first evidences of desertion were coming upon the beach. The people were thinning out, several of the hot dog places had been shuttered and nailed, and the wind, as always, had been waiting there to sing for us.

I almost saw Mama sitting on the sand as she used to sit. I had that feeling again of wanting to be alone. But I could not force myself to say it to Margaret. I only held onto her and waited.

It got late in the day. Most of the children had gone home, and only a few men and women remained basking in the windy sun.

The life-guard boat pulled up on the shore. The life-

guard stepped out of it, slowly, with something in his
arms.

I froze there. I held my breath and I felt small, only
twelve years old, very little, very infinitesimal and
afraid. The wind howled. I could not see Margaret. I
could see only the beach, the life-guard slowly emerg-
ing from his boat with a gray sack in his hands, not
very heavy, and his face almost as gray and lined.

"Stay here, Margaret," I said. I don't know why I
said it.

"But why?"

"Just stay here, that's all—"

I walked slowly down the sand to where the life-
guard stood. He looked at me.

"What is it?" I asked.

The life-guard kept looking at me for a long time
and he couldn't speak. He put the gray sack down on
the sand, the water whispered wet around it and went
back.

"What is it?" I insisted.

"She's dead," said the life-guard quietly.

I waited.

"Funny," he said softly, "funniest thing I ever saw.
She's been dead—a long time."

I repeated his words. "A long time?"

"Ten years, I'd say. There haven't been any children drowned here *this* year. There were twelve
children drowned here since 1933, but we recovered

71

all their bodies before a few hours had passed. All except one, I remember. This body here, why it must be ten years in the water. It's not—pleasant."

"Open it," I said. I don't know why I said it. The wind was louder.

He fumbled with the sack. "The way I know it's a little girl, is because she's still wearing a locket. There's nothing much else to tell by—"

"Hurry, man *open it!*" I cried.

"I better not do that," he said. Then maybe he saw the way my face must have looked. "She was such a little girl—"

He opened it only part way. That was enough.

The beach was deserted. There was only the sky and the wind and the water and the autumn coming on lonely. I looked down at her there.

I said something, over and over. The life-guard looked at me. "Where did you find her?" I asked.

"Down the beach, in the shallow water. Down that way. It's a long, long time for her, ain't it?"

I shook my head.

"Yes, it is. Oh, God, yes it is."

I thought, people grow. I have grown. But she has not changed. She is still small. She is still young. Death does not permit growth or change. She still has golden hair. She will be forever young and I will love her forever, oh God, I will love her forever.

The life-guard tied up the sack again.

Down the beach, a few moments later, I walked by

myself. I found something I didn't really expect. This is where the life-guard found her body, I said to myself.

There, at the water's edge, lay a sand-castle, only half built. Just like Tally and I used to make them. She—half. And I—half.

I looked at it. This is where they found Tally. I knelt beside the sand-castle and saw the little prints of feet coming in from the lake and going back out to the lake again—and not returning ever.

Then—I knew.

"I'll help you to finish it," I said.

I did. I built the rest of it up very slowly, and then I arose and turned away and walked off, so as not to watch it crumble in the waves, as all things crumble.

I walked back up the beach to where a strange woman named Margaret waited for me, smiling. . . .

Sir Arthur Quiller-Couch

A Pair of Hands

*Have a tissue ready when you read this story, for
when you're done you'll surely shed a tear for little
Margaret.*

"Yes," said Miss Le Petyt, gazing into the deep fireplace and letting her hands and her knitting lie for the
moment idle in her lap. "Oh, yes, I have seen a ghost.
In fact I have lived in a house with one for quite a
long time."

"How you *could*—!" began one of my host's daugh-
ters; and "You, Aunt Emily?" cried the other at the
same moment.

Miss Le Petyt, gentle soul, withdrew her eyes from
the fireplace and protested with a gay little smile.
"Well, my dears, I am not quite the coward you take
me for. And, as it happens, mine was the most harm-
less ghost in the world. In fact"—and here she looked
at the fire again—"I was quite sorry to lose her."

"It was a woman, then? Now *I* think," said Miss Blanche, "that female ghosts are the horridest of all. They wear little shoes with high red heels, and go about *tap, tap*, wringing their hands."

"This one wrung her hands, certainly. But I don't know about the high red heels, for I never saw her feet. Perhaps she was like the Queen of Spain, and hadn't any. And as for the hands, it all depends *how* you wring them. There's an elderly shopwalker at Knightbridge, for instance—"

"Don't be prosy, you know that we're just dying to hear the story."

Miss Le Petyt turned to me with a small deprecating laugh. "It's such a little one."

"The story, or the ghost?"

"Both."

And this was Miss Le Petyt's story:

"It happened when I lived down in Cornwall, at Tresillack on the south coast. Tresillack was the name of the house, which stood quite alone at the head of a coombe, within sound of the sea but without sight of it; for though the coombe led down to a wide open beach, it wound and twisted half a dozen times on its way, and its overlapping sides closed the view from the house, which was advertised as "secluded." I was very poor in those days. Your father and all of us were poor then, as I trust, my dears, you will never be; but I was young enough to be romantic and wise enough

75

to like independence, and this word "secluded" took my fancy.

"The misfortune was that it had taken the fancy, or just suited the requirements, of several previous tenants. You know, I dare say, the kind of person who rents a secluded house in the country? Well, yes, there are several kinds; but they seem to agree in being odious. No one knows where they come from, though they soon remove all doubt about where they're "going to," as the children say. "Shady" is the word, is it not? Well, the previous tenants of Tresillack (from first to last a bewildering series) had been shady with a vengeance.

"I knew nothing of this when I first made application to the landlord, a solid yeoman inhabiting a farm at the foot of the coombe, on a cliff overlooking the beach. To him I presented myself fearlessly as a spinster of decent family and small but assured income, intending a rural life of combined seemliness and economy. He met my advances politely enough, but with an air of suspicion which offended me. I began by disliking him for it: afterwards I set it down as an unpleasant feature in the local character. I was doubly mistaken. Farmer Hosking was slow-witted, but as honest a man as ever stood up against hard times; and a more open and hospitable race than the people on that coast I never wish to meet. It was the caution of a child who had burnt his fingers, not once but many times. Had I known what I afterwards learned of Farmer Hosking's tribulations as landlord of a 'secluded country resi- dence,' I should have approached him with the bash- fulness proper to my suit and faltered as I undertook to prove the bright exception in a long line of painful experiences. He had bought the Tresillack estate twenty years before—on mortgage, I fancy—because the land adjoined his own and would pay him for tillage. But the house was a nuisance, an incubus; and had been so from the beginning.

" 'Well, miss,' he said, 'you're welcome to look over it; a pretty enough place inside and out. There's no trouble about keys, because I've put in a housekeeper, a widow-woman, and she'll show you round. With your leave I'll step up the coombe so far with you, and put you in your way.' As I thanked him he paused and rubbed his chin. 'There's one thing I must tell you, though. Whoever takes the house must take Mrs. Car- keek along with it.'

" 'Mrs. Carkeek?' I echoed dolefully. 'Is that the housekeeper?'

" 'Yes: she was wife to my late hind. I'm sorry, miss,' he added, my face telling him no doubt what sort of woman I expected Mrs. Carkeek to be; 'but I had to make it a rule after—after some things that happened. And I dare say you won't find her so bad. Mary Car- keek's a sensible comfortable woman, and knows the place. She was in service there to Squire Kendall when he sold up and went: her first place it was.'

" 'I may as well see the house, anyhow,' said I dejectedly. So we started to walk up the coombe. The path, which ran beside a little chattering stream, was narrow for the most part, and Farmer Hosking, with an apology, strode on ahead to beat aside the brambles. But whenever its width allowed us to walk side by side I caught him from time to time stealing a shy inquisitive glance under his rough eyebrows. Courteously though he bore himself, it was clear that he couldn't sum me up to his satisfaction or bring me square with his notion of a tenant for his 'secluded country residence.'

" 'I don't know what foolish fancy prompted it, but about halfway up the coombe I stopped short and asked:

" 'There are no ghosts, I suppose?'

"It struck me, a moment after I had uttered it, as a supremely silly question; but he took it quite seriously. 'No; I never heard tell of any *ghosts*.' He laid a queer sort of stress on the word. 'There's always been trouble with servants, and maids' tongues will be runnin'. But Mary Carkeek lives up there alone, and she seems comfortable enough.'

"We walked on. By-and-by he pointed with his stick. 'It don't look like a place for ghosts, now, do it?'

"Certainly it did not. Above an untrimmed orchard rose a terrace of turf scattered with thorn-bushes, and above this a terrace of stone, upon which stood the prettiest cottage I had ever seen. It was long and low and thatched; a deep verandah ran from end to end.

Clematis, Banksia roses and honeysuckle climbed the posts of this verandah, and big blooms of the Maréchal Niel were clustered along its roof, beneath the lattices of the bedroom windows. The house was small enough to be called a cottage, and rare enough in features and in situation to confer distinction on any tenant. It suggested what in those days, we should have called 'elegant' living. And I could have clapped my hands for joy.

"My spirits mounted still higher when Mrs. Carkeek opened the door to us. I had looked for a Mrs. Gummidge, and I found a healthy middle-aged woman with a thoughtful but contented face, and a smile which, without a trace of obsequiousness, quite bore out the farmer's description of her. She was a comfortable woman; and while we walked through the rooms together (for Mr. Hosking waited outside) I 'took to' Mrs. Carkeek. Her speech was direct and practical; the rooms, in spite of their faded furniture, were bright and exquisitely clean; and somehow the very atmosphere of the house gave me a sense of well-being, of feeling at home and cared for; yes, *of being loved*. Don't laugh, my dears; for when I've done you may not think this fancy altogether foolish.

"I stepped out into the verandah, and Farmer Hosking pocketed the pruning-knife which he had been using on a bush of jasmine.

" 'This is better than anything I had dreamed of,' said I.

" 'Well, miss, that's not a wise way of beginning a bargain, if you'll excuse me.'

"He took no advantage, however, of my admission; and we struck the bargain as we returned down the coombe to his farm, where the hind chaise waited to convey me back to the market town. I had meant to engage a maid of my own, but now it occurred to me that I might do very well with Mrs. Carkeek. This, too, was settled in the course of the next day or two, and within the week I had moved into my new home.

"I can hardly describe to you the happiness of my first month at Tresillack; because (as I now believe) if I take the reasons which I had for being happy, one by one, there remains over something which I cannot account for. I was moderately young, entirely healthy; I felt myself independent and adventurous; the season was high summer, the weather glorious, the garden in all the pomp of June, yet sufficiently unkempt to keep me busy, give me a sharp appetite for meals, and send me to bed in that drowsy stupor which comes of the odors of earth. I spent the most of my time out of doors, winding up the day's work as a rule with a walk down the cool valley along the beach and back.

"I soon found that all housework could be safely left to Mrs. Carkeek. She did not talk much; indeed her only fault (a rare one in housekeepers) was that she talked too little, and even when I addressed her seemed at times unable to give me her attention. It was as though her mind strayed off to some small job she had forgotten, and her eyes wore a listening look, as though she waited for the neglected task to speak and remind her. But as a matter of fact she forgot nothing. Indeed, my dears, I was never so well attended to in my life.

"Well, that is what I'm coming to. That, so to say, is just *it*. The woman not only had the rooms swept and dusted, and my meals prepared to the moment. In a hundred odd little ways this orderliness, these preparations, seemed to read my desires. Did I wish the roses renewed in a bowl upon the dining-table, sure enough at the next meal they would be replaced by fresh ones. Mrs. Carkeek (I told myself) must have surprised and interpreted a glance of mine. And yet I could not remember having glanced at the bowl in her presence. And how on earth had she guessed the very roses, the very shapes and colors I had lightly wished for? This is only an instance, you understand. Every day, and from morning to night, I happened on others, each slight enough, but all together bearing witness to a ministering intelligence as subtle as it was untiring.

"I am a light sleeper, as you know, with an uncomfortable knack of waking with the sun and roaming early. No matter how early I rose at Tresillack, Mrs. Carkeek seemed to have preceded me. Finally I had to conclude that she arose and dusted and tidied as soon as she judged me safely a-bed. For once, finding the drawing-room (where I had been sitting late) 'redded-up' at four in the morning, and no trace of a plate

81

of raspberries which I had carried thither after dinner and left overnight, I determined to test her, and walked through to the kitchen, calling her by name. I found the kitchen as clean as a pin, and the fire laid, but no trace of Mrs. Carkeek. I walked upstairs and knocked at her door. At the second knock a sleepy voice cried out, and presently the good woman stood before me in her nightgown, looking (I thought) very badly scared.

" 'No,' I said, 'it's not a burglar. But I've found out what I wanted, that you do your morning's work overnight. But you mustn't wait for me when I choose to sit up. And now go back to your bed like a good soul, whilst I take a run down to the beach."

"She stood blinking in the dawn. Her face was still white.

" 'Oh, miss,' she gasped. 'I was sure you must have seen something!'

" 'And so I have,' I answered, 'but it was neither burglars nor ghosts.'

" 'Thank God!' I heard her say as she turned her back to me in her gray bedroom—which faced the north. And I took this for a carelessly pious expression and ran downstairs, thinking no more of it.

"A few days later I began to understand.

"The plan of Tresillack house (I must explain) was simplicity itself. To the left of the hall as you entered was the dining-room; to the right the drawing-room, with a boudoir beyond. The foot of the stairs faced the front door and beside it, passing a glazed inner door, you found two others right and left, the left opening on the kitchen, the right on a passage which ran by a store-cupboard under the bend of the stairs to a neat pantry with the usual shelves and linen-press, and under the window (which faced north) a procelain basin and brass tap. On the first morning of my tenancy I had visited this pantry and turned the tap; but no water ran. I supposed this to be accidental. Mrs. Carkeek had to wash up glassware and crockery, and no doubt Mrs. Carkeek would complain of any failure in the water supply.

"But the day after my surprise visit (as I called it) I had picked a basketful of roses, and carried them into the pantry as a handy place to arrange them in. I chose a china bowl and went to fill it at the tap. Again the water would not run.

"I called Mrs. Carkeek. 'What is wrong with this tap?' I asked.

" 'I don't know, miss. I never use it.'

" 'But there must be a reason; and you must find it a great nuisance washing up the plate and glasses in the kitchen. Come around to the back with me, and we'll have a look at the cisterns.'

" 'The cisterns'll be all right, miss. I assure you I don't find it a trouble.'

"But I was not to be put off. The back of the house stood ten feet from a wall which was really but a stone face built against the cliff cut away by the architect. Above the cliff rose the kitchen garden, and from its lower path we looked over the wall's parapet upon the cisterns. There were two—a very large one, supplying the kitchen and the bathroom above the kitchen; and a small one, obviously fed by the other, and as obviously leading, by a pipe which I could trace, to the pantry. Now the big cistern stood almost full, and yet the small one, though on a lower level, was empty.

" 'It's as plain as daylight,' said I. 'The pipe between the two is choked.' And I clambered onto the parapet.

" 'I wouldn't, miss. The pantry tap is only cold water, and no use to me. From the kitchen boiler I gets it hot, you see.'

" 'But I want the pantry water for my flowers.' I bent over and groped. 'I thought as much!' said I, as I wrenched out a thick plug of cork and immediately the water began to flow. I turned triumphantly on Mrs. Carkeek, who had grown suddenly red in the face. Her eyes were fixed on the cork in my hand. To keep it more firmly wedged in its place somebody had wrapped it round with a rag of calico print; and, discolored though the rag was, I seemed to recall the pattern (a lilac sprig). Then, as our eyes met, it occurred to me that only two mornings before Mrs. Carkeek had worn a print gown of that same sprigged pattern.

"I had the presence of mind to hide this very small discovery, sliding over it some quite trivial remark; and presently Mrs. Carkeek regained her composure. But I own I felt disappointed in her. It seemed such a paltry thing to be disingenuous over. She had deliberately acted a fib before me; and why? Merely because she preferred the kitchen to the pantry tap. It was childish. 'But servants are all the same,' I told myself. 'I must take Mrs. Carkeek as she is; and, after all, she is a treasure.'

"On the second night after this, and between eleven and twelve o'clock, I was lying in bed and reading myself sleepy over a novel of Lord Lytton's, when a small sound disturbed me. I listened. The sound was clearly that of water trickling; and I set it down to rain. A shower (I told myself) had filled the water pipes which drained the roof. Somehow I could not fix the sound. There was a water-pipe against the wall just outside my window. I rose and drew up the blind.

"To my astonishment no rain was falling; no rain had fallen. I felt the slate window-sill: some dew had gathered there—no more. There was no wind, no cloud: only a still moon high over the eastern slope of the coombe, the distant splash of waves, and the fragrance of many roses. I went back to bed and listened again. Yes, the trickling sound continued, quite distinct in the silence of the house, not to be confused for a moment with the dull murmur of the beach. After a while it began to grate on my nerves. I caught up my candle, flung my dressing-gown about me, and stole softly downstairs.

"Then it was simple. I traced the sound to the pantry. 'Mrs. Carkeek has left the tap running,' said I: and, sure enough, I found it so—a thin trickle steadily running to waste in the procelain basin. I turned off the tap, went contentedly back to bed, and slept.

"—for some hours. I opened my eyes in darkness, and at once knew what had awakened me. The tap was running again. Now it had shut easily in my hand, but not so easily that I could believe it had slipped open again of its own accord. 'This is Mrs. Carkeek's doing,' said I; and am afraid I added 'Bother Mrs. Carkeek!'

"Well, there was no help for it: so I struck a light, looked at my watch, saw that the hour was just three o'clock, and descended the stairs again. At the pantry door I paused. I was not afraid—not one little bit. In fact the notion that anything might be wrong had never crossed my mind. But I remember thinking, with my hand on the door, that if Mrs. Carkeek were in the pantry I might happen to give her a severe fright.

"I pushed the door open briskly. Mrs. Carkeek was not there. But something *was* there, by the porcelain basin—something which might have sent me scurrying upstairs two steps at a time, but which as a matter of fact held me to the spot. My heart seemed to stand still—so still! And in the stillness I remember setting down the brass candlestick on a tall nest of drawers beside me.

"Over the porcelain basin and beneath the water trickling from the tap I saw two hands.

"That was all—two small hands, a child's hands. I cannot tell you how they ended.

"No: they were not cut off. I saw them quite distinctly: just a pair of small hands and the wrists, and after that—nothing. They were moving briskly—washing themselves clean. I saw the water trickle and splash over them—not *through* them—but just as it would on real hands. They were the hands of a little girl, too. Oh, yes, I was sure of that at once. Boys and girls wash their hands differently. I can't just tell you what the difference is, but it's unmistakable.

"I saw all this before my candle slipped and fell with a crash. I had set it down without looking—for my eyes were fixed on the basin—and had balanced it on the edge of the nest of drawers. After the crash, in the darkness there, with the water running, I suffered some bad moments. Oddly enough, the thought uppermost with me was that I *must* shut off that tap before escaping. I *had* to. And after a while I picked up all my courage, so to say, between my teeth, and with a little sob thrust out my hand and did it. Then I fled.

"The dawn was close upon me: and as soon as the sky reddened I took my bath, dressed and went downstairs. And there at the pantry door I found Mrs. Carkeek, also dressed, with my candlestick in her hand.

" 'Ah!' said I, 'you picked it up.'

"Our eyes met. Clearly Mrs. Carkeek wished me to begin, and I determined at once to have it out with her.

" 'And you knew all about it. That's what accounts for your plugging up the cistern.'

" 'You saw . . . ?' she began.

" 'Yes, yes. And you must tell me all about it—never mind how bad. Is—is it—murder?'

" 'Law bless you, miss, whatever put such horrors in your head?'

" 'She was washing her hands.'

" 'Ah, so she does, poor dear! But—murder! And dear little Miss Margaret, that wouldn't go to hurt a fly!'

" 'Miss Margaret?'

" 'Eh, she died at seven year. Squire Kendall's only daughter; and that's over twenty years ago. I was her nurse, miss, and I know—diphtheria it was; she took it down in the village.'

" 'But how do you know it is Margaret?'

" 'Those hands—why, how could I mistake, that used to be her nurse?'

" 'But why does she wash them?'

" 'Well, miss, being always a dainty child—and the housework, you see—'

"I took a long breath. 'Do you mean to tell me that all this tidying and dusting—' I broke off. 'Is it *she* who has been taking this care of me?'

"Mrs. Carkeek met my look steadily.

" 'Who else, miss?'

" 'Poor little soul!'

" 'Well now'—Mrs. Carkeek rubbed my candlestick

88

with the edge of her apron—'I'm so glad you take it like this. For there isn't really nothing to be afraid of—is there?' She eyed me wistfully. 'It's my belief she loves you, miss. But only to think what a time she must have had with the others!'

" 'The others?' I echoed.

" 'The other tenants, miss: the ones afore you.'

" 'Were they bad?'

" 'They were awful. Didn't Farmer Hosking tell you? They carried on fearful—one after another, and each one worse than the last.'

" 'What was the matter with them? Drink?'

" 'Drink, miss, with some of 'em. There was the Major—he used to go mad with it, and run about the coombe in his nightshirt. Oh, scandalous! And his wife drank too—that is, if she ever *was* his wife. Just think of that tender child washing up after their nasty doings!'

"I shivered.

" 'But that wasn't the worst by a long way. There was a pair here—from the colonies, or so they gave out—with two children, a boy and gel, the eldest scarce six. Poor mites!'

" 'Why, what happened?'

" 'They beat those children, miss—your blood would boil!—*and* starved, *and* tortured 'em, it's my belief. You could hear their screams, I've been told, away back in the high-road, and that's the best part of half a mile. Sometimes they was locked up without food for days together. But it's my belief that little Miss

Margaret managed to feed them somehow. Oh, I can see her, creeping to the door and comforting!'

" 'But perhaps she never showed herself when these awful people were here, but took to flight until they left.'

" 'You didn't never know her, miss. The brave she was! She'd have stood up to lions. She've been here all the while: and only to think what her innocent eyes and ears must have took in! There was another couple—' Mrs. Carkeek sunk her voice.

" 'Oh, hush!' said I, 'if I'm to have any peace of mind in this house!'

" 'But you won't go, miss? She loves you, I know she do. And think what you might be leaving her to— what sort of tenant might come next. For she can't go. She've been here ever since her father sold the place. He died soon after. You mustn't go!'

"Now I had resolved to go, but all of a sudden I felt how mean this resolution was.

" 'After all,' said I, 'there's nothing to be afraid of.'

" 'That's it, miss; nothing at all. I don't even believe it's so very uncommon. Why, I've heard my mother tell of farmhouses where the rooms were swept every night as regular as clockwork, and the floors sanded, and the pots and pans scoured, and all while the maids slept. They put it down to the piskies; but we know better, miss, and now we've got the secret between us we can lie easy in our beds, and if we hear anything, say 'God bless the child!' and go to sleep.'

" 'Mrs. Carkeek,' said I, 'there's only one condition I have to make.'

" 'What's that?'

" 'Why, that you let me kiss you.'

" 'Oh, you dear!' said Mrs. Carkeek as we embraced: and this was as close to familiarity as she allowed herself to go in the whole course of my acquaintance with her.

"I spent three years at Tresillack, and all that while Mrs. Carkeek lived with me and shared the secret. Few women, I dare to say, were ever so completely wrapped around with love as we were during those three years. It ran through my waking life like a song: it smoothed my pillow, touched and made my table comely, in summer lifted the heads of the flowers as I passed, and in winter watched the fire with me and kept it bright.

"Why did I ever leave Tresillack? Because one day, at the end of three years, Farmer Hosking brought me word that he had sold the house—or was about to sell it; I forget which. There was no avoiding it, at any rate; the purchaser being a Colonel Kendall, a brother of the old Squire.

" 'A married man?' I asked.

" 'Yes, miss; with a family of eight. As pretty children as ever you see, and the mother a good lady. It's the old home to Colonel Kendall.'

" 'I see. And that is why you feel bound to sell.'

" 'It's a good price, too, that he offers. You mustn't think but I'm sorry enough—'

" 'To turn me out? I thank you, Mr. Hosking; but you are doing the right thing.'

"Since Mrs. Carkeek was to stay, the arrangement lacked nothing of absolute perfection—except, perhaps, that it found no room for me.

" '*She*—Margaret—will be happy,' I said; 'with her cousins, you know.'

" 'Oh yes, miss, she will be happy, sure enough,' Mrs. Carkeek agreed.

"So when the time came I packed up by boxes, and tried to be cheerful. But on the last morning, when they stood corded in the hall, I sent Mrs. Carkeek upstairs upon poor excuse, and stepped alone into the pantry.

"'Margaret!' I whispered.

"There was no answer at all. I had scarcely dared to hope for one. Yet I tried again, and, shutting my eyes this time, stretched out both hands and whispered:

" 'Margaret!'

"And I will swear to my dying day that two little hands stole and rested—for a moment only—in mine."

Edward Page Mitchell

An Uncommon Sort of Spectre

While ghosts of the past are what we've seen so far,
here's a story that provides a new direction.

I

The ancient castle of Weinstein, on the upper Rhine, was, as everybody knows, inhabited in the autumn of 1352 by the powerful Baron Kalbsbraten, better known in those parts as Old Twenty Flasks, a sobriquet derived from his reputed daily capacity for the product of the vineyard. The baron had many other admirable qualities. He was a genial, whole-souled, public-spirited gentleman, who robbed, murdered, burned, pillaged, and drove up the steep sides of the Weinstein his neighbors' cattle, wives, and sisters, with a hearty bonhomie that won for him the unaffected esteem of his contemporaries.

One evening the good baron sat alone in the great hall of Weinstein, in a particularly happy mood. He had dined well, as was his habit, and twenty empty bottles stood before him in a row upon the table, like a train of delightful memories of the recent past. But the baron had another reason to be satisfied with himself and with the world. The consciousness that he had that day become a parent lit up his countenance with a tender glow that mere wine cannot impart.

"What ho! Without! Hi! Seneschal!" he presently shouted, in a tone that made the twenty empty bottles ring as if they were musical glasses, while a score of suits of his ancestors' armor hanging around the walls gave out in accompaniment a deep metallic bass. The seneschal was speedily at his side.

"Seneschal," said Old Twenty Flasks, "you gave me to understand that the baroness was doing finely?"

"I am told," replied the seneschal, "that her ladyship is doing as well as could be expected."

The baron mused in silence for a moment, absently regarding the empty bottles. "You also gave me to understand," he continued, "that there were—"

"Four," said the seneschal, gravely. "I am credibly informed that there are four, all boys."

"That," exclaimed the baron, with a glow of honest pride, bringing a brawny fist down upon the table— "That, in these days, when the abominable doctrines of Malthus are gaining ground among the upper classes, is what I call creditable—creditable, by Saint Christopher. If I do say it!" His eyes rested again upon the empty bottles. "I think, Seneschal," he added, after a brief pause, "that under the circumstances we may venture—"

"Nothing could be more eminently proper," rejoined the seneschal. "I will fetch another flask forthwith, and of the best. What says Your Excellency to the vintage of 1304, the year of the comet?"

"But," hesitated the baron, toying with his mustache, "I understood you to say that there were four of 'em—four boys?"

"True, my lord," replied the seneschal, snatching the idea with the readiness of a well-trained domestic. "I will fetch four more flasks."

As the excellent retainer deposited four fresh bottles upon the table within the radius of the baron's reach, he casually remarked, "A pious old man, a traveler, is in the castle yard, my lord, seeking shelter and a supper. He comes from beyond the Alps, and fares toward Cologne."

"I presume," said the baron, with an air of indifference, "that he has been duly searched for plunder."

"He passed this morning," replied the retainer, "through the domain of your well-born cousin, Count Conrad of Schwinkenfels. Your lordship will readily understand that he has nothing now save a few beggarly Swiss coins of copper."

"My worthy cousin Conrad!" exclaimed the baron, affectionately. "It is the one great misfortune of my life that I live to the leeward of Schwinkenfels. But you relieved the pious man of his copper?"

"My lord," said the seneschal, with an apologetic smile, "it was not worth the taking."

"Now by my soul," roared the baron, "you exasperate me! Coin, and not worth the taking! Perhaps not for its intrinsic value, but you should have cleaned him out as a matter of principle, you fool!"

The seneschal hung his head and muttered an explanation. At the same time he opened the twenty-first bottle.

"Never," continued the baron, less violently but still severely, "if you value my esteem and your own paltry skin, suffer yourself to be swerved a hair's breadth from principle by the apparent insignificance of the loot. A conscientious attention to details is one of the fundamental elements of a prosperous career—in fact, it underlies all political economy."

The withdrawal of the cork from the twenty-second bottle emphasized this statement.

"However," the baron went on, somewhat mollified, "this is not a day on which I can consistently make a fuss over a trifle. Four, and all boys! This is a glorious day for Weinstein. Open the two remaining flasks, Seneschal, and show the pious stranger in. I fain would amuse myself with him."

II

Viewed through the baron's twenty-odd bottles, the stranger appeared to be an aged man—eighty years, if a day. He wore a shabby gray cloak and carried a palmer's staff, and seemed an innocuous old fellow, cast in too commoplace a mold to furnish even a few minutes' diversion. The baron regretted sending for him, but being a person of unfailing politeness, when not upon the rampage, he bade his guest be seated and filled him a beaker of the comet wine.

After an obeisance, profound yet not servile, the pilgrim took the glass and critically tasted the wine. He held the beaker up athwart the light with trembling hand, and then tasted again. The trial seemed to afford him great satisfaction, and he stroked his long white beard.

"Perhaps you are a connoisseur. It pleases your palate, eh?" said the baron, winking at the full-length portrait of one of his ancestors.

"Proper well," replied the pilgrim, "though it is a trifle syrupy from too long keeping. By the bouquet and the tint, I should pronounce it of the vintage of 1304, grown on the steep slope south southeast of the castle, in the fork of the two pathways that lead under the hill. The sun's rays reflected from the turret give a peculiar excellence to the growth of that particular spot. But your rascally varlets have shelved the bottle on the wrong side of the cellar. It should have been put on the dry side, near where your doughty grandsire Sigismund von Weinstein, the Hairy Handed, walled up his third wife in preparation for a fourth."

The baron regarded his guest with a look of amazement. "Upon my life!" said he, "but you appear to be familiar with the ins and outs of this establishment."

"If I do," rejoined the stranger, composedly sipping his wine, " 'tis no more than natural, for I lived more than sixty years under this roof and know its every leak. I happen to be a Von Weinstein myself."

The baron crossed himself and pulled his chair a little further away from the bottles and the stranger.

"Oh no," said the pilgrim, laughing; "quiet your fears. I am aware that every well-regulated castle has an ancestral ghost, but my flesh and blood are honest. I was lord of Weinstein till I went, twelve years ago, to study metaphysics in the Arabic schools, and the cursed scriveners wrote me out of the estate. Why, I know this hall from infancy! Yonder is the fireplace at which I used to warm my baby toes. There is the identical suit of armor into which I crawled when a boy of six and hid till my sainted mother—heaven rest her!— nigh died of fright. It seems but yesterday. There on the wall hangs the sharp two-handed sword of our ancestor, Franz, the One-Eared, with which I cut off the mustaches of my tipsy sire as he sat muddled over his twentieth bottle. There is the very casque—but perhaps these reminiscences weary you. You must pardon the garrulity of an old man who has come to revisit the home of his childhood and prime."

The baron pressed his hand to his forehead. "I have lived in this castle myself for half a century," said he, "and am tolerably familiar with the history of my immediate progenitors. But I can't say that I ever had the pleasure of your acquaintance. However, permit me to fill your glass."

"It is good wine," said the pilgrim, holding out his glass. "Except, perhaps, the vintage of 1392, when the grapes—"

The baron stared at his guest. "The grapes of 1392," said he dryly, "lack forty years of ripening. You are aged, my friend, and your mind wanders."

"Excuse me, worthy host," calmly replied the pilgrim. "The vintage of 1392 has been forty years cellared. You have no memory for dates."

"What call you this year?" demanded the baron.

"By the almanacs, and the stars, and precedent, and common consent, it is the year of grace 1433."

"By my soul and hope of salvation," ejaculated the baron, "it is the year of grace 1352."

"There is evidently a misunderstanding somewhere," remarked the venerable stranger. "I was born here in the year 1352, the year the Turks invaded Europe."

"No Turk has invaded Europe, thanks be to heaven," replied Old Twenty Flasks, recovering his self-control. "You are either a magician or an imposter. In either case I shall order you drawn and quartered as soon as we have finished this bottle. Pray proceed with your very interesting reminiscences, and do not spare the wine."

"I never practice magic," quietly replied the pilgrim, "and as to being an imposter, scan well my face. Don't you recognize the family nose, thick, short, and generously colored? How about the three lateral and two diagonal wrinkles on my brow? I see them there on yours. Are not my chaps Weinstein chaps? Look closely. I court investigation."

"You do look damnably like us," the baron admitted.

"I was the youngest," the stranger went on, "of quadruplets. My three brothers were puny, sickly things and did not long survive their birth. As a child I was the idol of my poor father, who had some traits worthy of respectful mention, guzzling old toper and unconscionable thief though he was."

The baron winced.

"They used to call him Old Twenty Flasks. It is my candid opinion, based on memory, that Old Forty Flasks would have been nearer the truth."

"It's a lie!" shouted the baron, "I rarely exceeded twenty bottles."

"And as for his standing in the community," the pilgrim went on, without taking heed of the interruption, "it must be confessed that nothing could be worse. He was the terror of honest folk for miles around. Property rights were extremely insecure in this neighborhood, for the rapacity of my lamented parent knew no bounds. Yet nobody dared to complain aloud, for lives were not much safer than sheep or ducats. How the people hated his shadow, and roundly cursed him behind his back! I remember well that, when I was about fourteen—it must have been in '66, the year the

Grand Turk occupied Adrianople—tall Hugo, the miller, called me up to him, and said: 'Boy, thou has a right pretty nose.' 'It is a pretty nose, Hugo,' said I, straightening up. 'Is it on firm and strong?' asked Hugo, with a sneer. 'Firm enough, and strong enough, I dare say,' I answered; 'but why ask such a fool's question?' 'Well, well, boy,' said Hugo, turning away, 'look sharp with thine eyes after thy nose when thy father is un-occupied, for he has just that conscience to steal the nose off his son's face in lack of better plunder.'"

"By St. Christopher!" roared the baron, "tall Hugo, the miller, shall pay for this. I always suspected him. By St. Christopher's burden, I'll break every bone in his villainous body."

" 'Twould be an ignoble vengeance," replied the pilgrim, quietly, "for tall Hugo has been in his grave these sixty years."

"True," said the baron, putting both hands to his head, and gazing at his guest with a look of utter helplessness. "I forget that it is now next century—that is to say, if you be not a spectre."

"You will excuse me, my respected parent," returned the pilgrim, "if I subject your hypothesis to the test of logic, for it touches me upon a very tender spot, impugning, as it does, my physical verity and my status on an actual individualized ego. Now, what is our relative position? You acknowledge the date of my birth to have been the year of grace 1352. That is a matter in which your memory is not likely to be at fault. On the other hand, with a strange inconsistency, you maintain, in the face of almanacs, chronologies, and the march of events, that it is still the year of grace 1352. Were you one of the seven sleepers, your hallucination (to use no harsher term) might be pardoned, but you are neither a sleeper nor a saint. Now, every one of the eighty years that are packed away in the carpet bag of my experience protests against your extraordinary error. It is I who have a prima facie right to question your physical existence, not you mine. Did you ever hear of a ghost, spectre, wraith, apparition, eldolon, or spook coming out of the future to haunt, annoy, or frighten individuals of an earlier generation?"

The baron was obliged to admit that he never had.

"But you have heard of instances where apparitions, ghosts, spooks, call them what you will, have invaded the present from out the limbo of the past?"

The baron crossed himself a second time and peered anxiously into the dark corners of the apartment. "If you are a genuine Von Weinstein," he whispered, "you already know that this castle is overrun with spectres of that sort. It is difficult to move about after nightfall without tumbling over half a dozen of them."

"Then," said the placid logician, "you surrender your case. You commit what, my revered preceptor in dialectics, the learned Arabian Ben Dusty, used to style syllogistic suicide. For you allow that, while ghosts out of the future are unheard of, ghosts from the past are not infrequently encountered. Now I submit to you as a man, this proposition: That it is infinitely more probable that you are a ghost than that I am one!"

The baron turned very red. "Is this filial," he demanded, "to deny the flesh and blood of your own father?"

"Is it paternal," retorted the pilgrim, not losing his composure, "to insinuate the unrealness of the son of your own begetting?"

"By all the saints!" growled the baron, growing still redder, "this question shall be settled, and speedily. Halloo, there, Seneschal!" He called again and again, but in vain.

"Spare your lungs," calmly suggested the pilgrim. "The best-trained domestic in the world will not stir from beneath the sod for all your shouting."

Twenty Flasks sank back helplessly in his chair. He tried to speak, but his tongue and throat repudiated their functions. They only gurgled.

"That is right," said his guest, approvingly. "Conduct yourself as befits a venerable and respectable ghost from the last century. A well-behaved apparition neither blusters nor is violent. You can well afford to be peaceable in your deportment now; you were turbulent enough before your death."

"My death?" gasped the baron.

"Excuse me," apologized the pilgrim, "for referring to that unpleasant event."

"My death!" stammered the baron, his hair standing

103

on end. "I should like to hear the particulars."

"I was hardly more than fifteen at the time," said the pilgrim musingly; "but I shall never forget the most trifling circumstances of the great popular arising that put an end to my worthy sire's career. Exasperated beyond endurance by your outrageous crimes, the people for miles around at last rose in a body, and, led by my old friend tall Hugo, the miller, flocked to Schwinkenfels and appealed to your cousin, Count Conrad, for protection against yourself, their natural protector. Von Schwinkenfels heard their complaints with great gravity. He replied that he had long watched your abominable actions with distress and consternation; that he had frequently remonstrated with you, but in vain; that he regarded you as the scourge of the neighborhood; that your castle was full of blood-stained treasure and shamefully acquired booty; and that he now regarded it as the personal duty of himself, the conservator of lawful order and good morals, to march against Weinstein and exterminate you for the common good."

"The hypocritical pirate!" exlaimed Twenty Flasks.

"Which he proceeded to do," continued the pilgrim, "supported not only by his retainers but by your own. I must say that you made a sturdy defense. Had not your rascally seneschal sold you out to Schwinkenfels and let down the drawbridge one evening when you were as usual fuddling your brains with your twenty bottles, perhaps Conrad never would have gained an entrance, and my young eyes would have been spared the horrid task of watching the body of my venerated parent dangling at the end of a rope from the topmost turret of the northwest tower."

The baron buried his face in his hands and began to cry like a baby. "They hanged me, did they?" he faltered.

"I am afraid no other construction can be put on it," said the pilgrim. "It was the inevitable termination of such a career as yours had been. They hanged you, they strangled you, they choked you to death with a rope; and the unanimous verdict of the community was Justifiable Homicide. You weep! Behold, Father, I also weep for the shame of the house of Von Weinstein! Come to my arms."

Father and son clasped each other in a long, affectionate embrace and mingled their tears over the disgrace of Weinstein. When the baron recovered from his emotion he found himself alone with his conscience and twenty-four empty bottles. The pilgrim had disappeared.

III

Meanwhile, in the apartments consecrated to the offices of maternity, all had been confusion, turmoil, and distress. In four huge armchairs sat four experienced matrons, each holding in her lap a pillow of swan's-down. On each pillow had reposed an infinitesimal fraction of humanity, recently added to the sum total of Von Weinstein. One experienced matron had dozed over her charge; when she awoke the pillow in her lap was unoccupied. An immediate census taken by the alarmed attendants disclosed the startling fact that, although there were still four armchairs, and four sage women, and four pillows of swan's-down, there were but three infants. The seneschal, as an expert in mathematics and accounts, was hastily summoned from below. His reckoning merely confirmed the appalling suspicion. One of the quadruplets was gone.

Prompt measures were taken in this fearful emergency. The corners of the rooms were ransacked in vain. Piles of bedclothing and baskets of linen were searched through and through. The hunt extended to other parts of the castle. The seneschal even sent out trusted and discreet retainers on horseback to scour the surrounding country. They returned with downcast countenances; no trace of the lost Von Weinstein had been found.

During one terrible hour the wails of the three neglected infants mingled with the screams of the hysterical mother, to whom the attention of the four sage women was exclusively directed. At the end of the hour her ladyship had sufficiently recovered to implore her attendants to make a last, though hopeless count. On three pillows lay three babies howling lustily in unison. On the fourth pillow reposed a fourth infant, with a mysterious smile upon his face, but cheeks that bore traces of recent tears.

Edward Lucas White

The House of the Nightmare

The car crash and the haunted house seemed bad enough, but the biggest shock was yet to come.

I first caught sight of the house from the brow of the mountain as I cleared the woods and looked across the broad valley several hundred feet below me, to the low sun sinking toward the far blue hills. From that momentary viewpoint I had an exaggerated sense of looking almost vertically down. I seemed to be hanging over the checker-board of roads and fields, dotted with farm buildings, and felt the familiar deception that I could almost throw a stone upon the house. I barely glimpsed its slate roof.

What caught my eyes was the bit of road in front of it, between the mass of dark-green shade trees about the house and the orchard opposite. Perfectly straight it was, bordered by an even row of trees, through which I made out a cinder side path and a low stone wall.

Conspicuous on the orchard side between two of the flanking trees was a white object, which I took to be a tall stone, a vertical splinter of one of the tilted limestone reefs with which the fields of the region are scarred.

The road itself I saw plain as a box-wood ruler on a green baize table. It gave me a pleasurable anticipation of a chance for a burst of speed. I had been painfully traversing closely forested, semi-mountainous hills. Not a farmhouse had I passed, only wretched cabins by the road, more than twenty miles of which I had found very bad and hindering. Now, when I was not many miles from my expected stopping-place, I looked forward to better going, and to that straight, level bit in particular.

As I sped cautiously down the sharp beginning of the long descent the trees engulfed me again, and I lost sight of the valley. I dipped into a hollow, rose on the crest of the next hill, and again saw the house, nearer, and not so far below.

The tall stone caught my eye with a shock of surprise. Had I not thought it was opposite the house, next the orchard? Clearly it was on the left-hand side of the road toward the house. My self-questioning lasted only the moment as I passed the crest. Then the outlook was cut off again; but I found myself gazing ahead, watching for the next chance at the same view.

At the end of the second hill I saw the bit of road only obliquely and could not be sure, but, as at first, the tall stone seemed on the right of the road.

At the top of the third and last hill I looked down the stretch of road under the overarching trees, almost as one would look through a tube. There was a line of whiteness which I took for the tall stone. It was on the right.

I dipped into the last hollow. As I mounted the farther slope I kept my eyes on the top of the road ahead of me. When my line of sight surmounted the rise I marked the tall stone on my right hand among the serried maples. I leaned over, first on one side, then on the other, to inspect my tires, then I threw the lever.

As I flew forward I looked ahead. There was the tall stone—on the left of the road! I was really scared and almost dazed. I meant to stop dead, take a good look at the stone, and make up my mind beyond peradventure whether it was on the right or the left—if not, indeed, in the middle of the road.

In my bewilderment I put on the highest speed. The machine leaped forward; everything I touched went wrong; I steered wildly, slewed to the left, and crashed into a big maple.

When I came to my senses I was flat on my back in the dry ditch. The last rays of the sun sent shafts of golden green light through the maple boughs overhead. My first thought was an odd mixture of appreciation of the beauties of nature and a disapproval of my own conduct in touring without a companion—a fad I had regretted more than once. Then my mind cleared and I sat up. I felt myself from the head down. I was not bleeding; no bones were broken; and, while much shaken, I had suffered no serious bruises.

Then I saw the boy. He was standing at the edge of the cinderpath, near the ditch. He was stocky and solidly built; barefoot, with his trousers rolled up to his knees; wore a sort of butternut shirt, open at the throat; and was coatless and hatless. He was tow-headed, with a shock of tousled hair; was much freckled, and had a hideous harelip. He shifted from one foot to the other, twiddled his toes, and said nothing whatever, though he stared at me intently.

I scrambled to my feet and proceeded to survey the wreck. It seemed distressingly complete. It had not blown up, nor even caught fire; but otherwise the ruin appeared hopelessly thorough. Everything I examined seemed worse smashed than the rest. My two hampers alone, by one of those cynical jokes of chance, had escaped—both had pitched clear of the wreckage and were unhurt, not even a bottle broken.

During my investigations the boy's faded eyes followed me continuously, but he uttered no word. When I convinced myself of my helplessness I straightened up and addressed him:

"How far is it to a blacksmith shop?"

"Eight mile," he answered. He had a distressing

case of cleft palate and was scarcely intelligible.

"Can you drive me there?" I inquired.

"Nary team on the place," he replied; "nary horse, nary cow."

"How far to the next house?" I continued.

"Six mile," he responded.

I glanced at the sky. The sun had set already. I looked at my watch: it was going—seven thirty-six.

"May I sleep in your house tonight?" I asked.

"You can come in if you want to," he said, "and sleep if you can. House all messy; ma's been dead three year, and dad's away. Nothin' to eat but buckwheat flour and rusty bacon."

"I've plenty to eat," I answered; picking up a hamper. "Just take that hamper, will you?"

"You can come in if you're a mind to," he said, "but you got to carry your own stuff." He did not speak gruffly or rudely, but appeared mildly stating an inoffensive fact.

"All right," I said, picking up the other hamper; "lead the way."

The yard in front of the house was dark under a dozen or more immense ailanthus trees. Below them many smaller trees had grown up, and beneath these a dank underwood of tall, rank suckers out of the deep, shaggy, matted grass. What had once been, apparently, a carriage-drive left a narrow, curved track, disused and grass-grown, leading to the house. Even here were some shoots of the ailanthus, and the air was unpleasant with the vile smell of the roots and suckers and the insistent odor of their flowers.

The house was of gray stone, with green shutters faded almost as gray as the stone. Along its front was a veranda, not much raised from the ground, and with no balustrade or railing. On it were several hickory splint rockers. There were eight shuttered windows toward the porch, and midway of them a wide door, with small violet panes on either side of it and a fanlight above.

"Open the door," I said to the boy.

"Open it yourself," he replied, not unpleasantly nor disagreeably but in such a tone that one could not but take the suggestion as a matter of course.

I put down the two hampers and tried the door. It was latched, but not locked, and opened with a rusty grind of its hinges, on which it sagged crazily, scraping the floor as it turned. The passage smelt moldy and damp. There were several doors on either side; the boy pointed to the first on the right.

"You can have that room," he said.

I opened the door. What with the dusk, the interlacing trees outside, the piazza roof, and the closed shutters, I could make out little.

"Better get a lamp," I said to the boy.

"Nary lamp," he declared cheerfully. "Nary candle. Mostly I get abed before dark."

I returned to the remains of my conveyance. All four of my lamps were merely scrap metal and splintered glass. My lantern was mashed flat. I always, however, carried candles in my valise. This I found split and crushed, but still holding together. I carried it to the porch, opened it, and took out three candles.

Entering the room, where I found the boy standing just where I had left him, I lit the candle. The walls were white-washed, the floor bare. There was a mildewed, chilly smell, but the bed looked freshly made up and clean, although it felt clammy.

With a few drops of its own grease I stuck the candle on the corner of a mean, rickety little bureau. There was nothing else in the room save two rush-bottomed chairs and a small table. I went out on the porch, brought in my valise, and put it on the bed. I raised the sash of each window and pushed open the shutters. Then I asked the boy, who had not moved or spoken, to show me the way to the kitchen. He led me straight through the hall to the back of the house. The kitchen was large, and had no furniture save some pine chairs, a pine bench, and a pine table.

I stuck two candles on opposite corners of the table. There was no stove or range in the kitchen, only a big hearth, the ashes in which smelt and looked a month old. The wood in the wood-shed was dry enough, but even it had a cellary, stale smell. The ax and hatchet were both rusty and dull, but usable, and I quickly made a big fire. To my amazement, for the mid-June evening was hot and still, the boy, a wry smile on his ugly face, almost leaned over the flame, hands and arms spread out, and fairly roasted himself.

"Are you cold?" I inquired.

"I'm allus cold," he replied, hugging the fire closer than ever, till I thought he must scorch.

I left him toasting himself while I went in search of water. I discovered the pump, which was in working order and not dry on the valves; but I had a furious struggle to fill the two leaky pails I had found. When I had put water to boil I fetched my hampers from the porch.

I brushed the table and set out my meal—cold fowl, cold ham, white and brown bread, olives, jam, and cake. When the can of soup was hot and the coffee made I drew up two chairs to the table and invited the boy to join me.

"I ain't hungry," he said; "I've had supper."

He was a new sort of boy to me; all the boys I knew were hearty eaters and always ready. I had felt hungry myself, but somehow when I came to eat I had little appetite and hardly relished the food. I soon made an end of my meal, covered the fire, blew out the candles, and returned to the porch, where I dropped into one of the hickory rockers to smoke. The boy followed me silently and seated himself on the porch floor, leaning against a pillar, his feet on the grass outside.

"What do you do," I asked, "when your father is away?"

"Just loaf 'round," he said. "Just fool 'round."

"How far off are your nearest neighbors?" I asked.

"Don't no neighbors never come here," he stated. "Say they're afeared of the ghosts."

I was not at all startled; the place had all those aspects which lead to a house being called haunted. I was struck by his odd matter-of-fact way of speaking— it was as if he had said they were afraid of a cross dog.

"Do you ever see any ghosts around here?" I continued.

"Never see 'em," he answered, as if I had mentioned tramps or partridges. "Never hear 'em. Sort o' feel 'em 'round sometimes."

"Are you afraid of them?" I asked.

"Nope," he declared. "I ain't skeered o' ghosts; I'm skeered o' nightmares. Ever have nightmares?"

"Very seldom," I replied.

"I do," he returned. "Allus have the same nightmare—big sow, big as a steer, trying to eat me up. Wake up so skeered I could run to never. Nowheres to run to. Go to sleep, and have it again. Wake up worse skeered than ever. Dad says it's buckwheat cakes in summer."

"You must have teased a sow sometime," I said.

"Yep," he answered. "Teased a big sow wunst, holding up one of her pigs by the hind leg. Teased her too long. Fell in the pen and got bit up some. Wisht I hadn't 'a' teased her. Have that nightmare three times a week sometimes. Worse'n being burnt out. Worse'n ghosts. Say, I sorter feel ghosts around now."

115

He was not trying to frighten me. He was as simply stating an opinion as if he had spoken of bats or mosquitoes. I made no reply, and found myself listening involuntarily. My pipe went out. I did not really want another, but felt disinclined for bed as yet, and was comfortable where I was, while the smell of the ailanthus blossoms was very disagreeable. I filled my pipe again, lit it, and then, as I puffed, somehow dozed off for a moment.

I awoke with a sensation of some light fabric trailed across my face. The boy's position was unchanged.

"Did you do that?" I asked sharply.

"Ain't done nary a thing," he rejoined. "What was it?"

"It was like a piece of mosquito-netting brushed over my face."

"That ain't netting," he asserted; "that's a veil. That's one of the ghosts. Some blow on you; some touch you with their long, cold fingers. That one with the veil she drags acrosst your face—well, mostly I think it's ma."

He spoke with the unassailable conviction of the child in *We Are Seven*. I found no words to reply, and rose to go to bed.

"Good night," I said.

"Good night," he echoed. "I'll set out here a spell yet."

I lit a match, found the candle I had stuck on the corner of the shabby little bureau, and undressed. The

116

bed had a comfortable husk mattress, and I was soon asleep.

I had the sensation of having slept some time when I had a nightmare—the very nightmare the boy had described. A huge sow, big as a dray horse, was reared up on her forelegs over the foot-board of the bed, trying to scramble over to me. She grunted and puffed, and I felt I was the food she craved. I knew in the dream that it was only a dream, and strove to wake up.

Then the gigantic dream-beast floundered over the foot-board, fell across my shins, and I awoke.

I was in darkness as absolute as if I were sealed in a jet vault, yet the shudder of the nightmare instantly subsided, my nerves quieted; I realized where I was, and felt not the least panic. I turned over and was asleep again almost at once. Then I had a real nightmare, not recognizable as a dream, but appallingly real—an unutterable agony of reasonless horror.

There was a Thing in the room; not a sow, or any other nameable creature, but a Thing. It was as big as an elephant, filled the room to the ceiling, was shaped like a wild boar, seated on its haunches, with its forelegs braced stiffly in front of it. It had a hot, slobbering, red mouth, full of big tusks, and its jaws worked hungrily. It shuffled and hunched itself forward, inch by inch, till its vast forelegs straddled the bed.

The bed crushed up like wet blotting-paper, and I felt the weight of the Thing on my feet, on my legs, on my body, on my chest. It was hungry, and I was what it was hungry for, and it meant to begin on my face. Its dripping mouth came nearer and nearer.

Then the dream-helplessness that made me unable to call or move suddenly gave way, and I yelled and awoke. This time my terror was positive and not to be shaken off.

It was near dawn: I could descry dimly the cracked, dirty window-panes. I got up, lit the stump of my candle and two fresh ones, dressed hastily, strapped my ruined valise, and put it on the porch against the wall near the door. Then I called the boy. I realized quite suddenly that I had not told him my name or asked his.

I shouted "Hello!" a few times, but won no answer. I had had enough of that house. I was still permeated with the panic of the nightmare. I desisted from shouting, made no search, but with two candles went out to the kitchen. I took a swallow of cold coffee and munched a biscuit as I hustled my belongings into my hampers. Then, leaving a silver dollar on the table, I carried the hampers out on the porch and dumped them by my valise.

It was now light enough to see to walk, and I went out to the road. Already the night-dew had rusted much of the wreck, making it look more hopeless than before. It was, however, entirely undisturbed. There was not so much as a wheel-track or a hoof-print on the road. The tall, white stone, uncertainty about which had caused my disaster, stood like a sentinel opposite where I had upset.

I set out to find that blacksmith shop. Before I had gone far the sun rose clear from the horizon, and almost at once scorching. As I footed it along I grew very much heated, and it seemed more like ten miles than six before I reached the first house. It was a new frame house, neatly painted and close to the road, with a whitewashed fence along its garden front.

I was about to open the gate when a big black dog with a curly tail bounded out of the bushes. He did not bark, but stood inside the gate wagging his tail and regarding me with a friendly eye; yet I hesitated with my hand on the latch, and considered. The dog might not be as friendly as he looked, and the sight of him made me realize that except for the boy I had seen no creature about the house where I had spent the night; no dog or cat; not even a toad or bird. While I was ruminating upon this a man came from behind the house.

"Will your dog bite?" I asked.

"Naw," he answered; "he don't bite. Come in."

I told him I had had an accident to my automobile, and asked if he could drive me to the blacksmith shop and back to my wreckage.

"Cert," he said. "Happy to help you. I'll hitch up foreshortly. Wher'd you smash?"

"In front of the gray house about six miles back," I answered.

"That big stone-built house?" he queried.

"The same," I assented.

"Did you go a-past here?" he inquired astonished. "I didn't hear ye."

"No," I said; "I came from the other direction."

"Why," he meditated, "you must 'a' smashed 'bout sunup. Did you come over them mountains in the dark?"

"No," I replied; "I came over them yesterday evening. I smashed up about sunset."

"Sundown!" he exclaimed. "Where in thunder've ye been all night?"

"I slept in the house where I broke down."

"In that there big stone-built house in the trees?" he demanded.

"Yes," I agreed.

"Why," he quavered excitedly, "that there house is haunted! They say if you have to drive past it after dark, you can't tell which side of the road the big white stone is on."

"I couldn't tell even before sunset," I said.

"There!" he exclaimed. "Look at that, now! And you slep' in that house! Did you sleep, honest?"

"I slept pretty well," I said. "Except for a nightmare, I slept all night."

"Well," he commented, "I wouldn't go in that there house for a farm, nor sleep in it for my salvation. And you slep'! How in thunder did you get in?"

"The boy took me in," I said.

"What sort of a boy?" he queried, his eyes fixed on

120

me with a queer, countrified look of absorbed interest.

"A thick-set, freckle-faced boy with a harelip," I said.

"Talk like his mouth was full of mush?" he demanded.

"Yes," I said; "bad case of cleft palate."

"Well!" he exclaimed. "I never did believe in ghosts, and I never did half believe that house was haunted, but I know it now. And you slep'!"

"I didn't see any ghosts," I retorted irritably.

"You seen a ghost for sure," he rejoined solemnly. "That there harelip boy's been dead six months."

Ellen Glasgow

The Shadowy Third

*A child's feelings toward her mother may be as close
as anyone can ever come to undying love.*

When the call came I remember that I turned from
the telephone in a romantic flutter. Though I had spoken only once to the great surgeon, Roland Maradick,
I felt on that December afternoon that to speak to him
only once—to watch him in the operating-room for a
single hour—was an adventure which drained the color
and the excitement from the rest of life. After all these
years of work on typhoid and pneumonia cases, I can
still feel the delicious tremor of my young pulses; I can
still see the winter sunshine slanting through the hospital windows over the white uniforms of the nurses.

"He didn't mention me by name. Can there be a
mistake?" I stood, incredulous yet ecstatic, before the
superintendent of the hospital.

"No, there isn't a mistake. I was talking to him

before you came down." Miss Hemphill's strong face softened while she looked at me. She was a big, resolute woman, a distant Canadian relative of my mother's, and the kind of nurse, I had discovered in the month since I had come up from Richmond, that Northern hospital boards, if not Northern patients, appear instinctively to select. From the first, in spite of her hardness, she had taken a liking—I hesitate to use the word "fancy" for a preference so impersonal— to her Virginia cousin. After all, it isn't every Southern nurse, just out of training, who can boast a kinswoman in the superintendent of a New York hospital.

"And he made you understand positively that he meant me?" The thing was so wonderful that I simply couldn't believe it.

"He asked particularly for the nurse who was with Miss Hudson last week when he operated. I think he didn't even remember that you had a name. When I asked if he meant Miss Randolph, he repeated that he wanted the nurse who had been with Miss Hudson. She was small, he said, and cheerful-looking. This, of course, might apply to one or two of the others, but none of these was with Miss Hudson."

"Then I suppose it is really true?" My pulses were tingling. "And I am to be there at six o'clock?"

"Not a minute later. The day nurse goes off duty at that hour, and Mrs. Maradick is never left by herself for an instant."

"It is her mind, isn't it? And that makes it all the

stranger that he should select me, for I have had so few mental cases."

"So few cases of any kind," Miss Hemphill was smiling, and when she smiled I wondered if the other nurses would know her. "By the time you have gone through the treadmill in New York, Margaret, you will have lost a good many things besides your inexperience. I wonder how long you will keep your sympathy and your imagination? After all, wouldn't you have made a better novelist than a nurse?"

"I can't help putting myself into my cases. I suppose one ought not to?"

"It isn't a question of what one ought to do, but of what one must. When you are drained of every bit of sympathy and enthusiasm, and have got nothing in return for it, not even thanks, you will understand why I try to keep you from wasting yourself."

"But surely in a case like this—for Doctor Maradick?"

"Oh, well, of course—for Doctor Maradick." She must have seen that I implored her confidence, for, after a minute, she let fall carelessly a gleam of light on the situation: "It is a very sad case when you think what a charming man and a great surgeon Doctor Maradick is."

Above the starched collar of my uniform I felt the blood leap in bounds to my cheeks. "I have spoken to him only once." I murmured, "but he is charming, and so kind and handsome, isn't he?"

"His patients adore him."

"Oh, yes, I've seen that. Everyone hangs on his visits." Like the patients and the other nurses, I also had come by delightful, if imperceptible, degrees to hang on the daily visits of Doctor Maradick. He was, I suppose, born to be a hero to women. From my first day in his hospital, from the moment when I watched, through closed shutters, while he stepped out of his car, I have never doubted that he was assigned to the great part in the play. If I had been ignorant of his spell—of the charm he exercised over his hospital—I should have felt it in the waiting hush, like a drawn breath, which followed his ring at the door and preceded his imperious footstep on the stairs. My first impression of him, even after the terrible events of the next year, records a memory that is both careless and splendid. At that moment, when, gazing through the chinks in the shutters, I watched him, in his coat of dark fur, cross the pavement over the pale streaks of sunshine, I knew beyond any doubt—I knew with a sort of infallible prescience—that my fate was irretrievably bound up with his in the future. I knew this, I repeat, though Miss Hemphill would still insist that my foreknowledge was merely a sentimental gleaning from indiscriminate novels. But it wasn't only first love, impressionable as my kinswoman believed me to be. It wasn't only the way he looked. Even more than his appearance—more than the shining dark of his eyes, the silvery brown of his hair, the dusky glow in his face—even more than his charm and his magnificence, I think, the beauty and sympathy in his voice won my heart. It was a voice, I heard someone say afterwards, that ought always to speak poetry.

So you will see why—if you do not understand at the beginning, I can never hope to make you believe impossible things!—so you will see why I accepted the call when it came as an imperative summons. I couldn't have stayed away after he sent for me. However much I may have tried not to go, I know that in the end I must have gone. In those days, while I was still hoping to write novels, I used to talk a great deal about "destiny" (I have learned since then how silly all such talk is), and I suppose it was my "destiny" to be caught in the web of Roland Maradick's personality. But I am not the first nurse to grow love-sick about a doctor who never gave her a thought.

"I am glad you got the call, Margaret. It may mean a great deal to you. Only try not to be too emotional." I remember that Miss Hemphill was holding a bit of rose-geranium in her hand while she spoke—one of the patients had given it to her from a pot she kept in her room, and the scent of the flower is still in my nostrils—or my memory. Since then—oh, long since then—I have wondered if she also had been caught in the web.

"I wish I knew more about the case." I was pressing for light. "Have you ever seen Mrs. Maradick?"

"Oh, dear, yes. They have been married only a little

over a year, and in the beginning she used to come sometimes to the hospital and wait outside while the doctor made his visits. She was a very sweet-looking woman then—not exactly pretty, but fair and slight, with the loveliest smile, I think, I have ever seen. In those first months she was so much in love that we used to laugh about it among ourselves. To see her face light up when the doctor came out of the hospital and crossed the pavement to his car, was as good as a play. We never tired of watching her—I wasn't superintendent then, so I had more time to look out of the window while I was on day duty. Once or twice she brought her little girl in to see one of the patients. The child was so much like her that you would have known them anywhere for mother and daughter."

I had heard that Mrs. Maradick was a widow, with one child, when she first met the doctor, and I asked now, still seeking an illumination I had not found, "There was a great deal of money, wasn't there?"

"A great fortune. If she hadn't been so attractive, people would have said, I suppose, that Doctor Maradick married her for her money. Only," she appeared to make an effort of memory, "I believe I've heard somehow that it was all left in trust away from Mrs. Maradick if she married again. I can't, to save my life, remember just how it was; but it was a queer will, I know, and Mrs. Maradick wasn't to come into the money unless the child didn't live to grow up. The pity of it—"

A young nurse came into the office to ask for something—the keys, I think, of the operating-room, and Miss Hemphill broke off inconclusively as she hurried out of the door. I was sorry that she left off just when she did. Poor Mrs. Maradick! Perhaps I was too emotional, but even before I saw her I had begun to feel her pathos and her strangeness.

My preparations took only a few minutes. In those days I always kept a suitcase packed and ready for sudden calls; and it was not yet six o'clock when I turned from Tenth Street onto Fifth Avenue, and stopped for a minute, before ascending the steps, to look at the house in which Doctor Maradick lived. A fine rain was falling, and I remember thinking, as I turned the corner, how depressing the weather must be for Mrs. Maradick. It was an old house, with damp-looking walls (though that may have been because of the rain) and a spindle-shaped iron railing which ran up the stone steps to the black door, where I noticed a dim flicker through the old-fashioned fanlight. Afterwards I discovered that Mrs. Maradick had been born in the house—her maiden name was Calloran—and that she had never wanted to live anywhere else. She was a woman—this I found out when I knew her better—of strong attachments to both persons and places; and though Doctor Maradick had tried to persuade her to move uptown after her marriage, she had clung, against his wishes, to the old house on lower Fifth Avenue. I dare say she was obstinate about it in spite of her gentleness and her passion for the doctor. Those sweet, soft women, especially when they have always been rich, are sometimes amazingly obstinate. I have nursed so many of them since—women with strong affections and weak intellects—that I have come to recognize the type as soon as I set eyes upon it.

My ring at the bell was answered after a little delay, and when I entered the house I saw that the hall was quite dark except for the waning glow from an open fire which burned in the library. When I gave my name, and added that I was the night nurse, the servant appeared to think my humble presence unworthy of illumination. He was an old negro butler, inherited perhaps from Mrs. Maradick's mother, who, I learned afterwards, was from South Carolina; and while he passed me on his way up the staircase, I heard him vaguely muttering that he "wa'n't gwinter tu'n on dem lights twel de chile had done playin'."

To the right of the hall, the soft glow drew me into the library, and crossing the threshold timidly, I stooped to dry my wet coat by the fire. As I bent there, meaning to start up at the first sound of a footstep, I thought how cozy the room was after the damp walls outside to which some bared creepers were clinging; and I was watching the strange shapes and patterns the firelight made on the old Persian rug, when the lamps of a slowly turning motor-car flashed on me through the white shades at the window. Still dazzled by the glare,

I looked round in the dimness and saw a child's ball of red and blue rubber roll towards me out of the gloom of the adjoining room. A moment later, while I made a vain attempt to capture the toy as it spun past me, a little girl darted airily, with peculiar lightness and grace, through the doorway, and stopped quickly, as if in surprise at the sight of a stranger. She was a small child—so small and slight that her footsteps made no sound on the polished floor of the threshold; and I remember thinking while I looked at her that she had the gravest and sweetest face I had ever seen. She couldn't—I decided this afterwards—have been more than six or seven years old, yet she stood there with a curious prim dignity, like the dignity of an elderly person, and gazed up at me with enigmatical eyes. She was dressed in Scotch plaid, with a bit of red ribbon in her hair, which was cut in a fringe over her forehead and hung very straight to her shoulders. Charming as she was, from her uncurled brown hair to the white socks and black slippers on her little feet, I recall most vividly the singular look in her eyes, which appeared in the shifting light to be of an indeterminate color. For the odd thing about this look was that it was not the look of childhood at all. It was the look of profound experience, of bitter knowledge.

"Have you come for your ball?" I asked; but while the friendly question was still on my lips, I heard the servant returning. In my confusion I made a second ineffectual grasp at the plaything, which had rolled away from me into the dusk of the drawing-room. Then, as I raised my head, I saw that the child also had slipped from the room; and without looking after her I followed the old negro into the pleasant study above, where the great surgeon awaited me.

Ten years ago, before hard nursing had taken so much out of me, I blushed very easily, and I was aware at the moment when I crossed Doctor Maradick's study that my cheeks were the color of peonies. Of course, I was a fool—no one knows this better than I do—but I had never been alone, even for an instant, with him before, and the man was more than a hero to me, he was—there isn't any reason now why I should blush over the confession—almost a god. At that age I was mad about the wonders of surgery, and Roland Maradick in the operating-room was magician enough to have turned an older and more sensible head than mine. Added to his great reputation and his marvelous skill, he was, I am sure of this, the most splendid-looking man, even at forty-five, that one could imagine. Had he been ungracious—had he been positively rude to me, I should still have adored him; but when he held out his hand, and greeted me in the charming way he had with women, I felt that I would have died for him. It is no wonder that a saying went about the hospital that every woman he operated on fell in love with him. As for the nurses—well, there wasn't a single one of them who had escaped his spell—not even Miss Hemphill, who could have been scarcely a day under fifty.

"I am glad you could come, Miss Randolph. You were with Miss Hudson last week when I operated?"

I bowed. To save my life I couldn't have spoken without blushing the redder.

"I noticed your bright face at the time. Brightness, I think, is what Mrs. Maradick needs. She finds her day nurse depressing." His eyes rested so kindly upon me that I have suspected since that he was not entirely unaware of my worship. It was a small thing, heaven knows, to flatter his vanity—a nurse just out of a training-school—but to some men no tribute is too insignificant to give pleasure.

"You will do your best, I am sure." He hesitated an instant—just long enough for me to perceive the anxiety beneath the genial smile on his face—and then added gravely, "We wish to avoid, if possible, having to send her away."

I could only murmur in response, and after a few carefully chosen words about his wife's illness, he rang the bell and directed the maid to take me upstairs to my room. Not until I was ascending the stairs to the third story did it occur to me that he had really told me nothing. I was as perplexed about the nature of Mrs. Maradick's malady as I had been when I entered the house.

I found my room pleasant enough. It had been arranged—at Doctor Maradick's request, I think—that I was to sleep in the house, and after my austere little bed at the hospital, I was agreeably surprised by the cheerful look at the apartment into which the maid led me. The walls were papered in roses, and there were curtains of flowered chintz at the window, which looked down on a small formal garden at the rear of the house. This the maid told me, for it was too dark for me to distinguish more than a marble fountain and a fir-tree, which looked old, though I afterwards learned that it was replanted almost every season.

In ten minutes I had slipped into my uniform and was ready to go to my patient: but for some reason—to this day I have never found out what it was that turned her against me at the start—Mrs. Maradick refused to receive me. While I stood outside her door I heard the day nurse trying to persuade her to let me come in. It wasn't any use, however, and in the end I was obliged to go back to my room and wait until the poor lady got over her whim and consented to see me. That was long after dinner—it must have been nearer eleven than ten o'clock—and Miss Peterson was quite worn out by the time she came for me.

"I'm afraid you'll have a bad night," she said as we went downstairs together. That was her way, I soon saw, to expect the worst of everything and everybody.

"Does she often keep you up like this?"

"Oh, no, she is usually very considerate. I never knew a sweeter character. But she still has this hallucination—"

Here again, as in the scene with Doctor Maradick, I felt that the explanation had only deepened the mystery. Mrs. Maradick's hallucination, whatever form it assumed, was evidently a subject for evasion and subterfuge in the household. It was on the tip of my tongue to ask, "What is her hallucination?"—but before I could get the words past my lips we had reached Mrs. Maradick's door, and Miss Peterson motioned me to be silent. As the door opened a little way to admit me, I saw that Mrs. Maradick was already in bed, and that the lights were out except for a night-lamp burning on a candle-stand beside a book and a carafe of water.

"I won't go in with you," said Miss Peterson in a whisper; and I was on the point of stepping over the threshold when I saw the little girl, in the dress of Scotch plaid, slip by me from the dusk of the room into the electric light of the hall. She held a doll in her arms, and as she went by she dropped a doll's workbasket in the doorway. Miss Peterson must have picked up the toy, for when I turned in a minute to look for it I found that it was gone. I remember thinking that it was late for a child to be up—she looked delicate, too—but, after all, it was no business of mine, and four years in a hospital had taught me never to meddle in things that do not concern me. There is nothing a nurse learns quicker than not to try to put the world to rights in a day.

When I crossed the floor to the chair by Mrs. Maradick's bed, she turned over on her side and looked at me with the sweetest and saddest smile.

"You are the night nurse," she said in a gentle voice; and from the moment she spoke I knew that there was nothing hysterical or violent about her mania—or hallucination, as they called it. "They told me your name, but I have forgotten it."

"Randolph—Margaret Randolph." I liked her from the start, and I think she must have seen it.

"You look very young, Miss Randolph."

"I am twenty-two, but I suppose I don't look quite my age. People usually think I am younger."

For a minute she was silent, and while I settled myself in the chair by the bed, I thought how strikingly she resembled the little girl I had seen first in the afternoon, and then leaving her room a few moments before. They had the same small, heart-shaped faces, colored ever so faintly; the same straight, soft hair, between brown and flaxen; and the same large, grave eyes, set very far apart under arched eyebrows. What surprised me most, however, was that they both looked at me with that enigmatical and vaguely wondering expression—only in Mrs. Maradick's face the vagueness seemed to change now and then to a definite fear—a flash, I had almost said, of startled horror.

I sat quite still in my chair, and until the time came for Mrs. Maradick to take her medicine not a word passed between us. Then, when I bent over her with the glass in my hand, she raised her head from the pillow and said in a whisper of suppressed intensity:

"You look kind. I wonder if you could have seen my little girl?"

As I slipped my arm under the pillow I tried to smile cheerfully down on her. "Yes, I've seen her twice. I'd know her anywhere by her likeness to you."

A glow shone in her eyes, and I thought how pretty she must have been before illness took the life and animation out of her features. "Then I know you're good." Her voice was so strained and low that I could barely hear it. "If you weren't good you couldn't have seen her."

I thought this queer enough, but all I answered was, "She looked delicate to be sitting up so late."

A quiver passed over her thin features, and for a minute I thought she was going to burst into tears. As she had taken the medicine, I put the glass back on the candle-stand, and bending over the bed, smoothed the straight brown hair, which was as fine and soft as spun silk, back from her forehead. There was something about her—I don't know what it was—that made you love her as soon as she looked at you.

"She always had that light and airy way, though she was never sick a day in her life," she answered calmly after a pause. Then, groping for my hand, she whispered passionately, "You must not tell him—you must not tell any one that you have seen her!"

"I must not tell any one?" Again I had the impression that had come to me first in Doctor Maradick's study, and afterwards with Miss Peterson on the staircase, that I was seeking a gleam of light in the midst of obscurity.

"Are you sure there isn't any one listening—that there isn't any one at the door?" she asked, pushing aside my arm and raising herself on the pillows.

"Quite, quite sure. They have put out the lights in the hall."

"And you will not tell him? Promise me that you will not tell him." The startled horror flashed from the vague wonder of her expression. "He doesn't like her to come back, because he killed her."

"Because he killed her!" Then it was that light burst on me in a blaze. So this was Mrs. Maradick's hallucination! She believed that her child was dead—the little girl I had seen with my own eyes leaving her room; and she believed that her husband—the great surgeon we worshipped in the hospital—had murdered her. No wonder they veiled the dreadful obsession in mystery! No wonder that even Miss Peterson had not dared to drag the horrid thing out into the light! It was the kind of hallucination one simply couldn't stand having to face.

"There is no use telling people things that nobody believes," she resumed slowly, still holding my hand in a grasp that would have hurt me if her fingers had not been so fragile. "Nobody believes that he killed her. Nobody believes that she comes back every day to the house. Nobody believes—and yet you saw her—"

"Yes, I saw her—but why should your husband have killed her?" I spoke soothingly, as one would speak to a person who was quite mad. Yet she was not mad, I could have sworn this while I looked at her.

For a moment she moaned inarticulately, as if the horror of her thoughts were too great to pass into speech. Then she flung out her thin, bare arm with a wild gesture.

"Because he never loved me!" she said. "He never loved me!"

"But he married you," I urged gently while I stroked her hair. "If he hadn't loved you, why should he have married you?"

"He wanted the money—my little girl's money. It all goes to him when I die."

"But he is rich himself. He must make a fortune from his profession."

"It isn't enough. He wanted millions." She had grown stern and tragic. "No, he never loved me. He loved someone else from the beginning—before I knew him."

It was quite useless, I saw, to reason with her. If she wasn't mad, she was in a state of terror and despondency so black that it had almost crossed the border-line into madness. I thought once that I would go upstairs and bring the child down from her nursery; but, after a moment's hesitation, I realized that Miss Peterson and Doctor Maradick must have long ago tried all these measures. Clearly, there was nothing to do except soothe and quiet her as much as I could; and this I did until she dropped into a light sleep which lasted well into the morning.

By seven o'clock I was worn out—not from work but from the strain on my sympathy—and I was glad, indeed, when one of the maids came in to bring me an early cup of coffee. Mrs. Maradick was still sleeping— it was a mixture of bromide and chloral I had given her—and she did not wake until Miss Peterson came on duty an hour or two later. Then, when I went downstairs, I found the dining-room deserted except for the old housekeeper, who was looking over the silver. Doctor Maradick, she explained to me presently, had his breakfast served in the morning-room on the other side of the house.

"And the little girl? Does she take her meals in the nursery?"

She threw me a startled glance. Was it, I questioned afterwards, one of distrust or apprehension?

"There isn't any little girl. Haven't you heard?"

"Heard? No. Why, I saw her only yesterday."

The look she gave me—I was sure of it now—was full of alarm.

"The little girl—she was the sweetest child I ever saw—died just two months ago of pneumonia."

"But she couldn't have died." I was a fool to let this out, but the shock had completely unnerved me. "I tell you I saw her yesterday."

The alarm in her face deepened. "That is Mrs. Maradick's trouble. She believes that she still sees her."

"But don't you see her?" I drove the question home bluntly.

"No." She set her lips tightly. "I never see anything."

So I had been wrong, after all, and the explanation, when it came, only accentuated the terror. The child was dead—she had died of pneumonia two months ago—and yet I had seen her, with my own eyes, playing ball in the library; I had seen her slipping out of her mother's room, with her doll in her arms.

"Is there another child in the house? Could there be a child belonging to one of the servants?" A gleam had shot through the fog in which I was groping.

"No, there isn't any other. The doctors tried bringing one once, but it threw the poor lady into such a state she almost died of it. Besides, there wouldn't be any other child as quiet and sweet-looking as Dorothea. To see her skipping along in her dress of Scotch plaid used to make me think of a fairy, though they say that fairies wear nothing but white or green."

"Has any one else seen her—the child, I mean— any of the servants?"

"Only old Gabriel, the colored butler, who came with

Mrs. Maradick's mother from South Carolina. I've heard that negroes often have a kind of second sight—though I don't know that that is just what you would call it. But they seem to believe in the supernatural by instinct, and Gabriel is so old and dotty—he does no work except answer the door-bell and clean the silver—that nobody pays much attention to anything that he sees—"

"Is the child's nursery kept as it used to be?"

"Oh, no. The doctor had all the toys sent to the children's hospital. That was a great grief to Mrs. Maradick; but Doctor Brandon thought, and all the nurses agreed with him, that it was best for her not to be allowed to keep the room as it was when Dorothea was living."

"Dorothea? Was that the child's name?"

"Yes, it means the gift of God, doesn't it? She was named after the mother of Mrs. Maradick's first husband, Mr. Ballard. He was the grave, quiet kind—not the least like the doctor."

I wondered if the other dreadful obsession of Mrs. Maradick's had drifted down through the nurses or the servants to the housekeeper; but she said nothing about it, and since she was, I suspected, a garrulous person, I thought it wiser to assume that the gossip had not reached her.

A little later, when breakfast was over and I had not yet gone upstairs to my room, I had my first interview with Doctor Brandon, the famous alienist who was in charge of the case. I had never seen him before, but from the first moment that I looked at him I took his measure almost by intuition. He was, I suppose, honest enough—I have always granted him that, bitterly as I have felt towards him. It wasn't his fault that he lacked red blood in his brain, or that he had formed the habit, from long association with abnormal phenomena, of regarding all life as a disease. He was the sort of physician—every nurse will understand what I mean—who deals instinctively with groups instead of with individuals. He was long and solemn and very round in the face; and I hadn't talked to him ten minutes before I knew he had been educated in Germany, and that he had learned over there to treat every emotion as a pathological manifestation. I used to wonder what he got out of life—what anyone got out of life who had analyzed away everything except the bare structure.

When I reached my room at last, I was so tired that I could barely remember either the questions Doctor Brandon had asked or the directions he had given me. I fell asleep, I know, almost as soon as my head touched the pillow; and the maid who came to inquire if I wanted luncheon decided to let me finish my nap. In the afternoon, when she returned with a cup of tea, she found me still heavy and drowsy. Though I was used to night nursing, I felt as if I had danced from sunset to daybreak. It was fortunate, I reflected, while I drank my tea, that every case didn't wear on one's sympathies as acutely as Mrs. Maradick's hallucination had worn on mine.

Through the day I did not see Doctor Maradick; but at seven o'clock when I came up from my early dinner on my way to take the place of Miss Peterson, who had kept on duty an hour later than usual, he met me in the hall and asked me to come into his study. I thought him handsomer than ever in his evening clothes, with a white flower in his buttonhole. He was going to some public dinner, the housekeeper told me, but, then, he was always going somewhere. I believe he didn't dine at home a single evening that winter.

"Did Mrs. Maradick have a good night?" He had closed the door after us, and turning now with the question, he smiled kindly, as if he wished to put me at ease in the beginning.

"She slept very well after she took the medicine. I gave her that at eleven o'clock."

For a minute he regarded me silently, and I was aware that his personality—his charm—was focussed upon me. It was almost as if I stood in the center of converging rays of light, so vivid was my impression of him.

"Did she allude in any way to her—to her hallucination?" he asked.

How the warning reached me—what invisible waves of sense-perception transmitted the message—I have never known; but while I stood there, facing the splendor of the doctor's presence, every intuition cautioned me that the time had come when I must take sides in the household. While I stayed there I must stand either with Mrs. Maradick or against her.

"She talked quite rationally," I replied after a moment.

"What did she say?"

"She told me how she was feeling, that she missed her child, and that she walked a little every day about her room."

His face changed—how I could not at first determine.

"Have you seen Doctor Brandon?"

"He came this morning to give me his directions."

"He thought her less well today. He has advised me to send her to Rosedale."

I have never, even in secret, tried to account for Doctor Maradick. He may have been sincere. I tell you only what I know—not what I believe or imagine—and the human is sometimes as inscrutable, as inexplicable, as the supernatural.

While he watched me I was conscious of an inner struggle, as if opposing angels warred somewhere in the depths of my being. When at last I made my decision, I was acting less from reason, I knew, than in obedience to the pressure of some secret current of thought. Heaven knows, even then, the man held me captive while I defied him.

"Doctor Maradick," I lifted my eyes for the first time

frankly to his, "I believe that your wife is as sane as I am—or as you are."

He started. "Then she did not talk freely to you?"

"She may be mistaken, unstrung, piteously distressed in mind"—I brought this out with emphasis—"but she is not—I am willing to stake my future on it—a fit subject for an asylum. It would be foolish—it would be cruel to send her to Rosedale."

"Cruel, you say?" A troubled look crossed his face, and his voice grew very gentle. "You do not imagine that I could be cruel to her?"

"No, I do not think that." My voice also had softened.

"We will let things go on as they are. Perhaps Doctor Brandon may have some other suggestion to make." He drew out his watch and compared it with the clock—nervously, I observed, as if his action were a screen for his discomfiture or perplexity. "I must be going now. We will speak of this again in the morning."

But in the morning we did not speak of it, and during the month that I nursed Mrs. Maradick I was not called again into her husband's study. When I met him in the hall or on the staircase, which was seldom, he was charming as ever; yet, in spite of his courtesy, I had a persistent feeling that he had taken my measure on that evening, and that he had no further use for me.

As the days went by Mrs. Maradick seemed to grow stronger. Never, after our first night together, had she mentioned the child to me; never had she alluded by so much as a word to her dreadful charge against her husband. She was like any woman recovering from a great sorrow, except that she was sweeter and gentler. It is no wonder that everyone who came near her loved her; for there was a mysterious loveliness about her like the mystery of light, not of darkness. She was, I have always thought, as much of an angel as it is possible for a woman to be on this earth. And yet, angelic as she was, there were times when it seemed to me that she both hated and feared her husband. Though he never entered her room while I was there, and I never heard his name on her lips until an hour before the end, still I could tell by the look of terror in her face whenever his step passed down the hall that her very soul shivered at his approach.

During the whole month I did not see the child again, though one night, when I came suddenly into Mrs. Maradick's room, I found a little garden, such as children make out of pebbles and bits of box, on the window-sill. I did not mention it to Mrs. Maradick, and a little later, as the maid lowered the shades, I noticed that the garden had vanished. Since then I have often wondered if the child were invisible only to the rest of us, and if her mother still saw her. But there was no way of finding out except by questioning, and Mrs. Maradick was so well and patient that I hadn't the heart to question. Things couldn't have been better with her than they were, and I was beginning to tell myself that she might soon go out for an airing, when the end came so suddenly.

It was a mild January day—the kind of day that brings the foretaste of spring in the middle of winter, and when I came downstairs in the afternoon, I stopped a minute by the window at the end of the hall to look down on the box maze in the garden. There was an old fountain, bearing two laughing boys in marble, in the centre of the gravelled walk, and the water, which had been turned on that morning for Mrs. Maradick's pleasure, sparkled now like silver as the sunlight splashed over it. I had never before felt the air quite so soft and springlike in January; and I thought, as I gazed down on the garden, that it would be a good idea for Mrs. Maradick to go out and bask for an hour or so in the sunshine. It seemed strange to me that she was never allowed to get any fresh air except the air that came through her windows.

When I went into her room, however, I found that she had no wish to go out. She was sitting, wrapped in shawls, by the open window, which looked down on the fountain; and as I entered she glanced up from a little book she was reading. A pot of daffodils stood on the window-sill—she was very fond of flowers and we tried always to keep some growing in her room.

"Do you know what I am reading, Miss Randolph?" she asked in her soft voice; and she read aloud a verse while I went over to the candlestand to measure out a dose of medicine.

" 'If thou hast two loaves of bread, sell one and buy daffodils, for bread nourisheth the body, but daffodils delight the soul.' That is very beautiful, don't you think so?"

I said "Yes," that it was beautiful; and then I asked her if she wouldn't go downstairs and walk about in the garden.

"He wouldn't like it," she answered; and it was the first time she had mentioned her husband to me since the night I came to her. "He doesn't want me to go out."

I tried to laugh her out of the idea; but it was no use, and after a few minutes I gave up and began talking of other things. Even then it did not occur to me that her fear of Doctor Maradick was anything but a fancy. I could see, of course, that she wasn't out of her head; but sane persons, I knew, sometimes have unaccountable prejudices, and I accepted her dislike as a mere whim or aversion. I did not understand then and—I may as well confess this before the end comes—I do not understand any better today. I am writing down the things I actually saw, and I repeat that I have never had the slightest twist in the direction of the miraculous.

The afternoon slipped away while we talked—she talked brightly when any subject came up that interested her—and it was the last hour of day—that grave, still hour when the movement of life seems to droop and falter for a few precious minutes—that brought us the thing I had dreaded silently since my first night in the house. I remember that I had risen to close the window, and was leaning out for a breath of the mild air, when there was the sound of steps, consciously softened, in the hall outside, and Doctor Brandon's usual knock fell on my ears. Then, before I could cross the room, the door opened, and the doctor entered with Miss Peterson. The day nurse, I knew, was a stupid woman; but she had never appeared to me so stupid, so armored and encased in her professional manner, as she did at that moment.

"I am glad to see that you are taking the air." As Doctor Brandon came over to the window, I wondered maliciously what devil of contradictions had made him a distinguished specialist in nervous diseases.

"Who was the other doctor you brought this morning?" asked Mrs. Maradick gravely; and that was all I ever heard about the visit of the second alienist.

"Someone who is anxious to cure you." He dropped into a chair beside her and patted her hand with his long, pale fingers. "We are so anxious to cure you that we want to send you away to the country for a fortnight or so. Miss Peterson has come to help you to get ready, and I've kept my car waiting for you. There couldn't be a nicer day for a trip, could there?"

The moment had come at last. I knew at once what he meant, and so did Mrs. Maradick. A wave of color flowed and ebbed in her thin cheeks, and I felt her body quiver when I moved from the window and put my arms on her shoulders. I was aware again, as I had been aware that evening in Doctor Maradick's study, of a current of thought that beat from the air around into my brain. Though it cost me my career as a nurse and my reputation for sanity, I knew that I must obey that invisible warning.

"You are going to take me to an asylum," said Mrs. Maradick.

He made some foolish denial or evasion: but before he had finished I turned from Mrs. Maradick and faced him impulsively. In a nurse this was flagrant rebellion, and I realized that the act wrecked my professional future. Yet I did not care—I did not hesitate. Something stronger than I was driving me on.

"Doctor Brandon," I said, "I beg you—I implore you to wait until tomorrow. There are things I must tell you."

A queer look came into his face, and I understood, even in my excitement, that he was mentally deciding in which group he should place me—to which class of morbid manifestations I must belong.

"Very well, very well, we will hear everything," he replied soothingly; but I saw him glance at Miss Peterson, and she went over to the wardrobe for Mrs. Maradick's fur coat and hat.

Suddenly, without warning, Mrs. Maradick threw the shawls away from her, and stood up. "If you send me away," she said, "I shall never come back. I shall never live to come back."

The gray of twilight was just beginning, and while she stood there, in the dusk of the room, her face shone out as pale and flower-like as the daffodils on the window-sill. "I cannot go away!" she cried in a sharper voice. "I cannot go away from my child!"

I saw her face clearly; I heard her voice; and then— the horror of the scene sweeps back over me!—I saw the door open slowly and the little girl run across the room to her mother. I saw the child lift her little arms, and I saw the mother stoop and gather her to her bosom. So closely locked were they in that passionate embrace that their forms seemed to mingle in the gloom that enveloped them.

"After this can you doubt?" I threw out the words almost savagely—and then, when I turned from the mother and child to Doctor Brandon and Miss Peterson, I knew breathlessly—oh, there was a shock in the discovery!—that they were blind to the child. Their blank faces revealed the consternation of ignorance, not of conviction. They had seen nothing except the vacant arms of the mother and the swift, erratic gesture with which she stooped to embrace some invisible presence. Only my vision—and I have asked myself since if the power of sympathy enabled me to penetrate the web of material fact and see the spiritual form of the child—only my vision was not blinded by the clay through which I looked.

"After this can you doubt?" Doctor Brandon had flung my words back to me. Was it his fault, poor man, if life had granted him only the eyes of flesh? Was it his fault if he could see only half of the thing there before him?

But they couldn't see, and since they couldn't see I realized that it was useless to tell them. Within an hour they took Mrs. Maradick to the asylum; and she went quietly, though when the time came for parting from me she showed some faint trace of feeling. I remember that at the last, while we stood on the pavement, she lifted her black veil, which she wore for the child, and said: "Stay with her, Miss Randolph, as long as you can. I shall never come back."

Then she got into the car and was driven off, while I stood looking after her with a sob in my throat. Dreadful as I felt it to be, I didn't, of course, realize the full horror of it, or I couldn't have stood there quietly on the pavement. I didn't realize it, indeed, until several months afterwards when word came that she had died in the asylum. I never knew what her illness was, though I vaguely recall that something was said about "heart failure"—a loose enough term. My own belief is that she died simply of the terror of life.

To my surprise Doctor Maradick asked me to stay on as his office nurse after his wife went to Rosedale: and when the news of her death came there was no suggestion of my leaving. I don't know to this day why he wanted me in the house. Perhaps he thought I should have less opportunity to gossip if I stayed under his roof; perhaps he still wished to test the power of his charm over me. His vanity was incredible in so great a man. I have seen him flush with pleasure when people turned to look at him in the street, and I know that he was not above playing on the sentimental weakness of his patients. But he was magnificent, heaven knows! Few men, I imagine, have been the objects of so many foolish infatuations.

The next summer Doctor Maradick went abroad for two months, and while he was away I took my vacation in Virginia. When we came back the work was heavier than ever—his reputation by this time was tremendous—and my days were so crowded with appointments, and hurried flittings to emergency cases, that I had scarcely a minute left in which to remember poor Mrs. Maradick. Since the afternoon when she went to the asylum the child had not been in the house; and at last I was beginning to persuade myself that the little figure had been an optical illusion—the effect of shifting lights in the gloom of the old rooms—not the apparition I had once believed it to be. It does not take long for a phantom to fade from the memory—especially when one leads the active and methodical life I was forced into that winter. Perhaps—who knows?— (I remember telling myself) the doctors may have been right, after all, and the poor lady may have actually been out of her mind. With this view of the past, my judgment of Doctor Maradick insensibly altered. It ended, I think, in my acquitting him altogether. And then, just as he stood clear and splendid in my verdict of him, the reversal came so precipitately that I grow breathless now whenever I try to live it over again. The violence of the next turn in affairs left me, I often fancy, with a perpetual dizziness of the imagination.

It was in May that we heard of Mrs. Maradick's death, and exactly a year later, on a mild and fragrant afternoon, when the daffodils were blooming in patches around the old fountain in the garden, the housekeeper came into the office, where I lingered over some accounts, to bring me news of the doctor's approaching marriage.

"It is no more than we might have expected," she concluded rationally. "The house must be lonely for him—he is such a sociable man. But I can't help feeling," she brought out slowly after a pause in which I felt a shiver pass over me, "I can't help feeling that it is hard for that other woman to have all the money poor Mrs. Maradick's first husband left her."

"There is a great deal of money, then?" I asked curiously.

"A great deal." She waved her hand, as if words were futile to express the sum. "Millions and millions!"

"They will give up this house, of course?"

"That's done already, my dear. There won't be a brick left of it by this time next year. It's to be pulled down and an apartment-house built on the ground."

Again the shiver passed over me. I couldn't bear to think of Mrs. Maradick's old home falling to pieces.

154

"You didn't tell me the name of the bride," I said. "Is she someone he met while he was in Europe?"

"Dear me, no! She is the very lady he was engaged to before he married Mrs. Maradick, only she threw him over, so people said, because he wasn't rich enough. Then she married some lord or prince from over the water; but there was a divorce, and now she has turned again to her old lover. He is rich enough now, I guess, even for her!"

It was all perfectly true, I suppose; it sounded as plausible as a story out of a newspaper: and yet while she told me I felt, or dreamed that I felt, a sinister, an impalpable hush in the air. I was nervous, no doubt; I was shaken by the suddenness with which the housekeeper had sprung her news on me; but as I sat there I had quite vividly an impression that the old house was listening—that there was a real, if invisible, presence somewhere in the room or the garden. Yet, when an instant afterwards I glanced through the long window which opened down to the brick terrace, I saw only the faint sunshine over the deserted garden, with its maze of box, its marble fountain, and its patches of daffodils.

The housekeeper had gone—one of the servants, I think, came for her—and I was sitting at my desk when the words of Mrs. Maradick on that last evening floated into my mind. The daffodils brought her back to me; for I thought, as I watched them growing, so still and golden in the sunshine, how she would have enjoyed them. Almost unconsciously I repeated the verse she had read to me:

"If thou hast two loaves of bread, sell one and buy daffodils"—and it was at this very instant, while the words were still on my lips, that I turned my eyes to the box maze, and saw the child skipping rope along the gravelled path to the fountain. Quite distinctly, as clear as day, I saw her come, with what children call the dancing step, between the low box borders to the place where the daffodils bloomed by the fountain. From her straight brown hair to her frock of Scotch plaid and her little feet, which twinkled in white socks and black slippers over the turning rope, she was as real to me as the ground on which she trod or the laughing marble boys under the splashing water. Starting up from my chair, I made a single step to the terrace. If I could only reach her—only speak to her— I felt that I might at last solve the mystery. But with the first flutter of my dress on the terrace, the airy little form melted into the quiet dusk of the maze. Not a breath stirred the daffodils, not a shadow passed over the sparkling flow of the water; yet, weak and shaken in every nerve, I sat down on the brick step of the terrace and burst into tears. I must have known that something terrible would happen before they pulled down Mrs. Maradick's home.

The doctor dined out that night. He was with the lady he was going to marry, the housekeeper told me; and it must have been almost midnight when I heard him come in and go upstairs to his room. I was down-stairs because I had been unable to sleep, and the book I wanted to finish I had left that afternoon in the office. The book—I can't remember what it was—had seemed to me very exciting when I began it in the morning; but after the visit of the child I found the romantic novel as dull as a treatise on nursing. It was impossible for me to follow the lines, and I was on the point of giving up and going to bed, when Doctor Maradick opened the front door with his latch-key and went up the staircase. "There can't be a bit of truth in it," I thought over and over again as I listened to his even step ascending the stairs. "There can't be a bit of truth in it." And yet, though I assured myself that "there couldn't be a bit of truth in it," I shrank, with a creepy sensation, from going through the house to my room in the third story. I was tired out after a hard day, and my nerves must have reacted morbidly to the silence and the darkness. For the first time in my life I knew what it was to be afraid of the unknown, of the unseen; and while I bent over my book in the glare of the electric light, I became conscious presently that I was straining my senses for some sound in the spacious emptiness of the rooms overhead. The noise of a passing motor-car in the street jerked me back from the intense hush of expectancy; and I can recall the wave of relief that swept over me as I turned to my book again and tried to fix my distracted mind on its pages.

I was still sitting there when the telephone on my desk rang, with what seemed to my overwrought nerves a startling abruptness, and the voice of the superintendent told me hurriedly that Doctor Maradick was needed at the hospital. I had become so accustomed to these emergency calls in the night that I felt reassured when I had rung up the doctor in his room and had heard the hearty sound of his response. He had not yet undressed, he said, and would come down immediately while I ordered back his car, which must just have reached the garage.

"I'll be with you in five minutes!" he called as cheerfully as if I had summoned him to his wedding.

I heard him cross the floor of his room; and before he could reach the head of the staircase, I opened the door and went out into the hall in order that I might turn on the light and have his hat and coat waiting. The electric button was at the end of the hall, and as I moved towards it, guided by the glimmer that fell from the landing above, I lifted my eyes to the staircase, which climbed dimly, with its slender mahogany balustrade, as far as the third story. Then it was, at the very moment when the doctor, humming gaily, began his quick descent of the stairs, that I distinctly saw—I will swear to this on my deathbed—a child's skipping rope lying loosely coiled, as if it had dropped from a careless little hand, in the bend of the staircase. With a spring I had reached the electric button, flooding the hall with light; but as I did so, while my arm was still outstretched behind me, I heard the humming voice change to a cry of surprise or terror, and the figure on the staircase tripped heavily and stumbled with groping hands into emptiness. The scream of warning died in my throat while I watched him pitch forward down the long flight of stairs to the floor at my feet. Even before I bent over him, before I wiped the blood from his brow and felt for his silent heart, I knew that he was dead.

Something—it may have been, as the world believes, a misstep in the dimness, or it may have been, as I am ready to bear witness, an invisible judgment— something had killed him at the very moment when he most wanted to live.

H. F. Brinsmead

The Twilight Road

*Read this story only if you care to be haunted by
some questions never answered.*

Four little girls scrawled and scattered along a white
sand ribbon of road that ran towards darkness.

It was blurred with time, frayed at its edges, where
water had washed over it or growth impinged; for it
was the old, convict-built mountain trail. Only a few
old-timers, now, or the lonely, self-sufficient children
of the Candlebark Country, could find the place where
it turned aside from the used highway; only they knew
where it shrugged away over the soft-shouldered
foothills, then up and up, over a cold stream, ever
upward bound, pushing into the dark forest, quickly
smothering into the coming night.

The old road etched with its faint finger the monkey-
puzzle mountains, the ragged ridges—the poorlands

of the sandstone country that followed the candle-barks—at last to lose itself among lush volcanic peaks, somber with white ash, sassafras pungent and damp, and the abrasive trunks of tree ferns.

The four little girls knew the Old Road well. They, who could find where wild violets spawned, and cray-fish shadowed the stones of streams, had eyes for the wraith-like trail, built long ago by the chain-gangs, before the days of Starlight the Bushranger, and the coaches of Cobb and Co. It was their secret place; their place of twilight.

"Look! There's a snake!" Hazel, the second eldest, brought them to a halt as she started backwards.

"It's only a black stick!" said Celia.

"It moved! I *saw* it—!"

Susan broke in. "It *did* move!" She peered at the black question mark on the white sand.

"Silly!" scoffed Celia. "It's only a crooked stick!"

She stooped and put out her hand to pick it up. Her curlicue back showed a row of cotton-reels beneath her summer dress. Then when her hand almost touched it, the black stick straightened. It flowed from its crooked shape and slid away over the sand, and so to the rocky wastes, by clumps of old-man's-beard and the hard foliage of geebung bushes.

Celia gasped with shock, shuddering and half-sobbing. Oh, the fright of it! The others comforted her.

"Never mind, Celi—never mind."

"It's all right now, Celi—it's gone, all gone."

"Mind you—" said Hazel, "I *said* it was a snake! I *told* you—!"

Susan nudged her urgently.

"Come, let's go home, do let's."

"Yes." Celia wiped her eyes. "I want to go home."

"Steffy?" Susan looked around them, for the fourth child.

"Steffany! Wherever has she gone?"

The three girls called their sister, looking up and down the road—to the right, where it traced back towards the highway—to the left, where it clambered out of the sandstone poorlands, blurring into the labyrinth of the rain-forest.

"She must have gone home already, of course," said Hazel. "She's such a scary-cat, she must have run off as soon as she saw the snake!"

"Most likely." Susan nodded. "Oh, isn't she naughty! I wonder why we didn't see her?"

"Because we were looking at the snake, of course! Do come!"

The girls ran off—three of them, at least—down towards the farmhouse at the edge of the Candlebark Country, where a light burned in a window, pale in the evening.

But the youngest—Steffany—ran light-footed, up into the distance, where the Old Road tunnelled into the deep-sea gloom, suffused with a sulphurous glow beneath the heavy leaves of the rain-forest.

Here the whistling grew clearer.

It was a tiny sound of a whistle that she had heard, walking with her sisters back where the road was clear and white. Then it had been faint and uncertain, no more than a ghost of a memory of a song. But it had called to her, pleading about her ears—a faint, far sound of a whistled tune. . . .

The child ran between walls of living growth, her face set in a tight mask of fear. As she moved through the void, she knew not what horrors could lurk in the forest's half-seen depths, at this strange hour. Swinging overhead, the sky was a narrow swathe of luminous silk, a gibbous moon woven into its texture, and faintly watermarked with the odd star or two. The air was heavy and cloying with silence—except for her own footfalls, and the fitful piping tune.

Now the close trees gave way for a small space, to a narrow shelf, where a spring stream indented the mountain-side before the last, steep crest. Here, all that was left of the road was a milestone; it was half-buried in long grass.

A fire glowed jewel-bright in the dusk. A figure was seated by the stone. shapeless and bulky. A man. His clothes were ragged. His eyes caught the red light of the fire. His lips were pursed. His fingers held to them a battered penny whistle.

Beside the man's fire was his meager swag and a

thin, black dog had taken possession of it with familiar presumption; it lay gazing into the flames, muzzle on paws, pensive, only its eyes reflecting the same red gleams of light that flickered from the fire into those of his master.

The child stopped short for a moment, then timidly drew closer to the pair.

At sight of her the man made a quick movement, as though for flight, his hand above his head in a defensive gesture. Then, seeing her alone, his figure half-relaxed; only his eyes were still wary and irrational, with their red gleam.

Steffany saw now that, beneath the rough husk of his unkempt poverty, he was no more than a boy. The dog crept close to him, cowering against his legs. Fear drained away from the child, leaving only fascination and a deep pity; she did not know why.

"Please—" she said awkwardly. "I—I—heard you playing."

"You alone?" He spoke in a rasping whisper.

She nodded, eyes round with wonder.

"Are you followed?"

"Oh, no—no, truly. Please, don't be afraid. There's only me."

She drew closer still; then, taking her courage, sat down on the milestone.

"Would you play for me again?" she asked softly. "I'd like to know your tune."

"Sure and I daren't play it, girleen. Only a small,

little bit of an ave I played—and look how it's brought you! No more, not a note dare I pipe. They'd hear it for sure and they'd be after coming for me."

"Coming for you? Who'd come for you?"

Terror seemed to grip his ravaged face.

"Och, the Redcoats, dear love you. I've not had the heart to play me whistle since I found it, mind—not until this night."

"But what Redcoats? And why would they come for you?"

He looked around furtively, put his lips close to her ear and whispered: "I've broken loose, then! It was for the dog here I done it, not for meself, I swear be the Finn! Had it not been for the dog's sake I'd have borne the lash and whatever, so I would!"

"Tell me about it," said the child. "I'll never harm you, cross my heart and spit my death."

Hesitantly he began, gaining confidence until his words dropped with a rhythm into the lap of the dusk, all in a strange brogue that she could not remember having heard before.

"In the road gangs I was, you'll understand. Shipped for life, I was, because of me father's coat of green. He wore the green, d'you see. So it was here in the chain-gang I fetched up, aworkin' on the road buildin', down to Taberag Ridge. The overseer was a great man for the whip, I'm telling you. Ah, a cruel man of iron, and no mistake. It's that cold in the winter-time, girleen, when there's snow on the wind. It's then that the hunger seems to eat into you, and the bruises ache bad. But—you'll be for lookin' at this dog now. A stray, he was. Left behind by a bullock train. Well, he took up with us convicts; and he stuck by us, so he did. Fed himself on rabbits and such—and me, too, sometimes. He slept with us at night to keep us warm. He'd lick our sores for us. This dog, see, he's a proper Christian and 'tis meself will swear to it.

"So it's when the overseer takes to him with the lash, girleen—" (Here the boy put his hand over his eyes, and the dog looked up lovingly, as though he heard and understood every word, and suffered with his master.)

"It's then—and may the holy angels forgive me— that a kind of red anger came into me brain, like. It took hold of me. I could not fight against it." His voice broke. Then in a moment he went on.

"I struck him down," he whispered.

"I wrested the lash from his hands. It was as though I had the strength of ten—as though possessed of devils I was, may the Gentle Mother help me.

"And I lashed the man.

"Ah, I gave him one for poor Jake Donegal, that died in the winter of the cough. And I lashed him for Ted Barnaby, that had gangrene of his leg iron. I lashed him for the heathen black that he rode down for a Sunday's sport. But most of all—I lashed him for this dog here. You'll maybe think it no reason. But I could not help it, as I tell you. I lashed him for this innocent creature, that is a friend to man with every hair of his body—so I did."

The boy covered his face, and the firelight seemed a place of dark tragedy. Then slowly, he took away his hands.

"So—" he shispered. "So—then—I stopped. Because—he was dead, see. I'd killed him."

The child drew away and tried to look into his face, in the flickering firelight. The boy said:

"I wrenched out of me leg iron. It was loose with the starvation, no doubt. And—then I took to the ridges. I went up all the time—always up. And so I came here. Now I'm spent. But if they catch me 'twill be me for the Hanging Tree on Taberag Ridge."

At first the child had no words to lighten the burden on the conscience of the ragged boy. But she placed her warm arm across his back, where every bone made the bars of a cage, as though in protection. After a while she said, "Don't be afraid. Whatever happens— don't be afraid. You did what you had to do. See—I am not afraid of you. The dog and I, we love you."

"If the soldiers take me," he said, "I'll remember that. Yes, I'll remember that."

Then he thrust into her pinafore his queer, rusted penny whistle.

"Keep it," he said. "Maybe some day it will be you who'll play—and I who'll hear, and come."

167

Quite suddenly, darkness gathered, and a drowsiness took hold of her. Tides of sleep came swirling like smoke before her eyes. . . .

They found her—the search party—high on the mountains, just as the dawn was breaking.

"But, Steffy," asked her father. "How did you light a fire? Did you have matches, then? Tell us how you came to be lost, my girl. Tell us how you endured through the night."

She shook her head. It seemed only full of a confused dreaming.

A queer, rusted whistle was in her pocket. A quaint, old-fashioned penny whistle, the like of which had not been seen around for many a year.

Even when she was grown, Steffany kept the whistle, as a curio; a souvenir of the time in childhood, when she wandered off alone, at dusk, on the Old Convicts' Road.

But she never played it, of course. It was too rusted. And so old, there was no one to teach her how to bring forth its tune.

Howard Goldsmith

The Voices of
El Dorado

The boy knew he heard voices in El Dorado . . .
but whose?

I can't blame anyone but myself for the jam I got
myself into. Rusty threw down the challenge, but it
was my own big mouth that drove him to dare me.
And you know how hard it is to back down from a
dare, especially when you've been boasting like a puffed-
up, loose-tongued bullfrog.

The episode with Rusty took place on a hike one
sunny afternoon in early spring. We were returning
home from a camping trip through Logan Forest. Our
group had never explored that neck of the woods before.

As Rusty unfolded a map of the terrain and checked
it against his compass, I remarked that I didn't need
any old map to find my way back to Central City. "And

only a tenderfoot has to use a compass," I added for good measure.

Rusty's face reddened. It matched the color of his tousled hair. "Well, wise guy, how would *you* get home?" he snapped.

"That's simple enough," I replied offhandedly. "Just by watching the sun and getting directions from its changing position in the sky. And," I added, "by observing what side moss grows on trees."

Rusty threw his head back and gave an imitation of a hog snorting.

I knew what he was thinking. Rusty sometimes led our entire troop on expeditions, and he never let any of us forget it. And he took great pride in the number of merit badges he had earned. I always teased him by saying that Daniel Boone never earned any badges, and he made out pretty well as a scout. And now, finally, I had the chance to show Rusty who was Daniel Boone and who was the tenderfoot.

Rusty leaned forward, the tip of his freckled nose an inch from mine. His chin jutted out challengingly. "If you're so smart, let's see you make it back home all by yourself." His lips curled in a sneering grin.

I smiled inwardly. Rusty was falling right into my trap. I couldn't resist the chance to show him up at scouting, even though I didn't like the idea of traveling home without the other kids.

"Okay," I answered casually, handing him my compass. "Please take care of this for me. Some people are born campers, and others just don't have what it takes. I'll be glad to give you a demonstration of practical know-how."

Rusty stood there fuming as I slung my pack over my back, gave a careless wave, and set off jauntily into the forest.

I glanced back over my shoulder. Our leader hadn't noticed my abrupt departure. Rusty's face had broken out into red blotches. One of his feet beat an angry tattoo on the ground. The other kids were laughing and enjoying his discomfort.

What I had concealed from Rusty was the fact that my father had taken me on an overnight hike through Logan Forest the previous summer. We had camped near the very spot where the group was now staying. Dad had pointed out that Clear Creek, which was located close by, narrowed to a stream that led straight to Central City. It would be a cinch to find Clear Creek, and from there it would be smooth sailing.

There was no trail to guide me, but I was pretty sure of my bearings. I remembered the clump of oak trees my father and I had passed through. I plunged deeper and deeper into the forest.

Sunlight painted the woods a blaze of gold and green. Feathery branches cast lacy shadows along the ground. On leafy boughs, birds twittered and jerked their heads in my direction, and grasshoppers darted and disappeared in the shadows.

After groping around in the brush for half an hour,

my confidence began to wilt. I knew how to make it home from the creek. The only problem was that the creek seemed to have disappeared.

I had been heading east. I veered about sharply and struck off in a westerly direction. But after trudging for an hour, I began to wonder if I'd ever make it home. Suddenly I heard the sound of water rippling in the distance. I raced through a thicket in the direction of the gurgling sounds and emerged at the edge of a stream.

"You see," I said to myself, with a deep sigh of relief, "there was nothing to worry about. You just temporarily lost your sense of direction. It could happen to anyone. Now, if I follow the stream north, I'll reach home within an hour. And will I gloat the next time I see Rusty!"

I walked steadily for an hour. I just had to be approaching Central City. But there were no signs of civilization. Instead, the forest became denser and darker. I began a slow jog.

It wasn't long before I was out of breath. I stumbled along, panting and staggering under the weight of my pack. My face was grimy and prickly with sweat. My legs ached and my feet burned. I would certainly remember this hike for a long time to come!

My watch indicated that I'd been following the stream for two hours, and Central City was still nowhere in sight. Suddenly it dawned on me that I must have been following an entirely different stream, one that had been leading me farther into the depths of the forest.

I stopped abruptly. I tried to keep cool and consider my position. I forced my mind to work against the mounting numbness that invaded it. I could double back along the path of the stream. But even if I managed to locate my starting point, which way would I then turn?

I decided to continue tracking the unfamiliar stream. It must lead *somewhere*. Perhaps to another town. Turning back might only land me in a deeper muddle.

The sun was beginning to set. The sky glowed with streaks of florid color. The dying glow of sunset lent a pale, mysterious cast to the forest. Arching trees engulfed me in their dark, leafy foliage.

Then, through a break in the woods, I spied a dark jumble of buildings off in the distance. A town! At last!

When I finally reached the clearing, I could see that the town was situated about a hundred yards west of a range of hills that enclosed a deep canyon. I ran toward the town with all the strength that remained in my wobbly legs.

As I approached the nearest houses, I stopped short. The buildings stretched out before me now—if you could call those ramshackle boxes "buildings." The town was completely deserted! With a heavy, sinking feeling, I read the name of the town on an old weathered sign that swung from a rusty nail: EL DORADO.

I stamped my foot in disgust. It was just my luck

to have discovered a ghost town! I marched wearily down its gloomy street, kicking up clouds of dust.

El Dorado must have been one of the many mining towns that had sprung up during the Gold Rush of the 1850s. Prospectors, seeking the precious metal, had trooped through the hills of Colorado by the thousands. The town had probably been abandoned more than a hundred years ago.

Well, a ghost town was better than no town at all—providing there were no real ghosts in it! Anyway, it was only a matter of spending the night.

I walked up and down the street, examining the old frame buildings. Most of them looked ready to collapse with the slightest shove. I picked out the one that seemed the sturdiest. At least there weren't any big holes in the roof.

Weeds grew up to the threshold and pressed against the door. I turned the doorknob. The door scraped open with a rusty scream of its hinges. A spider skittered out of my way and scurried up the opposite wall. The dusky interior had the dank, musty odor of rotted wood. One side of the shack had a blank rectangle for a window. Long, shadowy fingers stretched across the floor.

Up to that moment, I had forgotten how long it was since I had last eaten. I dumped my knapsack on the floor, took out a sandwich, and made quick work of it. Then I unfolded my bedroll and lay down to sleep.

Through the empty window, icy moonbeams fell upon

my face. Outside it was deathly still. I felt the presence of the vast, gaping canyon nearby. It was like being alone on the edge of the earth.

I tried not to let my imagination run away with me, or I'd soon be seeing strange shapes and hearing unearthly sounds. I had enough real, practical problems without inventing imaginary ones.

I was getting a grip on myself when a howling wind suddenly rustled up from the canyon. It played with the shack like an angry child with a dollhouse, rattling it to and fro. I buried my head deep into my bedroll. The boards of the shack groaned and creaked around me.

All at once, my ears caught a strange sound. Sitting up straight, I strained to hear.

Miaow . . . miaow!

A *cat?* Out here in a ghost town? Couldn't be! A mountain lion maybe!

Terror seized me. Cold shivers ran up my spine. With trembling fingers, I drew my Boy Scout knife from its sheath. Staring at the open window, I waited for whatever it was to spring through.

The cry came again, more distinctly this time. I cocked my ear.

It wasn't *miaow*, but a girl's voice!

"MOTHER! MOTHER!"

Another voice followed—the unmistakable cry of a boy. "FATHER! FATHER!"

What was going on? Who could they be? What were

they doing out here in this desolate place?

"Who is it?" I called.

No answer.

"Who is it?" I shouted louder.

Still no answer.

I fumbled around in my knapsack for a flashlight. Gripping it tightly, I scrambled out of the bedroll, sprang to my feet, and swung the door open.

I flashed a beam along the dark, dusty street.

"Who's out there?" I yelled.

No reply.

My flashlight probed every corner and crevice of the street. No one was there.

I turned around and crept back into the shack. No sooner had I lain down than the voices began again, urgently and insistently.

"MOTHER! MOTHER!"

"FATHER! FATHER!"

On and on the voices wailed.

"SAVE US! SAVE US!"

"COME BACK! COME BACK!"

I leaped up and rushed to the door. But the moment I opened it, the voices ceased.

"Who's calling?" I shouted hoarsely. "Why won't you answer me?"

No reply.

I didn't know what to think. Puzzled and frightened, I went back in again. How could I help them if they wouldn't answer? They seemed to be playing a cat-and-mouse game with me.

I lay down, resolved not to pay attention if the voices returned.

The wind picked up, whipping billows of dust through the open window. The voices came floating back on the midnight air. The strange, pitiful cries were louder than ever before.

"MOTHER! MOTHER!"

"SAVE US! SAVE US!"

I buried myself in my bedroll and lay there quivering. I pressed my hands over my ears, but the eerie voices droned on and on.

I sat up, grabbed a roll of gauze from my pack, ripped off two pieces, and stuffed them in my ears. But the voices would not be muffled. One barely stopped when the other began. Minutes ticked by endlessly as I tossed and turned, unable to sleep.

Finally, toward dawn, I dozed off. But my dreams were troubled, and when I awoke, I felt almost as tired as the night before. My bones ached. I stood up, stretched, and yawned.

The empty window made a brilliant rectangle of light on the floor.

I opened the door, inhaled the dry, thin mountain air, and shook the cobwebs out of my head. I felt better in the clear light of morning.

My legs itched to get moving, but I had no idea how

to find my way home from this place. If I set out into the woods, I might end up walking in circles and, by nightfall, find myself in an even worse predicament. And there was no telling when there might be a sharp drop in temperature. But here, at least, was shelter. I had enough food in my pack to last me for a few days, if necessary, and there was a stream nearby for water. I really shouldn't worry so much—a rescue party was surely combing the woods for me at that very moment.

But though I brightened a bit at this thought, I still felt completely, desolately alone. And the possibility of spending another night in that shack filled me with dread. I couldn't figure out where the voices had come from. Why had the boy and girl ignored my calls?

I decided to look for them. I poked around inside the empty shacks. The floors were caked with dust and windblown sand. There was no sign that anyone had entered them in years.

My thoughts returned to the rescue party. Perhaps they would send a helicopter to scour the terrain. I raced into the woods, gathered up some kindling, and stacked it in a small pile on the edge of town. I ran back into the shack and took a box of matches out of my pack. After stuffing the matches into my pocket, I felt better. The moment I heard the distant whine of a motor, I would dash to the woodpile and set it aflame.

But what if the kindling failed to ignite? Then I'd

wave my arms like a windmill. I practiced revolving my arms until they ached. I thought I'd better save them for the crucial moment.

Now that I'd reviewed my situation, I began to feel a bit more cheerful. I'd surely be rescued before evening. With a light spring to my step, I set out for a stroll around the rim of the canyon.

The vast cavity yawned up at me. Sharp-ridged hills rose to towering heights around me. I edged closer to the rim for a better look. "Careful," I told myself, "that's a drop of three hundred feet, at least."

Taking a step back, I began to test the canyon for echoes. I shouted my name, "Tim, Tim."

As my voice rebounded, I was shocked to hear another voice follow it. "HUSH, HUSH."

And then another. "BE STILL, STILL."

"Who is it?" I cried. "IT? IT?" my voice echoed.

There was no answer.

"I heard you," I called again. "YOU, YOU," pealed my voice in slowly dying eddies.

"I know you're there. THERE, THERE."

Still no answer.

I thought of a trick. I turned around and started back to the shack. But after walking thirty yards, I ducked swiftly behind a bush and waited.

After a few minutes, I heard the echo of a girl's voice reverberating through the canyon. "HE'LL NEVER FIND US, FIND US."

"NEVER, NEVER," a boy responded.

"HE HAS NO RIGHT HERE, HERE," echoed the girl's voice.

"THE MOUNTAINS BELONG TO US, US," replied the boy.

I sprang out of hiding and dashed to the rim of the canyon. "Who are you? YOU, YOU?"

"SHHH! THE BOY! BOY!"

"HE'S BACK! BACK!"

A volley of echoes bounced along the walls of the canyon.

"HA, HA, HA."

"HE THINKS HE'LL FIND US, FIND US."

I whirled about with dizzy speed. The voices were in back of me, now in front, now in back again. They were taunting me. The boy and girl must have been able to see me, but however hard I tried, I couldn't see them. "I must find them," I told myself.

"HE'LL NEVER FIND US, FIND US," came a voice, as if reading my mind.

But now I thought I was on to them. Their voices seemed to come from one of the hollows dug into the side of the canyon. I leaned over the edge to get a better view and then stepped gingerly onto an overhanging shelf. I was just easing my second foot down when the shelf suddenly gave way and crumbled beneath my feet! With a shock of terror, I found myself slipping down the slope. Frantically, I searched for a foothold, but there was not a fissure or cleft to support me. My hands clutched and clawed at the hill as it raced by my groping fingers. I plunged screaming down the hill until, suddenly, I landed with an abrupt thud.

Shaken and bruised, I couldn't help but be relieved. At least I hadn't landed in the deep rocky pit of the canyon. But when I looked around, creeping fear rippled along my arms, legs, my whole body. I found myself on a slightly projecting ledge, with only about four feet of rocky floor beneath me!

Clinging desperately to the side of the hill, not knowing what to do next, I looked up, hopelessly searching the crest of the hill. I didn't know what I was looking for. There was no way I could get back to the top. My breath came in heaving gasps. My head was spinning. I strained my neck farther upward. I had to keep my eyes away from what loomed below me. Then, slowly, something took shape before my eyes. I blinked again and again, trying to get the dust out. Then I realized I had been staring at a dwarf birch tree that jutted out at an angle from a ridge near the top of the rise. Could I possibly reach it? I really didn't know. It rose almost seven feet above the far end of the ledge I stood on. If I could only grab it, I might be able to pull myself up to safety. It was perilous but not impossible. I was good at high jumping. I had to take the risk. There was no telling how long I could remain erect on that narrow ledge.

Cautiously I sidled along the ledge, hugging the slope of the hill. "Slowly, slowly," I told myself. "There's no hurry. Easy does it."

181

Dripping perspiration, I finally reached the spot. I stared up at the tree. My heart pounded wildly. I gritted my teeth and said a silent prayer. Then, straining upward as high as my arms could reach, I vaulted up at the tree. Slap! My hands made contact. I locked my fingers firmly around the trunk. Using every ounce of strength, I drew myself up, inch by painful inch.

All at once the tree began to bend and sway. I bobbed up and down like a puppet. Praying that the scrawny birch was strong enough to support me, I continued pulling myself up until I succeeded in wrapping both my arms around it. But suddenly the tree gave a wrench and pitched sharply downward. It was tearing loose from its roots!

I hung suspended over the canyon, my eyes shut tight. I dared not breathe. The tree was shaking violently. And as my heart drummed and my head whirled, those same mysterious voices swelled throughout the canyon.

"HE'S FALLING! FALLING!" The echoes had lost their taunt, suddenly.

"HELP HIM! HELP HIM!" came the girl's voice. It was, unexpectedly, almost gentle.

"WE MUST, MUST, MUST."

The tree snapped erect, as if held by invisible bands. Without a moment's hesitation, I pulled myself up. My arms encircled the trunk. The tree was still holding firm. I could hardly believe it. With one last supreme effort, I heaved myself up and over the cliff. Then, as if suddenly released from the grip of an unseen power, the tree tore loose and plunged down the hill.

I stretched out on the ground, panting and sobbing with relief. In my mind there was no doubt that some friendly force had kept the tree from falling until I had climbed to safety. A picture of two children, a boy and a girl, flashed before my eyes. I could imagine them straightening the tree as I hung suspended over the canyon. I owed my life to them.

"Thank you! Thank you!" I cried fervently. My voice reverberated as I stumbled to my feet.

I waited expectantly, but no answer came. Still I waited, standing there for minutes, hoping. But not a sound disturbed the pervading stillness of the yawning canyon.

Finally, I lowered my head dejectedly and turned to leave. As I did, voices rang out behind me.

"WE ARE ONLY ECHOES, ECHOES, ECHOES."

I spun about sharply. "You have no bodies? BODIES?"

A girl's voice cried, "WE ARE ONLY ECHOES, ECHOES, ECHOES."

And then came a boy's voice. "WAITING, WAITING, WAITING."

And then silence.

There was no use. They didn't want me to know who they were. I trudged on back to the shack.

Pacing back and forth in the shack, wondering what to do next, I suddenly heard footsteps.

"Tim! Tim!" a man's voice called. It was my father's voice!

I raced out the door. There was my father striding down the street at the head of a rescue party. His face was drawn and anxious. I ran into his arms. He examined me to see if I was all right.

"Tim," he said, "we were worried sick about you. We've been out searching all night. Then Mr. Bailey remembered this old ghost town and figured you might have come here. It was a good guess."

He turned to Mr. Bailey and thanked him. Mr. Bailey's leathery, weather-beaten face creased into a big grin.

Breathlessly I blurted out my experience with the echoes. Everyone gave me a strange look. They thought I was out of my mind with fatigue and fright. All except Mr. Bailey, who leaned forward with a look of keen interest.

"Hmm," he said, stroking his chin thoughtfully. "You know, I recall an old legend that used to circulate around mining camps. This is reaching far back in my memory. These hills are pitted with scores of caves and recesses, you know. The story has it that two children once wandered into a cave in this very canyon. Rescue parties searched for days, but all their efforts amounted to nothing. From time to time, they caught the distant sound of voices echoing on the wind. But the faint cries never lasted long enough to be located. The poor tykes must have weakened pretty quickly without food or water. The story has it that their rest-less spirits haunt the canyon, their plaintive cries for-ever echoing through the hills. According to the Legend of the Lost Children, they linger as echoes to keep vigil until their parents return to find them."

Mr. Bailey held us spellbound with his tale.

"Oh, who believes those old miners' tales," scoffed a gravel-voiced, barrel-chested man with dark stubble covering his face. "They're just campfire stories in-vented to pass the time. Nobody puts any stock in 'em."

Everyone nodded in agreement except Mr. Bailey. He scratched his face and drawled, "I wouldn't be so sure."

As we prepared to leave, we suddenly heard my name called. "TIM, TIM."

Everyone gave a start. "What was that?" they asked with one voice.

Then they all stared at me. They knew, suddenly, that Mr. Bailey's story was true.

I whispered good-bye to the children, relieved that they had been there to save me from death but more than a little sad that they had not ever had anyone to help them.

And as we drove off, the dust kicking behind us, I thought that I heard the sound of weeping.

Rod Serling
Adapted by Anne Serling

The Changing of the Guard

The old Professor wondered if his life had been worthwhile and found the answer in his shadowy past.

PROLOGUE

What you are about to read is not just the story of the end of a semester. It happens to be the end of an era. Professor Ellis Fowler, a teacher of literature, a gentle, bookish, guide to the young, is about to find a package under his Christmas tree . . . and not a pleasant one. He doesn't realize it yet, but after half a century of planting seeds of wisdom, and then watching the fruits of his harvest, he is to discover that he has come to the end of the field and is about to be discarded. And that the campus of Rock Hill School for Boys lies on a direct path to another institution commonly referred to as . . . The Twilight Zone.

The Rock Hill School for Boys was located in a small town in Connecticut. There was nothing particularly unique about the school, nothing to differentiate it from any other boys' school of the time. The ivy clung to the brick walls, its thick carpet broken only in a few places where dusty, diamond-shaped panes of glass could be seen. The boys looked the same. The classrooms contained the same, wooden desks, lined up in rows, with names and thoughts of the time carved deep into the wood. The long, dark corridors retained the same musty smells that never dissipated, even on sunny days. The halls echoed with the same laughter, the same angers, the same disappointments that one might find in any other school. No, there was nothing really distinctive, nothing except Professor Ellis Fowler.

Professor Fowler was seventy-seven, with a great gray mop of hair and a beard the same color that moved up and down as he spoke. He had a kindly, tremendously intelligent old face with sparkling blue eyes that still questioned. His glasses constantly slipped down over the bridge of his nose and he intermittently, though fruitlessly, tried to push them back where they should be. He was thin and angular, not unlike a deflated Santa Claus.

His classroom was filled, on this the last day of the term. His students, a handful of young teenagers, sat in various postures of semi-bored lethargy before him.

Professor Fowler peered at the book in his hand and, looking like a kindly old owl, began the morning.

"You'll remember that we've talked of the work of Alfred Edward Houseman, born . . . what year, Mr. Graham?"

Graham, a sixteen-year-old linebacker, whose body had grown without him, blinked and suddenly came to attention. "What year, sir?"

There was a thin trickle of laughter. Graham shifted in his seat, looked out of the window, and fingered his varsity letter. "Ah, sometime this century. I think."

Professor Fowler smiled and nodded. "Close, Mr. Graham. Closer than usual. Sometime this century." He looked off thoughtfully, scratched his beard, and addressed the class. "Mr. Graham's career is laid out for him. He will be a second assistant in the Information Booth at Kennedy Airport."

The class laughed and, anticipating a bit of fun, sat up and centered their attention on Fowler. The Professor peered at Graham over his glasses. "The date of Alfred Houseman's birth, Mr. Graham, and for the benefit of the rest of the class, was eighteen fifty-nine. His death occurred . . . what year, Mr. Butler?"

An exuberant runty little enthusiast, who had the kind of head that looked like it would spend the rest of its life wearing a beanie, jumped to his feet with alacrity. "Sir, around nineteen hundred."

Professor Fowler straightened his glasses and again scratched his beard. " 'Pon my word, young Mr. Butler, you and Mr. Graham are kindred spirits. Alfred Houseman died in nineteen thirty-six. Now, with yours and Mr. Graham's permission, this is somewhat less moving than a screen pass or what a T-formation quarterback tells his line in a huddle, but I hope you'll bear with me for a moment of truth. All of you will recall, no doubt, 'A Shropshire Lad,' a little of which I will now read to you:

> "When I was one-and-twenty
> I heard a wise man say,
> 'Give crowns and pounds and guineas
> But not your heart away;' "

He continued to recite but his eyes left the book, moved over the heads of the students, and fastened on some far distant corner of the universe.

> " 'Give pearls away and rubies
> But keep your fancy free.'
> But I was one-and-twenty,
> No use to talk to me."

The book slowly lowered in his hand and he continued.

> " 'The heart out of the bosom
> Was never given in vain;
> 'Tis paid with sighs a-plenty
> And sold for endless rue.'
> And I am two-and-twenty,
> And oh, 'tis true, 'tis true."

Professor Fowler smiled and nodded and was lost for a protracted moment in which he was several thousand miles away, responding to a truth. He was suddenly aware of the boys looking at him and closed the book. He took off his glasses, checked them, blew on them, wiped them off, and smiled from face to face. Clearing his throat, he said, "It is quite an odd phenomenon, really, how you react to that poem much as your fathers did. It is a fact that I've been reading it for fifty-one years to various classes who failed to get its meaning at all. Said meaning, is, simply: Give sparingly of your youth. Embrace it for the precious thing it is. It's the most fleeting chapter in the book of your lives." He leaned over his desk and peered at the students. "You will, I am sure, at some future moment of your lives, understand precisely what I'm getting at."

Then, smiling, he said, "Now, gentlemen, this being the last day of the semester, and this being just three days before the Christmas holidays, I thought it might behoove me to show at least a minute degree of compassion and let you out early. I might add, here, that while your final exam papers are not ready to be returned to you, you have all—amazingly enough—passed. My delight is surpassed only by my sense of the shock. It is rare, young men, that in some fifty-one years of teaching I have ever encountered such a class of dunderheads." He looked down, then up over his glasses, and his eyes were twinkling. "But nice dunderheads, and potentially fine young men who will make their marks, and leave their marks. God bless you all. And a Merry Christmas!"

The boys rose and Professor Fowler started down the aisle nodding, smiling, and shaking an occasional hand as the students filed out into the hall. Their voices lifted in youthful laughter, as thoughts of Christmas and holiday and going home sent spirit through the halls. Locker doors were slammed shut. Books and papers were stashed away with great haste and exuberant shouts of "freedom" echoed through the building.

Professor Fowler walked through the hall, exchanging nods and hellos with the boys. He was about to pass the Headmaster's Office when the door opened and the Headmaster called out. He was a tweedy young man still rather new to the job and somewhat smug about it. He pointed an overlarge briar pipe at the Professor. "I say, Fowler, could you step in for a moment?"

Fowler nodded. "Why, of course."

The Headmaster walked over to his desk and sat down, lighting his pipe. "Sit down, Fowler. Be comfortable."

Professor Fowler sat down in the overstuffed chair, looked around the office and at the Headmaster's desk—neat and tidy and all together unused appearing. He took his pocket watch out and peered at it.

The Headmaster, watching him closely, asked, "Am I keeping you?"

Professor Fowler replied, "No, no, no. There is going to be a broadcast of *Messiah* at five o'clock, but I have plenty of time. It's a lovely thing. Very Yule-like."

The Headmaster, his pomposity oozing out of him, replied, "I agree. I agree." He then arranged the papers on his desk, straightened them again, lined them up, and laid them back down. "This won't take long."

There was a long silence. Fowler sat quietly, expectantly. The Headmaster ran a long finger down the wooden desk, sucked up his pipe, moved some more paper, and then, finally, reluctantly, looked up. "You . . . aaah . . . you did not respond to the letter that the Trustees sent you last week."

The Professor pushed his glasses further up his nose and with a thoughtful pause said, "Letter? I'm terribly sorry, Headmaster. It suddenly occurs to me that I haven't opened my mail for the last few weeks. Final exams, grading, preparation for the holiday . . . that sort of thing." He smiled and continued. "Though I'm rather certain I know the contents of that letter."

The Headmaster looked away. "And . . . aaah . . . your reactions, Professor?"

The Professor took off his glasses and went through the ritual of checking and cleaning them. "Well, I'll naturally go along."

The Headmaster beamed and rubbed his hands. "Well, I think that's very perspicacious of you, Professor. Then I'll tell the Trustees that you received the com-

munication and agreed to it. Now, as to your replace-
ment—"

Professor Fowler was not listening to the Headmaster now. He was smiling a little vacantly and interrupted without being aware he was interrupting.
"I told my housekeeper, not a week ago, that I should
very likely teach in this place until I'm a hundred years
old. Two years ago I actually taught the grandson of
one of my earlier students. I venture to say that I'll
live to teach a great-grandson one of these days. It
was the Reynolds boy. You know him. His father was
Damon Reynolds and his grandfather—a regular rascal of a boy who persisted in calling me 'weird beard.' "
He chuckled and wiped his glasses. " 'Weird beard'
didn't know that I knew that that's what he was calling
me. Oh, a regular rascal of a boy. Went into the stock
market. Made himself a fortune. Came back for his
twentieth reunion. Shook my hand and said, 'Professor
Fowler, please forgive me for calling you 'weird beard.' "
Fowler looked up at the ceiling and shook his head and
smiled.

The Headmaster coughed slightly. His voice was
very low and tentative. "Professor Fowler. You'll forgive me, sir, but . . . I think you best read the communication that the Trustees sent."

Fowler looked at him and nodded, "Oh, indeed I
will. Though it's really an odd formality, this contract
signing year after year. You can tell them for me,

193

Headmaster, that old Fowler won't depart the ship. Oh, no, indeed. He'll stand at the wheel through fair weather and foul, and he'll watch the crews come aboard and then depart, come aboard and then depart. And he'll see that the ship will stay on course."

The Headmaster cut in. His voice was very quiet and not without some pity. "Professor Fowler, please hear me out, sir." He rose, walked behind the desk over to a window, and stared at the snow-filled day. "The communication that the Trustees sent you was not a contract." He turned away very slowly from the window. "As a matter of fact . . . it was a notice of termination. You've been on the faculty here for over fifty years. You've passed the normal retirement age several years ago. We decided at our winter meeting that perhaps a younger man . . ." He stopped and looked across the room to Fowler, who had risen to his feet. "If you could have been at the meeting, sir, you would have been very proud at the things said about you and your work. A teacher of incalculable value to all of us. But . . ." He turned and retraced his steps back to the desk and stood there with his head down. He did not want to look at the old man's face, but finally had to.

Professor Fowler's voice was almost a whisper, "Mr. Headmaster, am I to understand that my contract is not to be renewed? I'm discharged?"

The Headmaster began pacing the room. "Discharged? Please! Don't call it that. Retirement. *And* at half salary for the rest of your life."

Fowler very softly said, "For . . . the . . . rest . . . of . . . my . . . life?" Suddenly, he looked very old. He walked toward the door, then stopped, his back to the Headmaster. "Well, it . . . it certainly proves one thing, 'pon my word it does. A man should read his mail. He most certainly should read his mail." He walked out the door and down the corridor.

Two boys passed and smiled at him, "Merry Christmas, Professor. Have a happy holiday, sir."

Professor Fowler studied their faces. "Mr. Hallidy and Mr. McTavish." His voice was shaking, perceptibly. "I wish you a safe and happy journey and a happy reunion with your families. And I trust you will not eat too much turkey . . . and too much . . . too much stuffing. I've, I've known it to happen Christmas after Christmas, you young rascals go home and eat yourselves into insensi—insensibility."

The boys looked at one another as tears appeared in Professor Fowler's eyes.

With trembling fingers, the Professor touched each boy's face in turn. "You're both fine men. Have a Merry Christmas, both of you. Have a—" His voice broke. He turned and walked away from them a few feet, and leaned against a bulletin board, struggling for composure.

He heard the boys' voices behind him. "What's the matter with old 'weird beard'? He was crying. Did you see that? He was crying."

Fowler turned away from the bulletin board and

started a slow walk down the corridor. He ran his hand along the wall, feeling the carved molding that had been worn smooth through the years. He stopped and looked around for a moment, taking in the sights and sounds of this building he had virtually lived in for half a century. Finally, pushing open the heavy oak door, he walked outside and, oblivious to the bitter chill, started home. Once, he stopped to gaze behind him at the building that he had cherished so many years. It was dark in the evening twilight and the building was almost hidden by the falling snow.

With difficulty he climbed the steps to his house and stamped the snow off his feet, more from habit than conscious concern at that moment. He walked directly to the hall table. A little Christmas tree sat on it, laden with ornaments and growing more top-heavy each year. Each ornament had a history—a special meaning— because all were gifts from his "boys." After the Christmas season was over, each treasure was wrapped and stored on a high shelf with great ceremony. But Professor Fowler wasn't looking at the tree that night. He was looking at the letters lying beside the tree. Still in his hat and coat, he fumbled through them, the front door behind him still open to the winter chill.

From the dark recesses of the house, Mrs. Landers, the Professor's housekeeper, materialized. After twenty odd years of living with and caring for the Professor she had grown very fond of him and was used to his absentmindedness—almost expected it. She closed the door and straightened her hair that had been blown loose by a gust of wind, and turned to the Professor. "I didn't hear you come in. It's certainly snowing and blowing to beat the band, isn't it?"

But Fowler, having finally found the letter that he had been searching for, absentmindedly responded. "Well, I guess it is. I hadn't noticed."

Mrs. Landers studied the Professor's face, and, noting his stooped shoulders and ashen color with growing concern, asked him if anything was wrong.

The Professor shook his head and looked down at the letter. "I guess that would depend on the point of view. If you're a Trustee of this institution, anxious to inject new young blood into the faculty, I'm sure you'd think there was nothing wrong at all." He very slowly picked up the letter and stared at it. "But if you're an old man who has spent the better part of his life inside those halls, those classrooms—then you might be forgiven a degree of consternation."

He suddenly chuckled a long, low chuckle. "As a matter of fact, everything is *not* all right. Everything happens to be very wrong."

Mrs. Landers pointed to the letter in his hand. "What is it, Professor? What's happened?"

Professor Fowler looked down at the letter and read aloud from it. " 'And since it is the policy of the school to ensure our students the most up-to-date educational concepts, we think it advisable that you consider this retirement to be a mutually beneficial thing. Please understand the spirit in which this request is made and understand further that your contributions to Rock Hill School for Boys are a matter of record, as is our appreciation."

The housekeeper bit her lower lip, "Oh my word, Professor, that means . . ."

The Professor finished her thought. "That means, Mrs. Landers, stripped of some of its sophistry, its subtlety, its back-breaking effort to break it gently—that I'm canned." He walked towards his study and asked Mrs. Landers, "Were any of my boys here?"

Mrs. Landers, confused and somewhat shaken, looked at him, "Your boys, sir?"

"The students, Mrs. Landers. They had a wonderful tradition that went on for many years. On the last afternoon of the winter term, they would gather outside there and sing Christmas carols. I got to expecting it after a while."

Mrs. Landers very softly said, "They haven't done that in years, Professor. Not since before the war, as I recall."

Fowler nodded and turned away from her again. "Of course. I should have remembered." He removed his glasses, peered through them, started to clean them, then suddenly stopped, gripped them tightly, stared at them, and threw them on the table. "Mrs. Landers, I've become a worshipper of tradition and a fervent follower of ritual. I know it now. I know it and I can admit it. I guess that's why this whole thing has hit me so hard."

He walked across the worn oriental rug and sat down at his desk. "I'm an antique guarding antiques. I am the curator of a museum that houses nothing but some very fragile memories."

Mrs. Landers shook her head. She was close to tears. "Professor, you're the finest man. You're absolutely the finest man."

Professor Fowler smiled at her gratefully. "And you, Mrs. Landers, are the most loyal woman. Now, would you do me a favor? Would you brew me up some tea? Handel's *Messiah* is on the radio in a few minutes. I'd like to listen to it."

Fowler closed his eyes, rested on his elbows for a moment, and then sat back. His eyes scanned the desk and he very slowly took a key off his key chain, unlocked the lower right-hand drawer, rummaged through it, and took out a revolver. He stared at it for a long moment, placed it inside his sweater, and moved to the old rocking chair.

The gentle snow still falling from the night sky was visible through the windows behind the desk. Professor Fowler finished the tea Mrs. Landers had brought him and the empty cup sat on the table as he listened to *The Messiah*. The music ended on a triumphant sweeping note just as Mrs. Landers entered the room. Almost on tiptoe, she walked around to the other side of the chair and peered into Fowler's face. He opened his eyes.

"Yes, Mrs. Landers?"

Mrs. Landers, somewhat startled, said, "Oh, I thought you were asleep, Professor. Would you care for some more tea?"

Fowler shook his head, his mind a million miles away. "Thank you, no."

"I'll have dinner ready in half an hour. Why don't you take a little nap?"

Fowler reached over and turned off the radio. "I know I'm being very difficult, but could we put off dinner this evening? I haven't much of an appetite."

"Professor, you've got to eat something. I could keep it warm for you. Perhaps after your nap?"

Fowler looked at her kind, aging, lovely face and smiled a little. "Perhaps later."

He rose from the chair and walked across the room, over to the bookcase. Three of the shelves were devoted to the Rock Hill School Yearbooks; the wood that supported them sagged from their weight. The books dated back many years. Fowler went through his daily ritual of lightly dusting them, and touching them, as if through osmosis he could transform himself back through the years. He took one book out and carried it over to the desk. He very carefully opened it, thumbed through the pages, and studied the faces and names.

Mrs. Landers sat in the chair across from him. She

watched him adoringly, yet sadly, feeling his loss.

Fowler mused aloud. "Timothy Arnold. Never thought that one would pass. Had an incorrigible habit of chewing bubble gum and popping it. Sounded like a howitzer. 'Pon my word, it sounded like a howitzer. William Hood. Little Bill Hood . . . smallest boy ever to play varsity football here, and had a penchant for Shelley." He turned the page again and a smile lit up on his face. "Artie Beachcroft. Now there was a lad. There was a staunch lad. Full of heart, that one." He looked off thoughtfully. "Was he the one? Yes, yes— I recall now. His father sent me a letter. He was killed on Iwo Jima. Freckle-faced little fellow, always grinning. Never stopped grinning; most infectious grin. He'd walk into a classroom and you had to smile."

He continued turning the pages, and then finally closed the book. He looked down at it for a long moment. "They come and go like ghosts. Faces, names, smiles, the funny things they did—or sad things, or poignant ones. I gave them nothing at all. I realize that now. Poetry that left their minds as soon as they themselves left. Aged slogans that were already out of date when I taught them. Quotations that were so dear to me that were meaningless to them."

Fowler shook his head. "Mrs. Landers, I am a failure. I am an old relic that walks from class to class. Speaking by rote to unhearing ears, unwilling heads. I am an abject, dismal failure. I moved no one. I left no imprint on anyone. Now where do you suppose I got the idea that I was accomplishing anything?"

Tears began to brim in Mrs. Landers' eyes. She shook her head as if trying to protest, but no words came out. Fowler smiled at her, excusing her for her silence and understanding it. He left the desk and walked to the door. "I will take that nap now. And I hope I haven't inconvenienced you, putting off dinner like this." He walked out of the room with slow, measured footsteps.

Mrs. Landers touched his yearbook, almost fondling it, and carried it over to the bookcase. She went back to the desk and started to put things in order. She touched the pipe, the book, the glasses—all with a very special touch, indicative of love. Seeing some papers sticking out of one of the drawers she reached down, opened the drawer, and suddenly stopped, transfixed in horror. There, under the papers, she saw the empty gun holster. She picked it up, held it at arm's length, made a motion as if to run through the room, stopped, looked at the holster again, and then carefully put it back in the drawer. With a growing feeling of panic and desperation, she screamed, "Professor Fowler" and ran into the hall. The front door was wide open. She quickly picked up the telephone and dialed the Headmaster.

Fowler walked slowly across the campus, his footsteps echoing in the silence and his breath coming in short, quick gasps in the cold night air. His overcoat was awry and misbuttoned. He was hatless and looked lost and forlorn. Halfway across the campus he stopped in front of a full-sized bronze statue. Wiping some of the snow off the base so that the legend carved there was readable, he softly spoke the words: "Horace Mann, Educator. Seventeen-ninety-six to eighteen-fifty-nine." Fowler knelt down in the snow and very thoughtfully said, "I was just wondering if you had any self-doubts." He smiled and shook his head. "I'm sure not." He brushed some more snow off until he could see the rest of the quotation beneath Mann's name.

" 'Be ashamed to die until you have won some victory for humanity.' " He looked away, his face emotionless, and said, "I have won no victory. . . . No victory at all." He looked down at his coat pocket, his voice very low. "And now I am ashamed to die." Very slowly, he took out the revolver, clicked off the safety catch, and was about to raise it when his motion was stopped by the sound of distant, ringing bells that pealed a melodious, and strangely, urgent call.

Fowler turned abruptly and looked off in the direction of the bells. He musingly said, "Class bells? Now that's odd. Why would they ring now? There's no special assembly now. There's nothing of that sort."

In the distance, the bells began to ring again. Fowler started to walk toward the school, unconsciously putting the gun back into his pocket. He reached the main building, where the door stood curiously open. Inside, he looked into each empty classroom and then up toward the ceiling, as the bells continued ringing. He was completely alone. He stopped at the door to his classroom and then walked inside and started up the aisle between the desks. Halfway up, he stopped again and listened. There was a strange echoing hollow sound of boys talking and laughing, as if coming from some far distant place. He continued on to the front of the room, bewildered and perplexed and then, gradually, amazed. In each seat a figure began to emerge—first from a kind of ghostlike transparency and then into the flesh-and-blood figure of a boy, until each seat was filled, and a dozen boys were looking expectantly toward him.

Professor Fowler unbuttoned his coat, and his lips moved in soundless questions. "I . . . I don't understand. Forgive me, boys, but I'm not at all sure—what I mean is, I don't recollect how—"

The boys smiled at him and finally one rose. "Artie Beachcroft, sir. Second form. Class of forty-one. How have you been, Professor?"

Fowler looked at him and shook his head from side to side quizically. "How's that? How's that again? You say you're Artie Beachcroft?" He began to nod slowly. "Of course you are. I'd recognize you anywhere." He walked over to the boy, held out his hands, and grabbed the boy's hand. He sniffled and wiped away a tear. "I'm delighted to see you. I'm truly delighted to see you. I've missed you, Artie." He then stared at the boy and began shaking his head again. "But . . . but what are you doing here? Forgive me, but you shouldn't be here. You were—"

The boy smiled and finished the Professor's thought. "I was killed on Iwo Jima, sir. That's right, Professor." He reached into his pocket, took out a small case, opened it and displayed a medal. "I wanted to show this to you, sir. It's the Congressional Medal of Honor. It was given to me posthumously."

Fowler looked at it and then up into the boy's face. "A very prideful thing, Mr. Beachcroft, a very prideful thing, and I am indeed proud of you. You were always a fine young man. A *fine* young man." He stared at the boy, closed his eyes, shook his head, and then blinked his eyes open. "I . . . I don't understand."

A boy from across the room called out, "Professor?" Fowler turned toward him.

"I'm Bartlett. Third form. Class of twenty-eight. I died in Roanoke, Virginia. I was doing research on X-ray treatment for cancer. I was exposed to radioactivity. I contacted leukemia."

Fowler said softly, "I remember, Bartlett. I *do* remember. That was an incredibly brave thing you did, an incredibly brave thing."

The boy continued. "I kept remembering, Professor, something you'd said to me. A quote. A poet named Walter."

Fowler nodded knowingly. "Howard Arnold Walter. I remember."

Bartlett, in a strong voice, began quoting.

"I would be true, for there are those
    who trust me; I would be pure, for there
    are those who care; I would be strong,
    for there is much to suffer. I would be
    brave, for there is much to dare."

He looked at the Professor. "I never forgot that, Professor. It was something you left me. I never forgot."

Fowler's lips began to tremble. "How . . . how very decent of you, Bartlett, to say that."

Artie Beachcroft shared the sentiment. "That's why I brought the medal to show you, Professor Fowler, because it's partly yours. You taught me about courage. You taught me what it meant."

Fowler said, very, very softly, "Why . . . why, how incredible." His eyes scanned the room and stopped on a very small boy. He walked over to him and touched the boy's face. "Why, it's . . . it's Weiss, isn't it? Dickie Weiss? You were the first one, Dick—"

The boy got to his feet. "The first one to die, Professor. I was at Pearl Harbor on the *Arizona*. I was an ensign."

Fighting building emotion, Fowler said, "I remember, Dick. You saved a dozen men. You got them out of the boiler room after they were trapped, and lost your life doing it."

The boy smiled and nodded. "You were at my elbow

206

that day, Professor. You may not have known it, but there you were. It was a poem you had taught me.

> ". . . any man's death diminishes me,
> because I am involved in mankind;
> and therefore never send to know for
> whom the bell tolls; it tolls for
> thee."

Fowler smiled and looked at the boys, who were all looking up at him. His smile grew broader, his eyes brighter in the silence that ensued. The bell rung again, but this time very softly. He walked by the boys and they each in turn rose.

"I'm Thompson, sir; second form, class of thirty-nine. I died in New Guinea, but you taught me about patriotism."

"Rice, sir. Third form, class of nineteen-seventeen. I died of wounds at Château-Thierry. You taught me about courage."

"Hudson, sir. Second form, class of nineteen twenty-two. You taught me about loyalty."

"Whiting, sir. Fourth form, class of fifty-one. You taught me about ethics and honesty."

Fowler blinked back his tears, surveyed the class, sniffled, coughed, wiped his eyes, then took off his glasses, peered through them, cleaned them, and then put them back on.

Each boy watched this and smiled. They remembered this ritual fondly; none of them had ever forgotten it. For a moment there was a still silence.

Finally Beachcroft said, "We have to go back now, Professor, but we wanted to let you know that we were grateful—that we were forever grateful, that each of us has, in turn, carried with him something that you gave him. We wanted to thank you, Professor."

Once again, the figures of the boys took on a transparency and finally disappeared altogether. And once more, the bells began to ring.

Fowler walked down the aisle, looked at the desks, touching that one, pausing by another, and finally went out the door and into the snow. He pulled his coat closer in the chill and walked across the campus toward home.

When he arrived, Mrs. Landers was on the telephone. When she saw him, she broke into a relieved smile. She said into the telephone, "Yes, Headmaster, he's home now. He's all right. Yes, he's just fine. Thank you." She put the phone down, and Fowler smiled at her. They both suddenly looked up as they heard the sound of Christmas caroling from outside.

Fowler turned, and framed in the window, he saw the boys outside knee deep in snow and heard their voices lifted in the last refrain of a Christmas carol. They finished and one boy stepped in front of the group. "Merry Christmas, Professor! Merry Christmas to you!"

Fowler opened the window and called out, "And a

merry Christmas to you, young men, a very merry Christmas, indeed. And may I add how . . . how grateful I am to all of you. I've always thought that Christmas caroling is . . . is a wonderfully special tradition. Merry Christmas, boys, and God bless you!"

The boys smiled and waved as they walked off, beginning another song.

Fowler lowered the window and turned to Mrs. Landers. "I've had a chance to think it over, Mrs. Landers, I think I *will* retire. I do believe that I've taught all that I can teach. And I wouldn't want the returns to diminish."

He turned, once again, and stared out the window. He took off his glasses, went through the ritual of peering through them, then cleaning them, and then putting them back on. There was the sound of chimes from a distant tower and then a soft Christmas carol from beyond.

"Mrs. Landers, I do believe . . . I do believe that I may *have* left my mark. A few gauntlets of knowledge that I've thrown down—they've been picked up."

He smiled. " 'Be ashamed to die until you have won some victory for humanity.' Mrs. Landers, I didn't win them, but I helped others to win them. I believe that now. So in that way . . . even in a small measure . . . they are victories that I can share."

He turned back and looked out the window, smiling and nodding. "I've had a very good life, Mrs. Landers. A very rich life. A very fruitful life. This particular changing of the guard . . . I wouldn't have it any other way."

EPILOGUE

Professor Ellis Fowler, teacher. Who discovered, rather belatedly, something of his own value. A very small scholastic lesson from the campus of . . . The Twilight Zone

Asimov's Monsters

Asimov's Monsters was
first published in Great Britain
in a single volume
by Dragon Books in 1986

Acknowledgements

'Homecoming' by Ray Bradbury. Copyright © 1946, 1974 by Ray Bradbury. Reprinted by permission of Don Congdon Associates, Inc.

'Good-by, Miss Patterson' by Phyllis MacLennan. Copyright © 1972 by Phyllis MacLennan. From *The Magazine of Fantasy and Science Fiction*. Reprinted by permission of the author.

'The Wheelbarrow Boy' by Richard Parker. Copyright © 1953 by Richard Parker. Reprinted by permission of Curtis Brown Associates, Ltd.

'The Cabbage Patch' by Theodore R. Cogswell. Copyright © 1952 by Perspective; copyright © 1980 by Theodore R. Cogswell. Reprinted by permission of the author.

'The Thing Waiting Outside' by Barbara Williamson. Copyright © 1977 by Barbara Williamson. From *Ellery Queen's Mystery Magazine*, December, 1977. Reprinted by permission of the author.

'Red as Blood' by Tanith Lee. Copyright © 1979 by Mercury Press, Inc. From *The Magazine of Fantasy and Science Fiction*. Reprinted by permission of Don Congdon Associates, Inc.

'Fritzchen' by Charles Beaumont. Copyright © 1953, 1981 by Charles Beaumont. Reprinted by permission of Don Congdon Associates, Inc.

'The Young One' by Jerome Bixby. Copyright © 1953 by Ziff-Davis Publishing Co.; copyright © 1981 by Jerome Bixby. Reprinted by permission of Forrest J. Ackerman, 2495 Glendower Ave., Hollywood, California 90027.

'Optical Illusion' by Mack Reynolds. Copyright © 1953 by Standard Magazines, Inc.; copyright © 1981 by Mack Reynolds. Reprinted by permission of the Scott Meredith Literary Agency, Inc., 845 Third Avenue, New York, New York 10022.

'Idiot's Crusade' by Clifford D. Simak. Copyright © 1954 by Galaxy Publishing Corporation; copyright © 1982 by Clifford D. Simak. Reprinted by permission of Kirby McCauley, Ltd.

'One for the Road' by Stephen King. Copyright © 1977 by Maine Magazine Co., Inc. From *Nightshift* by Stephen King. Reprinted by permission of Doubleday & Company, Inc.

'Angelica' by Jane Yolen. Copyright © 1979 by Mercury Press, Inc. From *The Magazine of Fantasy and Science Fiction*. Reprinted by permission of Curtis Brown, Ltd.

Contents

The Power of Evil

by Isaac Asimov

Young people living in the United States or some other developed and industrial nation are used to inhabiting a universe ruled by the laws of science.

We know how to control the environment to what we think is our own benefit—to grow food more efficiently, to produce energy, and to control disaster. We know how to prevent many diseases from striking us, how to control or cure them if they do strike. We know how to lower the danger of lightning and how to make planes, cars, and machinery of all kinds quite safe to use.

Even when disaster does strike—when a plane crashes or a tornado hits or someone is murdered or gets an incurable disease—we know there are natural causes and, if we can, we try to find out exactly what those causes are and how to protect ourselves more efficiently against such unpleasant events.

How different things were in prescientific times—and, still are in many undeveloped regions today.

When science and modern thought did not exist, and

219

where they do not exist today, the universe is a strange and very frightening thing. There is no knowledge of the scientific laws that govern events. Things therefore take place without natural cause.

Floods come or droughts wither the landscape; storms batter at people or epidemics cut them down; lightning strikes or animals die of disease; somehow things go wrong.

Why? Why?

No one in nonscientific surroundings even dreams of seeking a natural cause. If something bad happens it must be because some intelligent being has caused it out of anger or spite. If the event is something no normal human being can bring about, then it must be some superhuman being who does it. One of the gods is angry because he or she hasn't been sacrificed to. A passing demon with a hatred for the human race inflicted them. An indifferent spirit is just amusing himself the way a child might when pulling wings off flies. Or perhaps the disaster is brought about by a just and kindly god who has been angered by sin, and who wishes to chastise the sinners.

But you don't know, you can't know, exactly what caused the event or how to prevent it. Does one beg the superhuman being for forgiveness, or threaten him, or make use of certain magical charms or rituals, or what?

And, of course, there is always the suspicion that some people are better informed on how to handle such gods and demons than others. Some people may have learned how to perform the rituals or how to say the charms in just the right way so as to prevent the supernaturally caused disasters or bring them to an end.

If these gifted ones are kindly, and are concerned with the good of the people, they are priests, seers, saints, wise men. But what if they are themselves selfish or evil and want to use their control over the supernatural to make themselves powerful or to punish anyone who offends them? Then they are wizards, witches, enchanters, necromancers.

Think how dangerous a universe would be if anyone you chanced to meet might be an enchanter, unknown to you. Some casual thing you say might annoy him and he might change you into a frog.

Then, too, once you become afraid of any stranger because he might be an enchanter, it doesn't take much to fear him (or her) because he might be a human being with horrifying abilities or habits—someone who looks like a human being, but who is so different in various ways that he might be considered a "monster."

What if he (or she) is not really alive, but is a ghost or spirit, an insubstantial remnant of a human being, who can take on the appearance of reality but who can disappear at will, and who means evil against you? Or what if he has the ability to change into a wolf (or some other animal) whenever he wants to; or what if he *must* undergo such a change even against his will at the time of the full moon. He is then a "werewolf." What if he eats dead bodies (he is then a "ghoul") or drinks blood (he is then a "vampire"), and what if he lives forever as long as he can indulge these appetites, or what if he has superhuman strength or other abilities in addition.

In a world in which the idea of scientific law is absent, you don't ask how human cells can change into wolf cells, or how hair can suddenly grow when a man becomes a wolf, and what happens to it when the wolf changes back to a man. You don't think that a diet of corpses might result in food poisoning, or that an exclusive diet of blood might result in vitamin deficiency or in an iron oversupply.

Anything is possible, and as people tell these stories and pass them along, they get more and more horrible and horrifying.

In this anthology, we have collected over a dozen well-done tales of young monsters, those who are children or teenagers. Some are sympathetically, even humorously, told, and some are grisly.

But why should we be interested in such tales? Surely, we, with our familiarity with the scientific view of the universe, don't believe that such things as vampires and ghouls and werewolves can exist?

Yes, but we can pretend. In fact, that's what makes it fun. In the days when we thought monsters *really* existed, tales about them would have scared us so badly we would have nightmares, or be afraid to go out-of-doors. We would jump at every sound or shrink at every unexpected movement. Such stories would be no fun.

Nowadays, though, we can experience the odd world of nonscience, and even get tense or scared *while reading*, but then, when the story is over, dismiss it and return to our normal world where things happen out of natural cause and where we know what is impossible and what is not. We have the fun of *temporary* fear.

Then, too, in a way, to read monster stories is to move into a world so different from ours as to be a relief. Our own world has its terrors, too, though they are different from those of the nonscientific world.

We don't expect a stranger to be a dangerous enchanter—but he might be a dangerous mugger. We don't expect to meet a ghost or ghouls when we are passing a cemetery at night, but we might meet a car with a drunken driver at the wheel. We might not expect an angry god or demon to destroy the world in a fit of anger or malevolence, but human beings in charge of governments might destroy the world by nuclear warfare in a fit of fear or anger—or simple misunderstanding.

In a way, it is a relief to turn from the very real power of evil that surrounds us today to the totally different kind of evil that existed in the nonscientific world of ghosts and spirits and enchanters and monsters.

After all, we know that monsters *don't* exist—and that criminals and war *do* exist.

224

Homecoming

by Ray Bradbury

Exactly who is a "monster" often depends entirely on your point of view.

"Here they come," said Cecy, lying there flat in her bed. "Where are they?" cried Timothy from the doorway. "Some of them are over Europe, some over Asia, some of them over the Island, some over South America!" said Cecy, her eyes closed, the lashes long, brown, and quivering.

Timothy came forward upon the bare plankings of the upstairs room. "Who are they?"

"Uncle Einar and Uncle Fry, and there's Cousin William, and I see Frulda and Helgar and Aunt Morgiana and Cousin Vivian, and I see Uncle Johann! They're all coming fast!"

"Are they up in the sky?" cried Timothy, his little gray eyes flashing. Standing by the bed, he looked no more than his fourteen years. The wind blew outside, the house was dark and lit only by starlight.

"They're coming through the air and traveling along the ground, in many forms," said Cecy, in her sleeping. She did not move on the bed; she thought inward on herself and told what she saw. "I see a wolflike thing coming over a dark river—at the shallows—just above a waterfall, the starlight shining up his pelt. I see a brown oak leaf blowing far up in the sky. I see a small bat flying. I see many other things, running through the forest trees and slipping through the highest branches, and they're *all* coming this way!"

"Will they be here by tomorrow night?" Timothy clutched the bedclothes. The spider on his lapel swung like a black pendulum, excitedly dancing. He leaned over his sister. "Will they all be here in time for the Homecoming?"

"Yes, yes, Timothy, yes," sighed Cecy. She stiffened. "Ask no more of me. Go away now. Let me travel in the places I like best."

"Thanks, Cecy," he said. Out in the hall, he ran to his room. He hurriedly made his bed. He had just awakened a few minutes ago, at sunset, and as the first stars had risen, he had gone to let his excitement about the party run with Cecy. Now she slept so quietly there was not a sound. The spider hung on a silvery lasso about Timothy's slender neck as he washed his face. "Just think, Spid, tomorrow night is Allhallows' Eve!"

He lifted his face and looked into the mirror. His was the only mirror allowed in the house. It was his mother's concession to his illness. Oh, if only he were not so afflicted! He opened his mouth, surveyed the poor, inadequate teeth nature had given him. No more than so many corn kernels—

round, soft and pale in his jaws. Some of the high spirit died in him.

It was now totally dark, and he lit a candle to see by. He felt exhausted. This past week the whole family had lived in the fashion of the old country. Sleeping by day, rousing at sunset to move about. There were blue hollows under his eyes. "Spid, I'm no good," he said, quietly, to the little creature. "I can't even get used to sleeping days like the others."

He took up the candleholder. Oh, to have strong teeth, with incisors like steel spikes. Or strong hands, even, or a strong mind. Even to have the power to send one's mind out, free, as Cecy did. But, no, he was the imperfect one, the sick one. He was even—he shivered and drew the candle flame closer—afraid of the dark. His brothers snorted at him. Bion and Leonard and Sam. They laughed at him because he slept in a bed. With Cecy it was different; her bed was part of her comfort for the composure necessary to send her mind abroad to hunt. But Timothy, did he sleep in the wonderful polished boxes like the others? He did not! Mother let him have his own bed, his own room, his own mirror. No wonder the family skirted him like a holy man's crucifix. If only the wings would sprout from his shoulder blades. He bared his back, stared at it. He sighed again. No chance. Never.

Downstairs were exciting and mysterious sounds. The slithering sound of black crepe going up in all the halls and on the ceilings and doors. The smell of burning black tapers crept up the banistered stairwell. Mother's voice, high and firm. Father's voice, echoing from the damp cellar. Bion walking from outside the old country house lugging vast two-gallon jugs.

"I've just got to go to the party, Spid," said Timothy. The spider whirled at the end of its silk, and Timothy felt alone. He would polish cases, fetch toadstools and spiders, hang crepe, but when the party started he'd be ignored. The less seen or said of the imperfect son the better.

All through the house below, Laura ran.

"The Homecoming!" she shouted gaily. "The Homecoming!" Her footsteps everywhere at once.

Timothy passed Cecy's room again, and she was sleeping quietly. Once a month she went belowstairs. Always she stayed in bed. Lovely Cecy. He felt like asking her, "Where are you now, Cecy? And *in* who? And what's happening? Are you beyond the hills? And what goes on there?" But he went on to Ellen's room instead.

Ellen sat at her desk, sorting out many kinds of blond, red and black hair and little scimitars of fingernail gathered from her manicurist job at the Mellin Village beauty parlor fifteen miles over. A sturdy mahogany case lay in one corner with her name on it.

"Go away," she said, not even looking at him. "I can't work with you gawking."

"Allhallows' Eve, Ellen—just think!" he said, trying to be friendly.

228

"Hunh!" She put some fingernail clippings in a small white sack, labeled them. "What can it mean to you? What do you know of it? It'll scare the hell out of you. Go back to bed."

His cheeks burned. "I'm needed to polish and work and help serve."

"If you don't go, you'll find a dozen raw oysters in your bed tomorrow," said Ellen, matter-of-factly. "Good-by, Timothy."

In his anger, rushing downstairs, he bumped into Laura. "Watch where you're going!" she shrieked from clenched teeth.

She swept away. He ran to the open cellar door, smelled the channel of moist earthy air rising from below. "Father?"

"It's about time," Father shouted up the steps. "Hurry down, or they'll be here before we're ready!"

Timothy hesitated only long enough to hear the million other sounds in the house. Brothers came and went like trains in a station, talking and arguing. If you stood in one spot long enough, the entire household passed with their pale hands full of things. Leonard with his little black medical case; Samuel with his large, dusty ebon-bound book under his arm, bearing more black crepe; and Bion excursioning to the car outside and bringing in many more gallons of liquid.

Father stopped polishing to give Timothy a rag and a scowl. He thumped the huge mahogany box. "Come on, shine this up, so we can start on another. Sleep your life away."

While waxing the surface, Timothy looked inside.

"Uncle Einar's a big man, isn't he, Papa?"

"Unh."

"How big is he?"

"The size of the box'll tell you."

"I was only asking. Seven feet tall?"

"You talk a lot."

About nine o'clock Timothy went out into the October weather. For two hours in the now-warm, now-cold wind, he walked the meadows collecting toadstools and spiders. His heart began to beat with anticipation again. How many relatives had Mother said would come? Seventy? One hundred? He passed a farmhouse. "If only you knew what was happening at our house," he said to the glowing windows. He climbed a hill and looked at the town, miles away, settling into sleep, the town hall clock high and round, white in the distance. The town did not know, either. He brought home many jars of toadstools and spiders.

In the little chapel belowstairs a brief ceremony was celebrated. It was like all the other rituals over the years, with Father chanting the dark lines, Mother's beautiful white ivory hands moving in the reverse blessings, and all the children gathered except Cecy, who lay upstairs in bed. But Cecy was present. You saw her peering, now from Bion's eyes, now Samuel's, now Mother's, and you felt a movement and now she was in you, fleetingly, and gone.

Timothy prayed to the Dark One with a tightened stomach. "Please, please, help me grow up, help me be like my sisters and brothers. Don't let me be different. If only I could put the hair in the plastic images as Ellen does, or make people fall in love with me as Laura does with people, or read strange books as Sam does, or work in a respected job like Leonard and Bion do. Or even raise a family one day, as Mother and Father have done. . . ."

At midnight a storm hammered the house. Lightning struck outside in amazing, snow-white bolts. There was a sound of an approaching, probing, sucking tornado, funneling and nuzzling the moist night earth. Then the front door, blasted half off its hinges, hung stiff and discarded, and in trooped Grandmama and Grandpapa, all the way from the old country!

From then on people arrived each hour. There was a flutter at the side window, a rap on the front porch, a knock at the back. There were fey noises from the cellar; autumn wind piped down the chimney throat, chanting. Mother filled the large crystal punch bowl with a scarlet fluid poured from the jugs Bion had carried home. Father swept from room to room lighting more tapers. Laura and Ellen hammered up more wolfsbane. And Timothy stood amidst this wild excitement, no expression to his face, his hands trembling at his sides, gazing now here, now there. Banging of doors, laughter, the sound of liquid pouring, darkness, sound of wind, the webbed thunder of wings, the padding of feet, the welcoming bursts of talk at the entrances, the transparent

231

rattlings of casements, the shadows passing, coming, going, wavering.

"Well, well, and *this* must be Timothy!"

"What?"

A chilly hand took his hand. A long, hairy face leaned down over him. "A good lad, a fine lad," said the stranger.

"Timothy," said his mother. "This is Uncle Jason."

"Hello, Uncle Jason."

"And over here—" Mother drifted Uncle Jason away. Uncle Jason peered back at Timothy over his caped shoulder, and winked.

Timothy stood alone.

From off a thousand miles in the candled darkness, he heard a high fluting voice; that was Ellen. "And my brothers, they *are* clever. Can you guess their occupations, Aunt Morgiana?"

"I have no idea."

"They operate the undertaking establishment in town."

"What!" A gasp.

"Yes!" Shrill laughter. "Isn't that priceless!"

Timothy stood very still.

A pause in the laughter. "They bring home sustenance for Mama, Papa and all of us," said Laura. "Except, of course, Timothy. . . ."

An uneasy silence. Uncle Jason's voice demanded. "Well? Come now. What about Timothy?"

"Oh, Laura, your tongue," said Mother.

Laura went on with it. Timothy shut his eyes. "Timothy doesn't . . . well . . . doesn't *like* blood. He's delicate."

"He'll learn," said Mother. "He'll learn," she said very firmly. "He's my son, and he'll learn. He's only fourteen."

"But I was raised on the stuff," said Uncle Jason, his voice passing from one room on into another. The wind played the trees outside like harps. A little rain spattered on the windows—"raised on the stuff," passing away into faintness.

Timothy bit his lips and opened his eyes.

"Well, it was all my fault." Mother was showing them into the kitchen now. "I tried forcing him. You can't force children, you only make them sick, and then they never get a taste for things. Look at Bion, now, he was thirteen before he . . ."

"I understand," murmured Uncle Jason. "Timothy will come around."

"I'm sure he will," said Mother, defiantly.

Candle flames quivered as shadows crossed and recrossed the dozen musty rooms. Timothy was cold. He smelled the hot tallow in his nostrils and instinctively he grabbed at a candle and walked with it around and about the house, pretending to straighten the crepe.

"*Timothy,*" someone whispered behind a patterned wall, hissing and sizzling and sighing the words, "*Timothy is afraid of the dark.*"

Leonard's voice. Hateful Leonard!

"I like the candle, that's all," said Timothy in a reproachful whisper.

More noise, more laughter, and thunder. Cascades of roaring laughter. Bangings and clickings and shouts and rustles of clothing. Clammy fog swept through the front door. Out of the fog, settling his wings, stalked a tall man.

"Uncle Einar!"

Timothy propelled himself on his thin legs straight through the fog, under the green webbing shadows. He threw himself across Einar's arms. Einar lifted him.

"You've wings, Timothy!" He tossed the boy light as thistles. "Wings, Timothy—fly!" Faces wheeled under. Darkness rotated. The house blew away. Timothy felt breezelike. He flapped his arms. Einar's fingers caught and threw him once more to the ceiling. The ceiling rushed down like a charred wall. "Fly, Timothy!" shouted Einar, loud and deep. "Fly with wings! Wings!"

He felt an exquisite ecstasy in his shoulder blades, as if roots grew, burst to explode and blossom into new, moist membrane. He babbled wild stuff; again Einar hurled him high.

The autumn wind broke in a tide on the house, rain crashed down, shaking the beams, causing chandeliers to tilt their enraged candle lights. And the one hundred relatives peered out from every black, enchanted room, circling inward, all shapes and sizes, to where Einar balanced the child like a baton in the roaring spaces.

234

"Enough!" shouted Einar, at last.

Timothy, deposited on the floor timbers, exaltedly, exhaustedly fell against Uncle Einar, sobbing happily. "Uncle, Uncle, Uncle!"

"Was it good, flying? Eh, Timothy?" said Uncle Einar, bending down, patting Timothy's head. "Good, good."

It was coming toward dawn. Most had arrived and were ready to bed down for the daylight, sleep motionlessly with no sound until the following sunset, when they would shout out of their mahogany boxes for the revelry.

Uncle Einar, followed by dozens of others, moved toward the cellar. Mother directed them downward to the crowded row on row of highly polished boxes. Einar, his wings like sea-green tarpaulins tented behind him, moved with a curious whistling through the passageway; where his wings touched they made a sound of drumheads gently beaten.

Upstairs, Timothy lay wearily thinking, trying to like the darkness. There was so much you could do in darkness that people couldn't criticize you for, because they never saw you. He *did* like the night, but it was a qualified liking; sometimes there was so much night he cried out in rebellion.

In the cellar, mahogany doors sealed downward, drawn in by pale hands. In corners, certain relatives circled three times to lie down, heads on paws, eyelids shut. The sun rose. There was a sleeping.

Sunset. The revel exploded like a bat nest struck full, shrieking out, fluttering, spreading. Box doors banked wide.

Steps rushed up from cellar damp. More late guests, kicking on front and back portals, were admitted.

It rained, and sodden visitors laid their capes, their water-pelleted hats, their sprinkled veils upon Timothy, who bore them to a closet. The rooms were crowd-packed. The laughter of one cousin shot from one room, angled off the wall of another, ricocheted, banked, and returned to Timothy's ears from a fourth room, accurate and cynical.

A mouse ran across the floor.

"I know you, Niece Leibersrouter!" exclaimed Father.

The mouse spiraled three women's feet and vanished into a corner. Moments later a beautiful woman rose up out of nothing and stood in the corner, smiling her white smile at them all.

Something huddled against the flooded pane of the kitchen window. It sighed and wept and tapped continually, pressed against the glass, but Timothy could make nothing of it; he saw nothing. In imagination he was outside staring in. The rain was on him, the wind at him, and the taper-dotted darkness inside was inviting. Waltzes were being danced; tall thin figures pirouetted to outlandish music. Stars of light flickered off lifted bottles; small clods of earth crumbled from casques, and a spider fell and went silently legging over the floor.

Timothy shivered. He was inside the house again. Mother was calling him to run here, run there, help, serve, out to the kitchen now, fetch this, fetch that, bring the plates, heap the food—on and on—the party happened around him but not to him. The dozens of towering people pressed in against him, elbowed him, ignored him.

Finally, he turned and slipped away up the stairs.

He called softly. "Cecy. Where are you now, Cecy?"

She waited a long while before answering. "In the Imperial Valley," she murmured faintly. "Beside the Salton Sea, near the mud pots and the steam and the quiet. I'm inside a farmer's wife. I'm sitting on a front porch. I can make her move if I want, or do anything or think anything. The sun's going down."

"What's it like, Cecy?"

"You can hear mud pots hissing," she said, slowly, as if speaking in a church. "Little gray heads of steam push up the mud like bald men rising in the thick syrup, head first, out in the broiling channels. The gray heads rip like rubber fabric, collapse with noises like wet lips moving. And feathery plumes of steam escape from the ripped tissue. And there is a smell of deep sulphurous burning and old time. The dinosaur has been abroiling here ten million years."

"Is he done yet, Cecy?"

"Yes, he's done. Quite done." Cecy's calm sleeper's lips turned up. The languid words fell slowly from her shaping mouth. "Inside this woman's skull I am, looking out, watching the sea that does not move and is so quiet it makes you afraid. I sit on the porch and wait for my husband to come home. Occasionally, a fish leaps, falls back, starlight edging it. The valley, the sea, the few cars, the wooden

237

porch, my rocking chair, myself, the silence."

"What now, Cecy?"

"I'm getting up from my rocking chair," she said.

"Yes?"

"I'm walking off the porch, toward the mud pots. Planes fly over, like primordial birds. Then it is quiet, so quiet."

"How long will you stay inside her, Cecy?"

"Until I've listened and looked and felt enough: until I've changed her life some way. I'm walking off the porch and along the wooden boards. My feet knock on the planks, tiredly, slowly."

"And now?"

"Now the sulphur fumes are all around me. I stare at the bubbles as they break and smooth. A bird darts by my temple, shrieking. Suddenly I am in the bird and fly away! And as I fly, inside my new small glass-bead eyes I see a woman below me, on a boardwalk, take one two three steps forward into the mud pots. I hear a sound as of a boulder plunged into molten depths. I keep flying, circle back. I see a white hand, like a spider, wriggle and disappear into the gray lava pool. The lava seals over. Now I'm flying home, swift, swift, swift!"

Something clapped hard against the window. Timothy started.

Cecy flicked her eyes wide, bright, full, happy, exhilarated.

"Now I'm *home!*" she said.

After a pause, Timothy ventured, "The Homecoming's on. And everybody's here."

238

"Then why are you upstairs?" She took his hand. "Well, ask me." She smiled slyly. "Ask me what you came to ask."

"I didn't come to ask anything," he said. "Well, almost nothing. Well, oh, Cecy!" It came from him in one long rapid flow. "I want to do something at the party to make them look at me, something to make me good as them, something to make me belong, but there's nothing I can do, and I feel funny and . . . well . . . I thought you might . . ."

"I might," she said, closing her eyes, smiling inwardly. "Stand up straight. Stand very still." He obeyed. "Now, shut your eyes and blank out your thoughts."

He stood very straight and thought of nothing, or at least thought of thinking nothing.

She sighed. "Shall we go downstairs now, Timothy?" Like a hand into a glove, Cecy was within him.

"Look everybody!" Timothy held the glass of warm red liquid. He held up the glass so that the whole house turned to watch him. Aunts, uncles, cousins, brothers, sisters!

He drank it straight down.

He jerked a hand at his sister Laura. He held her gaze, whispering to her in a subtle voice that kept her silent, frozen. He felt tall as the trees as he walked to her. The party now slowed. It waited on all sides of him, watching. From all the room doors the faces peered. They were not laughing. Mother's face was astonished. Father looked bewildered, but pleased and getting prouder every instant.

He nipped her, gently, over the neck vein. The candle

flames swayed drunkenly. The wind climbed around on the roof outside. The relatives stared from all the doors. He popped toadstools into his mouth, swallowed, then beat his arms against his flanks and circled. "Look, Uncle Einar! I can fly, at last!" Beat went his hands. Up and down pumped his feet. The faces flashed past him.

At the top of the stairs before knowing it, flapping. Timothy heard his mother cry, "Stop, Timothy!" far below. "Hey!" shouted Timothy, and leaped off the top of the well, thrashing.

Halfway down, the wings he thought he owned dissolved. He screamed. Uncle Einar caught him.

Timothy flailed whitely in the receiving arms. A voice burst out of his lips unbidden. "This is Cecy! This is Cecy!" it announced, shrilly. "Cecy! Come see me, all of you, upstairs, first room on the left!" followed by a long trill of high laughter. Timothy tried to cut it off with his tongue, his lips.

Everybody was laughing. Einar set him down. Running through the crowding blackness as the relatives flowed upstairs toward Cecy's room to congratulate her, Timothy banged the front door open. Mother called out behind him, anxiously.

"Cecy, I hate you, I hate you!"

By the sycamore tree, in deep shadow, Timothy spewed out his dinner, sobbed bitterly and threshed in a pile of autumn leaves. Then he lay still. From his blouse pocket, from the protection of the matchbox he used for his retreat, the spider crawled forth. Spid walked along Timothy's arm. Spid explored up his neck to his ear and climbed in the ear to tickle it. Timothy shook his head. "Don't, Spid. Don't."

The feathery touch of a tentative feeler probing his ear-drum set Timothy shivering. "Don't, Spid!" He sobbed somewhat less.

The spider traveled down his cheek, took a station under the boy's nose, looked up into the nostrils as if to seek the brain, and then clambered softly up over the rim of the nose to sit, to squat there peering at Timothy with green gem eyes until Timothy filled with ridiculous laughter. "Go away, Spid!"

Timothy sat up, rustling the leaves. The land was very bright with the moon. In the house he could hear the faint ribaldry as Mirror, Mirror was played. Celebrants shouted, dimly muffled, as they tried to identify those of themselves whose reflections did not, had not ever appeared in a glass.

"Timothy." Uncle Einar's wings spread and twitched and came in with a sound like kettledrums. Timothy felt himself plucked up like a thimble and set upon Einar's shoulder. "Don't feel badly, Nephew Timothy. Each to his own, each in his own way. How much better things are for you. How rich. The world's dead for us. We've seen so much of it, believe me. Life's best to those who live the least of it. It's worth more per ounce, Timothy, remember that."

The rest of the black morning, from midnight on, Uncle Einar led him about the house, from room to room, weaving

241

and singing. A horde of late arrivals set the entire hilarity off afresh. Great-great-great-great and a thousand more great-greats-Grandmama was there, wrapped in Egyptian cerements. She said not a word, but lay straight as a burnt ironing board against the wall, her eye hollows cupping a distant, wise, silent glimmering. At the breakfast, at four in the morning, one-thousand-odd-greats-Grandmama was stiffly seated at the head of the longest table.

The numerous young cousins caroused at the crystal punch bowl. Their shiny olive-pit eyes, their conical, devilish faces and curly bronze hair hovered over the drinking table; their hard-soft, half-girl half-boy bodies wrestling against each other as they got unpleasantly, sullenly drunk. The wind got higher, the stars burned with fiery intensity, the noises redoubled, the dances quickened, the drinking became more positive. To Timothy there were thousands of things to hear and watch. The many darknesses roiled, bubbled, the many faces passed and repassed. . . .

"Listen!"

The party held its breath. Far away the town clock struck its chimes, saying six o'clock. The party was ending. As if at a cue, in time to the rhythm of the clock striking, their one hundred voices began to sing songs that were four hundred years old, songs Timothy could not know. They twined their arms around one another, circling slowly, and sang, and somewhere in the cold distance of morning the town clock finished out its chimes and quieted.

Good-bys were said, there was a great rustling. Mother and Father and the brothers and sisters lined up at the door to shake hands and kiss each departing relative in turn. The sky beyond the open door colored and shone in the east. A cold wind entered.

The shouting and the laughing, bit by bit, faded and went away. Dawn grew more apparent. Everybody was embracing and crying and thinking how the world was becoming less a place for them. There had been a time when they had met every year, but now decades passed with no reconciliation. "Don't forget, we meet in Salem in 1970!" someone cried.

Salem. Timothy's numbed mind turned the word over. Salem, 1970. And there would be Uncle Fry and Grandmama and Grandpapa and a thousand-times-great-Grandmama in her withered cerements. And Mother and Father and Ellen and Laura and Cecy and Leonard and Bion and Sam and all the rest. But would he be there? Would he be alive that long? Could he be certain of living until then?

With one last withering wind blast, away they all went, so many scarves, so many fluttery mammals, so many sere leaves, so many wolves loping, so many whinings and clustering noises, so many midnights and ideas and insanities.

Mother shut the door. Laura picked up a broom.

"No," said Mother, "we'll clean up tonight. We need sleep first."

Father walked down into the cellar, followed by Laura

and Bion and Sam. Ellen walked upstairs, as did Leonard.

Timothy walked across the crepe-littered hall. His head was down, and in passing a party mirror he saw himself, the pale mortality of his face. He was cold and trembling.

"Timothy," said Mother.

He stopped at the stairwell. She came to him, laid a hand on his face. "Son," she said. "We love you. Remember that. We all love you. No matter how different you are, no matter if you leave us one day," she said. She kissed his cheek. "And if and when you die, your bones will lie undisturbed, we'll see to that. You'll lie at ease forever, and I'll come see you every Allhallows' Eve and tuck you in the more secure."

The house was silent. Far away the wind went over a hill with its last cargo of small dark bats echoing, chittering.

He walked up the steps, one by one, crying to himself all the way.

Good-by, Miss Patterson

by Phyllis MacLennan

Miss Patterson was a martinet who finally let a student drive her bats.

Miss Agnes Patterson's fifth-grade class sat rigid under the Gorgon eye of their teacher, waiting to be programmed into the next item on their tightly organized schedule. Motionless, backs straight, hands neatly folded on their desks, faces careful masks of respectful submission, they seemed unaware that it was the last day before Easter vacation, with school almost out and spring waiting for them beyond the open windows. The trees now lightly smudged with pink, the call of carefree birds, the rich warm smell of moist earth and new growing things seemed to hold no charm for them. Not one so much as glanced outside. Apart from discipline, there was something on the windowsill that they could not bear to look at: an empty hamster cage.

The cage awaited no new occupant. It was simply there, to remind them of their failure in their nature study project—a frippery of modern education that Miss Patterson had never quite approved of. The committee appointed to care for the little beast had forgotten to take it home with them over the Christmas vacation, and their teacher, seeing in this oversight a heaven-sent opportunity for a stern lesson on Responsibility, had left the animal to the fate its thoughtless guardians had abandoned it to. When they came back after their holiday, they found it dead, lying on its back, eyes closed, mouth open, stiff and cold. Miss Patterson's vivid description of the torments the hamster must have suffered as it starved and thirsted to death had left most of the children in hysterical tears. One thing was sure: none of them would turn his or her eyes in the direction of that reproaching cage, no matter what marvelous events might transpire beyond the window. They sat, subdued, fully under control. When their teacher cracked the whip, they would jump.

All except Corinna.

Defiant little witch Corinna! She sat in the corner like a cat wandered in on a whim, watching what went on with a cat's inscrutable smoldering stare, or turning her attention inward to mysterious thoughts of her own. She had a reputation as a troublemaker. She had been transferred from room to room all year as teacher after teacher refused to cope with her. Her parents had been called, but they refused to discuss the problem like good parents. They said that their daughter went to school because the law required it, and

246

let the law make her behave, if it could. It was no concern of theirs.

She had been in Miss Patterson's class for little more than a week, and though she had as yet done nothing overt, in her mere presence the group was beginning to disintegrate. The children were restless, uneasy, like sheep who scent the wolf. Her contempt for the activities in which they spent their days was obvious. She refused to answer questions when called on, did no homework, turned in blank papers; and with her example before them, the others were beginning, ever so slightly, to get out of hand.

Miss Patterson was not disturbed. She had been dealing with troublemakers for twenty years, and she knew how to break them. Her methods were not subtle, but they were effective, and Corinna had put her most effective weapon to her hand by turning in an arithmetic test with nothing on it but her name. Miss Patterson returned the tests and addressed her pupils in a voice like honey on a razor's edge.

"Elephants have giant brains, and so all those who had perfect papers are elephants. Stand up, elephants, so we can see you. . . . My, we have a lot of elephants, haven't we? . . . Mice have little brains and don't pay attention, and so they make mistakes, but they can squeeze by. Stand up, mice! . . . Fleas are little tiny parasites with no brains at all. They're really stupid. We don't have any fleas in *our* class, do we? . . . Oh, we *do* have one! Corinna didn't get one single answer on this test! She couldn't answer *any* of the questions! Stand up, Corinna. You must be a very tiny flea indeed!"

She smiled triumphantly, and looked to see Corinna crushed.

"If I'm a flea, you're an old bat."

It was unthinkable that such impertinence could be. Stunned, helplessly conscious of her mouth gone slack, her burning face, Miss Patterson sat paralyzed. Transfixed by Corinna's eyes, fierce and yellow and soulless as a hawk's, she knew—how could she not have known before? How could she not have seen what she now saw so clearly?— this was no child like other children.

"You are a bat," Corinna repeated ominously, her witch's eyes grown huge and luminous. She glided forward, reached the desk and slid around it like a snake. Behind her, suddenly aware, bonded with her, strengthening her with their united wills, the children converged on their teacher. They gathered around her desk, all of them staring . . .

. . . Did they grow larger? Was it she who shrank? They loomed above her, glaring down with savage joy.

Agnes Patterson fluttered off her chair and scuttled away between their feet, screaming for help in a voice too shrill for human ears to hear. The children, shrieking their triumph, raced after her, chivvying her from corner to corner, striking at her as she dove past them. Help came at last, brought by the pandemonium in the room—Mr. Morgan from across the hall.

"What's going on here!"

"It's our bat!" Corinna shouted. "Our nature study bat! It got away!"

"Yes, yes!" the children chorused. "We're trying to catch it and put it back in the cage!"

"Where's Miss Patterson? She should have told me she was stepping out so I could cover her . . . never mind." He pulled off his jacket and in one deft swoop captured the hysterically chittering creature and stuffed it into the cage. He closed its door and glanced at his watch. "It's nearly time for dismissal. You kids sit quiet. I'll be keeping an eye on you from my room."

They took their places and sat until the bell rang. They said nothing aloud, but gleeful eyes met and giggles were muffled behind their hands as they gloated over the small animal huddled panting at the back of its prison. When it was time to leave, they gathered their things and left silently, in impeccable order, attracting no attention to themselves and their unsupervised classroom. Corinna waited until the others had gone. She came then and stood in front of the cage. The captive shrank still further back, but there was no move to harm her.

"Good-by, Miss Patterson," Corinna whispered. "Have a nice vacation."

She tiptoed out and closed the door behind her.

The Wheelbarrow Boy

by *Richard Parker*

This is a story of a school where teachers learn to spell.

"Now see here, Thomis," I said. "I've just about had enough of you. If you haven't settled yourself down and started some work in two minutes' time I shall turn you into a wheelbarrow. I'm not warning you again."

Of course, Thomis was not the only one; the whole class had the fidgets; he just happened to be the one I picked on. It was a windy day, and wind always upsets kids and makes them harder to handle. Also, I happened to know that Thomis's father had won a bit of money on the Pools, so it was easy to understand the boy's being off balance. But it's fatal to start making allowances for bad behavior.

After about three minutes I called out, "Well, Thomis? How many sums have you done?"

"I'm just writing the date," said the boy sullenly.

"Right," I said. "You can't say I didn't warn you." And I changed him into a wheelbarrow there and then—a bright red metal wheelbarrow with a pneumatic tire.

The class went suddenly quiet, the way they do when you take a strong line, and during the next half hour we got a lot of work done. When the bell for morning break went, I drove them all out so as to have the room to myself.

"All right, Thomis," I said. "You can change back now."

Nothing happened.

I thought at first he was sulking, but after a while I began to think that something had gone seriously wrong. I went round to the Headmaster's office.

"Look," I said, "I just changed Thomis into a wheelbarrow and I can't get him back."

"Oh," said the Head and stared at the scattering of paper on his desk.

"Are you in a violent hurry about it?"

"No," I said. "It's a bit worrying, though."

"Which is Thomis?"

"Scruffy little fellow—pasty-faced—always got a sniff and a mouthful of gum."

"Red hair?"

"No, that's Sanderson. Black, and like a bird's nest."

"Oh, yes. I've got him. Well, now." He looked at the clock. "Suppose you bring this Thomis chap along here in about half an hour?"

"All right," I said.

I was a bit thoughtful as I went upstairs to the Staff Room. Tongelow was brewing the tea, and as I looked at him I remembered that he had some sort of official position in the Union.

"How would it be if I paid my Union dues?" I said.

He put the teapot down gently. "What've you done?" he asked. "Pushed a kid out of a second-floor window?"

I pretended to be hurt. "I just thought it was about time I paid," I said. "It doesn't do to get too much in arrears."

In the end he took the money and gave me a receipt, and when I had tucked that away in my wallet I felt a lot better.

Back in my own room Thomis was still leaning up in his chair, red and awkward, a constant reproach to me. I could not start any serious work, so after about ten minutes, I set the class something to keep them busy and then lifted Thomis down and wheeled him round to the Head.

"Oh, good," he said. "So the gardening requisition has started to come in at last."

"No," I said, dumping the barrow down in the middle of his carpet. "This is Thomis. I told you . . ."

"Sorry," he said. "I'd clean forgotten. Leave him there and I'll get to work on him straightaway. I'll send him back to you when he's presentable."

I went back to my class and did a double period of composition, but no Thomis turned up. I thought the Old Man must have forgotten again, so when the bell went at twelve I took a peep into his room to jog his memory. He was on his knees on the carpet, jacket and tie off, with sweat pouring off his face. He got up weakly when he saw me.

"I've tried everything," he said, "and I can't budge him. Did you do anything unorthodox?"

"No," I said. "It was only a routine punishment."

"I think you'd better ring the Union," he said. "Ask for Legal Aid—Maxstein's the lawyer—and see where you stand."

"Do you mean we're stuck with this?" I said.

"You are," said the Head. "I should ring now, before they go to lunch."

I got through to the Union in about ten minutes, and luckily Maxstein was still there. He listened to my story, grunting now and then.

"You are a member, I suppose?"

"Oh yes," I said.

"Paid up?"

"Certainly."

"Good," he said. "Now let me see. I think I'd better ring you back in an hour or so. I've not had a case quite like this before, so I'll need to think about it."

"Can't you give me a rough idea of how I stand?" I said.

"We're right behind you, of course," said Maxstein. "Free legal aid and all the rest of it. But . . ."

"Oh, good," I said. "But what?"

"But I don't fancy your chances," he said and rang off.

The afternoon dragged on, but there was no phone call from Maxstein. The Head got fed up with Thomis and had him wheeled out into the passage. At break-time I phoned the Union again.

"Sorry I didn't ring you," said Maxstein when I got

through to him again. "I've been very busy."

"What am I to do?" I asked.

"The whole thing," said Maxstein, "turns on the attitude of the parents. If they decide to prosecute I'll have to come down and work out some line of defense with you."

"Meanwhile," I said, "Thomis is still a wheelbarrow."

"Quite. Now here's what I suggest. Take him home to-night—yourself. See his people and try to get some idea of their attitude. You never know; they might be grateful."

"Grateful?" I said.

"Well, there was that case in Glasgow—kid turned into a mincing machine—and the mother was as pleased as could be and refused to have him changed back. So go round and see, and let me know in the morning."

"All right," I said.

At four o'clock I waited behind and then, when the place was empty, wheeled Thomis out into the street.

I attracted quite a lot of attention on the way, from which I guessed the story must have preceded me. A lot of people I did not know nodded or said "Good evening," and three or four ran out of shops to stare.

At last I reached the place, and Mr. Thomis opened the door. The house seemed to be full of people and noise, so I gathered it was a party in celebration of the Pools.

He stared at me in a glazed sort of way for a moment and then made a violent effort to concentrate.

"It's Teddy's teacher," he bawled to those inside. "You're

just in time. Come in and have a spot of something."

"Well, actually," I said, "I've come about Teddy . . ."

"It can wait," said Mr. Thomis. "Come on in."

"No, but it's serious," I said. "You see, I turned Teddy into a wheelbarrow this morning, and now . . ."

"Come and have a drink first," he said urgently.

So I went in, and drank to the healths of Mr. and Mrs. Thomis. "How much did you win?" I asked politely.

"Eleven thousand quid," said Mr. Thomis. "What a lark, eh?"

"And now," I said firmly, "about Teddy."

"Oh, this wheelbarrow caper," said Mr. Thomis. "We'll soon see about that."

He dragged me outside into the yard and went up to the wheelbarrow. "Is this him?" he said.

I nodded.

"Now look here, Teddy," said Mr. Thomis fiercely. "Just you come to your senses this minute, or I'll bash the day-lights out of you." And as he spoke he began to unbuckle a heavy belt that was playing second fiddle to his braces.

The wheelbarrow changed back into Teddy Thomis and nipped smartly down the garden and through a hole in the fence.

"There you are," said Mr. Thomis. "Trouble with you teachers is you're too soft with the kids. Here, come in and have another drink."

255

The Cabbage Patch

by *Theodore R. Cogswell*

"Ah, love! Where is thy sting?" It's an age-old question, but
here is the answer.

Aunt Hester sent me to bed early that night. I lay quietly
in the old four-poster, listening to the night sounds and
the soft sleepy hisses as the narns who lived in the old
fern tree underneath my window bedded themselves down
in their holes. I was supposed to settle down too, but the
tight, excited feeling inside my chest wouldn't go away. I
pulled the soft down pillow over my head and tried to make
everything black. I wanted to go to sleep right away so I
could wake up in time to see the birth-fairy when she came
down with my new sister.

Priscilla Winters said babies came from the cabbage patch
but I knew better. She brought a cabbage to school one
day to prove it, and that night when we were supposed to
be asleep she opened it up and showed me a baby inside.
It was squishy and white like all soon-babies are before
they make the change, but I knew it wasn't a real baby

256

because it didn't have any teeth. We made a birthing-box out of a jar and gave it some flies to eat but it wouldn't eat them, it just kept crawling around and waving its feelers as if it didn't like it there. When we woke up the next morning it had turned brown and was all dead.

The narns in the fern tree had stopped their whispering, but I still couldn't get to sleep. The little moon had chased the big one up over the horizon so far that its light was shining through the window right into my eyes. I got up and shut the blinds but even having the room dark again didn't help. I kept seeing pictures of the birth-fairy fluttering down like a beautiful butterfly, and then, after she'd put the babies safe in their birthing-box, flying off again with the year-father soaring after her on his fine new wings.

I wanted to see his wings but Mother wouldn't let me. For two months now she had kept him shut up in his room and she wouldn't even let me speak to him through the door. I wanted to say good-bye to him because, even if he was only a year-father, he'd been nice to me. I was never supposed to be with him unless Mother or Aunt Hester were around, but sometimes I'd slip into the kitchen when they were away and we'd talk about things. I liked being with him best when he was baking preska because he'd give me bits of the dough and let me make funny things out of them.

Once Aunt Hester caught me alone with him and her face got all hard and twisted and she was going to call the patrol and have him beaten, but Mother came in just then. She sent the year-father to his room and then took me into the parlor. I knew that she was getting ready for one of her heart-to-heart talks but there wasn't anything I could do about it, so I just sat there and listened. Mother's talks always got so wound in on themselves that when she was through I usually couldn't figure out what all the fuss had been about.

First she asked me if I'd felt anything funny when I was alone with the year-father. I asked her what she meant by "funny" and she sort of stuttered and her face got all red. Finally she asked me a funny question about my stinger and I said no. Then she started to tell me a story about the wasps and the meem but she didn't get very far with that either. She wanted to but she got all flustered and her tongue wouldn't work. Aunt Hester said nonsense, that I was still a little girl and next year would be soon enough. Mother said she wished she could be sure, then she made me promise that if ever my stinger felt funny when I was around a year-father, I'd run and tell her about it right away because if I didn't, something terrible might happen.

My pillow got all hot so I went and sat in my chair. The more I thought about the year-father, the more I wanted to go and see his new wings. Finally I went over to the door and listened. I could hear Mother and Aunt Hester talking in the front of the house so I tiptoed down the back stairs. When I got to the landing I stopped and felt around with my foot until I found the part of the next stair that was right against the railing. That's a bad stair because if you step in the middle of it without thinking, it gives a loud squeak that you can hear all over the house.

The year-father's room is right next to the kitchen. I gave a little scratch on the door so he would know who it was and not be frightened. I stood there in the dark waiting for him to open up but he didn't so I went inside and felt for him in his nest. He wasn't there.

First I thought maybe I should go back up and get in bed because Aunt Hester said that if she ever again caught me up at night when I was supposed to be sleeping, she'd give me a licking that I'd never forget. But then I started to think of what would happen to the year-father if he'd gone outside and the patrol caught him wandering around alone at night, and I decided that I'd better tell Mother right away, even if I did get a walloping afterward.

Then I thought that first I'd better look in the kitchen for him. It was dark in there too, so I shut the hall door and lit the lamp on the kitchen table. The stone floor was awfully cold on my feet and I began to wish that I'd remembered to put on my slippers before I came downstairs. Once my eyes got used to the light I looked all around, but the year-father wasn't there either. I was about to blow out the lamp and go and tell Mother when I heard a funny sound coming from the nursery.

I know it sounds funny to have a nursery in the kitchen, but since soon-babies have to be locked away in a dark place until it's time for them to make the change, Mother said we might as well use the old pantry instead of going to all the trouble of blacking out one of the rooms upstairs.

The big, thick door that Mother had put on was shut but she'd forgotten to take the key away so I went over and opened it a crack. I was real scared because at birthing time nobody is allowed to go in the nursery, not even Aunt Hester. Once the little ones are in the birthing-box, Mother locks the door and doesn't ever open it up again until after they've changed into real people like us.

At Priscilla's house they've got an honest-to-goodness nursery. There's a little window on the door that they uncover after the first month. It's awful dark inside but if you look real hard you can see the soon-babies crawling around inside. Priscilla let me look in once when her mother was downtown. They had big ugly mouths and teeth.

The sound came again so I opened the door. It was so dark inside that I couldn't see a thing so I went back and got the lamp. The noise seemed to be coming from the birthing-box so I went over and looked in. The year-father was hunched up in the bottom of it. He didn't have any wings.

He blinked up at me in the lantern light. He'd been crying and his face was all swollen. He motioned to me to go away but I couldn't. I'd never seen a father without his clothes on before and I kept staring and staring.

I knew that I should run and get Mother but somehow I couldn't move. Something terrible was happening to the year-father. His stomach was all swollen up and angry red, and every once in a while it would knot up and twist as if there were something inside that didn't like it there. When that would happen he'd roll his head back and bite down on his lower lip real hard. He seemed to want to yell but he'd choke it back until nothing came out but a little whimper.

There was a nasty half-healed place on his stomach that looked as if he'd fallen on a sharp stick and hurt himself real bad. He kept pushing his hands against it as if he was trying to hold back something that was inside trying to get out.

I heard Mother's voice calling from the kitchen and then Aunt Hester's voice saying something real sharp but I couldn't look up or answer. Blood was trickling out through the year-father's locked fingers. Suddenly he emptied out in a raw scream and fell back so limp that it looked as if all his bones were gone. His hands dropped away and from inside his stomach something tore at the half-healed place until it split and opened like a big mouth. Then I could see the something. I knew it for what it was and I felt sick and scared in a different sort of way. It inched its way out and wiggled around kind of lost-like, until it finally lost its balance and fell to the bottom of the box. It didn't move for a minute and I thought maybe it was dead, but then the feelers around its mouth began to reach out as if they were trying to find something. And then all of a sudden it started a fast wobbly crawl as if it knew just where it was going. I saw teeth as it found the year-father and nuzzled up to him. It was hungry.

Aunt Hester slammed and locked the pantry door. Then she made me a glass of hot milk and sent me up to bed. Mother came into my room a little later and stood by my bed, looking down at me to see if I was asleep. I pretended I was because I didn't want to talk to her, and she finally left. I wanted to cry but I couldn't because if I did she'd hear me and come back up again. I pulled the pillow down over my face real tight until I could hardly breathe and there were little red flashes of light in the back of my eyes and a humming, hive sound in my head. I knew what my stinger was for and I didn't want to think about it.

When I did get to sleep I didn't dream about the year-father, I dreamed about the wasps and the meem.

The Thing Waiting Outside

by Barbara Williamson

Here it is . . . good advice on how to really hound your parents.

A cold wind came down from the hills that night, and in their room under the peaked roof the children turned their faces toward the sound.

"It's only the wind," the father said.

"Just the wind," said the mother.

There were two beds in the room, a dresser painted white, and under the windows, a table with small bright chairs.

The walls of the room were light yellow, like the first spring sunlight. In their glow the dolls and fire engines, the pasteboard castle with its miniature knights, even the sad-faced Harlequin puppet shimmered with warmth. The plush animals became as soft as down, and the mane on the rocking horse was a crest of foam.

The children, a boy of eight and a girl of six, were already in their beds. The light glistened on their faces, their pale silken hair. They were beautiful children. Everyone said so, even strangers, and their parents always smiled and placed proud hands on their shining heads.

Now, in the yellow light, with the wind brushing the windows, the children listened to their father.

He sat on the side of the boy's bed and spoke quietly. The mother sat with the girl, her fingers now and then touching the sleeve of her daughter's nightgown. The faces of both parents were troubled.

The father said, "You do understand about the books? Why I had to take them away?"

The boy did not turn his eyes from his father's face, but he could feel the emptiness of the shelves across the room.

He said, "Will you ever put them back?"

His father laid a hand on the boy's shoulder. "Yes, of course," he said. "In time. I *want* you to read, to enjoy your books." He looked now at the girl and smiled. "I'm very proud of both of you. You read so well and learn so quickly."

The mother smiled too and gave the girl's hand a gentle squeeze.

The father said, "I think maybe this whole thing is my fault. I gave you too many books, encouraged you to read to the point of neglecting other things that are important. So for a while the only books I want you to read are your school books. You'll do other things—paint pictures, play games. I'll teach you chess, I think. You'll both like that."

"And we'll do things together," the mother said. "Take

bike rides and walks up into the hills. And when it's spring, we'll have a croquet set on the lawn. And we'll go on picnics."

The children looked at their parents with wide dark eyes. And after a moment the boy said, "That will be nice."

"Yes," said the girl. "Nice."

The mother and father glanced at each other, and then the father leaned over and cupped a hand under the boy's chin.

"You know now, don't you, that you did not really see and speak to the people in the books. They were only here in your imagination. You did not *see* the Lilliputians or *talk* to the Red Queen. You did not *see* the cave dwellers or *watch* the tiger eat one of them. They were not *here* in this room. You know that now, don't you?"

The boy looked steadily into his father's eyes.

"Yes," he said, "I know."

The girl nodded her head when the father turned to her.

"We know," she said.

"Imagination is a wonderful thing," the father said to both of them. "But it has to be watched, or like a fire, it can get out of control. You'll remember that, won't you?"

"Yes," the boy said, and again the girl nodded, her long hair gleaming in the light.

The father smiled and got to his feet. The mother rose too and smoothed the blankets on both beds. Then they each kissed the children good night with little murmurs of love and reassurance.

265

"Tomorrow," the father said, "we'll make some plans."

"Yes," the children said, and closed their eyes.

After the mother and father were gone and the room was dark, the children lay still for what seemed to them a long time. The wind rattled the windows, and beyond the hills the moon began to rise.

At last the girl turned to her brother. "Is it time?" she asked.

The boy didn't answer. Instead, he threw back his blanket and crossed the room to the windows. Below, the fields were silvered by the moon, but the hills were a black hulk against the sky.

"Anything could come down from there," he said. "Anything."

The girl came to stand beside him, and together they looked out into the night and thought about the thing waiting outside.

Then the girl said, "Will you take them the book now?"

"Yes," the boy said.

He turned from the windows and went to the dresser. Kneeling on the floor, he pulled open a bottom drawer and felt carefully beneath the socks and undershirts. The girl came over and knelt beside him. Their white faces flowered in the darkness of the room.

They both smiled when the boy took the book out of its hiding place. They rose from the floor, and the boy clasped the book in his arms. He said, "Don't start until I get back."

266

"Oh, I won't," the girl said. "I wouldn't."

Still holding the book close, the boy went to the door of the room, opened it softly, and stepped out into the hall.

It was a large house and very old, and deep inside it the wind was only a whisper of sound. The boy listened for a moment, then started down the stairs. The carpet was thick under his bare feet, and the railing felt as cold as stone beneath his hand.

Downstairs, a faint spicy smell from the day's baking still lingered in the air. He walked to the back of the house, past dark rooms where mirrors winked from the light in the hall, and night lay thick across the floors.

The mother and father were in the room next to the kitchen. There was a fire in a small grate and empty coffee cups on a table. On the walls were photographs of the children. They looked out into the room with secret smiles.

The mother was seated on the sofa near a shaded lamp. Her lap was full of pink yarn and her knitting needles flashed in the firelight.

The father leaned back in a big leather chair, his eyes on the ceiling, his fingers curled around the bowl of his favorite pipe.

The fire sighed and sparks rose up the chimney. The boy's eyes flicked to the corners of the room where the shadows had retreated from the firelight.

From the doorway he said, "I couldn't sleep until I brought you this." And he went into the room toward his parents, holding the book out to them.

"I hid it, but that wasn't right, was it?"

They came to him then. His mother took him into her arms and kissed him, and his father said that he was a fine honest boy.

The mother held him in her lap for a few minutes and warmed his feet with her hands, and her eyes glistened in the light of the fire. They spoke softly to him for a time and he listened and answered "yes" and "no" at the right times, and then he yawned and said that he was sleepy and could he please go back to bed?

They took him to the stairs and kissed him, and he went up alone without looking back.

In the room at the top of the house the girl was waiting for him. He nodded his head, and then they climbed into their beds and joined hands across the narrow space between. Moonlight lay on the floor in cold slabs, and the wind now washed against the windows with a shushing sound.

"Now," the boy said, gripping the girl's hand tightly. "And, remember, it's harder when the book is somewhere else."

They did not move for a long time. Their eyes stared at the ceiling without blinking. Sweat began to glisten on their faces, and their breathing grew short and labored. The room flowed around them. Shadow and light merged and parted like streams in the sea.

When the sounds from below began to reach them, they still did not move. Their joined hands, slick with sweat, held firm. Their muscles strained and corded. Their eyes burned and swam with the shifting light and darkness.

At last the sounds from the bottom of the house stopped. Silence fell around them, cooling their faces, soothing their feverish eyes.

The boy listened and then said, "It's done. You know what to do now, don't you?"

"Yes," the girl said. She slid her hand out of his, brushed her hair back from her face, and closed her eyes. She smiled and thought of a garden filled with flowers. There was a table in the center of the garden, and on the table were china plates. Each plate held a rainbow of iced cakes. There were pink ones and yellow ones and some thick with chocolate. Her tongue flicked over her lips as she thought of how sweet they would taste.

The boy thought of ships—tall ships with white sails. He brought a warm wind out of the south and sent the ships tossing on a sea that was both blue and green. Waves foamed over the decks and the sailors slipped and laughed, while above their heads gulls wheeled in the sky, their wings flashing in the sun.

At the time agreed upon, just as the windows began to lighten, the children rose from their beds and went downstairs.

The house was very cold. The shadows were turning to gray, and in the room next to the kitchen the fire was dead, its coals turned to feathery ash.

The mother lay in a corner of the room, near the outside

wall. The father was a few feet away. He still held the fire-place poker in his hand.

The boy's eyes moved over the room quickly. "I'll find the book," he said. "You go open the door to the terrace."

"Why that one?"

The boy gave her a hard look. "Because that's the one with the catch that slips. It had to get in some way, didn't it?"

The girl turned, then she looked back and said, "Then can we have breakfast?"

The boy had begun moving around the room, looking under tables, poking under the sofa. "There's no time," he said.

"But I'm hungry!"

"I don't care," the boy said. "It's the cleaning lady's day, and we have to be asleep when she gets here. We'll eat later."

"Maybe pancakes? With syrup?"

The boy didn't look at her. "Maybe," he said. "Now go open the door like I told you."

The girl stuck her tongue out at him. "I wish I was the oldest," she said.

"Well, you're not," the boy said, turning and glaring at her. "Now go and do like I said."

The girl tossed her hair back in a gesture of defiance, but she left the room, not hurrying, and in the hall she began to hum a little tune to annoy him.

The boy did not notice. He was becoming anxious now. Where could the book be? It wasn't on the table. And it couldn't be out of the room. He saw it then, on the floor, under the shattered lamp.

He hurried to it and his hands were shaking when he picked it up, brushing the bits of glass away. He examined it carefully, turning the pages, running his fingers over the smooth binding, the embossed letters of that title. Then he smiled. It was all right. There weren't even any spatters of blood.

He closed the covers and hugged the book to his chest. A great joy welled inside him. It was one of his favorite stories. Very soon, he promised himself, he would read *The Hound of the Baskervilles* again.

Red as Blood

by Tanith Lee

A fairy tale! A fairy tale! And finally one with bite.

The beautiful Witch Queen flung open the ivory case of
the magic mirror. Of dark gold the mirror was, dark gold
as the hair of the Witch Queen that poured down her back.
Dark gold the mirror was, and ancient as the seven stunted
black trees growing beyond the pale blue glass of the window.

"*Speculum, speculum,*" said the Witch Queen to the
magic mirror. "*Dei gratia.*"

"*Volente Deo. Audio.*"

"Mirror," said the Witch Queen. "Whom do you
see?"

"I see you, mistress," replied the mirror. "And all in
the land. But one."

"Mirror, mirror, who is it you do not see?"

"I do not see Bianca."

The Witch Queen crossed herself. She shut the case of the mirror and, walking slowly to the window, looked out at the old trees through the panes of pale blue glass.

Fourteen years ago, another woman had stood at this window, but she was not like the Witch Queen. The woman had black hair that fell to her ankles; she had a crimson gown, the girdle worn high beneath her breasts, for she was far gone with child. And this woman had thrust open the glass casement on the winter garden, where the old trees crouched in the snow. Then, taking a sharp bone needle, she had thrust it into her finger and shaken three bright drops on the ground. "Let my daughter have," said the woman, "hair black as mine, black as the wood of these warped and arcane trees. Let her have skin like mine, white as this snow. And let her have my mouth, red as my blood." And the woman had smiled and licked at her finger. She had a crown on her head; it shone in the dusk like a star. She never came to the window before dusk; she did not like the day. She was the first Queen, and she did not possess a mirror.

The second Queen, the Witch Queen, knew all this. She knew how, in giving birth, the first Queen had died. Her coffin had been carried into the cathedral and masses had been said. There was an ugly rumor—that a splash of holy water had fallen on the corpse and the dead flesh had smoked. But the first Queen had been reckoned unlucky

273

for the kingdom. There had been a strange plague in the land since she came there, a wasting disease for which there was no cure.

Seven years went by. The King married the second Queen, as unlike the first as frankincense to myrrh.

"And this is my daughter," said the King to his second Queen.

There stood a little girl child, nearly seven years of age. Her black hair hung to her ankles, her skin was white as snow. Her mouth was red as blood, and she smiled with it.

"Bianca," said the King, "you must love your new mother."

Bianca smiled radiantly. Her teeth were bright as sharp bone needles.

"Come," said the Witch Queen, "come, Bianca. I will show you my magic mirror."

"Please, Mama," said Bianca softly, "I do not like mirrors."

"She is modest," said the King. "And delicate. She never goes out by day. The sun distresses her."

That night, the Witch Queen opened the case of her mirror.

"Mirror, whom do you see?"

"I see you, mistress. And all in the land. But one."

"Mirror, mirror, who is it you do not see?"

"I do not see Bianca."

The second Queen gave Bianca a tiny crucifix of golden

filigree. Bianca would not accept it. She ran to her father and whispered: "I am afraid. I do not like to think of Our Lord dying in agony on His cross. She means to frighten me. Tell her to take it away."

The second Queen grew wild white roses in her garden and invited Bianca to walk there after sundown. But Bianca shrank away. She whispered to her father: "The thorns will tear me. She means me to be hurt."

When Bianca was twelve years old, the Witch Queen said to the King, "Bianca should be confirmed so that she may take Communion with us."

"This may not be," said the King. "I will tell you, she has not even been christened, for the dying word of my first wife was against it. She begged me, for her religion was different from ours. The wishes of the dying must be respected."

"Should you not like to be blessed by the church," said the Witch Queen to Bianca. "To kneel at the golden rail before the marble altar. To sing to God, to taste the ritual bread and sip the ritual wine."

"She means me to betray my true mother," said Bianca to the King. "When will she cease tormenting me?"

The day she was thirteen, Bianca rose from her bed, and there was a red stain there, like a red, red flower.

"Now you are a woman," said her nurse.

"Yes," said Bianca. And she went to her true mother's jewel box, and out of it she took her mother's crown and set it on her head.

When she walked under the old black trees in the dusk, the crown shone like a star.

The wasting sickness, which had left the land in peace for thirteen years, suddenly began again, and there was no cure.

The Witch Queen sat in a tall chair before a window of pale green and dark white glass, and in her hands she held a Bible bound in rosy silk.

"Majesty," said the huntsman, bowing very low.

He was a man, forty years old, strong and handsome, and wise in the hidden lore of the forests, the occult lore of the earth. He would kill too, for it was his trade, without faltering. The slender fragile deer he could kill, and the moonwinged birds, and the velvet hares with their sad, foreknowing eyes. He pitied them, but pitying, he killed them. Pity could not stop him. It was his trade.

"Look in the garden," said the Witch Queen.

The hunter looked through a dark white pane. The sun had sunk, and a maiden walked under a tree.

"The Princess Bianca," said the huntsman.

"What else?" asked the Witch Queen.

The huntsman crossed himself.

"By Our Lord, Madam, I will not say."

"But you know."

"Who does not?"

"The King does not."

"Or he does."

"Are you a brave man?" asked the Witch Queen.

"In the summer, I have hunted and slain boar. I have slaughtered wolves in winter."

"But are you brave enough?"

"If you command it, Lady," said the huntsman, "I will try my best."

The Witch Queen opened the Bible at a certain place, and out of it she drew a flat silver crucifix, which had been resting against the words: *Thou shalt not be afraid for the terror by night. . . . Nor for the pestilence that walketh in darkness.*

The huntsman kissed the crucifix and put it about his neck, beneath his shirt.

"Approach," said the Witch Queen, "and I will instruct you in what to say."

Presently, the huntsman entered the garden, as the stars were burning up in the sky. He strode to where Bianca stood under a stunted dwarf tree, and he kneeled down.

"Princess," he said. "Pardon me, but I must give you ill tidings."

"Give them then," said the girl, toying with the long stem of a wan, night-growing flower which she had plucked.

"Your stepmother, that accursed, jealous witch, means to have you slain. There is no help for it but you must fly the palace this very night. If you permit, I will guide you to the forest. There are those who will care for you until it may be safe for you to return."

Bianca watched him, but gently, trustingly.

"I will go with you, then," she said.

They went by a secret way out of the garden, through a passage under the ground, through a tangled orchard, by a broken road between great overgrown hedges.

Night was a pulse of deep, flickering blue when they came to the forest. The branches of the forest overlapped and intertwined like leading in a window, and the sky gleamed dimly through like panes of blue-colored glass.

"I am weary," sighed Bianca. "May I rest a moment?"

"By all means," said the huntsman. "In the clearing there, foxes come to play by night. Look in that direction, and you will see them."

"How clever you are," said Bianca. "And how handsome."

She sat on the turf, and gazed at the clearing.

The huntsman drew his knife silently and concealed it in the folds of his cloak. He stopped above the maiden.

"What are you whispering?" demanded the huntsman, laying his hand on her wood-black hair.

"Only a rhyme my mother taught me."

The huntsman seized her by the hair and swung her about so her white throat was before him, stretched ready for the knife. But he did not strike, for there in his hand he held the dark golden locks of the Witch Queen, and her face laughed up at him and she flung her arms about him, laughing.

"Good man, sweet man, it was only a test of you. Am I not a witch? And do you not love me?"

The huntsman trembled, for he did love her, and she was pressed so close her heart seemed to beat within his own body.

"Put away the knife. Throw away the silly crucifix. We have no need of these things. The King is not one half the man you are."

And the huntsman obeyed her, throwing the knife and the crucifix far off among the roots of the trees. He gripped her to him, and she buried her face in his neck, and the pain of her kiss was the last thing he felt in this world.

The sky was black now. The forest was blacker. No foxes played in the clearing. The moon rose and made white lace through the boughs, and through the backs of the huntsman's empty eyes. Bianca wiped her mouth on a dead flower.

"Seven asleep, seven awake," said Bianca. "Wood to wood. Blood to blood. Thee to me."

There came a sound like seven huge rendings, distant by the length of several trees, a broken road, an orchard, an underground passage. Then a sound like seven huge single footfalls. Nearer. And nearer.

Hop, hop, hop, hop. Hop, hop, hop.

In the orchard, seven black shudderings.

On the broken road, between the high hedges, seven black creepings.

Brush crackled, branches snapped.

Through the forest, into the clearing, pushed seven warped, misshapen, hunched-over, stunted things. Woody-black mossy fur, woody-black bald masks. Eyes like glitter-

279

ing cracks, mouths like moist caverns. Lichen beards. Fingers of twiggy gristle. Grinning. Kneeling. Faces pressed to the earth.

"Welcome," said Bianca.

The Witch Queen stood before a window of glass like diluted wine. She looked at the magic mirror.

"Mirror. Whom do you see?"

"I see you, mistress. I see a man in the forest. He went hunting, but not for deer. His eyes are open, but he is dead. I see all in the land. But one."

The Witch Queen pressed her palms to her ears.

Outside the window the garden lay, empty of its seven black and stunted dwarf trees.

"Bianca," said the Queen.

The windows had been draped and gave no light. The light spilled from a shallow vessel, light in a sheaf, like the pastel wheat. It glowed upon four swords that pointed east and west, that pointed north and south.

Four winds had burst through the chamber, and three arch-winds. Cool fires had risen, and parched oceans, and the gray-silver powders of Time.

The hands of the Witch Queen floated like folded leaves on the air, and through dry lips the Witch Queen chanted.

"Pater omnipotens, mittere digneris sanctum Angelum tuum de Infernis."

The light faded, and grew brighter.

There, between the hilts of the four swords, stood the Angel Lucefiel, somberly gilded, his face in shadow, his golden wings spread and blazing at his back.

"Since you have called me, I know your desire. It is a comfortless wish. You ask for pain."

"You speak of pain, Lord Lucefiel, who suffer the most merciless pain of all. Worse than the nails in the feet and wrists. Worse than the thorns and the bitter cup and the blade in the side. To be called upon for evil's sake, which I do not, comprehending your true nature, son of God, brother of The Son."

"You recognize me, then. I will grant what you ask."

And Lucefiel (by some named Satan, Rex Mundi, but nevertheless the left hand, the sinister hand of God's design) wrenched lightning from the ether and cast it at the Witch Queen.

It caught her in the breast. She fell.

The sheaf of light towered and lit the golden eyes of the Angel, which were terrible, yet luminous with compassion, as the swords shattered and he vanished.

The Witch Queen pulled herself from the floor of the chamber, no longer beautiful, a withered, slobbering hag.

Into the core of the forest, even at noon, the sun never shone. Flowers propagated in the grass, but they were colorless. Above, the black-green roof hung down nets of thick, green twilight through which albino butterflies and moths feverishly drizzled. The trunks of the trees were smooth as the stalks of underwater weeds. Bats flew in the daytime, and birds who believed themselves to be bats.

There was a sepulcher, dripped with moss. The bones had been rolled out, had rolled around the feet of seven twisted dwarf trees. They looked like trees. Sometimes they moved. Sometimes something like an eye glittered, or a tooth, in the wet shadows.

In the shade of the sepulcher door sat Bianca, combing her hair.

A lurch of motion disturbed the thick twilight.

The seven trees turned their heads.

A hag emerged from the forest. She was crook-backed and her head was poked forward, predatory, withered, and almost hairless, like a vulture's.

"Here we are at last," grated the hag, in a vulture's voice.

She came closer, and cranked herself down on her knees, and bowed her face into the turf and the colorless flowers.

Bianca sat and gazed at her. The hag lifted herself. Her teeth were yellow palings.

"I bring you the homage of witches, and three gifts," said the hag.

"Why should you do that?"

"Such a quick child, and only fourteen years. Why? Because we fear you. I bring you gifts to curry favor."

Bianca laughed. "Show me."

The hag made a pass in the green air. She held a silken

cord worked curiously with plaited human hair.

"Here is a girdle which will protect you from the devices of priests, from crucifix and chalice and the accursed holy water. In it are knotted the tresses of a virgin, and of a woman no better than she should be, and of a woman dead. And here—" a second pass and a comb was in her hand, lacquered blue over green—"a comb from the deep sea, a mermaid's trinket, to charm and subdue. Part your locks with this, and the scent of ocean will fill men's nostrils and the rhythm of the tides their ears, the tides that bind men like chains. Last," added the hag, "that old symbol of wickedness, the scarlet fruit of Eve, the apple red as blood. Bite, and the understanding of sin, which the serpent boasted of, will be made known to you." And the hag made her last pass in the air and extended the apple, with the girdle and the comb, toward Bianca.

Bianca glanced at the seven stunted trees.

"I like her gifts, but I do not quite trust her."

The bald masks peered from their shaggy beardings. Eyelets glinted. Twiggy claws clacked.

"All the same," said Bianca. "I will let her tie the girdle on me, and comb my hair herself."

The hag obeyed, simpering. Like a toad she waddled to Bianca. She tied on the girdle. She parted the ebony hair. Sparks sizzled, white from the girdle, peacock's eye from the comb.

"And now, hag, take a little bite of the apple."

"It will be my pride," said the hag, "to tell my sisters I

shared this fruit with you." And the hag bit into the apple, and mumbled the bite noisily, and swallowed, smacking her lips.

Then Bianca took the apple and bit into it.

Bianca screamed—and choked.

She jumped to her feet. Her hair whirled about her like a storm cloud. Her face turned blue, then slate, then white again. She lay on the pallid flowers, neither stirring nor breathing.

The seven dwarf trees rattled their limbs and their bear-shaggy heads, to no avail. Without Bianca's art they could not hop. They strained their claws and ripped at the hag's sparse hair and her mantle. She fled between them. She fled into the sunlit acres of the forest, along the broken road, through the orchard, into a hidden passage.

The hag reentered the palace by the hidden way, and the Queen's chamber by a hidden stair. She was bent almost double. She held her ribs. With one skinny hand she opened the ivory case of the magic mirror.

"*Speculum, speculum. Dei gratia.* Whom do you see?"

"I see you, mistress. And all in the land. And I see a coffin."

"Whose corpse lies in the coffin?"

"That I cannot see. It must be Bianca."

The hag, who had been the beautiful Witch Queen, sank into her tall chair before the window of pale, cucumber green and dark white glass. Her drugs and potions waited, ready to reverse the dreadful conjuring of age the Angel Lucefiel had placed on her, but she did not touch them yet.

The apple had contained a fragment of the flesh of Christ, the sacred wafer, the Eucharist.

The Witch Queen drew her Bible to her and opened it randomly.

And read, with fear, the word: *Resurcat.*

It appeared like glass, the coffin, milky glass. It had formed this way. A thin white smoke had risen from the skin of Bianca. She smoked as a fire smokes when a drop of quenching water falls on it. The piece of Eucharist had stuck in her throat. The Eucharist, quenching water to her fire, caused her to smoke.

Then the cold dews of night gathered, and the colder atmospheres of midnight. The smoke of Bianca's quenching froze about her. Frost formed in exquisite silver scroll-work all over the block of misty ice that contained Bianca.

Bianca's frigid heart could not warm the ice. Nor the sunless, green twilight of the day.

You could just see her, stretched in the coffin, through the glass. How lovely she looked, Bianca. Black as ebony, white as snow, red as blood.

The trees hung over the coffin. Years passed. The trees sprawled about the coffin, cradling it in their arms. Their eyes wept fungus and green resin. Green amber drops hardened like jewels in the coffin of glass.

"Who is that lying under the trees?" the Prince asked, as he rode into the clearing.

He seemed to bring a golden moon with him, shining about his golden head, on the golden armor and the cloak of white satin blazoned with gold and blood and ink and sapphire. The white horse trod on the colorless flowers, but the flowers sprang up again when the hoofs had passed. A shield hung from the saddle-bow, a strange shield. From one side it had a lion's face, but from the other, a lamb's face.

The trees groaned, and their heads split on huge mouths.

"Is this Bianca's coffin?" asked the Prince.

"Leave her with us," said the seven trees. They hauled at their roots. The ground shivered. The coffin of ice-glass gave a great jolt, and a crack bisected it.

Bianca coughed.

The jolt had precipitated the piece of Eucharist from her throat.

Into a thousand shards the coffin shattered, and Bianca sat up. She stared at the Prince, and she smiled.

"Welcome, beloved," said Bianca.

She got to her feet, and shook out her hair, and began to walk toward the Prince on the pale horse.

But she seemed to walk into a shadow, into a purple room, then into a crimson room whose emanations lanced her like knives. Next she walked into a yellow room where

286

she heard the sound of crying, which tore her ears. All her body seemed stripped away; she was a beating heart. The beats of her heart became two wings. She flew. She was a raven, then an owl. She flew into a sparkling pane. It scorched her white. Snow white. She was a dove.

She settled on the shoulder of the Prince and hid her head under her wing. She had no longer anything black about her, and nothing red.

"Begin again now, Bianca," said the Prince. He raised her from his shoulder. On his wrist there was a mark. It was like a star. Once a nail had been driven in there.

Bianca flew away, up through the roof of the forest. She flew in at a delicate wine window. She was in the palace. She was seven years old.

The Witch Queen, her new mother, hung a filigree crucifix around her neck.

"Mirror," said the Witch Queen. "Whom do you see?"

"I see you, mistress," replied the mirror. "And all in the land. I see Bianca."

Gabriel-Ernest

by *Saki (H. H. Munro)*

It's sad but true that what is not believed is seldom seen.

"There is a wild beast in your woods," said the artist Cunningham, as he was being driven to the station. It was the only remark he had made during the drive, but as Van Cheele had talked incessantly, his companion's silence had not been noticeable.

"A stray fox or two and some resident weasels. Nothing more formidable," said Van Cheele. The artist said nothing.

"What did you mean about a wild beast?" said Van Cheele later, when they were on the platform.

"Nothing. My imagination. Here is the train," said Cunningham.

That afternoon Van Cheele went for one of his frequent rambles through his woodland property. He had a stuffed bittern in his study and knew the names of quite a number of wild flowers, so his aunt had possibly some justification in describing him as a great naturalist. At any rate, he was a great walker. It was his custom to take mental notes of everything he saw during his walks, not so much for the purpose of assisting contemporary science as to provide topics for conversation afterwards. When the bluebells began to show themselves in flower, he made a point of informing everyone of the fact; the season of the year might have warned his hearers of the likelihood of such an occurrence, but at least they felt that he was being absolutely frank with them.

What Van Cheele saw on this particular afternoon was, however, something far removed from his ordinary range of experience. On a shelf of smooth stone overhanging a deep pool in the hollow of an oak coppice, a boy of about sixteen lay asprawl, drying his wet brown limbs luxuriously in the sun. His wet hair, parted by a recent dive, lay close to his head, and his light-brown eyes, so light that there was an almost tigerish gleam in them, were turned toward Van Cheele with a certain lazy watchfulness. It was an unexpected apparition, and Van Cheele found himself engaged in the novel process of thinking before he spoke. Where on earth could this wild-looking boy hail from? The miller's wife had lost a child some two months ago, supposed to have been swept away by the millrace, but that had been a mere baby, not a half-grown lad.

"What are you doing there?" he demanded.

"Obviously, sunning myself," replied the boy.

"Where do you live?"

"Here, in these woods."

"You can't live in the woods," said Van Cheele.

"They are very nice woods," said the boy, with a touch of patronage in his voice.

"But where do you sleep at night?"

"I don't sleep at night; that's my busiest time."

Van Cheele began to have an irritated feeling that he was grappling with a problem that was eluding him.

"What do you feed on?" he asked.

"Flesh," said the boy, and he pronounced the word with slow relish, as though he were tasting it.

"Flesh! What flesh?"

"Since it interests you, rabbits, wild-fowl, hares, poultry, lambs in their season, children when I can get any; they're usually too well locked in at night, when I do most of my hunting. It's quite two months since I tasted child-flesh."

Ignoring the chaffing nature of the last remark, Van Cheele tried to draw the boy onto the subject of possible poaching operations.

"You're talking rather through your hat when you speak of feeding on hares." (Considering the nature of the boy's toilet, the simile was hardly an apt one.) "Our hillside hares aren't easily caught."

"At night I hunt on four feet" was the somewhat cryptic response.

"I suppose you mean that you hunt with a dog?" hazarded Van Cheele.

The boy rolled slowly over onto his back and laughed a weird low laugh that was pleasantly like a chuckle and disagreeably like a snarl.

"I don't fancy any dog would be very anxious for my company, especially at night."

Van Cheele began to feel that there was something positively uncanny about the strange-eyed, strange-tongued youngster.

"I can't have you staying in these woods," he declared authoritatively.

"I fancy you'd rather have me here than in your house," said the boy.

The prospect of this wild, nude animal in Van Cheele's primly ordered house was certainly an alarming one.

"If you don't go, I shall have to make you," said Van Cheele.

The boy turned like a flash, plunged into the pool, and in a moment had flung his wet and glistening body halfway up the bank where Van Cheele was standing. In an otter the movement would not have been remarkable; in a boy Van Cheele found it sufficiently startling. His foot slipped as he made an involuntary backward movement, and he found himself almost prostrate on the slippery weed-grown bank, with those tigerish yellow eyes not very far from his own. Almost instinctively he half-raised his hand to his throat. The boy laughed again, a laugh in which the snarl had nearly driven out the chuckle, and then, with another of his astonishing lightning movements, plunged out of view into a yielding tangle of weed and fern.

"What an extraordinary wild animal!" said Van Cheele as he picked himself up. And then he recalled Cunningham's remark, "There is a wild beast in your woods."

Walking slowly homeward, Van Cheele began to turn over in his mind various local occurrences which might be traceable to the existence of this astonishing young savage.

Something had been thinning the game in the woods lately, poultry had been missing from the farms, hares were growing unaccountably scarcer, and complaints had reached him of lambs being carried off bodily from the hills. Was it possible that this wild boy was really hunting the countryside in company with some clever poacher dog? He had spoken of hunting "four-footed" by night, but then again, he had hinted strangely at no dog caring to come near him, "especially at night." It was certainly puzzling. And then, as Van Cheele ran his mind over the various depredations that had been committed during the last month or two, he came suddenly to a dead stop, alike in his walk and his speculations. The child missing from the mill two months ago—the accepted theory was that it had tumbled into the millrace and been swept away; but the mother had always declared she had heard a shriek on the hill side of the house, in the opposite direction from the water. It was unthinkable, of course, but he wished that the boy had not made that uncanny remark about child-flesh eaten two months ago. Such dreadful things should not be said even in fun.

Van Cheele, contrary to his usual wont, did not feel disposed to be communicative about his discovery in the wood. His position as a parish councillor and justice of the peace seemed somehow compromised by the fact that he was harboring a personality of such doubtful repute on his property; there was even a possibility that a heavy bill of damages for raided lambs and poultry might be laid at his door. At dinner that night he was quite unusually silent.

"Where's your voice gone to?" said his aunt. "One would think you had seen a wolf."

Van Cheele, who was not familiar with the old saying, thought the remark rather foolish; if he *had* seen a wolf on his property, his tongue would have been extraordinarily busy with the subject.

At breakfast next morning Van Cheele was conscious that his feeling of uneasiness regarding yesterday's episode had not wholly disappeared, and he resolved to go by train to the neighboring cathedral town, hunt up Cunningham, and learn from him what he had really seen that had prompted the remark about a wild beast in the woods. With this resolution taken, his usual cheerfulness partially returned, and he hummed a bright little melody as he sauntered to the morning room for his customary cigarette. As he entered the room, the melody made way abruptly for a pious invocation. Gracefully asprawl on the ottoman, in an attitude of almost exaggerated repose, was the boy of the woods. He was drier than when Van Cheele had last seen him, but no other alteration was noticeable in his toilet.

"How dare you come here?" asked Van Cheele furiously.

"You told me I was not to stay in the woods," said the boy calmly.

"But not to come here. Supposing my aunt should see you!"

And with a view to minimizing that catastrophe Van Cheele hastily obscured as much of his unwelcome guest as possible under the folds of a *Morning Post*. At that moment his aunt entered the room.

"This is a poor boy who has lost his way—and lost his memory. He doesn't know who he is or where he comes from," explained Van Cheele desperately, glancing apprehensively at the waif's face to see whether he was going to add inconvenient candor to his other savage propensities.

Miss Van Cheele was enormously interested.

"Perhaps his underlinen is marked," she suggested.

"He seems to have lost most of that, too," said Van Cheele, making frantic little grabs at the *Morning Post* to keep it in its place.

A naked, homeless child appealed to Miss Van Cheele as warmly as a stray kitten or derelict puppy would have.

"We must do all we can for him," she decided; and in a very short time a messenger, dispatched to the rectory, where a page-boy was kept, had returned with a suit of pantry clothes, and the necessary accessories of shirt, shoes, collar, etc. Clothed, clean and groomed, the boy lost none of his uncanniness in Van Cheele's eyes, but his aunt found him sweet.

"We must call him something till we know who he really is," she said. "Gabriel-Ernest, I think; those are nice suitable names."

Van Cheele agreed, but he privately doubted whether they were being grafted on to a nice suitable child. His misgivings were not diminished by the fact that his staid and elderly spaniel had bolted out of the house at the first incoming of the boy and now obstinately remained shivering and yapping at the farther end of the orchard, while the canary, usually as vocally industrious as Van Cheele himself, had put itself on an allowance of frightened cheeps. More than ever he was resolved to consult Cunningham without loss of time.

As he drove off to the station, his aunt was arranging that Gabriel-Ernest should help her to entertain the infant members of her Sunday-school class at tea that afternoon.

Cunningham was not at first disposed to be communicative.

"My mother died of some brain trouble," he explained, "so you will understand why I am averse to dwelling on anything of an impossibly fantastic nature that I may see or think that I have seen."

"But what *did* you see?" persisted Van Cheele.

"What I thought I saw was something so extraordinary that no really sane man could dignify it with the credit of having actually happened. I was standing, the last evening I was with you, half-hidden in the hedgegrowth by the orchard gate, watching the dying glow of the sunset. Suddenly I became aware of a naked boy, a bather from some neighboring pool, I took him to be, who was standing out on the bare hillside also watching the sunset. His pose was so suggestive of some wild faun of Pagan myth that I instantly wanted to engage him as a model, and in another moment I think I should have hailed him. But just then the sun dipped out of view, and all the orange and pink slid out of the landscape, leaving it cold and gray. And at the same moment an astounding thing happened—the boy vanished too!"

"What! Vanished away into nothing?" asked Van Cheele excitedly.

"No, that is the dreadful part of it," answered the artist. "On the open hillside where the boy had been standing a second ago, stood a large wolf, blackish in color, with gleaming fangs and cruel, yellow eyes. You may think—"

But Van Cheele did not stop for anything as futile as thought. Already he was tearing at top speed toward the station. He dismissed the idea of a telegram. "Gabriel-Ernest is a werewolf" was a hopelessly inadequate effort at conveying the situation, and his aunt would think it was a code message to which he had omitted to give her the key. His one hope was that he might reach home before sundown. The cab that he chartered at the other end of the railway journey bore him with what seemed exasperating slowness along the country roads, which were pink and mauve with the flush of the sinking sun. His aunt was putting away some unfinished jams and cake when he arrived.

"Where is Gabriel-Ernest?" he almost screamed.

"He is taking the little Toop child home," said his aunt. "It was getting so late, I thought it wasn't safe to let him go back alone. What a lovely sunset, isn't it?"

But Van Cheele, although not oblivious of the glow in the western sky, did not stay to discuss its beauties. At a speed for which he was scarcely geared, he raced along the narrow lane that led to the home of the Toops. On one side ran the swift current of the millstream, on the other rose the stretch of bare hillside. A dwindling rim of red sun showed still on the skyline, and the next turning must bring him in view of the ill-assorted couple he was pursuing. Then the color went suddenly out of things, and a gray light settled itself with a quick shiver over the landscape. Van Cheele heard a shrill wail of fear and stopped running.

Nothing was ever seen again of the Toops' child or Gabriel-Ernest, but the latter's discarded garments were found lying in the road, so it was assumed that the child had fallen into the water, and that the boy had stripped and jumped in, in a vain endeavor to save him. Van Cheele and some workmen who were nearby at the time testified to having heard a child scream loudly just near the spot where the clothes were found. Mrs. Toop, who had eleven other children, was decently resigned to her bereavement, but Miss Van Cheele sincerely mourned her lost foundling. It was on her initiative that a memorial brass was put up in the parish church to "Gabriel-Ernest, an unknown boy, who bravely sacrificed his life for another."

Van Cheele gave way to his aunt in most things, but he flatly refused to subscribe to the Gabriel-Ernest memorial.

Fritzchen

by *Charles Beaumont*

Only after a few days did the little monster's problems become apparent.

It had once been a place for dreaming. For lying on your back in the warm sand and listening to the silence and making faraway things seem real. The finest place in all the world for all the reasons that ever were.

But it had stopped being this long ago. Now, he supposed, it wasn't much more than a fairly isolated cove, really; a stretch of land bleeding into the river at one of its wide points, cut off like a tiny peninsula; a grey, dull place, damp and unnatural from its nights beneath the tidewaters—decaying, sinking slowly, glad to be eaten by the river. As Edna had put it: Just a lot of dirty wet sand. Not a place for dreaming anymore.

Mr. Peldo shifted his position and sighed as he remembered. He took from his mouth the eviscerated end of a lifeless cigar, flipped it away distastefully, watched as the

298

mud whitened and oozed where it landed, and the spiders lumbered clumsily away in fright.

The spiders made him think of his snakes. And soon he was thinking, too, of rabbits and goldfish and ooo wow-wow puppy dogs, all flop-eared and soft, common as a blade of grass—and his bread-and-butter. His living.

He was almost relieved to hear Edna's coarse voice beside him.

"Jake."

She would now make some complaint about the foolishness of this whole trip, adding that it made her sinuses runny.

"Yes, Chicken, what is it?"

"Go and see to Luther."

Go-and-see-to-Luther. Eight-year-old kid ought to be able to see to himself, by God.

"All right. Where'd he go?"

"Somewhere over in that direction, there by the trees. I'm worried he might think of going in the water or get lost."

Mr. Peldo grunted softly as he pulled his weight erect. Exertion. Oh well, that was all right. Soon he would have started with the frustration, thinking about the lousy pet shop and his lousy life. Better to hunt in the trees for spoiled brats.

It was hard going. Had to end in a few yards, of course, but still, it *was* . . . exciting, in a small, tired, remembering way. He pushed aside a drenched fern, and another, needles of wet hitting him.

"Luther."

Mr. Peldo continued for a few feet, until he could distinctly hear the current. A wall of leaves rose at the curve, so he stopped there, let the last of the thrill fall loose from him, then listened.

"Luther. Hustle, boy."

Only the water. The vibrant, treacherous river water, hurrying to join the Sound and to go with it to the ocean.

"Hey, *Luu-therr.*"

Mr. Peldo stabbed his hands into the foliage and parted it. From the window, by peering close, he could see his son's back.

"Boy, when your father calls you, *answer* him, hear!"

Luther looked around disinterestedly, frowned and turned his head. He was sitting in the mud, playing.

Mr. Peldo felt the anger course spastically through him. He pushed forward and stopped, glared.

"Well?"

Then he glimpsed what his son had been playing with. Only a glimpse, though.

"Fritzchen!" Luther pronounced defiantly, shielding something in his hands. "Fritzchen—like I wanted to call Sol's birdie."

Mr. Peldo felt his eyes smart and rubbed them. "What have you got there?"

"Fritzchen, Fritzchen," the boy wailed. There was another sound then. A sound like none Mr. Peldo had ever heard: high-pitched, whiny, discordant. The sound an animal makes when it is in pain.

Mr. Peldo reached down and slapped at his son's mouth, which had fastened like a python's about the calf of his left leg. Then, by holding his thumb and forefinger tightly on Luther's nose, he forced him to drop the thing he had been hiding.

It fell onto the slime and began to thrash.

Mr. Peldo gasped. He stared for a moment, like an idiot at a lampshade, his mouth quite open, and his eyes bulged.

A thin voice from across the trees called: "Jake, is there anything wrong? Answer me!"

He pulled off his sport coat and threw it about the squirmy thing. "No, no, everything's okay. Kid's just acting up is all. Hold your horses!"

"Well, hurry! It's getting dark!"

Mr. Peldo blocked Luther's charge with his foot.

"Where did you get that?"

Luther did not answer. He glowered sullenly at the ground, mumbling, "He's mine. I found him. You can't have him."

"Where did it come from?" Mr. Peldo demanded.

Luther's lower lip resembled a bloated sausage. Finally he jerked his thumb in the direction of the riverbank.

"You can talk!"

Luther whimpered, tried once again to get at the wriggling bundle on the sand, sat down and said, "I found him in the water. I snuck up on him and grabbed him when he wasn't looking. Now he's mine and you can't have—"

But Mr. Peldo, having recovered himself, had plucked off the coat and was staring.

A place for dreaming.

Roadsters that would go over two hundred miles per hour. Promontoried chateaus with ten bathrooms. Coveys of lithe young temptresses, vacant-minded, full-bodied, infinitely imaginative, infinitely accessible . . .

"JAAAAke! Are you trying to scare me to death? It's cold and my sinuses are beginning to run!"

Luther looked at his father, snorted loudly and started for the trees.

"He's Fritzchen and he's *mine!*" he called back as he ran. "All right—I'll get even! You'll see!"

Mr. Peldo watched the small creature, fascinated, as all its legs commenced to move together, dwarfed, undeveloped legs, burrowing into the viscous ground. Shuddering slightly, he replaced the coat, gathered it into the form of a sack and started through the shrubbery.

Edna's nose had turned red. He decided not to show Fritzchen to her, for a while.

"Got no empties," Sol said slowly, eying the bundle Mr. Peldo held at arms' length. Sol didn't care for animals. He was old; his mind had fallen into a ravine; it paced the ravine, turned and paced, like a contented baboon. He was old.

302

Mr. Peldo waited for Edna and Luther to go around to the living quarters in the back. "Put the capuchin in with Bess," he said. "Ought to have a stout one. Hop to it, Sol, I can't stand here holding this all day."

" 'nother stray?"

"You . . . might say."

Sol shrugged and transferred the raucous little monkey from his carved wood cage to the parrot dome.

Then he looked back. Mr. Peldo was holding the jacket-bundle down on a table with both hands. Whatever was inside was moving in violent spasms, not the way a dog moves or a rabbit. There were tiny sounds.

"Give me a hand," Mr. Peldo said, and Sol helped him put the bundle, jacket and all, into the cage. They locked it.

"This'll do for a while," Mr. Peldo said, "until I can build a proper one. Now mind, Sol, you keep your mouth strictly shut about this. Shut."

Sol didn't answer. His nose had snapped upward and he held a conched hand behind his ear.

"Listen, you," Sol said.

Mr. Peldo took his fingers off the sport coat, which had begun to show a purplish stain.

"First time it ever happened in sixteen years," Sol said.

The silence roared. The silent pet shop roared and burst and pulsed with tension, quiet electric tension. The animals didn't move anywhere in the room. Mr. Peldo's eyes darted from cage to cage, seeing the second strangest thing he had

303

ever seen: unmoving snakes, coiled or supine, but still, as though listening; monkeys hidden in far corners, haunched; rabbits—even their noses quiet and frozen; white mice huddled at the bottom of mills that turned in cautious, diminishing arcs, frightened, staring creatures.

The phlegm in Mr. Peldo's throat racked loose.

Then it was quiet again. Though not exactly quiet.

Sol quit his survey of the animals and turned back to the occupant of the capuchin's cage. The sport jacket glistened with stain now, and from within the dark folds there was a scrabbling and a small gurgling sound.

Then the jacket fell away.

"Tom-hell, Jake!" Sol said.

The animals had begun to scream, all of them, all at once.

"Not a word to anyone now, Sol! Promise?"

Mr. Peldo feasted. He stared and stared, feeling satisfaction.

"What in glory is it?" Sol inquired above the din.

"A pet," Mr. Peldo answered, simply.

"Pet, hey?"

"We'll have to build a special cage for it." Mr. Peldo beamed. "Say, bet there ain't many like this one! No, sir. We'll have to read up on it so's we can get the feeding right and all . . ."

"*You* read up." Sol's eyes were large. The air was filled with the wild beating of birds' wings.

Mr. Peldo was musing. "By the way, Sol, what you suppose it could be?"

The old man cocked his head to one side, peered from slitted eyes, picked out the crumpled sport jacket quickly and let it fall to the floor. It dropped heavily and exuded a sick water smell. Sol shrugged.

"Cross between a whale," he said, "and a horsefly, near's I can see."

"Maybe it's valuable—you think?" Mr. Peldo's ideas were growing.

"Couldn't say. Most likely not, in the face of it."

The chittering sound rose into a sort of staccato wail, piercing, clear over the frantic pets.

"Where in thunder you get it?"

"*He* didn't. *I* did." It was Luther, scowling, in his nightclothes.

"Go to bed. Go away."

"I found Fritzchen in the water. He likes me."

"*Out!*"

"Dirty stinking rotten lousy rotten stealer!"

Sol put his fingers into his ears and shut his eyes.

Luther made a pout and advanced toward Fritzchen's cage. The sobbing noises ceased.

"He hadda lock you up. Yeah. *I* was gonna let you loose again." The boy glared at his father. "See how he loves me." Luther put his face up to the cage, and as he did so, the small animal came forward, ponderously, with suction-like noises from its many legs.

Mr. Peldo looked disinterested. He inspected his watch stem. Neither he nor Sol saw what happened.

Luther stamped his foot and yelled. The right side of his face was covered with something that gathered and dripped down.

"Luther!" It was Mr. Peldo's wife. She ran into the room and looked at the cage. "Oh, that nasty thing!" She stormed out, clutching her son's pink ear.

"Damn woman will drive me crazy," Mr. Peldo said. Then he noticed that the shop was quiet again. Sol had thrown the damp jacket over Fritzchen's cage. There was only the sobbing.

"Funny!"

Mr. Peldo bent down, lifted the end of the coat and put his face close. He jerked back with abnormal speed, swabbing at his cheek.

There was a sound like a drowning kitten's purr.

Luther stood in the back doorway. Hate and astonishment contorted his features. "That's all he cares about me when I only wanted to be good to him! Now he loves *you*, dirty rotten—"

"Look, boy, your father's getting mighty tired of—"

"Yeah, well, he'll be sorry."

Fritzchen began to chitter again.

When Mr. Peldo returned to the shop after dinner, he found a curious thing. Bess, the parrot, lay on her side, dead.

Everything else was normal. The animals were wakeful or somnolent but normal. Fritzchen's cage was covered with a canvas, and there was silence from within.

Mr. Peldo inspected Bess and was horrified to discover the bird's condition. She lay inundated in an odd miasmic jelly which had hardened and was now spongey to the touch. It covered her completely. What was more, extended prodding revealed that something had happened to Bess's insides.

They were gone.

And without a trace. Even the bones. Bess was little more than skin and feathers.

Mr. Peldo recalled the substance that had struck his face when he examined Fritzchen's cage the last time. In a frenzy he pulled off the tarpaulin. But Fritzchen was there, and the cage was as securely locked as ever.

And easily twenty feet from the parrot dome.

He went back and found the capuchin staring at him out of quizzical eyes.

Luther, of course. Monster boy. Spoiled bug of a child. He had an active imagination. Probably rigged the whole thing, like the time he emasculated the parakeet in an attempt to turn it inside out.

Mr. Peldo was ungratified that the animals had not yet gotten used to Fritzchen. They began their harangue, so he switched off the light and waited for his eyes to accustom themselves to the moonlight. Moonlight comes fast to small towns near rivers.

Fritzchen must be sleeping. Curled like a baby anaconda, legs slender filaments adhering to the cage floor, the tender tiny tail tucked around so that the tip rested just inside the immense mouth.

Mr. Peldo studied the animal. He watched the mouth especially, noting its outsized relationship to the rest of the body.

But—Mr. Peldo peered—could it actually be that Fritzchen was *larger?* Surely not. The stomach did seem fatter, yet the finely ground hamburger, the dish of milk, the oysters, sat to one side, untouched. Nor had the accommodating bathing and drinking pool been disturbed.

Then he noticed, for the first time, that the mouth had no teeth. There did not appear to be a gullet! And the spiny snout, with its florid green cup, was not a nose after all, for the nose was elsewhere.

But most curious of all, Fritzchen had grown. Oh, yes, grown. No doubt about it.

Mr. Peldo retired hours later with sparkling visions of wealth. He would contact—somebody appropriate—and sell his find for many hundreds of thousands of dollars. Then he would run away to Europe and play with a different woman every night until he died of his excesses.

He was awakened a short time later by Sol, who informed him that the bird of paradise and one dalmatian pup had died during the night. He knew because he'd heard the racket from clean across the street.

"Oh, not the ooo wow-wow," said Edna. "Not the liddle puppy!"

Luther sat up in bed, interested.

"How'd it happen?" Mr. Peldo said.

"Don't know. No good way for definite sure." Sol's eyelids almost closed. "Their innards is gone."

Edna put her head beneath the covers.

"Fritzchen?"

"Guess. Y'ought'a do somethin' with that crittur. Bad actor."

"He got out—that it?"

"Hey-up. Or somebody let him out. Cage is all locked up tight as wax, 'n it wailin' like a banshee."

Mr. Peldo whirled to face his son, who stuck out his tongue.

"See here, young fellow, we're going to get to the bottom of this. If I find out that you—"

"Don't think t'was the lad," Sol said.

"Why not?"

"Wa'l . . . that there thing is thrice the size 'twas yesterday when you brung 'er in."

"No."

"No nothin'. Stomach's pooched out like it's fit to bust."

Mr. Peldo got up and rubbed his hand over his bald head.

"But look, Sol, if it didn't get out, and—Luther, you didn't let it out, did you?"

"No, ma'am."

"—then how we going to blame it? Maybe there's a disease going around."

"*I* know, *I* know," Luther sang, swinging his feet in the air. "His nose can go longer."

"Be still, boy."

"Well, it *can*! I saw it. Fritzchen did it on the beach— hit a bird way out over the water, and he didn't move out of my hands."

"What happened to the bird, Luther?"

"Well, it got stuck up with this stuff Fritzchen has inside him, so it couldn't do anything. Then when it was all glued, Fritzchen pulled it back closer to him and shot out his nose and put his nose inside the bird's mou—"

Mr. Peldo felt his cheek, where the molasses had gathered that time. Both he and Luther had thought of it as an affectionate gesture, no worse than a St. Bernard leaping and pawing over you, raking your face, covering you with friendly, doggy slobber.

That's why Luther had gotten angry.

But Fritzchen wasn't being affectionate. It didn't work only because Fritzchen was too small, or they had been too big.

Mr. Peldo remembered Bess.

Edna poked her head out of the covers and said, "You listen to that! The neighbors will kill us!"

The sounds from the shop were growing stronger and louder and more chaotic.

Mr. Peldo dashed to the hall and returned with a telephone book. "Here," he said, tossing it to his wife, "get the numbers of all the zoos and museums."

"He's mine, he's mine!" Luther screeched.

Sol, who was old, said, "Jake, you never you mind about that. You just fished up something quaar, is all, and the best thing you can do is chuck 'er smack back where she come from."

"Edna—get those numbers, do you hear me? All the museums in the state. I'll be back."

The wailing had reached a crescendo now.

And Luther had disappeared.

Mr. Peldo put on a robe and hurried across the frosty lawn to the back door of the shop.

"Luther!"

The small boy had a box of kitchen matches. Holding a cluster of them in his hands, he lit them and hurled them into Fritzchen's cage. The fiery sticks landed; there was a cry of pain, and then the matches spluttered out against moist skin.

"Luther!"

"I wanted to be good to you," Luther was saying, "but then you hadda take up with *him!* Yeah, well, now you'll see!"

Mr. Peldo threw his son out the door.

The painful wail became an intermittent cry—a strange cry, not unmelodious.

Mr. Peldo looked into the great jeweled milk-white eyes of the creature and dodged as the snout unrolled like a party favor, spraying a fine crystal glaze of puce jam.

Fritzchen stood erect. He—it—had changed. There were antennae where no antennae had been; many of the legs had developed claws; the mouth, which had been toothless the day before, was now filled with sharp brown needles. Fritzchen had been fifteen inches high when Mr. Peldo first saw him. Now he stood over thirty inches.

Still time, though. Time for everything.

Mr. Peldo looked at the animal until his eyes hurt; then he saw the newspaper on the floor. It was soaked with what looked like shreds of liquid soap-jelly, greenish, foul with the odor of seaweed and other things. On it lay a bird and a small dog.

He felt sad for a moment. But then he thought again of some of the things he had dreamed a long time ago, of what he had now, and he determined to make certain telephone calls.

A million dollars, or almost, probably. They'd—oh, they'd stuff Fritzchen, at all odds, or something like that.

"Dirty rotten lousy—"

Luther had come back. He had a crumpled-up magazine saturated with oil and lighter fluid. The magazine was on fire.

The monkeys and the rabbits and the mice and the goldfish and the cats and birds and dogs shrilled in fear. But Fritzchen didn't.

Fritzchen howled only once. Or lowed—a deep sound from somewhere in the middle of his body that seemed to come from his body and not just his mouth. It was an eerily mournful sound that carried a new tone, a tone of helplessness. Then the creature was silent.

By the time Mr. Peldo reached the cage, Luther had thrown in the paper and was squirting inflammable fluid from a can. The fire burned fiercely.

"I *told* you," Luther said, pettishly.

When the fire was pulled and scattered and trampled out, an ugly thing remained in the cage. An ugly blackened thing that made no noise.

Luther began to cry.

Then he stopped.

And Mr. Peldo stopped chasing him.

Sol and Edna, in the doorway, didn't move either.

They all listened.

It could have been a crazed elephant shambling madly through a straw village . . .

Or a whale blind with the pain of sharp steel, thrashing and leaping in illimitable waters . . .

Or it could have been a massive hawk swooping in outraged vengeance upon the killers of her young . . .

The killers of her young!

In that moment, before the rustling sound grew huge; before the windows shattered and the great nightmarish shadow came into the shop, Mr. Peldo understood the meaning of Fritzchen's inconsolable cries.

They were the cries of a lost infant for its mother . . .

The Young One

by Jerome Bixby

As we grow, we learn our roles in life. That isn't always good.

Old Buster was suddenly crouched on stiff legs, right up out of a sound sleep, and his ears were laid back flat against his head, and he was letting out the deep, wet-sounding growl he always used on rattlers.

Young Johnny Stevens looked up in surprise.

The new kid was standing out in the middle of the road, about ten feet away. He'd come up so silently Johnny hadn't even known he was there—until old Buster let out that growl.

Johnny stopped whittling. He sat there on the damp, tree-shaded grass in front of the Stevens farmhouse, his big silver-mounted hunting knife in one hand, the shaved stick in the other, and stared at old Buster.

The dog's head was down, his eyes were up and slitted on the new kid. His lips were curled back tight against his teeth.

Johnny started to reach for Buster's scruff, afraid he was getting set to attack. But Buster gave him a mean, panicky, sideways glance, and Johnny pulled back his hand, because he knew his dog. Then Buster whined. His tail went between his legs and he started to walk backward, one slow step after another. He emerged from the shade of the big elm, where he'd been sleeping at Johnny's feet ever since lunch, and kept going backward until he was about twenty feet up the lawn toward the house. Then he stopped and threw back his head as if to howl—but he didn't. He held the pose for a second, his eyes glaring on the new kid down along the sides of his muzzle, and then he turned and ran around the corner of the house.

Buster had never even run from bear. Johnny had once had to drag him off the scent of one.

Johnny turned to look at the new kid, mad clear through and curious as heck at the same time.

The kid looked friendly, curious—and kind of lost. He was dark and thin, with big eyes. His short, stiff, black hair fit his long skull like a cap. His voice had a funny accent, and it was kind of hesitant, almost like he was afraid to talk.

"Hello," he said.

Johnny Stevens stood up. Wood shavings spilled off his lap onto the grass.

"What'd you do to Buster?" he demanded.

"I . . . I don't know. Dogs just don't like me. I'm sorry I frightened him."

315

Johnny scowled. "You didn't frighten him," he denied formally. "He musta seen something across the road."

"It was me," said the new kid softly.

Johnny turned to look at the corner of the house. Buster was poking his head around, low down, ears still back. The new kid looked over that way too, and Buster ducked out of sight like he was yanked. A second later, Johnny heard the dog's claws gallop across the cellar door along the side of the house and knew Buster must be heading for the field out back, where he went and hid whenever he was punished.

Johnny scowled harder. "Who're you?"

"Kovacs. Hello."

Johnny didn't answer—just stared suspiciously.

"What are you making?" Kovacs asked, after a minute.

"I dunno," Johnny said. Then, because that didn't sound smart, he added, "A cane, maybe. Or a fishing rod. Kovacs what?"

"Bela."

"That's a funny name."

"What is yours?"

"Johnny Stevens."

"Hello, Johnny," Kovacs Bela said again, hopefully.

"Hello," Johnny said sourly.

Kovacs Bela came to the edge of the road, where it gave onto a slope of rock and root-studded dirt that rose a few feet to the Stevens lawn. There he stopped, his thin shadow lying up the slope in front of him, as if he were waiting to be invited.

Johnny sat down again, still scowling. He didn't say anything.

Kovacs half-turned, looking down the road over his shoulder, as if sorry he'd stopped.

They watched a couple of robins chase each other through the sun-bleached rails of the fence across the road. Summer heat danced along the waving tips of wheat in the field beyond, and shimmered up the green-brown sides of the low hillocks that lined the old creek-bed.

Johnny started whittling again.

"You from that new family who bought the old Burman place?" he asked.

"Yes."

"Moved in last week, din'cha? I heard about it."

"Yes."

The robins tired of darting through the fence-rails and set off across the wheatfield, wings blurring, bodies almost brushing the carpet of tips.

"We played around there a lot." Johnny grunted. "The Burman place. Guess we can't now . . . 'cause you moved in."

Kovacs Bela was silent.

"We used the silo for a robber hideout," Johnny said accusingly.

"Silo . . . ?"

"Don't you know what that is?"

Kovacs shook his dark head.

"It's the big round building, like a tin can. You're kinda dumb."

Kovacs bit his lip and stood silently, his big, dark eyes unhappy. "Do you want me to go away?" he asked.

"Sure," said Johnny, still feeling mean.

Kovacs started to turn away, with that aimless look to his movements that means one is going no place in particular—just leaving.

Johnny relented a little. "I was just kiddin' . . . c'mon and sit down."

Kovacs Bela stood for a moment, then smiled hesitantly and came up the dirt slope into the shade of the trees. He sank to the grass and curled his legs under him with an oddly graceful motion. "Thank you," he said.

Johnny peeled a long sliver of bark off the stick with his big, razor-sharp knife. "I wanna know what you did to Buster. How'd you make him act that way?"

"Animals just don't like me."

"Why?"

"My father once said it is the way we sme . . ." Kovacs' voice trailed off. "I don't know. They don't like us."

"Us? You mean your whole family?"

"I—yes."

"You're a funny guy. Where you from, they don't have silos? You talk funny too."

318

"I am from Hungary."

Johnny looked closely at Kovacs Bela, taking in the dark features, the big eyes, the soft mouth. There was something about the face that disturbed him, but he couldn't pin it down.

"Where's Hungry?" he asked.

"In Europe."

"Oh . . . a foreigner. I guess Buster never saw a foreigner before."

The two robins, or another pair, came hedgehopping back over the wheatfield, arced up over the fence, over the road and into the uppermost branches of the tree directly overhead. They set up a loud chirping, and commenced flitting from branch to branch.

"Where are you from?" Kovacs Bela asked.

"Right here. Michigan." Johnny thought for a second, balancing his big knife on one finger, the heavy blade on one side, the silver-mounted handle on the other. "There's Bela Lugosi in the movies. He's always a monster or something. But Bela's his *first* name."

"It is my first name too. In Hungary, the first name comes last. I should have said my name is Bela Kovacs . . . that is the way you would say it here."

Johnny shook his head, as if wondering at the crazy things foreigners did—and the crazy way they must smell, to wake old Buster up and send him kiting the way he had.

Without being obvious about it, he tried to get a whiff

319

of Bela Kovacs—but he couldn't smell a thing. Well, dogs could smell lots more than people. Old Buster sure must have.

Bela Kovacs had noticed the headshake. He said a little defensively, "I talk English well, don't I?"

Johnny started to deprecate; but he said instead, honestly, "Yeah. I gotta admit, you talk pretty good."

"We have been in America for almost a year. In New York. And my father taught English to me and my mother before we came."

Johnny was working up considerable interest in his first foreigner. "You mean your father's English?"

"He is Hungarian. He had to teach himself first. It took him a long time. But he said we had to move, and America was the best place for us to go. We brought over some paintings, and my father sold them to buy the farm."

"Your father paints pitchers?"

"My grandfather painted them. He was a famous artist in Hungary."

"What d'you mean, you *had* to move?"

"We . . . we just had to. We had to move to a new country. That's what Father said." Bela Kovacs looked around at the blue summer sky, the heat-shimmering hillocks, the groves of trees that lay along the landscape like clean green cushions, the dusty road that wound through low hills to Harrisville thirty miles to the east. "I am glad we finally moved out here. I did not like New York. In Hungary, we lived in the country."

The two robins had been hopping lower and lower in the tree overhead, and now they dropped side by side from the bottom branches to the lawn, where they began searching the thick grass for insects.

One hopped to within a few feet of Bela Kovacs, who still sat with his legs curled under him in that relaxed yet curiously steel-spring position.

Suddenly the robin froze—cocked its head—regarded the boy with a startled beady eye.

Then it chirped a thin note, and both birds streaked away across the lawn as fast as they could go.

Johnny stared after them.

"I like birds," Bela Kovacs said wistfully. "I would not hurt them. I wish they liked me. I wish animals did not hate us."

Johnny began to work up even more interest in his first foreigner—because maybe it wasn't the way he smelled after all.

Because birds could hardly smell anything.

Then he noticed something funny. Bela Kovacs was still looking at the place where the robins had vanished, and Johnny saw what it was that had disturbed him about Bela's face ever since he'd first seen it.

"You have funny eyebrows," he said. "They're awful thick, and they meet in the middle. They grow all the way across."

Bela didn't look at him. The remark seemed to have brought back his shyness. He lowered his head and raised one slender hand to the side of his face, as if wanting to conceal the eyebrows.

After a second, Johnny was sorry he'd said anything.

"Heck, that's okay," he said. "Look—I haven't got any end on this finger." He held up the pinkie he'd caught in the wheel on the well two years ago.

Bela Kovacs stared at the smooth pink end and his straight bar of brows rose at the outsides.

"We're all different," Johnny said—and realized that, curiously, where he had before been teasing this new kid, he was now trying almost to console him. And he wondered, more than ever, what could be wrong with Bela Kovacs to make him act so funny. Guilty, almost—like he was ashamed of something—something he was maybe afraid people would find out.

Bela was sitting in the same position, but somehow he seemed smaller than before, like he was huddled into himself. His hand was still up to his face.

"We're all different," Johnny said again. "My dad always tells me that . . . and he says it doesn't matter. He says for me never to care where anybody comes from, or how funny they look, or anything like that. That's why I don't mind you being a foreigner. I'm sorry Buster acted the way he did."

Bela Kovacs said muffledly, "I'm *so* different."

"Naw."

"I am." Bela looked at Johnny's finger. "I was *born* different."

"Naw," Johnny said again, because he couldn't think of anything else to say. Heck, he knew Bela Kovacs *was* different—anybody could see that. And he was itching to know what the mystery was all about.

He said uncomfortably, "Want to hike or something?"

"Hike?"

"Go walking." Johnny stood up and shoved the hunting knife in his belt. "C'mon, Bela. There's lots of swell places to play—I'll show 'em to you. There's the hollow tree, and the injun fort, and—"

"A real Indian fort?" Bela said, looking up finally, dark eyes wide.

"Naw. We built it outa rocks. And there's the caves, back in the hills . . . miles of 'em. You go in through a little chink that don't look like nothin' at all, and then you flash your light around and there's walls that look like waving cloth, all pink and green and blue, and secret passages and stalatites and stagmites and holes where you can't even see the bottom they're so deep."

"That sounds wonderful," Bela Kovacs said. "Will you take me there, Johnny?"

"Sure. C'mon, I'll pick up my flashlight." Johnny started up the lawn toward the house.

Bela rose gracefully to his feet, as if the steel-spring had suddenly uncoiled, and walked a few steps after Johnny. Then he stopped and looked up at the high summer sun.

"What is the time?" he asked.

"Oh . . . 'bout three o'clock, I guess."

"Is it far—to the caves?"

"Two, three miles."

Bela looked at the grass at his feet. "I have to be home by seven o'clock."

"We can make it easy. C'mon." Johnny started off again. Bela fell into step. "Johnny—"

"Yeah?"

"I *have* to be home by seven."

"Why?"

"I . . . I just have to. My parents will be terribly angry if I'm not. We will not get lost, or go too far away, will we?"

"Heck, no. I know the caves better'n anybody." Johnny glanced sideways at Bela. "Won't your parents let you play at night? *Mine* do."

"It's—only on certain days that I can't go out at night. Certain times of the month."

"Why?"

"I can't tell you. But I have to be home by seven."

Johnny was intrigued by this new addition to the mystery. "Don't worry," he said. "Nothing'll happen."

They reached the front porch.

"Wait here," said Johnny.

He went into the house and into the kitchen, where Mom was already working on supper, because the Youngs were coming over for bridge tonight, and supper was always something special for guests.

Johnny got his flashlight from under the sink.

Mom looked up from the chicken she was stuffing. "What are you doing, dear?"

"Goin' to the caves."

Mom frowned. "I wish you'd stay away from that place, Johnny. I wish your father would do something to make you. It's so dangerous . . . they go on for miles. Suppose you got lost sometime?"

"I won't get lost," Johnny said contemptuously. "I know every inch."

"Suppose the flashlight failed?"

"Aw, Mom, don't worry . . . I'm just going to show the new kid around."

"The new kid?"

"Bela Kovacs . . . his family bought the old Burman place."

Mom looked surprised and a little pleased. "So they have a little boy! Now you'll have a new playmate. Is he a nice boy?"

Johnny juggled the flashlight. "Well, he's kinda funny. He's a foreigner from Hungry. That's in Europe. I guess he's all right."

"I'd like to meet him."

"He's right outside waitin' . . . c'mon, I'll interduce you."

Johnny started through the house toward the porch where he'd left Bela. Mom smiled and wiped her hands on a towel and followed.

They were just passing through the front room when they heard old Buster barking and snarling like he'd gone crazy.

Buster had Bela Kovacs backed against the porch steps, and was snaking back and forth in front of the boy as if he wanted to attack worse than anything else in the world, but was afraid to.

Bela's dark face had gone bone-colored, and he was half-crouched in an almost animal position, looking ready to move instantly in any direction, including straight up.

Johnny Stevens dropped over the porch-rail and lit beside Bela and shouted, "Buster! Cut it out! *Stop* it!"

Old Buster looked at him with the red-lamp eyes of a mad dog. Watery froth dripped from his stretched lips. His tail was curled so hard between his legs that it pressed up along his belly. He trembled so hard he could hardly stand—but Johnny knew that scared or not, Buster was set to attack any second.

Johnny hissed and clapped his hands in front of him, hard and fast. That meant Buster had better git, or end up with a sore rump.

Buster took a prowling, back-high, head-low step forward. His lips were so curled that his head seemed half teeth.

Mom screamed from the porch, "Johnny, come away!" and Johnny turned his head frantically to look at her, and Buster chose that moment to charge Bela Kovacs.

Then everything happened almost too fast to see.

Johnny felt a tug at his belt, where he'd stuck the hunting

knife, and saw Bela Kovacs swing the heavy blade at Buster's head.

Old Buster lost heart, and turned and ran again, howling his heart out.

Bela Kovacs screamed, *"Silver . . . the knife is silver!"* and he dropped the knife and ran off across the lawn, crying and flapping the hand he'd grabbed the knife-handle with. He turned and ran down the road, faster than Johnny had ever seen a kid run.

Johnny's mother was off the porch and on her knees, frantically examining Johnny to see if he'd been bitten; and Johnny's father drove up just then in the station wagon, craned his neck after Bela Kovacs, and asked what in hell was going on.

After supper, the grown-ups sat around and talked about the new family before starting to play bridge.

Everybody who had met either Mr. or Mrs. Kovacs seemed to like them all right—that was the consensus. Mrs. Young said that McIntyre, the grocer, who was generally looked up to as a pretty good judge of character, had let it be known yesterday that Mr. Kovacs had impressed him favorably, Mr. Kovacs had come in to stock up on food and some implements, and McIntyre had tried to pump him, and Mr. Kovacs had answered the right questions and resisted the rest pleasantly, and McIntyre had liked that.

And Mrs. Kovacs had waited outside the store in the Kovacs' '42 Dodge, and three townsladies said she looked like a nice woman, if a little foreign-looking.

And Junior Murdock, at the gas station, said that the Kovacs Dodge was in very good shape for its age, and showed signs of recent careful overhauling—and Murdoch liked people who cared for their cars, particularly old cars that someone else might lose pride in. He thought it told a lot about them.

Nobody thought them too strange, it seemed—just foreign.

Mrs. Young and Johnny's Mom decided, on the basis of the evidence, to suggest at the next meeting of the Ladies' Club that Mrs. Kovacs be invited to join.

Then the talk got around to what had happened this afternoon.

Old Buster had come back around five o'clock, sneaking out of his hideaway in the field and looking around each time before he put his paw down for a step.

While Mom and Johnny had stayed inside and watched through the front window, and Johnny had blinked back tears of worry, Dad had gone out with his pistol in one hand and coaxed Buster over to him and, with the gun to the animal's head, examined him carefully. Dad knew a lot about animals.

Old Buster wagged his tail and took a couple of laps out of the pan of water Dad carried in his other hand.

Dad came back and said, "He's okay. I don't know what got into him. There are some people animals just hate, and

I guess the Kovacs boy is one of them. It's nothing against him . . . from what Johnny says, he likes animals himself. They just don't like *him.*"

"He tried to kill Buster," Johnny said. He'd been mad about that all afternoon. "He took my knife and tried to kill Buster."

Dad said, "You shouldn't be angry about that, Johnny. It was an instinctive thing to do . . . the kid was probably scared silly. Buster was out for blood, God knows why, and Bela grabbed the knife and took a swipe in self-defense. He's probably sorry he did it."

"I don't care," Johnny said sullenly. "He tried to kill him."

Dad sighed. "It's just lucky that Buster saw the knife and lit out—and that Bela missed with the knife. Bela didn't get bitten, and Buster's all right."

"It wasn't the knife," Johnny said. "Buster ain't scared of my knife. He was scared of *Bela* . . . he ran before he even saw the knife."

"Well," Dad said, "maybe. Anyway, everything's all right now. Nothing really bad happened." He paused. "You know, I feel a little sorry for the kid . . . animals hating him like that. No wonder he acts a little strange. A kid ought to be able to have a pet. Maybe he feels a little inferior to kids who can."

But Johnny was still mad. After Dad finished talking to him, he was less mad than before—but he still resented

329

anyone taking a knife to his dog. No matter what the provocation. And *his* knife to boot.

"I wonder why he dropped the knife and ran," Mom mused. "He yelled that it was silver and acted like it burned his hand."

"Oh," Dad said, "he probably said 'sliver.' Maybe he got a sliver from the knife handle."

Johnny started to object, but let it go. His knife handle was of smooth, worn, hard wood and silver strips—he knew darned well there weren't any slivers on it. But still, he let it go. He'd settle the whole thing in his own way.

When Dad suggested that he go over the next day and apologize to Bela Kovacs for Buster's behavior, and show the new boy that nobody held his actions against him, Johnny said all right.

Because, though he knew Dad was absolutely right and it hadn't been Bela's fault, he still wanted to get back at Bela for trying to kill Buster—and he had a good idea of how to do it.

He'd scare the living daylights out of the kid—and maybe find out what the mysterious reason was why Bela had to be home every night by that time at certain times of the month.

The grownups finally started their bridge game, and Johnny went outside and sat on the porch with Buster and looked up at the big, yellow full moon that rode the night sky like a spotlight.

Buster had spent the last two hours prowling around the lawn, smelling everyplace where Bela Kovacs had walked, growling deep in his throat and every so often letting out a scared-sounding howl.

Now Johnny scratched Buster's ears, and thought about tomorrow.

It was a good idea. He'd scare Bela spitless—and then tell him why he'd done it and make friends with him again. Because Bela really wasn't a bad guy . . . he was just a little queer.

The next day Johnny took his flashlight and went over to the old Burman place around three o'clock. He went cross-country instead of down the road, and as he came out of the weed-grown cornfield that old Burman had once tended so lovingly, he saw Bela Kovacs playing in the yard by the windmill.

When Bela saw him, he stood stock-still, dark eyes wide, again with that animal look to him, as if he were ready to run.

Johnny said, "I came over to say I'm sorry Buster tried to bite you."

"Oh." Bela blinked. He had his hands cupped in front of him, about belt-level.

Johnny waited for Bela to say something else, but he didn't. Johnny looked curiously at Bela's cupped hands. "What you got?" he asked.

Bela's mouth twisted. He lifted the top hand, and Johnny

331

saw that he held a mouse. It was curled into a ball, and its mouth hung wide open—but Johnny noticed it wasn't trying to bite its way loose. Tiny black eyes glittered up in terror.

"I caught it," Bela said. "In the barn."

"What d'you want to catch a *mouse* for?" Johnny said disgustedly. "Why not get a cat?"

Bela blinked again, and Johnny suddenly wondered if Bela hadn't been just about to cry or something, before Johnny showed up, and if he wasn't holding it back now.

"I wanted to make friends with it," Bela said softly. "But it is no different in America. All the animals hate me—fear me."

"Heck, any mouse'd be scared, caught and held that way."

"Not this frightened." Bela knelt and gently placed the mouse on the ground. For a second it stayed there, a huddled gray ball—then legs erupted and it bounded off so fast that halfway to the barn it tripped and rolled over twice, and when it reached a gap between two boards in the side of the barn, it bounced off hard because of bad aim. Then it vanished, hind legs scrabbling.

"See?" said Bela. "It runs in terror. So would a cat. I have never had a pet." He straightened and gave Johnny his shy, lonely smile. "I am sorry about yesterday too, Johnny. I am sorry I tried to hurt your dog. I did not mean—"

"Aw," Johnny said uncomfortably, remembering how Dad had felt sorry for Bela last night—and remembering what he planned to do today in the caves. "Aw . . . forget it."

Bela took Johnny into the farmhouse to meet his parents.

Mr. Kovacs was a big, handsome, middle-aged man who moved the same smooth way Bela did. And Mrs. Kovacs moved that way too—Johnny noticed it the instant he came through the front door into the living room, for Bela's parents had just been finishing their lunch, and when they saw Johnny come in, they rose from the table with Old World courtesy. And with that strange animal grace.

"Father and Mother," said Bela, "this is Johnny Stevens, the boy I met yesterday."

Mr. Kovacs took Johnny's hand and shook it firmly and gently—and Johnny could tell, from the size of Mr. Kovacs' hand and the hard feel of its palm against his own, that Mr. Kovacs was very, very strong.

And a funny thing—when Johnny took his hand away, the ends of his fingers rubbed against something sort of bristly in Mr. Kovacs' hard palm. It felt almost like Dad's cheek, just after he shaved—like short whisker stubble.

But that was silly. Nobody had hair on their palms. He'd probably just felt dried skin peeling away from work calluses . . .

Mrs. Kovacs, a slim, pretty woman, nodded pleasantly and said, with an accent much more pronounced than Bela's, "How do you do, Mr. Stevens."

Johnny swelled a little. It was the first time anyone had ever called him Mr. Stevens.

"I'm pleased to meet you," he said.

"Bela has told us what happened yesterday," Mr. Kovacs said. "Please, may we add our apologies to his? It is unfortunate—but animals just do not like us. It is a peculiarity of our family."

"Heck," Johnny said. "*I* came over to apologize. And to play with Bela."

Mrs. Kovacs smiled and said almost exactly what Johnny's mother had said the day before: "How nice . . . for Bela to have such a nice boy his own age to play with."

It was Johnny's turn to smile shyly. He looked away and for the first time got a look at the inside of the Kovacs home.

The last time he'd been in this house, about three weeks ago, it had been bare walls and refuse-cluttered floors. Now there was furniture—mostly ordinary stuff. But there were some things—the round table in the middle of the room, for instance, and that big bookcase-desk against the wall—that were pretty foreign-looking. And the pictures—most of them were in fancier, heavier frames than any he'd ever seen, and a lot of them were of funny foreign buildings. And the tablecloth, and the candlesticks and lamps and the rug—oh, lots of the smaller things around the room had a foreign look. A sort of solid, warm, old look.

Mr. Kovacs, noting Johnny's interest, said in a deep bass voice. "We brought many of our things from Hungary."

"It looks nice," Johnny said.

"Thank you," said Mr. Kovacs gravely.

Mrs. Kovacs commenced to clear the table, and Johnny glanced casually at the plates . . . and when he saw what the lunch had consisted of, his jaw sagged, and he looked again.

Raw meat. A roast of beef, it looked like—except it wasn't roasted. And nothing else. A big platter of red, blood-juicy beef in the middle of the table, three red-stained plates at the chair-places, glasses, and a pitcher of water.

Again Mr. Kovacs noted Johnny's interest. Or his amazement.

"Raw meat," he said, a little heavily, "is good for the blood. We eat raw beefsteak once or twice a week, young man."

"Oh," said Johnny, trying not to stare so hard. "I guess I read about that someplace myself—'bout raw meat being good for you. But I don't think . . ." His voice trailed off.

"You do not think you would like it," Mrs. Kovacs smiled, picking up the plates. "But you are too polite to say so."

Johnny nodded uncomfortably.

"Now," said Mr. Kovacs, "come here, young man."

Johnny moved to stand before the man's chair. He didn't know exactly why—except that he felt somehow that Mr. Kovacs was a friendly man.

Mr. Kovacs looked appreciatively—almost critically—at Johnny's well-muscled arms and firm neck and clear eyes.

"You are in good health," he said.

"I . . . I guess so."

"You will make a good playmate for our Bela," Mr. Kovacs said. "He is very active. Do you know the country here?"

"I've lived here all my life."

"Good. You will tell Bela of any dangers that exist, yes?"

"Sure."

"Good. Now, Bela, why don't you show your new friend around the house?"

Mrs. Kovacs began to remove the platter of raw beef. Mr. Kovacs reached out and took one of the remaining chunks and bit into it with teeth that, when he opened his mouth wide, were startlingly long and white and, from the way the meat tore, sharp.

He chewed and looked at Johnny again, a little reflectively. Johnny and Bela were over by the bookcase by the stairs. Bela was showing Johnny what Hungarian writing looked like.

Mrs. Kovacs looked too, and her large eyes—now they were almost luminous—traveled up and down Johnny's body, along the muscular arms and legs, dwelt on the tanned throat. She licked her lips.

"In the old country . . ." she sighed in Hungarian.

"Eva," said Mr. Kovacs, softly but warningly, also in Hungarian.

"Ah, *imadot* Ferenc, I am only thinking. But *look* at him . . ."

Mr. Kovacs smiled at the expression on her face. "Sh-h, now, Eva. We have left all that behind . . . it is best not even to think."

"*Sajnos* . . ." Mrs. Kovacs picked up a small piece of beef and bit into it with teeth as long and sharp as her husband's. She sighed again. "A new country, a new life . . . I know, my dear."

"You are unhappy, Eva?"

"Unhappy?" Eva Kovacs smiled down at him, and since her lower lip concealed the points of her teeth, it was quite a pleasant smile. "Only my belly suffers. I am happy that we are safe, Ferenc."

He took her hand and pressed it against his shoulder. "The old country, the old life . . . it is impossible to live that way any longer, Eva. We are known. Not you, perhaps, nor I, nor little Bela, but *we* . . . all of us . . . known by signs familiar to the smallest child. While here—here they do not know us, or even believe in us—and we must let it remain so. We must forsake the old ways."

"You are not disappointed in America, then."

He shook his massive head. "America is best, in every way. There is no tradition to expose us. The political situation is good. And living conditions, and opportunity. No, mamma, I am well content here—except—" he put his big hands palms up on the table before him and flexed them and then slowly made fists around the clean-shaven stubble on the palms—"except at this time of the month, when the moon turns her full face to us . . ."

"Yes," said Eva Kovacs softly. "Yes."

"But beef does not taste so bad my dear. Not so bad at least, as a silver bullet."

Mrs. Kovacs popped the last of the beef into her mouth, chewed powerfully, and swallowed. She seemed to be tasting it in her throat, feeling it, almost analyzing it as it went toward her stomach. "No," she said slowly. "Once you are used to it, it is not bad. But—"

"Do not think about it, Eva."

"We cannot even chase the cow," she said softly. "We must go and buy—"

"I know."

Mrs. Kovacs looked across the room again at Johnny Stevens, and her large eyes grew larger.

"Eva," Mr. Kovacs said, a little sharply. "You would not think of—"

"No, no," she said, and licked blood from fingers which seemed to have grown just a little hairier, and the nails a little longer. "Of course not, *imadot* Ferenc. It is just when I remember . . ."

"We must forget."

"And they are so *healthy* here . . ."

"We must never *change* again, Eva. Never."

"And Bela?"

Ferenc Kovacs sighed. "He is too young yet—too young to know. We must be sure that he is always with us when he *changes*. Soon he will be old enough to control the *change*, as we do—then we must worry no longer in our new home."

338

Bela had been showing Johnny his room, which held an old posterbed, a very old maple bureau, and a carved chest full of fascinating toys such as Johnny had never seen before.

Now the boys came back to the living room, and Bela said, "Mother, we are going out to play."

"All right, Bela. But remember—come home before seven o'clock."

"Yes, mamma."

"You know what time of the month this is, don't you?"

"Yes, mamma." Bela looked uncomfortably at Johnny. "I will be back."

"You *must*," said Mr. Kovacs. "Just as you did in New York. You know why, Bela . . ." He turned to Johnny. "You will not keep our Bela out late, will you? You see—he is not well . . . that is why it is very important that he return home before nightfall."

"Oh," said Johnny. "I'll be careful. I mean, I'll . . . I won't . . ." And he looked away in confusion, thinking of what he planned to do in the cave.

Mr. Kovacs' big eyes were still on his face when he looked up, and Johnny felt they were looking right through his own eyes at the inside of his skull.

"I think," said Mr. Kovacs, "that you had better be."

Bela's parents came to the door and stood in the sunshine, and as Johnny and Bela turned to wave at them from the edge of the cornfield, Johnny noticed for the first time that their eyebrows were just like Bela's—straight, thick bars of hair that ran right across their foreheads.

The entrance to the caves was just a black chink in the rocks on the hillside. They climbed up toward it, leaping from one big boulder to the next under the afternoon sun.

They reached the black hole, and felt the coolness of it on their faces, even in the sunshine.

Bela hung back when Johnny started to go right in.

"Johnny . . ." he said.

"Yeah?"

"Don't forget . . . I *have* to be back before seven."

Johnny put his hands on his hips. "Well, f'gosh sakes, yes! I heard it enough. What's so awful that'll happen to you if you don't? D'you have to take medicine or something?"

Bela shook his head. "I can't tell you. But . . . you won't get lost or anything, will you?"

"No," said Johnny emphatically, crossing his fingers behind his back.

"You heard what my parents said . . . I have to be home before the moon rises."

"The *moon!* What's the moon got to do with it?"

Bela just looked nervously at the black hole in the hillside.

And Johnny didn't ask about it again. He just sniffed. "The moon, f'gosh sakes!" as if he were dismissing it as something else crazy that foreigners—especially Hungarians—worried about. Because he knew he had a better way of finding out.

"Johnny . . . perhaps I had better not go in. Not now."

Johnny put a jeer in his voice. "Scared?"

"Not for the reasons you think," Bela said, dark eyes flashing. "You do not understand."

"Well, come on, then . . . I promise—" the crossed fingers again—"I won't get lost."

Johnny started again into the black chink. Bela hesitated for a second, and then followed.

Actually, Johnny thought, as they made their way through the narrow fissure into increasing darkness, the crossed fingers weren't necessary—because he wasn't planning to really get lost; only to *pretend* to get lost.

And he wasn't sure he was going to do even that, now—not if Bela was *sick*. That was different. Maybe it explained a lot—even old Buster's behavior. Dogs sometimes got funny around sick people.

But he wasn't sure that that *was* the explanation. It sounded a little fishy to him. Why all the mystery, if Bela was just sick? Or was it some awful-to-*gosh* disease? If so, why was Bela let out to play and maybe give the disease to someone else? And Mr. Kovacs had said that Bela was very active. That didn't sound like he was sick. And Bela sure didn't look sick.

Johnny decided he'd wait and decide what to do later.

The floor of the chink dipped down and turned at a right angle, and they were inside the caves.

Johnny turned on his flashlight. And heard Bela gasp.

All around them were curtains and draperies and carpets and fountains of stone—gray, pink, blue, green, lavender, stretching from where they stood to a sharp sixty-foot down-slope ahead of them, which led to the cave floor below and off into inky shadows that looked almost like solids.

Johnny played the beam of light around, giving Bela a good look at everything worth seeing here near the entrance. Then he said, "Let's start down."

They made their way across ripples of pastel-shaded stone to where the down-slope began. The sounds they made started to echo, and the air was very dry and cool.

The beam of the flashlight was hard and bright, and the blackness pressed in on it as if trying to squash it down to pencil-thinness—but the beam moved like lightning, cutting like a knife, and wherever it opened the blackness it revealed wonders of color and shape.

"The waves in the slope make steps," Johnny said, pointing the light downward. "See? We can go down that way. How do you like it?"

"It is beautiful," Bela whispered.

They started down, Johnny keeping the light always on their footing and guiding their progress down the face of rock by familiar rippling formations and splashes of color.

At last they reached the bottom, and Johnny said, "This way."

As they started across the uneven floor of the cave, Bela asked, "Do you know the time, Johnny?"

" 'Bout four . . . you got lotsa time."

And soon the caves became so beautiful that Bela forgot entirely to worry about the time.

They passed fountains and sprays and mists and museums of stone, gleaming with colors purer and more delicate than any ever seen on Earth's surface. They passed marching stalagmites of green and blue and bright orange, here and there united with drooping stalactites to form arching passageways and gardens of pillars. They moved slowly beneath walls of rippled stone, as if blue or pink or purple lava had been frozen in midflow.

They passed lakes of blue-black water, so still and smooth that one had almost to touch them to be convinced that they weren't glass.

They moved up vast slopes of colored stone, like insects up a giant Christmas tree ornament, and when they reached the top, Johnny would select this dark passage or that and lead them on into royal chambers of purple and white, and then up a curving crimson staircase to a balcony of coral, pink and green, where more passages offered further mysteries to be explored.

They moved along the edges of crevices so deep that a penny dropped made no sound—not even the whisper of an echo.

Once Johnny turned off his light and told Bela to stand still, and they listened to the silence which cannot be qualified, the silence which is absolute—the silence that exists only underground.

They heard their own hearts beating.

At last Johnny was sure the time must be about six o'clock. "We'd better get started back," he told Bela. "If you're going to get home by seven. This way."

And he led the way back to the place where they had entered the caves. And there he pretended to get lost.

It was easy. Bela was new to the caves. He probably wouldn't recognize the entrance even if Johnny flashed his light up the long slope right to the chink where they'd come in.

Johnny wasn't sure yet whether he wanted to keep up the pretense for more than a few minutes—maybe he'd just throw a short scare into Bela, and then take him on out of the caves so he could go home by seven. After all, if Bela was sick . . .

But he wasn't sure about that. It still sounded fishy. And he was more curious than ever to know what the mystery was all about—even if it *was* some kind of disease.

He said worriedly, "Bela . . . I . . . I'm not sure which way we go from here. I think maybe I'm lost . . ."

And he looked to see what effect it would have on the Hungarian boy.

Bela's eyes grew huge. "Oh, *no* . . . Johnny, you do not mean it! You *promised!*"

Johnny pretended to be confused—even afraid. "I . . . I'm sorry," he stammered. "I just lost the way. I was so interested showing you around. Gosh, Bela—"

"But, Johnny, I *have* to get out. I have to get home before . . ."

"Come on," Johnny said, making his voice worried. "Maybe . . . maybe it's this way."

And he led Bela in a huge circle through the pillars and passages and hanging stone curtains that surrounded the entrance. It took about half an hour, and then they were right back where they'd started from—within a hundred feet of the entrance.

Johnny said, "I just don't know where we *are!*"

"What time do you think it is?" Bela asked, his voice terrified.

"Six-thirty, about."

Bela shuddered and looked at Johnny, his eyes shining enormously in the light. "Johnny, I have to get *out* . . ."

Johnny put panic in his voice. "Well, what can *I* do? I'm sorry! I'm scared too! Maybe we'll *never* get out!"

"Try," Bela begged. "Try, Johnny . . . can't you remember the way?"

Looking at Bela in the light, at the big dark eyes and smooth brown skin and white straight teeth and lithe body, Johnny decided abruptly that the story about Bela's being sick must be phony. It was something *else*—there was some other reason why Bela was so frantic about being home by seven, and why his parents were so emphatic on the same point. Some real strange, funny reason—and Johnny wanted to know what.

He decided to do as he'd originally planned—keep Bela down here and watch to see what happened.

He turned around as if in indecision. "I think . . . I think maybe it's off this way. Come on!"

And he led Bela in a circle the other way around, by a

slightly different route, and they ended up by the entrance again.

Johnny knew it must be nearly seven by now. He kept a sharp eye on Bela while pretending to search for the entrance chink that was really right up the slope over their heads.

Would Bela know, somehow, when seven o'clock had arrived? And was it something that would happen to him right at seven that he was afraid of? But how could he know the time? . . . and what could happen down here in the caves? Or was it something his parents would do to him later, as punishment for not getting home by that time?

"Johnny!" Bela said suddenly, close by Johnny in the blackness, a quaver in his voice.

Johnny stopped his pretense of searching, and put the beam of light on Bela. "Yeah?"

Bela was trembling all over, and he was looking up at the roof of the cave. As Johnny watched, he hunched his shoulders a little—sort of cringed—and his face got even tighter, as if he saw something horrible coming at him right down through the blackness, the solid rock.

"It is almost seven . . . Johnny . . . *do something* . . . it is going to *happen!*"

"What's going to happen? *What* can I do?"

"I do not know," Bela cried, and echoes came back, *I do not know, do not know* . . .

"You don't know what I can do?"

"I do not know . . ." . . . *do notknow, notknow, know, know* . . .

"You don't know what's going to happen?"

"I do not know! I am frightened . . . it never happened to me away from home before . . . Johnny, you *promised* . . . ah, mamma, mamma, *mamma*—" and Bela began to cry. He sank to a heap on the colored stone floor, and tears rolled down his cheeks and splashed on the stone and made the colors deeper, and he wailed things in Hungarian until he could hardly talk any more but just cried.

"You don't know what's going to happen?" Johnny asked, amazed.

Bela choked trying to talk, and coughed hard, and the echoes came back like footsteps across his frantic voice. "Yes, I know—but I do not know what it is, or why, it just *happens* . . . ah, mamma, *mamma* . . ."

Suddenly his back stiffened, and his hands clawed out in front of him. His streaming eyes rolled up to Johnny's face. He whined like an animal. "Johnny . . . it is seven . . . the moon is rising . . . I can feel it . . ."

"*Feel* the moon? Down *here?* How can—"

"It does not matter where . . . I can *feel* it . . . I can feel . . . mamma, mamma—ah, ah, *ah!*"

And Bela's face twisted into an expression of such terror and agony that Johnny was suddenly chilled—and he decided that his joke had gone far enough. In fact, all of a sudden he was pretty darned scared—he hadn't expected anything like this! Golly, if Bela really *was* sick . . .

He bent over the huddled figure on the cave floor and pointed his flashlight upward.

"Bela, look!" he said loudly. "Look up there . . . *there's* where we came in! Come on—let's go out!"

Bela didn't answer.

"Bela . . . *c'mon.*"

Bela moved, and his fingernails scratched the rock so hard it sounded like they'd tear off.

Johnny began to tremble. He looked down, the flashlight still pointing up.

Bela's eyes gleamed up at him from the floor—enormous, yellowish in the reflected light, glassy, fixed—somehow baleful.

As Johnny watched, they seemed to move closer together and get yellower.

Johnny was so startled he dropped the flashlight. It thumped on the stone at his feet, and glass broke and the light went out.

In the blackness—the utter thick blackness—Johnny heard a scuffling sound near his feet, and a low, soft, animal snarl.

He yelled and leaped back. His foot struck the flashlight, and even as he went down he got one hand on it, and with the other hand he dragged his big hunting knife out of his belt. He hit hard on his side. He pressed the flashlight button and prayed that it would work.

It did.

Bela was gone.

Wide-eyed, Johnny rolled over. Kneeling there, he darted the light this way and that. Finally he found his voice.

"B-Bela . . ." he quavered.

Nothing happened.

He got to his feet and stood shaking. "Bela?"

There was a claws-on-stone sound from the blackness behind him.

He whirled, his neck stiff and cold, and lashed the beam of light across the shadows. He held his hunting knife hard, the point straight out, ready to stab or slice from almost any angle.

At first he saw nothing. Rocks. Curtains and pillars of colored stone. Black shadows that seemed to lean toward him.

Then a low shadow moved at the corner of his vision. He swung the light that way.

Two yellow eyes, low against the stone floor, blazed back at him.

"B-Bela?" Johnny whispered, and lifted the light so that it shone directly on the possessor of the eyes.

The creature slitted the eyes and snarled to reveal sharp white fangs and charged.

Mr. and Mrs. Kovacs were looking both furious and terrified at the same time. They stood by the big table in the living room, where they'd been sitting playing some kind of game with big colored cards, when Johnny came bursting in to tell them what had happened in the caves.

"I'm sorry," Johnny said, for the dozenth time—and wiped a hand across his tear-stained cheeks.

"I didn't mean to do it . . . it was just a joke. Please, call Sheriff Morris and ask him to get a posse out . . . they'll find Bela, honest they will!"

Mr. Kovacs' large eyes were brilliant with anger—and his deep voice was almost a snarl. "*I* will go look for Bela, young man—and you had better go home. I do not think we want to see you any more!"

Johnny turned miserably toward the door.

There was a growl from the darkness right outside.

Mrs. Kovacs gasped, "*Bela . . .*"

The creature came panting through the open door and made a beeline for Johnny's leg.

Johnny said, "It isn't Bela . . . it's that darned wolf cub!"

He dodged and dropped to one knee and cuffed the cub playfully on the side of the head.

It snarled like a lapdog and backed off and put its belly against the floor. Its tiny ears were flat against its head, just as old Buster's had been when he'd first seen Bela, and its yellow eyes gleamed hungrily on Johnny's throat.

It charged again, stubby legs pumping.

Johnny caught it neatly by the scruff of the neck and shook it gently. It snapped and snarled and waved its legs.

"I'll be darned," he said, forgetting for the moment that Mr. Kovacs had practically ordered him out of the house. "The little feller must've followed me here . . ."

"You saw the little wolf tonight?" Mr. Kovacs said

350

sharply, eyes widening and glowing a little brighter.

"Sure. In the cave. Just after Bela ran off. It tried to bite me then too, and now it followed me all the way to your place." Johnny grinned feebly, looking from Mr. Kovacs' rather grim face to Mrs. Kovacs' somehow relieved one. "I guess it wants to eat me or something."

"I suppose," said Mr. Kovacs heavily, "it does."

"I'll take it outside and turn it loose again," Johnny said.

"Again?"

The cub swung from Johnny's grasp, rolling its yellow eyes hungrily at the nearest finger. Johnny nodded. "I carried it up out of the caves, after I gave up hollering for Bela. Figured it wasn't right to let it die down there. Maybe when it gets older, I'll shoot it if I see it . . . but now I figured to give it a chance, it's so young."

"Oh, give him to me, young man," said Mrs. Kovacs. "He's so cute!" And she took the wolf cub from Johnny's arms before Johnny could protest it was dangerous, and cuddled it in her own. It whined and looked up at her with its big yellow eyes, and didn't struggle at all to free itself.

Johnny was too unhappy to wonder at that, though, or even notice it.

"Now go home, young man," said Mr. Kovacs.

Johnny turned to the door again. "Will you turn it loose afterwards, Mr. Kovacs? You won't kill it, will you?"

"I will not kill it."

"And you better call the sheriff to help you look for Bela.

I'll help too, if . . . if you want. I know the caves like—"

"Bela will be all right," Mr. Kovacs said.

"When you find him, will you please tell him I'm sorry for what I did?"

"Yes."

Johnny had reached the front door when Mrs. Kovacs said something soft in Hungarian, and Mr. Kovacs grunted and said, "Young man."

Johnny turned. "Yes, sir?"

The wolf cub was on the table, and Mr. Kovacs was thoughtfully scratching the scruff of its neck.

"Young man," Mr. Kovacs said slowly. "I do not want to be harsh. I have thought it over. What you did was not very nice—but I think it is understandable. I think it may be forgiven. And you came to us immediately and told us about it—and now you have offered to help undo what you have done."

"Yes, sir?"

"You may come here as often as you wish, and play with our Bela."

Johnny brightened. "Yes, sir! Thank you!"

"Provided you never do anything like that again."

"Yes, sir. I mean, no, sir!"

"Now," said Mr. Kovacs a little intently. "I would like to make absolutely certain of what happened in the cave. It happened like this, yes? Our Bela became sick; you dropped your flashlight; when you turned the light on again, Bela was gone."

"That's right, sir."

"You did *not* see where Bela went."

"No, sir."

"And then you saw the little wolf."

"Uh, huh." Johnny grinned. "It was a dope to wander in there. Lucky I came along."

"M'm," said Mr. Kovacs. "Yes." His eyes, which had become a little larger as he questioned Johnny, lost some of their wary glow; and his fingers, which had become just a tiny bit hairier, relaxed. "Now, you had better go. I will . . . find Bela. Good night, young man."

"Good night, Mr. Kovacs. Good night, Mrs. Kovacs."

As Johnny turned to leave again, Mr. Kovacs said, "Another thing, young man."

Johnny paused.

"I was not entirely truthful with you. Our Bela is not really sick. It is just that at certain times of the month, he is expected to be home before nightfall because . . . well, I believe you might call it a custom. A Hungarian custom. An old family custom. It must be observed. Do you understand?"

"Yes, sir."

"We will not tell Bela what you did . . . if you will promise never to tell anyone what happened tonight."

"Yes, sir."

"We would not want to be thought queer by our neighbors. After all, young man, customs differ. We are all of us different."

"Yes, sir. My father taught me that."

"Did he teach you to keep promises?"

Johnny grinned. "He licks me when I don't."

"Do you promise, then?"

"Yes."

"You will make a good playmate for our Bela, as I said. Good night, young man."

Smiling, Johnny Stevens left. When he reached the edge of the cornfield, he began to whistle at the full moon overhead. He wondered if the moon always rose at seven in Hungary . . .

Naw. Maybe it was just a time set so Bela would always be home before it happened, and observe whatever the custom was. But, heck, lots of times the moon rose earlier than seven. Even the full moon, like tonight—it always rose when the sun set. Four o'clock sometimes, in winter.

Maybe—Johnny nodded, remembering something from school—maybe the Kovacs figured the time for Bela to be home by the seasons, by the months. Even by the—the—latitudes.

What a funny custom. Maybe someday Bela would tell him about it . . .

Mr. Kovacs looked thoughtfully at his son.

"We could have lost all," he told his wife, "but for a boy dropping a flashlight. Our new country is good to us. Now—the time has come when we must tell Bela what he is."

Optical Illusion

by Mack Reynolds

In acquiring followers, it is not always wise to depend upon blind faith.

Molly brought my plate, silver, and side dishes and placed them before me without fuss or comment. I was an old customer, and one of the things I liked about Molly was that she never fussed over me.

I usually make a practice of eating after the rush hour, but today I was early and the restaurant crowded. It was only a matter of time before someone would want to share my table.

I didn't look up when he asked, "Is this seat taken?" His voice was high, almost to the point of shrillness, in spite of his attempt to control it.

"No," I told him, "go right ahead."

He hung his cane, or umbrella, whatever it was, over the back of his chair and fumbled his hat underneath it before climbing to his seat. Then he picked up the menu from where it stood between the catsup and napkins.

"Nothing fit to eat," he muttered finally.

I said, "The pot pie is quite good today."

Molly came up and he said to her, "I'll have the swiss steak, miss. Green peas, french fries. I'll decide on the dessert later."

"Coffee?"

"Milk."

I don't know what it was that first gave me the idea that the person seated across the table from me wasn't a midget at all. Not a midget or dwarf, but a child pretending adulthood and doing a fantastically good job of it. As I say, I don't know what it was that gave me the hint, possibly I'm more susceptible to such intuitiveness than the next man.

But whatever it was, he knew almost as soon as I did.

That is, he knew that I'd caught on to him, and somehow it frightened me. The whole idea was so bizarre—a child, not yet in his teens, passing himself off, for some reason of his own, as a mature, if stunted, adult.

"So," he said, his shrill voice almost a hiss. He put down his fork. "So . . ."

How can I describe that cold voice? The voice of a child . . . but not a child. Not a child as we know one.

I reached for the sugar, which was there where it always is at the end of the table next to the salt and pepper and the mustard jar. I measured out a spoonful very carefully without looking up at him. As I have said, somehow I was afraid.

He said, still softly, "So at last a stupid human has penetrated my disguise."

A *human,* he had said.

His voice was a child's, but his words dug into me viciously. "Ah, so that surprises you, my curious friend. You wonder, eh?" There was a sneering quality now, a contemptuous overtone.

I cleared my throat, tried to cover my confusion by taking a gulp of the coffee. "I don't know what you mean . . . sir."

He chuckled and mimicked, "I don't know what you mean . . . sir." Then his voice snapped over at me, even as he kept his tone low. "Why did you hesitate before adding the *sir,* eh? Why?" He didn't wait for an answer. "I'll tell you why. Because somehow you've discovered that my age is less than I would have it known."

He was boiling with rage, and in spite of his size and the public nature of our whereabouts, I was afraid of him. Why, I didn't know. Somehow I sensed that—impossibly— he could destroy me at will.

I fumbled my cup back into its saucer, kept my face averted.

"You're terrified," he snapped again. "You recognize your master even as you wonder about him."

"My master?" I said. Who did he think . . .

"Your master," he repeated. "Mankind's master. The new race. The super-race, *Homo Superior,* if you will. He is here, my snooping friend, and you, you and your stupid nation-divided, race-divided, class-divided, religion-divided humanity will never stand before him."

It was hard for me to assimilate. I had come into my

favorite restaurant for my midday meal. It had been a routine day, and I had expected it to continue as one. Now, I had been startled so many times in the past few minutes that I felt I was in a state of shock.

"Oh, it's been suggested before," he went on, seemingly welcoming this opportunity to explain to me, to gloat over me. "The possibility that mutations would develop, a super-race, a super-humanity as far above man as man is above the ape."

"How . . . what . . ."

He cut me off. "What difference if it was the atomic bomb, laboratory experiments, or only nature's continual plodding advance? The fact remains, we are here, a considerable number of us, and in a few years, when we have developed our full capacities, man will hear from us. Ah, how he will hear!"

Long ago an icy hand had gripped my heart. Now it squeezed.

"Why," I stumbled. "Why tell me all this? Surely you wouldn't disguise yourself if you didn't wish to keep it all a secret."

He laughed mockingly. There was still much of the immature in him, super-race or nay.

"Because it doesn't make any difference," he whispered. "None at all. Ten minutes from now, you will remember nothing of this conversation. Hypnotism, my stupid *Homo sapiens,* can be a developed art when practiced on the lower orders."

His voice went hard and incisive. "Look up into my eyes," e ordered.

I had no power to resist. Slowly my face came up. I ould *feel* his eyes drill into mine.

"This you will forget," he ordered. "All of this conversa-ion, all of this experience, you will forget."

He came to his feet, took his time about securing his hings, and then left.

Molly came over later. "Gee," she said, "that little midget hat was just here, he sure tips good."

"I would imagine," I told her. I was still shaken. "He robably has a substantial source of income."

"Oh," Molly said, making conversation as she cleaned up. "You been talking to him?"

"Yes," I told her, "we had quite a discussion." I added houghtfully, "And as a result I have duties to perform."

I came to my own feet and reached up for my hat and cane, where they hung on their usual hook.

I thought: *possibly man has more of a chance than these hidden enemies realize. Mental powers beyond us they may have, although they would seem lacking in the more kindly qualities. But this one hadn't been as sharp as he liked to think himself. Hypnotic powers he might possess beyond our understanding, but that didn't prevent him from making a very foolish error. He hadn't caught on to the fact that I'm blind.*

Idiot's Crusade

by *Clifford D. Simak*

Is he good or is he bad? Read his story and decide.

For a long time I was the village idiot, but not any longer—although they call me "dummy" still and even worse than that.

I'm a genius now, but I won't let them know.

Not ever.

If they found out, they'd be on their guard against me.

No one has suspected me and no one will. My shuffle is the same and my gaze as vacant and my mumblings just as vague as they ever were. At times, it has been hard to remember to keep the shuffle and the gaze and mumblings as they were before, times when it was hard not to overdo them. But it's important not to arouse suspicion.

It all started the morning I went fishing.

I told Ma I was going fishing while we were eating breakfast, and she didn't object. She knows I like fishing. When I fish, I don't get into trouble.

"All right, Jim," she said. "Some fish will taste real good."

"I know where to get them," I told her. "That hole in the creek just past Alf Adams' place."

"Now don't you get into any fracas with Alf," Ma warned me. "Just because you don't like him—"

"He was mean to me. He worked me harder than he should have. And he cheated me out of my pay. And he laughs at me."

I shouldn't have said that, because it hurts Ma when I say someone laughs at me.

"You mustn't pay attention to what people do," said Ma, speaking kind and gentle. "Remember what Preacher Martin said last Sunday. He said—"

"I know what he said, but I still don't like being laughed at. People shouldn't laugh at me."

"No," Ma agreed, looking sad. "They shouldn't."

I went on eating my breakfast, thinking that Preacher Martin was a great one to be talking about humility and patience, knowing the kind of man he was, and how he was carrying on with Jennie Smith, the organist. He was a great one to talk about anything at all.

After breakfast, I went out to the woodshed to get my fishing tackle, and Bounce came across the street to help me. After Ma, Bounce is the best friend I have. He can't talk to me, of course—not actually, that is—but neither does he laugh at me.

I talked to him while I was digging worms and asked

him if he wanted to go fishing with me. I could see h
did, so I went across the street to tell Mrs. Lawson tha
Bounce was going along. He belonged to her, but he spen
most of his time with me.

We started out, me carrying my cane pole and all m
fishing stuff, and Bounce walking at my heels, as if I wer
someone he was proud to be seen walking with.

We went past the bank, where Banker Patton was sittin
in the big front window, working at his desk and lookin
like the most important man in all of Mapleton, which h
was. I went by slow so I could hate him good.

Ma and me wouldn't be living in the old tumbledow
house we're living in if Banker Patton hadn't foreclose
on our home after Pa died.

We went out past Alf Adams' place, which is the firs
farm out of town, and I hated him some, too, but not a
hard as Banker Patton. All Alf had done was work m
harder than he should have, then cheat me of my pay.

Alf was a big, blustery man and a good enough farmer
I guess—at least he made it pay. He had a big new barn
and it's just like him not to paint it red, the way any prope
barn is painted, but white with red trim. Who ever hear
of paint trim on a barn?

Just beyond Alf's place, Bounce and I turned off the roa
and went down across the pasture, heading for the big hol
in the creek.

Alf's prize Hereford bull was way off in another corne

362

of the pasture with the rest of the stock. When he saw us, he started coming for us, not mean or belligerent, but just investigating and ready for a fight if one was offered him. I wasn't afraid of him, because I'd made friends with him that summer I had worked for Alf. I used to pet him and scratch behind his ears. Alf said I was a crazy fool and someday the bull would kill me.

"You can never trust a bull," Alf said.

When the bull was near enough to see who it was, he knew we meant no harm, so he went back across the pasture again.

We got to the hole and I started fishing, while Bounce went up the stream to do some investigating. I caught a few fish, but they weren't very big and they weren't biting very often and I got disinterested. I like to fish, but to keep my interest up, I have to catch some.

So I got to daydreaming. I began wondering if you marked off a certain area of ground—a hundred feet square, say—and went over it real careful, how many different kinds of plants you'd find. I looked over a patch of ground next to where I was sitting, and I could see just ordinary pasture grass and some dandelions and some dock and a couple of violets and a buttercup which didn't have any flowers as yet.

Suddenly, when I was looking at the dandelion, I realized I could see *all* that dandelion, not just the part that showed above the ground!

* * *

I don't know how long I'd been seeing it that way before realizing it. And I'm not certain that "seeing" is the right word. Maybe "know" would be better. I *knew* how that dandelion's big taproot went down into the ground and how the little feathery roots grew out of it, and I knew where all the roots were, how they were taking water and chemicals out of the ground, how reserve food was stored in the root and how the dandelion used the sunlight to convert its food into a form it could use. And the funniest thing about it was that I had never known any of it before.

I looked at the other plants, and I could see all of them the same way. I wondered if something had gone wrong with my eyes and if I would have to go around looking into things instead of at them, so I tried to make the new seeing go away and it did.

Then I tried to see the dandelion root again and I saw it, just the way I had before.

I sat there, wondering why I had never been able to see that way before and why I was able to now. And while I was wondering, I looked into the pool and tried to see down into the pool and I could, just as plain as day. I could see clear to the bottom of it and into all the corners of it, and there were lunkers lying in there, bigger than any fish that ever had been taken from the creek.

I saw that my bait was nowhere near any of the fish, so I moved it over until it was just in front of the nose of one of the biggest ones. But the fish didn't seem to see it, or if he did, he wasn't hungry, for he just lay there, fanning the water with his fins and making his gills work.

I moved the bait down until it bumped his nose, but he still didn't pay any attention to it.

So I made the fish hungry.

Don't ask me how I did it. I can't tell you. I all at once knew I could and just how to do it. So I made him hungry and he went for that bait like Bounce grabbing a bone.

He pulled the cork clear under, and I heaved on the pole and hoisted him out. I took him off the hook and put him on the stringer, along with the four or five little ones I'd caught.

Then I picked out another big fish and lowered my bait down to him and made him hungry.

In the next hour and a half, I just about cleaned out all the big fish. There were some little ones left, but I didn't bother with them. I had the stringer almost full, and I couldn't carry it in my hand, for then the fish would have dragged along the ground. I had to sling it over my shoulder, and those fish felt awfully wet.

I called Bounce and we went back to town.

Everyone I met stopped and had a look at my fish and wanted to know where I'd got them and what I'd caught them on and if there were any left or had I taken them all. When I told them I'd taken all there was, they laughed fit to kill.

I was just turning off Main Street, on my way home, when Banker Patton stepped out of the barbershop. He smelled nice from the bottles of stuff that Jake, the barber, uses on his customers.

He saw me with my fish and stopped in front of me. He looked at me and looked at the fish, and he rubbed his fat hands together. Then he said, like he was talking to a child, "Why, Jimmy, where did you get all those fish?" He sounded a little bit, too, like I might not have a right to them and probably had used some low-down trick to get them.

"Out in the hole on Alf's place," I told him.

All at once, without even trying to do it, I saw him the same way I had seen the dandelion—his stomach and intestines and something that must have been his liver—and up above them all, surrounded by a doughy mass of pink, a pulsating thing that I knew must be his heart.

I guess that's the first time anybody ever *really* hated someone else's guts.

I shot out my hands—well, not my hands, for one was clutching the cane pole and the other was busy with the fish—but it felt almost exactly as if I'd put them out and grabbed his heart and squeezed it hard.

He gasped once, then sighed and wilted, like all the starch had gone out of him, and I had to jump out of the way so he wouldn't bump into me when he fell.

He never moved after he hit the ground.

Jake came running out of his barbershop.

"What happened to him?" he asked me.

"He just fell over," I said.

Jake looked at him. "It's a heart attack. I'd know it anywhere. I'll run for Doc."

He took off up the street for Doc Mason while other people came hurrying out of the places along the street.

There was Ben from the cheese factory and Mike from the pool hall and a couple of farmers who were in the general store.

I got out of there and went on home, and Ma was pleased with the fish.

"They'll taste real good," she said, looking at them. "How did you come to catch that many, Jim?"

"They were biting good," I said.

"Well, you hurry up and clean them. We'll have to eat some right away, and I'll take some over to Preacher Martin's, and I'll rub salt in the others and put them in the cellar where it's good and cool. They'll keep for several days."

Just then, Mrs. Lawson ran across the street and told Ma about Banker Patton.

"He was talking to Jim when it happened," she told Ma.

Ma said to me, "Why didn't you tell me, Jim?"

"I never got around to it," I said. "I was showing you these fish."

So the two of them went on talking about Banker Patton, and I went out to the woodshed and cleaned the fish. Bounce sat alongside me and watched me do it, and I swear he was as happy over those fish as I was, just like he might have had a hand in catching them.

Now I don't want you to think I'm trying to make you believe Bounce actually talked, because he didn't. But it was just as if he'd said those very words.

"It was a nice day, Bounce," I said, and Bounce said he'd thought so, too. He recalled running up and down the stream and how he'd chased a frog and the good smell there was when he stuck his nose down to the ground and sniffed.

People all the time are laughing at me and making cracks about me and trying to bait me because I'm the village idiot, but there are times when the village idiot has it over all of them. They would have been scared they were going crazy if a dog talked to them, but I didn't think it was strange at all. I just thought how much nicer it was now that Bounce could talk and how I wouldn't have to guess at what he wanted to say. I never thought it was queer at all, because I always figured Bounce could talk if he only tried, being a smart dog.

So Bounce and I sat there and talked while I cleaned the fish. When I came out of the woodshed, Mrs. Lawson had gone home, and Ma was in the kitchen, getting a skillet ready to cook some of the fish.

"Jim, you . . ." she hesitated, then went on, "Jim, you didn't have anything to do with what happened to Banker

'atton, did you? You didn't push him or hit him or any-
hing?"

"I never even touched him," I said, and that was true.
certainly hadn't touched him.

In the afternoon, I went out and worked in the garden.
Ma does some housework now and then, and that brings
in some money, but we couldn't get along if it wasn't for
the garden. I used to work some, but since the fight I had
with Alf over him not paying me, she don't let me work
for anyone. She says if I take care of the garden and catch
some fish, I'm helping out enough.

Working in the garden, I found a different use for my
new way of seeing. There were worms in the cabbages, and
I could see every one of them, and I killed them all by
squeezing them, the way I'd squeezed Banker Patton. I
found a cloudy sort of stuff on some of the tomato plants
and I suppose it was some kind of virus, because it was
so small I could hardly see it at first. So I magnified it
and could see it fine, and I made it go away. I didn't squeeze
it like I did the worms. I just made it go away.

It was fun working in the garden, when you could look
down into the ground and see how the parsnips and radishes
were coming and could kill the cutworms you found there
and know just how the soil was and if everything was all
right.

We'd had fish for lunch and we had fish again for sup-

369

per, and after supper, I went for a walk.

Before I knew it, I was walking by Banker Patton's place and, going past, I felt the grief inside the house.

I stood out on the sidewalk and let the grief come into me. I suppose that outside any house in town, I could have felt just as easily whatever was going on inside, but I hadn' known I could and I hadn't tried. It was only because the grief in the Patton house was so deep and strong that I noticed it.

The banker's oldest daughter was upstairs in her room and I could feel her crying. The other daughter was sitting with her mother in the living room and neither of them was crying, but they seemed lost and lonely. There were other people in the house, but they weren't very sad. Some neighbors, probably, who'd come in to keep the family company.

I felt sorry for the three of them, and I wanted to help them. Not that I'd done anything wrong in killing Banker Patton, but I felt sorry for those women, because, after all, it wasn't their fault the way Banker Patton was, so I stood there, wishing I could help them.

And all at once I felt that perhaps I could, and I tried first with the daughter who was upstairs in her room. I reached out to her, and I told her happy thoughts. It wasn't easy to start with, but pretty soon I got the hang of it, and it wasn't hard to make her happy. Then I made the other two happy and went on my way, feeling better about what I'd done to the family.

I listened in on the houses I passed. Most of them were happy, or at least contented, though I found a couple that were sad. Automatically, I reached out my mind and gave them happiness. It wasn't that I felt I should do something good for any particular person. To tell the truth, I don't remember which houses I made happy. I just thought if I was able to do a thing like that, I should do it. It wasn't right for someone to have that kind of power and refuse to use it.

Ma was sitting up for me when I got home. She was looking kind of worried, the way she always does when I disappear for a long time and she don't know where I am.

I went up to my room and got into bed and lay awake for a long time, wondering how come I could do all the things I could and how, suddenly, today I was able to do them when I'd never been able to before. But finally I went to sleep.

The situation is not ideal, of course, but a good deal better than I had any reason to expect. It is not likely that one should find on every alien planet, a host so made to order for our purpose as is this one of mine.

It has accepted me without recognizing me, has made no attempt to deny itself to me or to reject me. It is of an order of intelligence which has enabled it, quickly and efficiently, to make use of those most-readily manipulated of my abilities,

371

and this has aided me greatly in my observations. It is fairly mobile and consorts freely with its kind, which are other distinct advantages.

I reckon myself fortunate, indeed, to have found so satisfactory a host so soon upon arrival.

When I got up and had breakfast, I went outside and found Bounce waiting for me. He said he wanted to go and chase some rabbits, and I agreed to go along. He said since we could talk now, we ought to make a good team. I could stand up on a stump or a pile of rocks or even climb a tree, so I could overlook the ground and see the rabbit and yell out to him which way it was going, and he could intercept it.

We went up the road toward Alf's place, but turned off down across the pasture, heading for some cutover land on the hill across the creek.

When we were off the road, I turned around to give Alf a good hating, and while I was standing there, hating him, a thought came into my mind. I didn't know if I could do it, but it seemed to be a good idea, so I tried.

I moved my seeing up to Alf's barn and went right through and came out in the middle of the haymow, with hay packed all around me. But all the time, you understand, I was standing out there in the pasture with Bounce, on our way to chase some rabbits.

I'd like to explain what I did next and how I did it,

ut mostly what worries me is how I knew enough to do
t—I mean enough about chemical reaction and stuff like
hat. I did something to the hay and something to the oxy-
gen, and I started a fire up there in the center of the haymow.
When I saw it was started good, I got out of there and
was in myself again, and Bounce and I went on across the
creek and up the hill.

I kept looking back over my shoulder, wondering if the
fire might not have gone out, but all at once there was a
little trickle of smoke coming out of the haymow, opening
up under the gable's end.

We'd got up into the cutover land by that time, and I
sat down on a stump and enjoyed myself. The fire had a
good start before it busted out and there wasn't a thing
that could be done to save the barn. It went up with a
roar and made the prettiest column of smoke you've ever
seen.

On the way home, I stopped at the general store. Alf
was there and he seemed much too happy to have just lost
his barn.

But it wasn't long until I understood why he was so happy.

"I had her insured," he told Bert Jones, the storekeeper,
"plumb up to the hilt. Anyhow, it was too big a barn, a
lot bigger than I needed. When I built it, I figured I was
going to go into milking heavier than I've done and would
need the space."

Bert chuckled. "Handy fire for you, Alf."

"Best thing that ever happened to me. I can build another barn and have some cash left over."

I was pretty sore about bungling it, but I thought of a way to get even.

After lunch, I went up the road again and out into Alf's pasture and hunted up the bull. He was glad to see me although he did a little pawing and some bellowing just to show off.

I had wondered all the way out if I could talk to the bull the way I talked to Bounce and I was afraid that maybe I couldn't, for Bounce was bound to be smarter than a bull.

I was right, of course. It was awful hard to make that bull understand anything.

I made the mistake of scratching behind his ears while I tried to talk to him, and he almost went to sleep. I could feel just how good the scratching felt to him. So I hauled off and kicked him in the ribs to wake him up, so he would pay attention. He did pay a little closer attention and even did a little answering, but not much. A bull is awful dumb.

But I felt fairly sure I'd got my idea across, for he started acting sore and feisty, and I'm afraid that I overdid it just a mite. I made it to the fence ahead of him and went over without even touching it. The bull stopped at the fence and stood there, pawing and raising Cain, and I got out of there as fast as I could go.

I went home fairly pleased with myself for thinking up

as smart a thing as that. I wasn't surprised in the least to hear that evening that Alf had been killed by his bull.

It wasn't a pretty way to die, of course, but Alf had it coming to him, the way he beat me out of my summer wages.

I was sitting in the pool hall when the news was brought in by someone, and they all talked about it. Some said Alf had always claimed you couldn't trust no bull, and someone else said he'd often said I was the only one who'd ever gotten along with this particular bull, and he was scared all the time I was there for fear the bull would kill me.

They saw me sitting there and they asked me about it and I acted dumb and all of them laughed at me, but I didn't mind their laughing. I knew something they didn't know. Imagine how surprised they'd be if they ever learned the truth!

They won't, of course.

I'm too smart for that.

When I went home, I got a tablet and a pencil and started to write down the names of all my enemies—everyone who had ever laughed at me or done mean things to me or said mean things about me.

The list was pretty long. It included almost everyone in town.

I sat there thinking and I decided maybe I shouldn't kill everyone in town. Not that I couldn't, for I could have, just as slick as anything. But thinking about Alf and Banker

Patton, I could see there wasn't any lasting satisfaction in killing people you hate. And I could see as plain as day that if you killed a lot of people, it could leave you pretty lonesome.

I read down through the list of names I'd made, and I gave a couple of them the benefit of a doubt and scratched them out. I read those that were left over, and I had to admit that every one of them was bad. I decided that if I didn't kill them, I'd have to do something else about them, for I couldn't let them go on being bad.

I thought about it a long time, and I remembered some of the things I'd heard Preacher Martin say, although, as I've mentioned before, he's a great one to be saying them. I decided I'd have to lay aside my hate and return good for evil.

I am puzzled and disturbed, although that, perhaps, is the normal reaction when one attaches oneself to an alien being. This is a treacherous and unprincipled species and, as such, an incalculably important one to study.

I am continually amazed at the facility with which my host has acquired the use of my talents, continually appalled by the use he makes of them. I am more than puzzled by his own conviction that he is less intelligent than his fellows; his actions during my acquaintance with him do not bear this out. I wonder if it may not be a racial trait, a sort of cult-attitude of inferiority, that it may be ill-mannered to think of oneself in any other way.

But I half suspect that he may have sensed me in some way without my knowing it and may be employing this strange concept as a device to force me from his mind. Under such a circumstance, it would not be prime ethics for me to remain with him—but he has proved to be such an excellent seat of observation that I am loath to leave him.

The fact is, I don't know. I could, of course, seize control of his mind and thus learn the truth of this and other matters which are perplexing me. But I fear that, in doing so, I would destroy his effectiveness as a free agent and thus impair his observational value. I have decided to wait before taking such a drastic measure.

I ate breakfast in a hurry, being anxious to get started. Ma asked me what I was going to do and I said just walk around a bit.

First off, I went to the parsonage and sat down outside the hedge between it and the church. Pretty soon, Preacher Martin came out and began to walk up and down in what he called his garden, pretending he was sunk in holy thought, although I always suspected it was just an act to impress old ladies who might see him.

I put out my mind real easy and finally I got it locked with his so neatly, it seemed that it was me, not him, who was walking up and down. It was a queer feeling, I can tell you, for all the time I knew good and well that I was sitting there back of the hedge.

He wasn't thinking any holy thoughts at all. He was going

over in his mind all the arguments he intended to use to hit up the church board for a raise in salary. He was doing some minor cussing out of some of the members of the board for being tightfisted skinflints and that I agreed with, because they surely were.

Taking it easy, just sort of stealing in on his thoughts, I made him think about Jennie Smith, the organist, and the way he was carrying on with her, and I made him ashamed of himself for doing it.

He tried to push me away, though he didn't know it was me; he just thought it was his own mind bringing up the matter. But I wouldn't let him push the thought away. I piled it on real heavy.

I made him think how the people in the church trusted him and looked to him for spiritual leadership, and I made him remember back to when he was a younger man, just out of seminary, and looked on his lifetime work as a great crusade. I made him think of how he'd betrayed all the things he'd believed in then, and I got him down so low, he was almost bawling. Then I made him tell himself that owning up was the only way he could absolve himself. Once he'd done that, he could start life over again and be a credit to himself and his church.

I went away, figuring I'd done a fair job of work on him, but knowing that I'd have to check up on him every now and then.

At the general store, I sat around and watched Bert Jones

sweep out the place. While he was talking to me, I sneaked into his mind and recalled to him all the times he'd paid way less than market prices for the eggs the farmers brought in, and the habit of sneaking in extra items on the bills he sent out to his charge customers, and how he'd cheated on his income tax. I scared him plenty on the income tax, and I kept working at him until he'd about decided to make it right with everyone he'd cheated.

I didn't finish the job airtight, but I knew I could come back any time I wanted to, and in a little while, I'd make an honest man of Bert.

Over at the barbershop, I watched Jake cut a head of hair. I wasn't too interested in the man Jake was working on—he lived four or five miles out of town—and at the moment, I figured that I'd better confine my work to the people in the village.

Before I left, I had Jake plenty worried about the gambling he'd been doing in the back room at the pool hall and had him almost ready to make a clean breast of it to his wife.

I went over to the pool hall. Mike was sitting back of the counter with his hat on, reading the baseball scores in the morning paper. I got a day-old paper and pretended to read it. Mike laughed and asked me when I'd learned to read, so I laid it on good and thick.

When I left, I knew, just as soon as I was out the door, he'd go down into the basement and dump all the moonshine down the drain, and before too long, I'd get him to close up the back room.

Over at the cheese factory, I didn't have much chance to work on Ben. The farmers were bringing in their milk and he was too busy for me to really get into his mind. But I did manage to make him think of what would happen if Jake ever caught him with Jake's wife. And I knew when I could catch him alone, I could do a top-notch job on him, for I saw he scared easy.

And that's the way it went.

It was tough work, and at times I felt it was just too much of a job. But then I'd sit down and remind myself that it was my duty to keep on—that for some reason this power had been given me, and that it was up to me to use it for all it was worth. And furthermore, I was not to use it for myself, for any selfish ends, but for the good of other people.

I don't think I missed a person in the village.

Remember how we wondered if there might not be unseen flaws in this plan of ours? We went over it most carefully and could find none, yet all of us feared that some might show up in actual practice. Now I can report there is one. It is this:

Accurate, impersonal observation is impossible, for as soon as one introduces one's self into a host, his abilities become available to the host and at once become a factor which upsets the norm.

As a result of this, I am getting a distorted picture of the culture of this planet. Reluctant to intervene before, I am now convinced that I must move to take command of the situation.

Bert, now that he's turned honest, is the happiest man you ever saw. Even losing all the customers who got sore at him when he explained why he paid them back some money, doesn't bother him. I don't know how Ben is getting along—he disappeared right after Jake took the shotgun to him. But, then, everyone agrees Ben was overdoing it when he went to Jake and told him he was sorry for what had been going on. Jake's wife is gone, too, and some folks say she followed Ben.

To tell the truth, I am well satisfied with the way everything's turned out. Everyone is honest, and no one is fooling around with anyone else, and there ain't a lick of gambling or drinking going on in town. Mapleton probably is the most moral village in the United States.

I feel that perhaps it turned out the way it did because I started out by conquering my own evil thoughts and, instead of killing all the folks I hated, set out to do them good.

I'm a little puzzled when I walk through the streets at night, because I don't pick up near as many happy thoughts as I used to. In fact, there are times when it keeps me busy almost all night long, getting them cheered up. You'd think honest folks would be happy folks. I imagine it's be-

cause, now they're good instead of bad, they're not so give
to giddy pleasures, but are more concerned with the solic
worthwhile side of life.

I'm a little worried about myself. While I did a lot o
good, I may have done it for a selfish reason. I did it, perhap
partly, to make up for killing Alf and Banker Patton. An
I did it not for just people, but for people I know. Tha
doesn't seem right. Why should only people I know benefit'

Help! Can you hear me? I'm trapped! I can neither contro
my host nor can I escape from him. Do not under any circum
stances let anyone else try to use another member of thi
race as a host!

Help!
Can you hear me?
Help!

I've sat up all night, thinking, and now the way is clear.

Having reached my decision, I feel important and humble,
both at once. I know I'm a chosen instrument for good
and must not let anything stop me. I know the village was
no more than a proving ground, a place for me to learn
what I could really do. Knowing now, I'm determined to
use the power to its utmost for the good of all humanity.

Ma's been saving up a little money for a long time for
a decent burial.

I know just where she hides it.

It's all she's got.

But it's enough to get me to the U.N.

One for the Road

by *Stephen King*

Here's why Downeasters don't like kissing.

It was quarter past ten and Herb Tooklander was thinking of closing for the night when the man in the fancy overcoat and the white, staring face burst into Tookey's Bar, which lies in the northern part of Falmouth. It was the tenth of January, just about the time most folks are learning to live comfortably with all the New Year's resolutions they broke, and there was one hell of a northeaster blowing outside. Six inches had come down before dark and it had been going hard and heavy since then. Twice we had seen Billy Larribee go by high in the cab of the town plow, and the second time Tookey ran him out a beer—an act of pure charity my mother would have called it, and my God knows she put down enough of Tookey's beer in her time. Billy told him they were keeping ahead of it on the main road, but the side ones were closed and apt to stay that way until next morning. The radio in Portland was forecasting another foot and a forty-mile-an-hour wind to pile up the drifts.

There was just Tookey and me in the bar, listening to the wind howl around the eaves and watching it dance the fire around on the hearth. "Have one for the road, Booth," Tookey says, "I'm gonna shut her down."

He poured me one and himself one and that's when the door cracked open and this stranger staggered in, snow up to his shoulders and in his hair, like he had rolled around in confectioner's sugar. The wind billowed a sand-fine sheet of snow in after him.

"Close the door!" Tookey roars at him. "Was you born in a barn?"

I've never seen a man who looked that scared. He was like a horse that's spent an afternoon eating fire nettles. His eyes rolled toward Tookey and he said, "My wife— my daughter—" and he collapsed on the floor in a dead faint.

"Holy Joe," Tookey says. "Close the door, Booth, would you?"

I went and shut it, and pushing it against the wind was something of a chore. Tookey was down on one knee holding the fellow's head up and patting his cheeks. I got over to him and saw right off that it was nasty. His face was fiery red, but there were gray blotches here and there, and when you've lived through winters in Maine since the time Woodrow Wilson was President, as I have, you know those gray blotches mean frostbite.

"Fainted," Tookey said. "Get the brandy off the back ~ar, will you?"

I got it and came back. Tookey had opened the fellow's ~oat. He had come around a little; his eyes were half open ~nd he was muttering something too low to catch.

"Pour a capful," Tookey says.

"Just a cap?" I asks him.

"That stuff's dynamite," Tookey says. "No sense over-~oading his carb."

I poured out a capful and looked at Tookey. He nodded. "Straight down the hatch."

I poured it down. It was a remarkable thing to watch. The man trembled all over and began to cough. His face got redder. His eyelids, which had been at half-mast, flew up like window shades. I was a bit alarmed, but Tookey only sat him up like a big baby and clapped him on the back.

The man started to retch, and Tookey clapped him again.

"Hold on to it," he says, "that brandy comes dear."

The man coughed some more, but it was diminishing now. I got my first good look at him. City fellow, all right, and from somewhere south of Boston, at a guess. He was wearing kid gloves, expensive but thin. There were probably some more of those grayish-white patches on his hands, and he would be lucky not to lose a finger or two. His coat was fancy, all right; a three-hundred-dollar job if ever I'd seen one. He was wearing tiny little boots that hardly came up over his ankles, and I began to wonder about his toes.

"Better," he said.

"All right," Tookey said. "Can you come over to the fire?"

"My wife and my daughter," he said. "They're out there. . . in the storm."

"From the way you came in, I didn't figure they were at home watching the TV," Tookey said. "You can tell us by the fire as easy as here on the floor. Hook on, Booth."

He got to his feet, but a little groan came out of him and his mouth twisted down in pain. I wondered about his toes again, and I wondered why God felt he had to make fools from New York City who would try driving around in southern Maine at the height of a northeast blizzard. And I wondered if his wife and his little girl were dressed any warmer than him.

We hiked him across to the fireplace and got him sat down in a rocker that used to be Missus Tookey's favorite until she passed on in '74. It was Missus Tookey that was responsible for most of the place, which had been written up in *Down East* and the *Sunday Telegram* and even once in the Sunday supplement of the Boston *Globe*. It's really more of a public house than a bar, with its big wooden floor, pegged together rather than nailed, the maple bar, the old barn-raftered ceiling, and the monstrous big field-tone hearth. Missus Tookey started to get some ideas in her head after the *Down East* article came out, wanted to start calling the place Tookey's Inn or Tookey's Rest, and I admit it has sort of a Colonial ring to it, but I prefer plain old Tookey's Bar. It's one thing to get uppish in the summer, when the state's full of tourists, another thing altogether in the winter, when you and your neighbors have to trade together. And there had been plenty of winter nights, like this one, that Tookey and I had spent all alone together, drinking scotch and water or just a few beers. My own Victoria passed on in '73, and Tookey's was a place to go where there were enough voices to mute the steady ticking of the deathwatch beetle—even if there was just Tookey and me, it was enough. I wouldn't have felt the same about it if the place had been Tookey's Rest. It's crazy but it's true.

We got this fellow in front of the fire and he got the shakes harder than ever. He hugged onto his knees and his teeth clattered together and a few drops of clear mucus spilled off the end of his nose. I think he was starting to realize that another fifteen minutes out there might have been enough to kill him. It's not the snow, it's the wind-chill factor. It steals your heat.

"Where did you go off the road?" Tookey asked him.

"S-six miles s-s-south of h-here," he said.

Tookey and I stared at each other, and all of a sudden I felt cold. Cold all over.

"You sure?" Tookey demanded. "You came six mile through the snow?"

He nodded. "I checked the odometer when we came through t-town. I was following directions . . . going to see my wife's s-sister . . . in Cumberland . . . never been there before . . . we're from New Jersey . . ."

New Jersey. If there's anyone more purely foolish than a New Yorker it's a fellow from New Jersey.

"Six miles, you're sure?" Tookey demanded.

"Pretty sure, yeah. I found the turnoff but it was drifted in . . . it was . . ."

Tookey grabbed him. In the shifting glow of the fire his face looked pale and strained, older than his sixty-six years by ten. "You made a right turn?"

"Right turn, yeah. My wife—"

"Did you see a sign?"

"Sign?" He looked up at Tookey blankly and wiped the end of his nose. "Of course I did. It was on my instructions. Take Jointer Avenue through Jerusalem's Lot to the 295 entrance ramp." He looked from Tookey to me and back to Tookey again. Outside, the wind whistled and howled and moaned through the eaves. "Wasn't that right, mister?"

"The Lot," Tookey said, almost too soft to hear. "Oh my God."

"What's wrong?" the man said. His voice was rising. "Wasn't that right? I mean, the road looked drifted in, but I thought . . . if there's a town there, the plows will be out and . . . and then I . . ."

388

He just sort of trailed off.

"Booth," Tookey said to me, low. "Get on the phone. Call the sheriff."

"Sure," this fool from New Jersey says, "that's right. What's wrong with you guys, anyway? You look like you saw a ghost."

Tookey said, "No ghosts in the Lot, mister. Did you tell them to stay in the car?"

"Sure I did," he said, sounding injured. "I'm not crazy."

Well, you couldn't have proved it by me.

"What's your name?" I asked him. "For the sheriff."

"Lumley," he says. "Gerard Lumley."

He started in with Tookey again, and I went across to the telephone. I picked it up and heard nothing but dead silence. I hit the cutoff buttons a couple of times. Still nothing.

I came back. Tookey had poured Gerard Lumley another tot of brandy, and this one was going down him a lot smoother.

"Was he out?" Tookey asked.

"Phone's dead."

"Hot damn," Tookey says, and we look at each other. Outside the wind gusted up, throwing snow against the windows.

Lumley looked from Tookey to me and back again.

"Well, haven't either of you got a car?" he asked. The anxiety was back in his voice. "They've got to run the engine to run the heater. I only had about a quarter of a tank of

gas, and it took me an hour and a half to . . . Look, wil
you *answer* me?" He stood up and grabbed Tookey's shirt

"Mister," Tookey says, "I think your hand just ran away
from your brains, there."

Lumley looked at his hand, at Tookey, then dropped it
"Maine," he hissed. He made it sound like a dirty word
about somebody's mother. "All right," he said. "Where's
the nearest gas station? They must have a tow truck—"

"Nearest gas station is in Falmouth Center," I said.
"That's three miles down the road from here."

"Thanks," he said, a bit sarcastic, and headed for the
door, buttoning his coat.

"Won't be open, though," I added.

He turned back slowly and looked at us.

"What are you talking about, old man?"

"He's trying to tell you that the station in the Center
belongs to Billy Larribee and Billy's out driving the plow,
you damn fool," Tookey says patiently. "Now why don't
you come back here and sit down, before you bust a gut?"

He came back, looking dazed and frightened. "Are you
telling me you can't . . . that there isn't . . . ?"

"I ain't telling you nothing," Tookey says. "You're doing
all the telling, and if you stopped for a minute, we could
think this over."

"What's this town, Jerusalem's Lot?" he asked. "Why
was the road drifted in? And no lights on anywhere?"

I said, "Jerusalem's Lot burned out two years back."

"And they never rebuilt?" He looked like he didn't believe it.

"It appears that way," I said, and looked at Tookey. "What are we going to do about this?"

"Can't leave them out there," he said.

I got closer to him. Lumley had wandered away to look out the window into the snowy night.

"What if they've been got at?" I asked.

"That may be," he said. "But we don't know it for sure. I've got my Bible on the shelf. You still wear your Pope's medal?"

I pulled the crucifix out of my shirt and showed him. I was born and raised Congregational, but most folks who live around the Lot wear something—crucifix, St. Christopher's medal, rosary, something. Because two years ago, in the span of one dark October month, the Lot went bad. Sometimes, late at night, when there were just a few regulars drawn up around Tookey's fire, people would talk it over. Talk around it is more like the truth. You see, people in the Lot started to disappear. First a few, then a few more, then a whole slew. The schools closed. The town stood empty for most of a year. Oh, a few people moved in—mostly damn fools from out of state like this fine specimen here—drawn by the low property values, I suppose. But they didn't last. A lot of them moved out a month or two after they'd moved in. The others . . . well, they disappeared. Then the town burned flat. It was at the end of a long dry fall.

They figure it started up by the Marsten House on the hill that overlooked Jointner Avenue, but no one knows how it started, not to this day. It burned out of control for three days. After that, for a time, things were better. And then they started again.

I only heard the word "vampires" mentioned once. A crazy pulp truck driver named Richie Messina from over Freeport way was in Tookey's that night, pretty well liquored up. "Jesus Christ," this stampeder roars, standing up about nine feet tall in his wool pants and his plaid shirt and his leather-topped boots. "Are you all so damn afraid to say it out? Vampires! That's what you're all thinking, ain't it? Jesus-jumped-up-Christ in a chariot-driven sidecar! Just like a bunch of kids scared of the movies! You know what there is down there in 'Salem's Lot? Want me to tell you? Want me to tell you?"

"Do tell, Richie," Tookey says. It had got real quiet in the bar. You could hear the fire popping, and outside the soft drift of November rain coming down in the dark. "You got the floor."

"What you got over there is your basic wild dog pack," Richie Messina tells us. "That's what you got. That and a lot of old women who love a good spook story. Why, for eighty bucks I'd go up there and spend the night in what's left of that haunted house you're all so worried about. Well, what about it? Anyone want to put it up?"

But nobody would. Richie was a loudmouth and a mean drunk and no one was going to shed any tears at his wake, but none of us were willing to see him go into 'Salem's Lot after dark.

"Be screwed to the bunch of you," Richie says. "I got my four-ten in the trunk of my Chevy, and that'll stop anything in Falmouth, Cumberland, *or* Jerusalem's Lot. And that's where I'm goin'."

He slammed out of the bar and no one said a word for a while. Then Lamont Henry says, real quiet, "That's the last time anyone's gonna see Richie Messina. Holy God." And Lamont, raised to be a Methodist from his mother's knee, crossed himself.

"He'll sober off and change his mind," Tookey said, but he sounded uneasy. "He'll be back by closin' time, makin' out it was all a joke."

But Lamont had the right of that one, because no one ever saw Richie again. His wife told the state cops she thought he'd gone to Florida to beat a collection agency, but you could see the truth of the thing in her eyes—sick, scared eyes. Not long after, she moved away to Rhode Island. Maybe she thought Richie was going to come after her some dark night. And I'm not the man to say he might not have done.

Now Tookey was looking at me and I was looking at Tookey as I stuffed my crucifix back into my shirt. I never felt so old or so scared in my life.

Tookey said again, "We can't just leave them out there, Booth."

"Yeah. I know."

We looked at each other for a moment longer, and then he reached out and gripped my shoulder. "You're a good man, Booth." That was enough to buck me up some. It seems like when you pass seventy, people start forgetting that you are a man, or that you ever were.

Tookey walked over to Lumley and said, "I've got a four-wheel-drive Scout. I'll get it out."

"For God's sake, man, why didn't you say so before?" He had whirled around from the window and was staring angrily at Tookey. "Why'd you have to spend ten minutes beating around the bush?"

Tookey said, very softly, "Mister, you shut your jaw. And if you get the urge to open it, you remember who made that turn onto an unplowed road in the middle of a goddamned blizzard."

He started to say something, and then shut his mouth. Thick color had risen up in his cheeks. Tookey went out to get his Scout out of the garage. I felt around under the bar for his chrome flask and filled it full of brandy. Figured we might need it before this night was over.

Maine blizzard—ever been out in one?

The snow comes flying so thick and fine that it looks like sand and sounds like that, beating on the sides of your car or pickup. You don't want to use your high beams because they reflect off the snow and you can't see ten feet in front of you. With the low beams on, you can see maybe fifteen feet. But I can live with the snow. It's the wind I don't like, when it picks up and begins to howl, driving the snow into a hundred weird flying shapes and sounding like all the hate and pain and fear in the world. There's death in the throat of a snowstorm wind, white death—and maybe something beyond death. That's no sound to hear when you're tucked up all cozy in your own bed with the shutters bolted and the doors locked. It's that much worse if you're driving. And we were driving smack into 'Salem's Lot.

"Hurry up a little, can't you?" Lumley asked.

I said, "For a man who came in half frozen, you're in one hell of a hurry to end up walking again."

He gave me a resentful, baffled look and didn't say anything else. We were moving up the highway at a steady twenty-five miles an hour. It was hard to believe that Billy Larribee had just plowed this stretch an hour ago; another two inches had covered it, and it was drifting in. The strongest gusts of wind rocked the Scout on her springs. The headlights showed a swirling white nothing up ahead of us. We hadn't met a single car.

About ten minutes later Lumley gasps: "Hey! What's that?"

He was pointing out my side of the car; I'd been looking dead ahead. I turned, but was a shade too late. I thought I could see some sort of slumped form fading back from the car, back into the snow, but that could have been imagination.

"What was it? A deer?" I asked.

"I guess so," he says, sounding shaky. "But its eyes—they looked red." He looked at me. "Is that how a deer's eyes look at night?" He sounded almost as if he were pleading.

"They can look like anything," I says, thinking that might be true, but I've seen a lot of deer at night from a lot of cars, and never saw any set of eyes reflect back red.

Tookey didn't say anything.

About fifteen minutes later, we came to a place where the snowbank on the right of the road wasn't so high because the plows are supposed to raise their blades a little when they go through an intersection.

"This looks like where we turned," Lumley said, not sounding too sure about it. "I don't see the sign—"

"This is it," Tookey answered. He didn't sound like himself at all. "You can just see the top of the signpost."

"Oh. Sure." Lumley sounded relieved. "Listen, Mr. Tooklander, I'm sorry about being so short back there. I was cold and worried and calling myself two hundred kinds of fool. And I want to thank you both—"

"Don't thank Booth and me until we've got them in this car," Tookey said. He put the Scout in four-wheel drive and slammed his way through the snowbank and onto Jointner Avenue, which goes through the Lot and out to 295. Snow flew up from the mudguards. The rear end tried to break a little bit, but Tookey's been driving through snow since Hector was a pup. He jockeyed it a bit, talked to it, and on we went. The headlights picked out the bare indication of other tire tracks from time to time, the ones made by Lumley's car, and then they would disappear again. Lumley was leaning forward, looking for his car. And all at once Tookey said, "Mr. Lumley."

"What?" He looked around at Tookey.

"People around these parts are kind of superstitious about 'Salem's Lot," Tookey says, sounding easy enough—but I could see the deep lines of strain around his mouth, and the way his eyes kept moving from side to side. "If your people are in the car, why, that's fine. We'll pack them up, go back to my place, and tomorrow, when the storm's over, Billy will be glad to yank your car out of the snowbank. But if they're not in the car—"

"Not in the car?" Lumley broke in sharply. "Why wouldn't they be in the car?"

"If they're not in the car," Tookey goes on, not answering, "we're going to turn around and drive back to Falmouth Center and whistle for the sheriff. Makes no sense to go wallowing around at night in a snowstorm anyway, does it?"

"They'll be in the car. Where else would they be?"

I said, "One other thing, Mr. Lumley. If we should see anybody, we're not going to talk to them. Not even if they talk to us. You understand that?"

Very slow, Lumley says, "Just what are these superstitions?"

Before I could say anything—God alone knows what I

would have said—Tookey broke in. "We're there."

We were coming up on the back end of a big Mercedes. The whole hood of the thing was buried in a snowdrift, and another drift had socked in the whole left side of the car. But the taillights were on and we could see exhaust drifting out of the tailpipe.

"They didn't run out of gas, anyway," Lumley said.

Tookey pulled up and pulled on the Scout's emergency brake. "You remember what Booth told you, Lumley."

"Sure, sure." But he wasn't thinking of anything but his wife and daughter. I don't see how anybody could blame him, either.

"Ready, Booth?" Tookey asked me. His eyes held on mine, grim and gray in the dashboard lights.

"I guess I am," I said.

We all got out and the wind grabbed us, throwing snow in our faces. Lumley was first, bending into the wind, his fancy topcoat billowing out behind him like a sail. He cast two shadows, one from Tookey's headlights, the other from his own taillights. I was behind him, and Tookey was a step behind me. When I got to the trunk of the Mercedes, Tookey grabbed me.

"Let him go," he said.

"Janey! Francie!" Lumley yelled. "Everything okay?" He pulled open the driver's-side door and leaned in. "Every-thing—"

He froze to a dead stop. The wind ripped the heavy door right out of his hand and pushed it all the way open.

"Holy God, Booth," Tookey said, just below the scream of the wind. "I think it's happened again."

Lumley turned back toward us. His face was scared and bewildered, his eyes wide. All of a sudden he lunged toward us through the snow, slipping and almost falling. He brushed me away like I was nothing and grabbed Tookey.

"How did you know?" he roared. "Where are they? What the hell is going on here?"

Tookey broke his grip and shoved past him. He and I looked into the Mercedes together. Warm as toast it was, but it wasn't going to be for much longer. The little amber low-fuel light was glowing. The big car was empty. There was a child's Barbie doll on the passenger's floormat. And a child's ski parka was crumpled over the seatback.

Tookey put his hands over his face . . . and then he was gone. Lumley had grabbed him and shoved him right back into the snowbank. His face was pale and wild. His mouth was working as if he had chewed down on some bitter stuff he couldn't yet unpucker enough to spit out. He reached in and grabbed the parka.

"Francie's coat?" he kind of whispered. And then loud, bellowing: "*Francie's coat!*" He turned around, holding it in front of him by the little fur-trimmed hood. He looked at me, blank and unbelieving. "She can't be out without her coat on, Mr. Booth. Why . . . why . . . she'll freeze to death."

"Mr. Lumley—"

He blundered past me, still holding the parka, shouting:

"Francie! Janey! Where are you? Where are youuu?"

I gave Tookey my hand and pulled him onto his feet. "Are you all—"

"Never mind me," he says. "We've got to get hold of him, Booth."

We went after him as fast as we could, which wasn't very fast with the snow hip-deep in some places. But then he stopped and we caught up to him.

"Mr. Lumley—" Tookey started, laying a hand on his shoulder.

"This way," Lumley said. "This is the way they went. Look!"

We looked down. We were in a kind of dip here, and most of the wind went right over our heads. And you could see two sets of tracks, one large and one small, just filling up with snow. If we had been five minutes later, they would have been gone.

He started to walk away, his head down, and Tookey grabbed him back. "No! No, Lumley!"

Lumley turned his wild face up to Tookey's and made a fist. He drew it back . . . but something in Tookey's face made him falter. He looked from Tookey to me and then back again.

"She'll freeze," he said, as if we were a couple of stupid kids. "Don't you get it? She doesn't have her jacket on and she's only seven years old—"

"They could be anywhere," Tookey said. "You can't follow those tracks. They'll be gone in the next drift."

"What do you suggest?" Lumley yells, his voice high and hysterical. "If we go back to get the police, she'll freeze to death! Francie *and* my wife!"

"They may be frozen already," Tookey said. His eyes caught Lumley's. "Frozen, or something worse."

"What do you mean?" Lumley whispered. "Get it straight, goddamn it! Tell me!"

"Mr. Lumley," Tookey says, "there's something in the Lot—"

But I was the one who came out with it finally, said the word I never expected to say. "Vampires, Mr. Lumley. Jerusalem's Lot is full of vampires. I expect that's hard for you to swallow—"

He was staring at me as if I'd gone green. "Loonies," he whispers. "You're a couple of loonies." Then he turned away, cupped his hands around his mouth, and bellowed, "*FRANCIE! JANEY!*" He started floundering off again. The snow was up to the hem of his fancy coat.

I looked at Tookey. "What do we do now?"

"Follow him," Tookey says. His hair was plastered with snow, and he *did* look a little bit loony. "I can't just leave him out here, Booth. Can you?"

"No," I says. "Guess not."

So we started to wade through the snow after Lumley as best we could. But he kept getting further and further ahead. He had his youth to spend, you see. He was breaking the trail, going through that snow like a bull. My arthritis began to bother me something terrible, and I started to

401

look down at my legs, telling myself: A little further, just a little further, keep goin', damn it, keep goin' . . .

I piled right into Tookey, who was standing spread-legged in a drift. His head was hanging and both of his hands were pressed to his chest.

"Tookey," I says, "you okay?"

"I'm all right," he said, taking his hands away. "We'll stick with him, Booth, and when he fags out he'll see reason."

We topped a rise and there was Lumley at the bottom, looking desperately for more tracks. Poor man, there wasn't a chance he was going to find them. The wind blew straight across down there where he was, and any tracks would have been rubbed out three minutes after they was made, let alone a couple of hours.

He raised his head and screamed into the night: *"FRAN-CIE! JANEY! FOR GOD'S SAKE!"* And you could hear the desperation in his voice, the terror, and pity him for it. The only answer he got was the freight-train wail of the wind. It almost seemed to be laughin' at him, saying: *I took them Mister New Jersey with your fancy car and camel's-hair topcoat. I took them and I rubbed out their tracks and by morning I'll have them just as neat and frozen as two strawberries in a deepfreeze . . .*

"Lumley!" Tookey bawled over the wind. "Listen, you never mind vampires or boogies or nothing like that, but you mind this! You're just making it worse for them! We got to get the—"

402

And then there *was* an answer, a voice coming out of the dark like little tinkling silver bells, and my heart turned cold as ice in a cistern.

"Jerry . . . Jerry, is that you?"

Lumley wheeled at the sound. And then *she* came, drifting out of the dark shadows of a little copse of trees like a ghost. She was a city woman, all right, and right then she seemed like the most beautiful woman I had ever seen. I felt like I wanted to go to her and tell her how glad I was she was safe after all. She was wearing a heavy green pullover sort of thing, a poncho, I believe they're called. It floated all around her, and her dark hair streamed out in the wild wind like water in a December creek, just before the winter freeze stills it and locks it in.

Maybe I did take a step toward her, because I felt Tookey's hand on my shoulder, rough and warm. And still—how can I say it?—I *yearned* after her, so dark and beautiful with that green poncho floating around her neck and shoulders, so exotic and strange as to make you think of some beautiful woman from a Walter de la Mare poem.

"Janey!" Lumley cried. *"Janey!"* He began to struggle through the snow toward her, his arms outstretched.

"No!" Tookey cried. *"No, Lumley!"*

He never even looked . . . but she did. She looked up at us and grinned. And when she did, I felt my longing, my yearning turn to horror as cold as the grave, as white and silent as bones in a shroud. Even from the rise we could see the sullen red glare in those eyes. They were less human than a wolf's eyes. And when she grinned you could see how long her teeth had become. She wasn't human anymore. She was a dead thing somehow come back to life in this black howling storm.

Tookey made the sign of the cross at her. She flinched back . . . and then grinned at us again. We were too far away, and maybe too scared.

"Stop it!" I whispered. "Can't we stop it?"

"Too late, Booth!" Tookey says grimly.

Lumley had reached her. He looked like a ghost himself, coated in snow like he was. He reached for her . . . and then he began to scream. I'll hear that sound in my dreams, that man screaming like a child in a nightmare. He tried to back away from her, but her arms, long and bare and as white as the snow, snaked out and pulled him to her. I could see her cock her head and then thrust it forward—

"Booth!" Tookey said hoarsely. "We've got to get out of here!"

And so we ran. Ran like rats, I suppose some would say, but those who would weren't there that night. We fled back down along our own backtrail, falling down, getting up again, slipping and sliding. I kept looking back over my shoulder to see if that woman was coming after us, grinning that grin and watching us with those red eyes.

We got back to the Scout and Tookey doubled over, holding his chest. "Tookey!" I said, badly scared. "What—"

"Ticker," he said. "Been bad for five years or more. Get

ne around in the shotgun seat, Booth, and then get us
he hell out of here."

I hooked an arm under his coat and dragged him around
and somehow boosted him up and in. He leaned his head
back and shut his eyes. His skin was waxy-looking and yellow.

I went back around the hood of the truck at a trot, and
I damned near ran into the little girl. She was just standing
there beside the driver's-side door, her hair in pigtails, wearing nothing but a little bit of a yellow dress.

"Mister," she said in a high, clear voice, as sweet as morning mist, "won't you help me find my mother? She's gone
and I'm so cold—"

"Honey," I said, "honey, you better get in the truck.
Your mother's—"

I broke off, and if there was ever a time in my life I
was close to swooning, that was the moment. She was standing there, you see, but she was standing *on top* of the snow
and there were no tracks, not in any direction.

She looked up at me then, Lumley's daughter Francie.
She was no more than seven years old, and she was going
to be seven for an eternity of nights. Her little face was a
ghastly corpse white, her eyes a red and silver that you
could fall into. And below her jaw I could see two small
punctures like pinpricks, their edges horribly mangled.

She held out her arms at me and smiled. "Pick me up,
mister," she said softly. "I want to give you a kiss. Then
you can take me to my mommy."

I didn't want to, but there was nothing I could do. I was leaning forward, my arms outstretched. I could see her mouth opening, I could see the little fangs inside the pink ring of her lips. Something slipped down her chin, bright and silvery, and with a dim, distant, faraway horror, I realized she was drooling.

Her small hands clasped themselves around my neck and I was thinking: Well, maybe it won't be so bad, not so bad, maybe it won't be so awful after a while—when something black flew out of the Scout and struck her on the chest. There was a puff of strange-smelling smoke, a flashing glow that was gone an instant later, and then she was backing away, hissing. Her face was twisted into a vulpine mask of rage, hate, and pain. She turned sideways and then . . . and then she was gone. One moment she was there and the next there was a twisting knot of snow that looked a little bit like a human shape. Then the wind tattered it away across the fields.

"Booth!" Tookey whispered. "Be quick, now!"

And I was. But not so quick that I didn't have time to pick up what he had thrown at that little girl from hell. His mother's Douay Bible.

That was some time ago. I'm a sight older now, and I was no chicken then. Herb Tooklander passed on two years ago. He went peaceful, in the night. The bar is still there, some man and his wife from Waterville bought it, nice peoble, and they've kept it pretty much the same. But I don't go by much. It's different somehow with Tookey gone.

Things in the Lot go on pretty much as they always have. The sheriff found that fellow Lumley's car the next day, out of gas, the battery dead. Neither Tookey nor I said anything about it. What would have been the point? And every now and then a hitchhiker or a camper will disappear around there someplace, up on Schoolyard Hill or out near the Harmony Hill cemetery. They'll turn up the fellow's packsack or a paperback book all swollen and bleached out by the rain or snow, or some such. But never the people.

I still have bad dreams about that stormy night we went out there. Not about the woman so much as the little girl, and the way she smiled when she held her arms up so I could pick her up. So she could give me a kiss. But I'm an old man and the time comes soon when dreams are done.

You may have an occasion to be traveling in southern Maine yourself one of these days. Pretty part of the countryside. You may even stop by Tookey's Bar for a drink. Nice place. They kept the name just the same. So have your drink, and then my advice to you is to keep right on moving north. Whatever you do, don't go up that road to Jerusalem's Lot.

Especially not after dark.

There's a little girl somewhere out there. And I think she's still waiting for her good-night kiss.

Angelica

by Jane Yolen

He was a boy with a fever he would never outgrow.

The boy could not sleep. It was hot and he had been sick for so long. All night his head had throbbed. Finally he sat up and managed to get out of bed. He went down the stairs without stumbling.

Elated at his progress, he slipped from the house without waking either his mother or father. His goal was the river bank. He had not been there in a month.

He had always considered the river bank his own. No one else in the family ever went there. He liked to set his feet in the damp ground and make patterns. It was like a picture, and the artist in him appreciated the primitive beauty.

Heat lightning jetted across the sky. He sat down on a fallen log and picked at the bark as he would a scab. He could feel the log imprint itself on his backside through the thin cotton pajamas. He wished—not for the first time—that he could be allowed to sleep without his clothes.

The silence and heat enveloped him. He closed his eyes and dreamed of sleep, but his head still throbbed. He had never been out at night by himself before. The slight touch of fear was both pleasure and pain.

He thought about that fear, probing it like a loose tooth, now to feel the ache and now to feel the sweetness, when the faint came upon him and he tumbled slowly from the log. There was nothing but river bank before him, nothing to slow his descent, and he rolled down the slight hill and into the river, not waking till the shock of the water hit him.

It was cold and unpleasantly muddy. He thrashed about. The sour water got in his mouth and made him gag.

Suddenly someone took his arm and pulled him up onto the bank, dragged him up the slight incline.

He opened his eyes and shook his head to get the lank, wet hair from his face. He was surprised to find that his rescuer was a girl, about his size, in a white cotton shift. She was not muddied at all from her efforts. His one thought before she heaved him over the top of the bank and helped him back onto the log was that she must be quite marvelously strong.

"Thank you," he said, when he was seated again, and then did not know where to go from there.

"You are welcome." Her voice was low, her speech precise, almost old-fashioned in its carefulness. He realized that she was not a girl but a small woman.

"You fell in," she said.

"Yes."

She sat down beside him and looked into his eyes, smiling. He wondered how he could see so well when the moon was behind her. She seemed to light up from within like some kind of lamp. Her outline was a golden glow and her blonde hair fell in straight lengths to her shoulder.

"You may call me Angelica," she said.

"Is that your name?"

She laughed. "No. No, it is not. And how perceptive of you to guess."

"Is it an alias?" He knew about such things. His father was a customs official and told the family stories at the table about his work.

"It is the name I . . ." she hesitated for a moment and looked behind her. Then she turned and laughed again. "It is the name I travel under."

"Oh."

"You could not pronounce my real name," she said.

"Could I try?"

"*Pistias Sophia!*" said the woman and she stood as she named herself. She seemed to shimmer and grow at her own words, but the boy thought that might be the fever in his head, though he hadn't a headache anymore.

"Pissta. . . ." he could not stumble around the name.

There seemed to be something blocking his tongue. "I guess I better call you Angelica for now," he said.

"For now," she agreed.

He smiled shyly at her. "My name is Addie," he said.

"I know."

"How do you know? Do I look like an Addie? It means . . ."

"Noble hero," she finished for him.

"How do you know *that?*"

"I am very wise," she said. "And names are important to me. To all . . . of us. Destiny is in names." She smiled, but her smile was not so pleasant any longer. She started to reach for his hand, but he drew back.

"You shouldn't boast," he said. "About being wise. It's not nice."

"I am not boasting." She found his hand and held it in hers. Her touch was cool and infinitely soothing. She reached over with the other hand and put it first palm, then back to his forehead. She made a "tch" against her teeth and scowled. "Your guardian should be Flung Over. I shall have to speak to Uriel about this. Letting you out with such a fever."

"Nobody *let* me out," said the boy. "I let myself out. No one knows I am here—except you."

"Well, there is one who *should* know where you are. And he shall certainly hear from me about this." She stood up and was suddenly much taller than the boy. "Come.

411

Back to the house with you. You should be in bed." She reached down the front of her white shift and brought up a silver bottle on a chain. "You must take a sip of this now. It will help you sleep."

"Will you come back with me?" the boy asked after taking a drink.

"Just a little way." She held his hand as they went.

He looked behind once to see his footprints in the rain-soft earth. They marched in an orderly line behind him. He could not see hers at all.

"Do you believe, little Addie?" Her voice seemed to come from a long way off, further even than the hills.

"Believe in what?"

"In God. Do you believe that he directs all our movements?"

"I sing in the church choir," he said, hoping it was the proof she wanted.

"That will do for now," she said.

There was a fierceness in her voice that made him turn in the muddy furrow and look at her. She towered above him, all white and gold and glowing. The moon haloed her head, and behind her, close to her shoulders, he saw something like wings, feathery and waving. He was suddenly desperately afraid.

"What are you?" he whispered.

"What do you think I am?" she asked, and her face looked carved in stone, so white her skin and black the features.

"Are you . . . the angel of death?" he asked and then looked down before she answered. He could not bear to watch her talk.

"For you, I am an angel of life," she said. "Did I not save you?"

"What kind of angel are you?" he whispered, falling to his knees before her.

She lifted him up and cradled him in her arms. She sang him a lullaby in a language he did not know. "I told you in the beginning who I am," she murmured to the sleeping boy. "I am Pistias Sophia, angel of wisdom and faith. The one who put the serpent into the garden, little Adolf. But I was only following orders."

Her wings unfurled behind her. She pumped them once, twice, and then the great wind they commanded lifted her into the air. She flew without a sound to the Hitler house and left the boy sleeping, feverless, in his bed.

Hairline Cracks
John Robert Taylor

Sam Lydney's mother knows too much. She has realized that a public inquiry into the safety of a local nuclear power station has been rigged and, despite his father's assurances, Sam is certain she's been kidnapped. He can trust no one except his resourceful friend Mo. They must work alone to piece together the clues and discover who has taken his mother and where she may be kept.

An Armada Original

On the Spot
Mark Daniel

Ben O'Connell has a problem. He is small. Humiliated at home and bullied at school, he seems a born loser. But Ben has a special talent for snooker and he's determined to reach the top.

It seems that no one can beat him and nothing will stand in his way – until scheming Perry Curling becomes his manager. To him, a boy like Ben is made for hustling round seedy snooker joints. Winning championships, says Curling, is the stuff dreams are made of. After all, this is tough '80s Merseyside.

But Ben is aiming for the top . . .

An Armada Original

The Pit
Ann Cheetham

The summer has hardly begun when Oliver Wright is plunged into a terrifying darkness. Gripped by fear when workman Ted Hoskins is reduced to a quivering child at a demolition site, Oliver believes something of immense power has been disturbed. But what?

Caught between two worlds – the confused present and the tragic past – Oliver is forced to let events take over.

An Armada Original